RETRIBUTION

Also by R. J. Pineiro

Siege of Lightning
Ultimatum

RETRIBUTION

R.J.PINEIRO

A Tom Doherty Associates Book
New York

RETRIBUTION

Copyright © 1995 by Rogelio J. Pineiro

This book is printed on acid-free paper.

A Forge Book
Published by Tom Doherty Associates, Inc.
175 Fifth Avenue
New York, N.Y. 10010

Forge® is a registered trademark of Tom Doherty Associates, Inc.

Library of Congress Cataloging-in-Publication Data

Pineiro, R. J.
    Retribution / R. J. Pineiro.
        p.   cm.
    ISBN 0-312-85940-6
    I. Title.
PS3566.I5215R48   1995
813'.54—dc20   95-22687
                                                          CIP

First edition: September 1995

Printed in the United States of America

0   9   8   7   6   5   4   3   2   1

For Lory Anne,

My fiercely loyal friend,
My beautiful wife,
My inspiration,

It makes me very happy to let the whole world know how much I love you.

ACKNOWLEDGMENTS

As always, there are many wonderful people to thank for their help throughout the process. Any errors that remain, of course, are my own.

Gary Muschla, for his feedback during the early stages of the project.

Lt. Comdr. Robert Lamanna, for his technical assistance, particularly in the proper use of night vision goggles aboard the F/A-18D Hornet.

My friend Dave, for his technical review of the manuscript, and also for an ongoing education in firearms.

Lt. Comdr. Michael Dunn, F-14 Tomcat Pilot and a graduate of the United States Navy Fighter Weapons School (TOPGUN), for keeping me technically honest. In addition to his flying background, Comdr. Dunn also happens to be one heck of a fiction writer.

Comdr. Gino Giannotti, U.S. Navy, Retired, for a crash course in the defense systems of a carrier battle group against a missile attack.

Matt Bialer, my super agent at William Morris, for guiding me through turbulent waters.

Andy Zack, for his accurate feedback and top-notch editorial work.

Robert Gleason, for his valuable ideas and suggestions.

Camille Cline, my loyal editor at Tor/Forge, for her total support and confidence.

Stephen de las Heras, for his diligent efforts during the production process.

Tom Doherty, for believing in my writing.

ACKNOWLEDGMENTS

St. Jude, Saint of the Impossible, for making it possible.

My parents, Rogelio and Dora, and my twin sisters, Irene and Dora, for a lifetime of coveted memories.

Mike and Linda Wiltz, terrific in-laws, for loving me as one of their own.

Bobby and Kevin Moser, and Michael Wiltz, three wonderful brothers-in-law, for reminding me what it was like to be a teenager.

My son, Cameron, for brightening every day of my life.

And . . .

Lory Anne, for her unconditional love, yesterday, today, and all tomorrows.

If injury ensues, thou shalt give life for life,
eye for eye, tooth for tooth, hand for hand.
— The Bible, Exodus 21:23–24

RETRIBUTION

PROLOGUE

The first stars sprang forth in the twilight as the crimson dusk faded into darkness. The yellow-and-orange glare of the burning complex contrasted sharply with the indigo sky high above the desert sands. Inky smoke rose up out of the thundering sounds of bitter defeat echoing across the desolated valley. A lonely vulture, riding the thermals in wide, lazy circles, kept a hungry eye on the rows and rows of charred soldiers lined up at the eastern edge of the complex. On the opposite edge, a small group stood near a waiting helicopter, surveying the destruction.

Wearing a starched, light brown uniform and black beret, his Russian Makarov secured in a polished black leather holster, Iraqi President Saddam Hussein al-Tikriti turned to the moonless sky, silently praying to Allah for strength.

Allahbad was gone now, just like Osirak, Tuwaitha, Tarmiyah, Al Fallujah, and his many other uranium enrichment facilities created for the development of nuclear weapons. Only the smell of gasoline fumes, burning rubber, and gunpowder hanging in the air told of its existence. His hope for a superweapon had vanished in the wake of an F-117 Stealth Fighter's bomb run.

Saddam walked slowly over the warm sand, where shadows danced from the reddish fire spewing out of a crater a half mile in diameter, the smoldering remnants of his underground nuclear facility.

A stiff wind blew clouds of dark smoke past the hill where he walked and down the fertile plains extending to the Euphrates. A week had passed since American jets had destroyed his underground complex, yet Allahbad continued to burn. The water mains feeding the complex had broken during the underground explosion, leaving the arriving troops and emergency personnel with nothing to fight the intense inferno, the hell on earth

that President Bill Clinton had created in Saddam Hussein's Mesopotamia.

Using the sleeve of his uniform to wipe a film of sweat off his forehead,
Saddam grimaced. The Americans had stripped him of the means to
achieve superpower status. It would have meant the ultimate protection
for the motherland, the supreme equalizer against the forces of the West,
the greatest tool of nationalism. The complex had already had four of the
thirty nuclear missiles fully assembled when the Americans came. *The
total destruction of the Zionists had been mine!*

Fury overwhelming him, the Iraqi leader unholstered his Makarov,
flipped the safety, and fired repeatedly into the hell he swore at that
moment to avenge in full. His startled staff of generals, standing to either
side of him, stepped back as Saddam emptied his eight-shot magazine into
the large crater, the muzzle flashes of his weapon dwarfed by his blazing
target. Pulling a fresh magazine from his belt, Saddam dropped the empty
one on the sand by his boots and jammed the new one in place. Sliding the
weapon back in its holster, he inhaled deeply. President Bill Clinton had
no idea what kind of demon he had awakened in Saddam Hussein.

Turning around, Saddam walked to his waiting helicopter, which
would take him back to Baghdad. Inside the Aérospatiale Puma medium
transport helicopter, Saddam eased himself into a comfortable seat in the
middle of the spacious rear section. His five generals silently took their
seats around him. Three of them had been promoted to their current rank
only the day before, after Saddam had personally put a bullet into the head
of each of their predecessors for failing to protect Allahbad. The Iraqi
president's automatic, a gift from Yuri Andropov shortly before his death
in 1984, had been directly responsible for the termination of hundreds of
Iraqi officers.

The Puma helicopter left the ground and hovered above Allahbad for a
moment before heading east, arriving in Baghdad an hour later.

Saddam Hussein led the silent group of generals across the concrete
ramp and toward three black Mercedes limousines. Saddam sat alone in
the rear of the middle limo. The caravan, escorted by four personnel
carriers packed with elite members of the Republican Guard, raced
through the streets of Baghdad toward the Ministry of Foreign Affairs.

Three Iraqi soldiers, guarding the main entrance to the two-story
ministry building, snapped to attention at the sight of more than thirty
Republican Guard soldiers jumping out of their personnel carriers and
forming a human shield around the three limousines.

Saddam stepped away from the Mercedes and walked up the steps just
as the foreign minister rushed outside, arms stretched out in front.

"Great One, how honored we are that you have taken time from your
holy work to come and visit us!" The minister, a short, bald, and skinny
man in his late fifties embraced the Iraqi leader. He wore a dark blue suit

that hung loosely from his coat hanger shoulders. Saddam gave him a light pat on the back.

"How, Great One? How can this loyal servant be of use to you at this moment?" the minister asked, as he led Saddam and a caravan of guards through the mahogany double doors.

Stepping inside the large office of the old foreign minister, Saddam sank into one of two black leather sofas while his subordinate quietly walked to his desk on the opposite side of the square room and picked up a picture frame, which he brought over to Saddam. The Iraqi leader noticed the beads of perspiration rolling down his minister's forehead and cheeks.

"I just became a grandfather for the seventh time, Great One. This time it was my oldest son."

Dropping an eyebrow at the foreign minister as he nervously pointed to the picture of a young man dressed in the uniform of the Republican Guard and holding an infant, Saddam slowly shook his head.

"I did not come here to kill you," Saddam said, the tenor of his voice echoing across the gray-and-white marble floors.

The foreign minister slowly breathed deeply before sitting down on a dark green sofa, the trembling fingers of his right hand clutching the five-by-seven silver frame tight against his chest. Only in Saddam's presence did the Iraqi leader ever see the veteran diplomat tremble like this. It reminded Saddam of himself many years ago, on one of the few occasions he had lost his nerve in the face of grave danger. In 1959 Saddam and a group of young Ba'ath activists ambushed Iraq's ruler, General al-Karim Qassem. Saddam, nervously holding a revolver with both hands, opened fire prematurely, confusing his partners and giving Qassem's bodyguards time to counterattack. Accidentally wounded by one of his own comrades, Saddam managed to escape Qassem's purges within the Ba'ath party by fleeing to Syria. The event had taught the young Saddam the merits of self-control, patience, and caution, values that he used time after time upon his return to Iraq years later.

"I need you to make a trip to Damascus," Saddam finally said.

The foreign minister leaned forward. "Damascus, Great One? What is my mission?"

Saddam understood the concern in the minister's voice. The intra-Arab rivalry between Syria and Iraq went back to 1966, when the Marxist faction of the Ba'ath party in Damascus rose to power through a military coup and then tried to influence the Iraqi Ba'ath party to do likewise. Unwilling to accept Damascus's authority, the Iraqi Ba'athists formed their own pan-Arab National Command, dividing the unified Ba'ath party and upsetting the Syrian high command.

Fortunately for Saddam Hussein, Syrian President Hafez Assad not only viewed the West as the ultimate enemy of Islam, but the Syrian president was also a key member of the New Islamist International, the terrorist organization created by Iranian President Hashemi-Rafsanjani to consolidate all Islamic terrorist groups, such as the Armed Islamic Movement, the International Muslim Brotherhood, and the *HizbAllah*, under the umbrella of the New Islamist International. The NII was an organization inspired by Ayatollah Ruhollah Khomeini's vision of an ecumenical Islamic revolution. With its main headquarters in Teheran, the NII also had foreign headquarters in London, New York, Khartoum, and Damascus. With training centers in Sudan, Syria, Lebanon, Pakistan, Libya, and Afghanistan, Hashemi-Rafsanjani had under his direct control the largest terrorist network in the world. Since December 1991, the NII had steadily built up its terrorist infrastructure. The NII had expanded the number of terrorist training camps throughout Sudan, Syria, and Libya and had vastly improved the quality of the training. The NII now had more than twenty-five new state-of-the-art training facilities, where veteran terrorists, many of whom had trained with the *Mujahideen* in Pakistan and fought in Afghanistan, taught young recruits everything from armed ambushes and counterpolitical work to sophisticated bomb-making techniques.

Saddam, who had not participated in the making of the NII—he'd been preoccupied with the Iran-Iraq war of the eighties—wanted NII soldiers in America to work in coordination with Saddam's own terrorist network, which the Iraqi leader had deployed in several cities across the United States. The combined power of Islam in America would realize his vision of revenge against Bill Clinton.

"You will go to Syria to carry out the most important mission of your life," Saddam said.

Five minutes later, Saddam stepped back inside the Mercedes, headed for the Presidential Palace. Earlier in the day he had called Jafar Dhia Jafar, Saddam's top nuclear scientist, minister of industry and military industrialization, chairman of the Iraq Atomic Energy Commission, and director of reactor physics at Allahbad. Jafar had been the brains behind not just Allahbad, but the entire Iraqi nuclear project, most of which had been destroyed by coalition planes during the war of 1991. Luckily for Saddam, Jafar had not been in Allahbad a week ago but had been attending clandestine meetings with a black market arms dealer in Germany.

Jafar sat waiting for Saddam as the Iraqi leader stepped inside his office, followed by a river of bodyguards, who quickly left at a gesture of dismissal from Saddam.

Saddam glanced at his subordinate. Jafar did not wear fatigues. Neither did he wear the short-sleeved shirt and loose slacks preferred by the Iraqi scientific community, who often worked in buildings lacking air-conditioning. Jafar favored European haircuts and handmade silk suits.

Handpicked by Saddam himself in 1975, when Saddam was Iraq's vice president, Jafar Dhia Jafar had joined the Iraq Atomic Energy Commission during the construction of the French-supplied reactor called Osirak. By 1979, Jafar had become vice chairman of the IAEC and quickly became the young Iraqi leader's father figure.

"How is Marcos?" asked Saddam, as he turned around and inspected the Baghdad night skyline through the bulletproof glass windowpanes behind his large rosewood desk.

Jafar walked across the parquet floor to a table on the right corner of the office, near a pair of cream-colored sofas. A white pitcher of hot water, six teacups, and several bags of tea rested on a round silver tray. Raised and educated in England, Jafar had developed a taste for premium British tea, of which Saddam maintained a good stock in order to keep his top scientist happy.

Jafar put a tea bag in a cup and filled it with hot water. He walked over to his leader, who quietly stood with his hands behind his back, chin up and eyes glaring into the darkness.

"Marcos sends his regards," Jafar responded, taking a sip while enjoying the peaceful view of the city under a blanket of stars.

"And?"

"And he needs a few months to make the necessary arrangements, especially the ones in America."

Saddam nodded in silent acceptance. Marcos Dominguez was a Chilean arms dealer that had kept Iraq's war machine rolling in high gear during the Iran-Iraq war. But during the war of 1991, the CIA had nearly bankrupted his five-billion-dollar business. The same American government that had turned a blind eye to Marcos Dominguez while he clandestinely armed Iraq to fight against Iran had quickly changed its policy in the aftermath of the invasion of Kuwait. Marcos had been forced hurriedly to pack up what was left of his operations and unconfiscated bank accounts and flee to Europe, where his business was once again flourishing.

"The Russians or the Chinese?" Saddam asked, turning to his subordinate.

"It will be the Russians again. Marcos already has contacts in Moscow through Russians living in Germany and the United States," answered Jafar, while taking a sip of tea. "But this time we must change the rules of the game."

Saddam waited for Jafar to explain.

"We must bring most of the hardware to Iraq, of course," continued Jafar, "but some key components will be diverted to southern Europe for preassembly before being shipped to America for final assembly."

Saddam turned back to the night sky over Baghdad. "I take it that Marcos has a price in mind for this?"

Jafar nodded and told Saddam the amount of money Marcos wanted transferred to bank accounts in Zurich and the Cayman Islands. "As always, Marcos will do anything not only to help you, Great One, but also to get back at the CIA infidels for nearly ruining him in 1990. Like us, he, too, despises the Americans."

Although the images of Allahbad burned in Saddam's mind, the Iraqi leader managed a thin smile.

Soon, Saddam Hussein thought, the reflection of his face on the bulletproof glass becoming stern. *Soon the Americans will experience Allah's retribution.*

THE MEDITERRANEAN SEA.
One Month Later.

A full moon shone high above the waves, shedding its gray light on the peaceful wake of a blue-and-white yacht sailing twenty miles off the coast of southern France.

Aboard the vessel, a yacht measuring over a hundred feet from bow to stern, a man dressed in a pair of white slacks and a black, short-sleeved silk shirt walked alone on the main deck, his right hand holding a half-consumed bottle of Cerveza Regia, a popular Chilean beer. A cool breeze swirled his brown hair as he stopped, took a swig of the drink, and leaned over the metal railing, watching a light approach his vessel from out of the dark sky.

The helicopter came in from the west at two hundred feet, circling the yacht twice before hovering above the helipad near the stern. Taking a final swig from the beer bottle, the man threw it overboard as the chopper landed.

Marcos Eduardo Dominguez then walked up the steps to the upper deck as his guards brought the helicopter's passenger to him. This would be his second visitor tonight. The first had been a Greek businessman, from whom Marcos had purchased a one-year lease on a hilltop villa overlooking the Aegean Sea. The price had been steep, but it would be worth it. The place was not only secluded and low on the priority list of American surveillance satellites, but the hardware would be easily smuggled in and out of the country. Greek customs were lax, and Marcos had a number of high-ranking officials on his payroll.

As the short and overweight American approached him, Marcos could not help the feeling of hatred boiling up inside him, a feeling he knew he would have to control. The short, fat man with the double chin and lazy eyes which stared back at Marcos owned a large sugarcane plantation in southern Louisiana. The Chilean arms dealer, with the help of the Russian Mafia in America, had handpicked this location from a long list of possible spots across the United States because of the laid-back local law enforcement and the general economic recession of the state. Like the fat man in front of Marcos, desperate Louisiana landowners were quite willing to take the cash and look the other way when offered top dollar for their depreciating properties. This factor alone guaranteed Marcos the privacy he would need to carry out Saddam Hussein's plans.

Extending his right hand toward one of his guards, Marcos took a briefcase and handed it to the American.

"It's all there, *amigo,*" said Marcos in as friendly a tone as he could muster.

The American stared at the brown briefcase in his hands and, kneeling in front of Marcos, opened it. "Looks like it's all here," he said.

"Just as agreed," said Marcos.

Standing up, the American smiled at the Chilean arms dealer. "Looks like you got yourself a one-year lease on a fine Louisiana property."

Marcos nodded and motioned his guards to escort the American back to the helicopter. In another two minutes the craft was out of sight.

Facing the distant lights dotting the French coast, he smiled. Saddam had recently doubled the size of Marcos Dominguez's bank accounts, a task that would have taken the Chilean a few years to accomplish through his regular arms sales. But along with the money came the life-or-death responsibility of delivering as promised. Success meant the opportunity to live to spend that money. Failure meant his eventual execution at the hands of the *Mukhabarat,* Iraq's intelligence network.

DAMASCUS, SYRIA.

Syrian President Hafez Assad sat behind his desk as he regarded the gaunt Iraqi foreign minister with faint distaste. He did not trust Saddam Hussein but had to agree with the Iraqi leader's statement that only united would they succeed in preserving the spirit of Islam.

Assad leaned back on his leather chair and placed both hands on his lap, interlocking his fingers. The risky proposition, which had been carefully laid out by the aging diplomat sitting across the desk from him, held the promise of launching him to the status of a god among his people, if they could indeed pull this off.

"Who will coordinate the efforts of the expendables?" asked Assad.

The diplomat leaned forward and crossed his legs, placing both elbows on his thighs as he spoke. "We have a very seasoned spiritual leader already in place, Your Excellency. We have also contracted Marcos to handle the . . . logistics."

A look of concentration flashed across Assad's face. It had been Marcos's tanks and ammunition that had given Assad the hardware to crush the rebellious Muslim Brotherhood's stronghold in the Syrian city of Hama in 1982. Assad had ordered the complete demolition of a number of neighborhoods in that city. Overnight, tanks and soldiers, followed by bulldozers and dump trucks, leveled neighborhood after neighborhood, exterminating its inhabitants.

"He is a good ally," replied the Syrian leader. "A good ally."

"I've been requested to return to Baghdad with a response," the diplomat said in the friendliest of tones.

Assad stared into the distance, thinking of the terror that could be inflicted upon America if he agreed to assist with Saddam's plan.

With a simple nod of the head, President Hafez Assad committed every dormant NII soldier under his control in America to Saddam Hussein and his *Jihad*.

1

OLD DINOSAURS

The new and terrible dangers which man has created can only be controlled by man.

—John F. Kennedy

MOSCOW, RUSSIA.
One Year Later.

The quarter hour chimes of the massive bells atop Spassky Tower thundered across the Kremlin just as the dawning sun blazed above the dark horizon, bathing the Russian capital with a wan orange light. The Russian Big Ben, as the tallest of the towers along the redbrick wall surrounding the Kremlin was sometimes called, overlooked Red Square and St. Basil's Cathedral on the northwest end of this city within a city.

The dark and peaceful waters of the Moscow River hugged the south section of the wall between the Water Tower and Beklemishev Tower, which, like their bigger sister to the northwest, were also built during the latter portion of the previous century.

Across the river, near the west end of Gorky Park, a man leaned against the rusted yellow paint of a fifteen-year-old Skoda. Wearing a pair of dark slacks, a heavy woolen sweater, and a fur hat, with an old 35mm camera hanging from his neck, he looked just like any other provincial tourist getting an early start on his sight-seeing day in one of the most architecturally beautiful cities in the country. His eyes, however, were trained on his agent, Ukrainian General Vasili Krasilov, quietly smoking a cigarette a block away, at the corner of Pushikinskaya Embankment and Smolenskiy Boulevard. Krasilov stared at the onion domes atop the Cathedral of St. Michael the Archangel at the heart of the Kremlin.

The provincial tourist, a senior CIA case officer named Donald Bane, bit into a greasy, dough-wrapped sausage. His breakfast.

A large man, almost six-two, Bane tipped the scales at a hefty 260 pounds, forty pounds more than necessary, according to Jessica, his ex-wife. A fair-skinned man with a flat nose, strong chin, full lips, and a pair of black eyes on a square, heavily lined face, Bane looked like a retired boxer. His rugged features, all under thinning black hair shot with gray, added to his intimidating appearance.

But as he finished off his third sausage kabob of the morning, Donald Bane felt anything but intimidating. He felt very tired from the overnight trip from Washington. Bane had gotten word from the Moscow Station chief that General Krasilov had come across very critical information— too critical to discuss over the phone. After being handled by Bane for five of the past six years, the old and nervous general apparently wouldn't trust anyone with this information but his old case officer. Bane, who had moved back to Langley to work in counterterrorism, had made the overnight flight after it became clear that Krasilov wouldn't deal with anyone else.

In a way Bane wasn't at all surprised by Krasilov's demands. The Moscow Station seemed to be filled with too many young guns, too many wannabe officers with too much ego and not enough field experience. A whole generation of senior officers were retiring, and the gap was being filled by cocky, well-dressed junior officers who viewed seasoned officers like Bane as the last of the old dinosaurs.

But being an old dinosaur had its advantages. Donald Bane had learned to be very patient, and he had been around the block enough times to know that what goes around comes around. You just had to be patient, and make sure you didn't catch it in the ass when it did. So far, Bane hadn't been caught looking in the wrong direction.

He hadn't actually begun his career at the CIA, but at the FBI, back in 1968. J. Edgar Hoover, who had been director of the Bureau since 1924, was more interested in statistical accomplishments than in real law enforcement. Back in those days arresting a car thief carried as much weight as bringing down a Mafia boss. Every arrest was simply a number Hoover took to Congress as proof of his work to get more funding. So the young Donald Bane, then a first-office agent—on his first assignment after finishing training—in Boise, Idaho, started the Fifth of the Month Club. Once a month he awarded a fifth of Jack Daniel's to the local or state police officer who could provide Bane with the most stolen car cases in the state, so that he could claim them as FBI recoveries. This created a huge competition between the state and local police, and after a few months Donald Bane had most of the cops in Idaho working for the FBI. With a monthly output larger than the entire New York field office's, Donald Bane was transferred to the FBI headquarters in 1972, just a month before Hoover died of a heart attack and President Richard Nixon appointed L. Patrick Gray III as acting director.

Bane considered himself a "brick agent," an agent who enjoyed working the field, a "street agent." He grew attached to field operations and the men and women who participated in them. In Washington, Bane formed the Foreign Operations Group, a team of agents working in T-shirts, blue jeans, and sneakers, wearing long hair and beards, and specializing in surveillance of foreigners, particularly those from the Soviet bloc. This deviation from the clean-cut FBI standard of three-piece suits and trench coats would have been unheard of under Hoover, but during the seventies the Bureau was undergoing major changes.

In 1978, William Webster took the oath of office as FBI director. Bane received favorable notice from Webster during his nine years in the position. In 1987, when Webster left the FBI to fill the position of Director of Central Intelligence, he personally asked Donald Bane to come along and become the new Moscow Station chief. The station was in disarray at one of the worst possible moments in its history. The previous station chief had suffered a heart attack and several senior agents had suddenly reached retirement age, leaving the station in the hands of rookies. Webster, well aware of Bane's ability to adapt quickly to a new environment, had wasted no time, providing Bane with everything he needed to get up to speed, which Bane did in record time. It was under Bane's umbrella that foreign nationals like General Vasili Krasilov were recruited to spy for the CIA during the fall of communism at the turn of the decade. After seven successful years, Bane transferred back to Langley, where he had hoped to remain until his retirement. He had hated every single minute he'd spent outside the U.S. He loved America and hated Russia. It was that simple.

Bane grunted. *Now I'm back in this shithole.*

Although Bane realized the importance of this meeting—during their last meeting a year earlier, Krasilov had revealed that Iraq had purchased Russian nuclear weapons—he still didn't like being here. At fifty-two he was definitely feeling the mileage. He'd worked for the government since the age of twenty-one. Bane figured he'd already put in plenty of time, blood, and personal sacrifice for Uncle Sam. Now it should be his turn to kick off his shoes and let the young guns run the field show.

Fuck, I'm still hungry. Briefly glancing away from his contact toward the junior officer accompanying him, Bane's heavily pockmarked face changed into a grimace. Operations Officer Harvey Lee was petting a small black dog dressed in a little pink sweater. It apparently belonged to a nearby street actor setting up a gypsy-style dog show at this end of the park. Worse, the young Kansas native was not only petting the dog— which by some bizarre coincidence looked strikingly similar to his ex-wife's little yapper mutt—but his lips were moving.

Screw me blind!

"Harv, what'n the *fuck* are you doing? That's a damned mutt you're talking to." Bane's eyes remained glued to Krasilov's every movement. The old general had kept his fur hat on the entire time since arriving at the east end of the park twenty minutes ago. The Ukrainian finished his cigarette and lit up another while keeping his gaze on the Kremlin. Bane was not to approach the general until he removed his hat, signaling an absence of surveillance.

The red-haired, freckle-faced junior officer gave Bane an embarrassed smile. Over six inches shorter than Bane and roughly seventy pounds lighter, he reminded Bane of Opie, from "The Andy Griffith Show."

"Sorry, Chief. I grew up with—"

"Harv, you're still petting the mutt, aren't you? Does the Agency pay you to pet mangy mutts, Harv? You know I hate dogs, 'specially one that looks like Pookey, my ex-wife's fucking little dog. And what're you telling this mutt anyway?"

His subordinate smiled. "It's a she, Chief, and she's madly in love with you."

Bane fought a smile. He liked Harvey Lee, a highly dependable backup and a hell of a shot with any firearm. For security reasons, Bane had chosen to bring Harvey Lee, who was fluent in Russian, German, and French, with him rather than using an officer from the Moscow Station. In fact, Bane hadn't notified anyone but the Moscow Station chief that he had arrived, preferring to keep his presence in Moscow a secret until after this meeting. "Well, why don't you leave me and this little bitch alone and go fetch me another one of those sausage things."

"No problem." Lee patted the little dog once more and began to walk away.

"And Harv?"

"Yeah?"

"I know you're dying to practice your Russian, but don't be stopping and talking to street animals, would you? Something's about to happen. I can feel it."

Lee nodded and left. Wagging its tail, the little dog came up to Bane, who briefly looked at its owner, verified that he wasn't looking in Bane's direction, and proceeded to kick the dog in the rear. With a little yelp, the dog took off toward the safety of her master.

Talking to a dog. Jesus Christ!

Checking his watch, Bane frowned as he felt heartburn spread across his chest. He silently cursed the greasy Russian food. He found himself actually getting angrier with every passing second he spent on Russian soil, and he promised himself that he would duke it out with his superiors as soon as this case was over. The CIA owed him, dammit! Bane had lost his Jessica, gone to the hospital three times because of gunshot wounds and twice because of ulcers, spent several months walking in a therapeutic pool to regain full use of his right leg after some KGB asshole put a 9mm slug in his knee six years ago, gotten his ribs broken and his face kicked in during various raids, and had spent countless nights sleeping in shitholes that would make public-housing buildings look like a Hyatt Regency. The time had come to break in a good desk chair and figure out this thing called *Myst* everyone at Langley seemed to be playing. After all, the Cold War was over.

Harvey Lee returned with three sausage kabobs. "Here you go, Chief . . . say, where's the little dog? I bought her one too."

"Left. Little bitch couldn't stand my charming self," Bane said as he grabbed two kabobs from Lee's hands, devouring one in under a minute. He bit into the second greasy link, pulling off a chunk with his teeth.

"Pretty good stuff, huh?" Lee said, still working on his skewered sausage.

"It'll give you the shits for a week," said Bane, with a tilt of the head.

Lee suddenly stopped chewing.

"Subject's moving," commented Bane, dropping the food in the nearest garbage bin before moving up Smolenskiy Boulevard. Krasilov turned right on Pushikinskaya Embankment. Bane, quickly closing the gap to sixty feet with Harvey Lee in tow, also turned onto the two-lane street, which followed the curved contour of the river.

The dark, uneven cobblestones layering the embankment met a two-foot-high retaining wall overlooking the south bank of the Moscow River. Decrepit buildings lined the opposite side of the deserted street. Just one block away from the clean and cheerful Gorky Park, the streets of Moscow suddenly took on a menacing look.

"Why is he heading that way?" asked Harvey Lee. "Doesn't look like the best part of town."

Bane shrugged, silently sharing his subordinate's concern, and ran a hand behind his back, feeling one of two Sig Sauer automatics the Moscow Station chief had left for them inside a locker at the metro station near Sokolniki Park.

Krasilov stopped by a bench at the edge of the river and removed his hat. Bane breathed a bit easier and kept walking in the Ukrainian's direction.

Just as he took another step, a black Zil limousine turned onto the embankment two blocks away, its wheels spinning over the cobblestone as the vehicle headed toward Krasilov at full speed. Bane automatically reached behind his back, the fingers of his right hand curling around the stainless steel handle of the automatic.

"What in the—" Lee began to say.

"GUN!" screamed Bane, as he spotted the dark barrel extending through the rear window on the passenger side. Then the front window on the same side also lowered and another barrel appeared.

As Krasilov ran for the protection of the low stone wall bordering the river, Bane and Lee simultaneously leveled their weapons at the vehicle.

Bane fired five rounds in rapid succession, but missed the moving Zil. This was the first time in years he had used a Sig, and the weapon just didn't feel right. Lee hadn't fired yet. The young officer simply tracked the rapidly approaching vehicle with the automatic. The unmistakable rattle of an AK-47 thundered across the embankment.

"The wall!" screamed Bane, as he watched Krasilov's back explode with rounds. "Krasilov's been hit! Let's get to the wall!"

"Wait, Chief! I almost got the driver!"

Pulling Harvey Lee by the arm, Bane raced for the river. "Move it, kid!" screamed the seasoned CIA officer. Their handguns were no match for the assault rifles, which now pointed in their direction.

With the wind swirling his dark hair and the sound of rapid fire echoing across the winding embankment, Bane cut across to the stone wall. A cobblestone exploded to his left, then another to his right. Bullets ricocheted off the stone wall, their sound mixed with the harrowing screams of Harvey Lee.

Turning around and dropping to the ground, Bane watched his subordinate dragging himself over the cobblestones. Bane set his right knee on the street, raised the weapon once again toward the Zil, and let loose the rest of the fifteen-shot magazine.

Round after round left the Sig Sauer, the last few shots blowing out the front left tire, sending the limousine into a sharp left lurch, directly toward the CIA officer.

Bane dived away just as the Zil crashed through the retaining wall and plunged into the dark waters of the Moscow River.

The few seconds of silence that followed were broken by Harvey Lee. "Chief . . ."

Bane got to his side, but it only took a moment for the seasoned officer to realize that his young subordinate wasn't going to make it. Bleeding badly from his nose, ears, and mouth, Harvey Lee went into convulsions as his eyes rolled to the back of his head. A few moments later he went limp.

Bane shoved his weapon in the small of his back and knelt next to Lee, picking him up with both hands and cradling him like a mother holding an infant.

Bastards!

In his years with the Bureau and the Agency, Bane had lost three partners, and the experience never got any easier. The overwhelming guilt consumed him. As senior officer he was responsible for all the junior guys. This twenty-six-year-old kid had been his responsibility, and Bane felt he might have made the wrong call. He should have left Lee back at the corner covering his rear, instead of letting him close on Krasilov like this.

The limp body still in his arms, the professional in Donald Bane kicked into gear, reminding him that he couldn't get caught by the Moscow Police in this mess. If word got out that General Krasilov had been assassinated while meeting with the CIA, it would be all over for the general's family. With or without communism, the Russians and the Ukrainians knew of only one way to deal with the families of traitors.

It had been just under a minute since the firing started. He didn't have much time left. Frisking Harvey Lee, Bane verified that his former subordinate carried nothing but the few thousand rubles expected to be in the possession of a Russian tourist. Bane pocketed the money and Lee's Seiko to fake a robbery. He also grabbed the second Sig and tucked it in his pants. That done, Bane lifted the body and, draining his mind of any feeling, threw it into the river. Someone downstream would probably fish him out, and, with luck, Lee would become just another unfortunate tourist who had fallen victim to Moscow's rapidly increasing crime wave.

Quickly walking over to Krasilov, Bane opened the general's coat and pulled out a brown manila envelope, just as sirens blared in the distance.

Moscow Police.

Bane had little time to get out of sight. Without looking back, he raced down the embankment and disappeared around the corner.

2

THE DIRECTORATE OF OPERATIONS

If the Russians do an excellent job at retaining control over their stockpile of nuclear weapons, and they are ninety-six percent successful, that would mean you could still have as many as two hundred fifty warheads that they were not able to control.

—Defense Secretary Richard Cheney

CIA HEADQUARTERS. LANGLEY, VIRGINIA.

Robert Bourdeaux considered himself a risk manager. As the CIA's deputy director for operations, he viewed the intelligence collected by his directorate as risks, some worth taking, others worth forgoing. He believed that nothing worthwhile came free. If an intelligence report showed data that just looked too good to be true, it was probably a plant, information fed by a rival intelligence agency to get the CIA moving in the wrong direction. To collect solid intelligence one had to make certain compromises, just as in a game of chess. A pawn had to be sacrificed to capture the enemy's castle. A knight had to be sacrificed to captured the enemy's queen. The trick was to minimize the sacrifice and maximize the gain. Of course, the other side did likewise. And that was one of the biggest dilemmas in the espionage business: Which side was really getting the better end of the deal? Which side was winning the game? Right now, Bourdeaux didn't feel much like a winner.

Bourdeaux glanced at the computer printout of a flash report he had received from the Moscow Station. CIA agent Vasili Krasilov had been assassinated just as he was about to meet with Donald Bane. In the process, Officer Harvey Lee had been expended.

Sitting behind his large mahogany desk, Robert Bourdeaux read the three-paragraph report for the fifth time under the light of his halogen desk lamp. The overheads were off. Outside, thick rain pelted the windowpanes behind his desk.

His computer's clock had just chimed two o'clock in the morning, and the deputy director for operations was still embroiled in his work. The stack of reports and forms requiring his signature had shrunk from five inches to just under an inch thick, and Bourdeaux began to think, not for the first time, that he should change his micromanaging ways. He had a tendency to get involved in practically every aspect of his organization, always keeping an eye on what everyone was doing. But his directorate alone employed just over five thousand permanent employees and about four thousand contractors and hired agents. The number of reports that flowed through his desk every day was mind-numbing.

The Directorate of Operations carried the burden of collecting intelligence through the use of operations officers. Also known as Clandestine Services, the Directorate of Operations was the spy side of the CIA, the place where men and women changed from ordinary civilians into operations officers trained to violate the laws of foreign countries—friendly or not—by performing direct spying or by recruiting citizens from those countries to commit treason. These foreign nationals, or CIA agents, were the backbone of the CIA. Through their operations officers, they provided the Agency with vital intelligence on their own governments, sometimes at the price of execution for treason by their own countries.

Robert Bourdeaux had been one such operations officer. He'd started his clandestine life as a trainee at Camp Peary, outside of Williamsburg, Virginia. Mastering courses in explosives, small weapons, surveillance, counterterrorism, and the art of recruiting and running agents, Bourdeaux had transferred to Harvey Point, North Carolina, for additional weapons and explosives training. Assigned to the Baghdad Station during the eighties, Bourdeaux was instrumental in providing Iraqi troops with vital intelligence during the war with Iran. In the process, Bourdeaux recruited dozens of agents from the military, civilian, and local Kurd populations. These agents, particularly the Kurds, proved quite valuable for the CIA during Operation Desert Storm and also during the Allahbad nuclear weapons crisis.

His solid work with the Agency, particularly the year before, when his Kurdish contacts played a key role in the discovery and destruction of the Iraqi underground nuclear weapons assembly facility, had provided Robert Bourdeaux with the visibility required to move up quickly within the ranks of the Central Intelligence Agency. With President Clinton's personal endorsement, Bourdeaux had landed his current position as deputy director of operations.

Bourdeaux stood and stretched his arms above his tall, heavyset frame. At fifty-one years of age, he felt ten years older. Lack of exercise, poor eating habits, and eighteen-hour days were taking their toll. The chronic migraines that had started in his college days dogged him more than ever now.

Kicking off his shoes, he put down the flash report from Bane. Once again, General Krasilov had performed an invaluable service to the United States. The memos inside the manila envelope Bane had retrieved from Krasilov told a story that in many ways seemed quite reminiscent of a year earlier: enriched uranium spheres, graphite reflectors, neutron initiators, and other warhead components had been smuggled out of a storage facility in Serpuchov, a city one hundred miles south of Moscow, where Ukrainian nuclear weapons were being disassembled. General Krasilov was among the Ukrainian officers assigned by his government to oversee the destruction of the warheads.

Bourdeaux walked across the carpeted room to a small refrigerator in the corner of his office. Pulling out a bottle of mineral water, he twisted the cap and took a long swig. Closing his eyes as he swallowed, the DDO pressed an index finger against his right temple. He now regretted turning down the dinner invitation his new girlfriend, Kate, had extended earlier that day. A home-cooked meal and a good night's sleep were just what he needed. Along with one of Kate's incredible massages.

Robert Bourdeaux couldn't help but grin. He hadn't felt this way about a woman since his early college days, before he started taking life too seriously. The forty-five-year-old Kate Marston had literally turned Bourdeaux's world upside down since they had become involved six months earlier. Widowed a year before, right after Bourdeaux returned home from his successful assignment in Saudi Arabia, Kate Marston had caught the deputy director of operations' eye one afternoon as she walked down a hall dressed in black. The long legs, the long cinnamon hair, and the simple elegance with which that knee-high dress followed the curves of her smooth torso had captivated Robert Bourdeaux. But he had respected her mourning until the day color returned to her garments three months later, the day Robert Bourdeaux asked her out even though she also happened to be his superior's executive secretary. Kate had accepted immediately, and two months later they were regularly rolling under the sheets at his place or hers. They were so close now that Bourdeaux was seriously considering the possibility of proposing to this woman. Not only did they already have keys to each other's houses and cars, but they also kept half their wardrobes at each house. They had already shared toothpaste, shampoo, and deodorant. Soon Bourdeaux hoped to share everything with her.

Bourdeaux took another sip of mineral water and forced his thoughts away from Kate and back to his immediate problem. According to Bane, enough enriched uranium had disappeared to make several implosion-type nuclear bombs if the hardware fell into the hands of someone with the right skills. The last section of the report told the story that had given Bourdeaux a migraine that refused to go away: the official report from the Moscow Police indicated that the occupants of the Zil limousine were members of the Soltnevo Group, Russia's most powerful organized crime gang, controlling everything from black market arms sales to prostitution rings.

The prior month, the Moscow Station had linked four more former KGB officers to the powerful gang. That brought the CIA's count to over one hundred former government officials and high-ranking military officers who had simply vanished following the collapse of the Soviet Union, and Bourdeaux firmly believed that those missing men were at the heart of this criminal network.

The network had to be well connected, Bourdeaux reflected, in order to grow so fast. The Soltnevo Group was always a step ahead of the local police and government forces, and the only way to do that with such efficiency was to own people within the police and the government.

Outside, the rain dwindled. Security guards in dark raincoats and broad-brimmed hats patrolled the grounds with loaded M-16s in their hands and German shepherds at their sides.

Sitting down in his chair once more, Bourdeaux pinched the bridge of his nose and closed his eyes in thought. The problem, of course, was what to do about it. Russia currently possessed more than forty thousand nuclear weapons, a significant percentage of which were being disassembled and scheduled for destruction; the pressure to sell components to the highest bidder had to be overwhelming. And the actual selling price wouldn't have to be all that high either. The average Russian worker made the equivalent of four dollars a month, leaving the avenue for black market arms dealers and brokers wide open. To compound the problem, there were 125 metric tons of bomb-grade plutonium stored at Chelyabinsk and Tomsk—enough to make fifteen thousand more weapons. The excess plutonium, plus the one thousand metric tons of highly enriched uranium stashed in five facilities around the Rodina, gave the Russians the raw material to assemble forty-five thousand more bombs.

What a fucking nightmare!

The lines around his eyes deepened as Robert Bourdeaux grew angry. The very last section of the report commented on the strong ties between the Soltnevo Group and Marcos Eduardo Dominguez, the Chilean arms dealer and longtime supplier to Saddam Hussein. Even a novice chess player could see the potential threat.

Crashing a closed fist on the table, Bourdeaux cursed the sneaky Chilean dealer. Now Marcos supposedly operated out of Germany, a country whose industry was still driven by the remorseless greed of the Nazi years. German conglomerates like Degussa and Leybold, which for years had spread nuclear technology to Third World countries such as Iraq, Libya, Pakistan, Brazil, and North Korea, would be natural suppliers for the notorious arms dealer. But nobody knew Marcos's location for certain.

The headache flared.

Longing for Kate's warm and soothing embrace rather than the dreadful realities of his profession, Bourdeaux opened a drawer in his desk, snagged a bottle filled with 800mg orange caplets, took one, and downed it with another swig of mineral water. Again he leaned back on his chair and checked his watch.

A beeping noise on the computer terminal covering the left section of his large desk drew Bourdeaux's attention. He leaned forward. The screen came alive, prompting Bourdeaux for the access password. He entered it, and the message PLEASE STAND BY FOR FIELD REPORTXXD.B. flashed across the center of the screen. It was a message from Donald Bane.

Bourdeaux waited a few seconds, and the screen changed to:

XXXXXXXQLKJDFLEBPW OSJPW4EOHFEPWOF OFEOJO QWE OFJOPEFPEJ P'F EF FPO WEGTI7EJFE XS EFKE QPSLXH YAQ OJAPOEUIK OFWEJO MV2VJDA IEUEIC MJ3OOM OMFDLEB WMFOEQ REFS J KL9PEOMDOC DHDHTC SHSTCASJ HS LSPRUD SHSYEAR SHDGFR SJSDJDE DKLEDHFUR WDJHSFY ZIJSTJAJSTDSXXXXXXXX

Bourdeaux entered an eight-digit decoding password, and the characters on the screen changed to:

XXXXXXXMADE CONNECTION WITH S.G.XXXXTHREE MEN TRAVELING SOUTH TO-WARD SERPUCHOVXXXXXSUBJECTS SPENDING NIGHT AT LOCAL HOTELXXXXHAVE NOT ADVISED AUTHORITIES OR AMBASSADOR'S STAFFXXXXONLY MOSCOW CHIEF AND D.B. INVOLVEDXXXXREQUESTING INSTRUCTIONSXXXXXXXXX

His fingers tapped the side of the keyboard while he thought of a reply. Guilt began to creep up on Bourdeaux. He had promised to bring the seasoned CIA officer back to Langley right after his meeting with Krasilov, but Bourdeaux saw no other choice. Bane knew the Russians, knew the territory, and he was simply one hell of a handy son of a bitch. Bourdeaux had no other officer like Donald Bane operating in the region and, given the importance of this mission, he could not afford to replace him with an inexperienced gun from the Moscow Station. There was a very good reason why Bane had survived the shooting today and Lee had not. It was called field experience. Donald Bane, as much as he hated being in Russia, had plenty of experience under his belt to keep him alive on this very dangerous assignment.

Without entering a reply, which meant "continue monitoring the events and report as they develop," Bourdeaux terminated the connection. He leaned back in his chair and rubbed his tired eyes. *Sorry, Don. You gotta stay on it.*

Reaching back for the keyboard, Bourdeaux requested access to the file for the following morning's President's Daily Brief, a CIA summary of daily activities generated for President Clinton's eyes only.

The screen went blank for a few seconds as the request traveled through a maze of fiber optics to the basement, where Langley's powerful main-frame computers ran nonstop. The encoded PDB for the following morning appeared on the screen, and Bourdeaux had to enter a special password to decode and edit it. This was actually the fourth time today he had had to make an entry in the report. With over a third of the CIA's twenty-two thousand full-time employees reporting in to him, a day never went by without Bourdeaux writing at least one full page in the PDB. Tonight he was already up to two pages, and he had enough information to write a third, which he did, describing in full detail the events that had taken place less than twenty-four hours earlier in Moscow.

The indications were that Saddam Hussein was on the move again, and Bourdeaux saw it as his job to provide the president of the United States with a clear picture of the nearing danger, of the dark clouds that once again threatened to block out the sun above the nation's capital.

AIR FORCE ONE. THIRTY-FIVE THOUSAND FEET OVER THE PACIFIC OCEAN.

Four hours later, a fax machine aboard Air Force One came alive. A presidential aide stapled six sheets of paper faxed via a secured satellite link from Langley. Setting the sheets in a leather binder labeled PDB in large gold letters across the front, the presidential aide walked past a dozen men and women dressed in business suits who cruised the corridors of the Boeing 747. Some of them wore flesh-color earpieces with wires that coiled into their suits. They were members of the Presidential Security Detail, highly selected Secret Service agents with the task of keeping President Bill Clinton alive.

As the aide approached the presidential suite, one of four agents guarding the double doors let the aide through.

Sitting on a black leather sofa, President Bill Clinton sipped coffee and waited for a call from his defense secretary at the Pentagon while listening to his secretary of state's pitch about the upcoming nuclear nonproliferation meeting in Hiroshima, the site selected by the United Nations secretary-general to bring together over thirty countries involved at some level in nuclear research. Countries with the bomb, like the United States, Russia, Ukraine, Belarus, Israel, China, India, Pakistan, France, and England would ratify their nonproliferation stand, and also encourage those countries actively pursuing bomb technology to halt their research. The countries in question, who had chosen to accept the U.N. invitation, included Iraq, Iran, Syria, and Brazil.

Dressed in a pair of khaki slacks and a white polo shirt, the chief executive put down the cup of steaming coffee on the glass cocktail table in front of him. He raised his right hand, palm facing the secretary of state, who, impeccably dressed in a gray pin-striped suit, stood next to the president. The secretary was reading from the notes he held in his hands.

The secretary removed his reading glasses and lowered his notes as the aide handed Clinton the PDB and left the suite. Having worked for the president since Clinton's first day in office, the secretary knew the importance the chief executive placed on those CIA reports. Sighing, the secretary turned around and walked across the suite to the breakfast cart, where he poured himself a cup of coffee, snatched a chocolate doughnut, and sat on the sofa opposite Clinton's, across from the hexagonal glass table.

President Bill Clinton, one hand holding the CIA summary, reached for his cup of coffee, but his hand never made it to the table. His eyes had already reached Bourdeaux's section of the report, which he read twice more before handing the report to his subordinate. Holding a cup of coffee in his right hand, the secretary of state picked up the PDB with his other hand and began to read.

Clinton stood up and walked to the side of the suite, where a round window gave him a clear view of one of six F-15 Eagles escorting Air Force One. Looking at his faint reflection on the thick glass, Clinton put a hand to his chin, his mind replaying the scenes of over a year ago, when Saddam Hussein had almost turned the Middle East into a nuclear wasteland. Allahbad indeed had had the nukes assembled and deployed, and the region had been spared by a combination of top-notch intelligence gathering and some luck. The intelligence gathering had been the work of Robert Bourdeaux, who had just informed the president of the strong possibility that Saddam Hussein was at it again.

"How do you discourage someone like Saddam Hussein?" Clinton asked without turning around. The president felt he already knew the answer but wanted to hear it from his top foreign policy adviser.

With his eyes fixed on the blue-gray F-15, Clinton heard the light clatter of fine china against glass as the veteran diplomat put down his cup of coffee on the table.

"A difficult question to answer, Mr. President," responded the secretary. "When I think of Saddam Hussein, I always think of a ruthless pragmatist. That, I believe, is the best way to describe the man. Saddam views the world as a hostile environment, where only the strongest and most violent survive. In his beleaguered mind, Saddam sees plots to assassinate him lurking around every corner. He views everyone as a potential enemy, even his closest associates, of which he has basically none because he trusts nobody. Saddam Hussein has perfected the art of exposing fabricated plots to assassinate him as a tool to detain and execute anyone he feels threatens his position as Iraq's strongman. So how do you deal with someone who not only views force as the only way to achieve true political control, but is also the master of great caution, endless patience, intense calculation, and utter ruthlessness? How do you deal with someone whose name itself means 'he who confronts'? Conventional ways, like economic sanctions, will not work with Saddam Hussein. He basically laughs at them. He drove his country to the very brink of total collapse during the war with Iran, and again during the Gulf War. He doesn't care about sanctions. He does covet, however, the idea of possessing a nuclear weapon. To him it's almost a religious matter, and he will push his country once more to the brink of total economic and military collapse to get it."

Clinton nodded. Saddam wasn't likely to give up his thirst for the ultimate weapon anytime soon. Unlike other nations aspiring to get the bomb, Iraq was quite well positioned in terms of technological know-how. Saddam had more than seven thousand nuclear scientists and engineers, many of them trained in England, France, Germany, and the United States. But the Iraqi leader lacked the basic ingredient: either enriched uranium or plutonium.

"What else should we be doing about controlling his source?" Clinton asked, hoping his secretary would reveal something the chief executive didn't already know. Clinton had already taken a giant leap in that direction by purchasing tons of excess uranium and plutonium from Russia to prevent them from falling into the wrong hands.

"President Yeltsin has fully bought in to our proposal to assist them in the disposition of the warheads. In fact, he welcomes the help with open arms. The problem is that there are too many warheads spread out in too many places, and their current inventory system is not refined enough to come up with accurate counts. Our country can account for every single gram of enriched uranium or plutonium we generate. In contrast, the granularity of the Russian count is in pellets, each of which varies in size by as much as a half pound. It would be quite easy for anyone to steal enriched uranium a few grams at a time over a period of several months and walk away with enough radioactive material to build a bomb as large as the one that we dropped on Hiroshima."

Clinton turned around and stared in the distance as the word *Hiroshima* momentarily filled his mind. The United States was the only country in the world that had actually used nuclear weapons against another nation, and it was now the same United States which headed the rally for nuclear nonproliferation. Although President Bill Clinton understood the unique situation in which the bomb was last used, he felt certain many countries, Iraq included, viewed the nonproliferation treaty as a farce, and the American stance on the policy as the ultimate act of hypocrisy. Why should the United States of America, a country that had nuked another, be allowed to keep its weapons while telling other countries that they could not develop them? And for the Arab world, the fact that Israel also had them only compounded the problem, making it appear quite lopsided to people like the paranoid Saddam Hussein.

But regardless of the past, or the way Third World countries viewed the United States and its vast nuclear arsenal, President Bill Clinton could not allow any other nation to get the bomb, particularly Iraq, a country with a history of indiscriminate use of nonconventional weapons.

The phone rang, and the secretary of state reached for the extension on the cocktail table and pressed the speaker button.

"Yes?" said the president.

"Good morning, Mr. President," came the voice of Clinton's defense secretary.

"I'm afraid we have a situation," said Clinton. "I just read this morning's PDB. What is your take on this?"

After a few seconds of silence, the defense secretary said, "Force, Mr. President. With any other country I would recommend diplomacy, followed by economic pressure, but not when it comes to Saddam Hussein."

Clinton looked at his secretary of state, whose heavily lined face slowly changed to a mask of agreement.

"What's the situation in the Gulf?" asked Clinton, referring to the USS *Kennedy* carrier force, currently patrolling the waters of the Persian Gulf.

"On full alert, Mr. President, as always. The carrier's sailing fifty miles off the coast of Bahrain."

"Good. Let's keep it there, but I also want to hear options for a possible air strike."

"There is also the issue of two divisions of the Republican Guard moving south," said the defense secretary.

Clinton recalled the prior day's PDB, in which Bourdeaux had included a satellite photo showing a deployment of forty thousand men to a location fifty miles southwest of Baghdad for no other apparent reason than to annoy the American president and make the Kuwaitis nervous.

"Did your men in Kuwait and Saudi Arabia get their supplies as requested?"

"Yes, Mr. President. We have the strike force aboard the *Kennedy,* the six F-15 fighter squadrons at Salman Assad in Saudi Arabia, and the Marine Corps' Hornets stationed at Al Jaber outside of Kuwait City. That gives us roughly three hundred planes in the region. About two-fifty land-based and another fifty carrier-based. Definitely more than enough to handle a much larger Iraqi force than the forty thousand troops south of Baghdad. In fact, our initial estimates indicate that we can lick 'em with just the Hornets in Kuwait."

Clinton pressed an index finger against his bottom lip. Ever since the Somalia fiasco, when American troops got slaughtered due to failure of the former defense secretary to provide the tanks and armored vehicles requested by the U.S. commander in the region, the Pentagon was quite sensitive to such requests from its overseas troop deployments. President Bill Clinton had recently approved the shipment of three hundred more tanks, two hundred additional Multiple Rocket Launching Systems, and tens of thousands of state-of-the-art artillery shells to the two thousand U.S. troops protecting American interests in Kuwait. With such strong air support, the ground troops should be able to accomplish their mission.

"A word of caution, Mr. President," said the secretary of state. "There are fifty-three U.N. inspectors currently in Iraq. Twenty-seven are American. If we get serious about sending Saddam a message, it might be wise to get them out of there before the strike."

Clinton checked his watch. He was scheduled to meet the U.N. secretary-general in another three hours.

"I'll take that advice under consideration when I speak to the secretary-general. In the meantime, I want to keep all my options open, including a possible air strike."

"Yes, sir."

The president turned his attention back to the F-15 fighter. In the end, force was the only language Saddam Hussein understood, and for the second time in his career, President Bill Clinton readied himself to remind the Iraqi leader that the American government would not tolerate any deviation from the nonproliferation treaty.

3

A CUT ABOVE THE REST

Be not afraid of greatness. Some are born great, some achieve greatness, and some have greatness thrust upon them.

—Shakespeare

SOUTHERN GREECE.

Under a star-filled sky, Khalela Yishaid readjusted a pair of night vision goggles before clutching a suppressed Uzi submachine gun. Swiftly and quietly, she moved away from the powered rubber boat, which she had used to reach this unpopulated section of rocky beach, and up the dry and winding ravine leading to the tall mountain wall she knew would be unguarded. No one would be crazy enough to approach the road, built on the side of the mountain four hundred feet above her, from this side, particularly the Iraqi agents patrolling the grounds at the top, or the bribed Greek soldiers stationed downhill from the mansion. Local Greek officials kept a detachment of men at the foot of the mountain to protect the Iraqi scientists inside the mansion.

Well adjusted to this environment after months of training in a similar terrain in northern Israel, she scanned the light forest, searching for anything that could jeopardize her mission.

Khalela was Jewish, but more than that, she was an officer of the Mossad, a trained operative for one of the finest intelligence agencies in the world. Taking its rightful place alongside the CIA, Britain's MI-6, and the old KGB, the Mossad was created by Prime Minister David Ben-Gurion in 1951. The Mossad shouldered the burden of "Special Assignments," whose proper execution often involved a multitude of difficult and dangerous activities. From the historic kidnapping in Argentina of Nazi war criminal Adolf Eichmann to the intelligence gathering that led to the legendary hostage rescue mission in Entebbe and the decisive victory against the Arabs in the Six-Day War in 1967, the Mossad had proved time and again to be one of Israel's most valuable weapons.

Khalela stopped as she reached the end of the ravine. Wearing a light jacket over a dark gray jumpsuit, she slowly climbed up the side. The traction of her sturdy climbing boots helped propel her 120-pound body all the way up to the edge of the ravine, where she walked to the foot of the high wall and softly rubbed a hand over it, feeling the texture of the granite.

Satisfied, she removed her backpack, unzipped it, and took out a roll of athletic tape. She pulled the tape off the roll and wrapped it across the knuckles of her right hand. Then she wrapped it across the palm and across the back of her hand, slightly overlapping the previous wrap. She repeated that a few more times, also wrapping it around the thumb every other time. She finished off at the wrist and tore the tape, then did the same to her left hand before checking the flexibility of both hands. The tape would protect her skin during the climb, when Khalela would have to stick her hands into cracks to lift herself.

Khalela removed the rest of her climbing gear and set it on the ground. She untied a padded adjustable sling and slid in a few key climbing tools she would need to reach the top. Not many, just enough to accomplish her goal. The metallic utensils rattled against each other as she tied the sling, which she hung over her left shoulder along with two coiled 10mm ropes. She had chosen the ropes carefully, deciding on a German brand for its flexibility and softness without compromising strength.

She stowed the Uzi in the backpack, which she donned before approaching the wall. During the climb she would rely on the friction between the rubber soles of her climbing boots and the smooth surface of the rock.

Khalela stepped back a few feet and inspected the lower section of the wall, mentally rehearsing her movements. She stepped close to the rock and reached for a crack a foot above her head. She jammed her left hand in it with the thumb up and outside the crack. Next she lifted her right leg, bent at the knee, and pressed the ball of the foot against the smooth rock surface. She pulled herself up and pressed the ball of her left foot against the rock. With her free hand she reached up for a small boulder and held on with her middle and index fingers. Her upper body leaned away from the rock, forcing her feet into it. Although she didn't have a real foothold, the pressure of the balls of her feet against the rock caused enough adhesion to support her weight. She maximized contact with the rock by keeping her heels as low as possible. That provided balance and temporarily rested her calf muscles. She continued by reaching farther up the long crack with her left hand, placing her right foot on a small boulder and pulling herself up again. Her left foot was pressed against the rock and her right hand found its way into another large crack.

For the next thirty minutes, hand jam after agonizing hand jam, Khalela continued her strenuous climb up the steep rocky incline, keeping her movements short and efficient. She mentally worked out her moves before trying them, knowing exactly where she was going and how she would get there. This little mental effort saved her from a lot of physical exertion and enabled her to keep her climbing at a steady pace for long periods of time.

She approached a wide, chimneylike crack and placed a hand and foot on each side of it, pressing hard to lever herself upward. Slowly, inches at a time, alternating between hands and feet, Khalela made her way up the long crack, developing a rhythm to keep her body in almost-constant motion and avoiding hesitating in mid-move. She knew that would be disastrous since her entire weight rested on only two limbs during transitions. A few minutes into it she had it down to a science, making her next move exactly when she reached the apogee of the previous one. Hands and feet moved in harmony at precise moments, keeping her momentum pointed upward and using her bone structure instead of her muscles to carry most of the load.

The top of the chimney ended in a ledge that protruded over it. Khalela pressed both legs against the sidewalls, relying solely on pressure and friction to keep her body from falling into the abyss. Perspiration ran down her forehead, neck, and in between her breasts as she reached up with both hands over the ledge. When she felt she had a good enough handhold, she reduced the pressure against the chimney walls and used her legs to help herself up and over the ledge. It was a swift but critical move. She rested on her back on the three-foot-wide ledge for a few moments, shaking each limb and allowing herself time to relax before climbing the final section of rock. She wiped the glistening sweat from her face and sat up to inspect her position from a different angle.

The waters of the Aegean Sea extended as far as Khalela could see. The light green hues of the sea as it met the dark green, jagged shore reminded Khalela that she only had five more hours of battery life in her Israeli-made night vision goggles.

Khalela estimated she was three-fourths of the way up. She could see sections of the ravine roughly three hundred feet below. If her calculations were accurate, the two two-hundred-foot-long ropes across her chest would barely make it. She looked at the glinting climbing tools hanging loose from the sling and smiled. She had been correct in assuming she would eventually need the hardware. The climb was going to be tricky from now on. As the wall reached the road above, it sloped outward, which meant she would have to rely more on strong hand and footholds and less on friction, since her body weight would be naturally pointing away from the rock. She was also too close to the road to hammer in a piton to use as anchor.

Khalela stood up on the ledge and briefly examined the section of wall above her. She selected a steel hex with a two-foot-long Kevlar attachment and carefully ran it across the wider portion of a vertical crack that narrowed at the bottom until the steel piece was firmly wedged halfway down the crack. Khalela checked the anchor and nodded approvingly. The large area of contact on both sides of the hex would make rotation under impact unlikely. She was relying on the anchor to hold her weight in case she fell during the final phase of the climb.

From the sling, she selected a steel link with a spring-loaded gate and attached it to the end of the Kevlar runner. Next she removed one of the carefully coiled nylon ropes and unwrapped the standing end. She looped the rope through the steel link until it reached the midpoint, and then attached both ends to her safety belt. She gave the setup one final inspection and continued her climb, convinced that she had clipped herself to a substantial anchor.

For another fifteen minutes, Khalela struggled to maintain her climbing rhythm while twisting her body to correspond with the imperfections of the rock wall. Her shoulders burned from the strain as she pulled herself up one last time, finally reaching the top, where she rested her drained body on the light underbrush and lay perfectly still for several minutes, allowing the grass's cool moisture to soothe and relax her muscles after the strenuous exercise.

Khalela retrieved the rope she had used for safety, tied the standing ends of both ropes together, and secured one end to the trunk of a thick tree by the edge of the rock, letting the rest of the rope fall to the bottom—her quick way out of there if anything went wrong.

Khalela took a deep breath. The air was thin, cool, and invigorating. A pine resin fragrance filled her lungs as a light breeze softly caressed her face. Wiping off the cool perspiration, Khalela scanned the uneven terrain, her catlike eyes carefully searching for sentries before slowly moving toward the edge of the forest.

The well-kept lawn belonged to the mansion on top of the hill. She continued upward, hiding in some thirty feet of forest between the mansion's grounds and the abyss.

Khalela's dark clothing blended well with the surroundings. The forest grew thinner as she approached the top. Quietly, she turned toward the clearing and frowned as her boots sank deep into the muddy terrain, creating a sucking sound. She slowed down, taking extra care when lifting her feet off the ground.

Removing her backpack and dropping to a crouch behind the light underbrush by the edge of the clearing, the Mossad operative removed her goggles and briefly rubbed her face. Although small and lightweight, after three hours of wear the goggles had lined her otherwise smooth skin. Blinking rapidly in a fruitless effort to adjust her vision in the pitch-black woods, she untied the canvas flap and grabbed a pair of night binoculars from the bottom of the sack. Crawling forward, she reached the trimmed lawn, powered up the binoculars, brought them to her eyes, and scanned the grounds.

Three, five, eight . . . eight, Khalela thought, expecting to spot exactly that many sentries guarding the grounds. Satellite surveillance had already given the Mossad this information. Shifting her gaze to the front of the mansion, Khalela quickly spotted six double French doors along the first floor that led to a large covered porch extending the entire length of the large house.

Scanning the vast clearing once more, she put the binoculars down, put the goggles back on, and reached into the small backpack, retrieving a powerful Automatic Directional Finder transmitter. A flip of the green switch on its side and the battery operated ADF unit began to transmit a 360-degree signal with a range of one hundred miles. She started the chronometer of her Casio G-Shock watch.

Carefully placing the ADF transmitter by the edge of the abyss to provide the incoming team with a clear homing signal, Khalela retraced her steps. After walking almost five hundred yards down the tree line, she slowly approached the edge of the narrow road connecting the mansion to the foot of the mountain.

She checked her watch. The team was due to arrive within an hour from the time she activated the ADF transmitter.

She heard the distant sounds of Greek music and singing down the road. Friday night. Bribed or not, the Greek men at the foot of the hill just over a mile away had started to drink and party.

The Iraqis won't be getting their money's worth tonight, Khalela thought, as she removed her backpack. She unzipped the top and removed two square blocks of high-explosive plastic, a roll of nylon fishing line, and a roll of duct tape. She quickly selected a tall pine leaning over the road and pounded both blocks of HEP into a pancake shape against the trunk at knee level. Satisfied, Khalela removed a hand grenade from the backpack and pressed it against the plastic compound until the pear-shaped object stuck in place. After further securing the grenade in place with the duct tape, she tied one end of the fishing line to the grenade's safety pin and quickly got up and ran across to the opposite side of the road, where she secured the line to another tree.

Khalela went back to her backpack and retrieved two pressurized canisters filled with a napalmlike gel. She used one canister to spray a river of the volatile fuel from the grenade to the center of the road, where she emptied the contents of the second canister.

Warily checking the road for signs of sentries, Khalela returned to the edge of the forest. She stowed away the remaining line, zipped up the backpack, and returned to the spot where she had left the ADF transmitter. Briefly checking the homing device, she returned to the edge of the road. Now she just had to wait.

ISRAELI AIR FORCE C-130 TRANSPORT. NEAR THE COAST OF GREECE.

For the tall and thin Jossele Dani, the senior Mossad operative in charge of Iraqi affairs, the word *flying* had taken an entirely different meaning since his introduction to hang gliders a few months earlier by Colonel

Menachem Ken-Dror, commander of the *Hashomer,* Israel Defense Forces' elite and highly secretive special operations group. Flying had meant just the means of getting from one place to the next, a way to reach the front lines, and an easy and comfortable way to return home.

Not anymore, decided Jossele as he held on to the side of a seat while the rest of the *Hashomer* gathered around Colonel Ken-Dror, a short, stocky man of forty-five with a bald head, a black mustache, and arms large enough to qualify as thighs.

"Weather is not ideal out there!" Ken-Dror shouted in a booming voice over the noise of the C-130 Hercules turboprops. "Down by the target things look quite mild, but up here the wind is gusting to thirty knots!" Ken-Dror paused for a few moments to let the information sink in.

Jossele inhaled deeply and briefly inspected the group's seasoned faces under the camouflage cream. None flinched at their commander's words. Jossele knew many of them had to be scared . . . *God, I'm scared,* he silently admitted. After twenty years with the Israeli intelligence agency, the veteran Jossele thought he could handle anything, but jumping out of a Hercules in a hang glider in the middle of a windy night over the Aegean Sea was definitely pushing the outer envelope of his tolerance. The *Hashomer* members, however, showed a degree of professionalism that made Jossele feel ashamed of his fear.

"The signal has arrived, Jossele!" Ken-Dror said to the Mossad operative. "Looks like your operative down there is in place."

Jossele simply nodded, not only forcing himself to look as calm as the others, but also showing no surprise at the news that the Mossad had once again come through for the military forces.

"All right, men!" Ken-Dror added, as he checked his watch. "Preflight check! We are leaving the plane in ten minutes!"

So there Jossele Dani stood, nervously preflighting his Rogallo-wings hang glider, whose fourteen-foot wingspan made it the narrowest glider ever built, and thus inherently unstable. But everyone in the team had to use it because of the Hercules's twenty-foot-wide rear cargo entrance, through which the unit would have to jump.

Jossele walked around the front of the airframe of the Rogallo glider and checked the tension on the stainless steel cables attached to the aluminum noseplate, where long tubes running along the leading edge of each wing met the keel, a tube that ran from the nose to the center point of the rear. He walked underneath the delta-shaped glider and verified that the crossbar, the aluminum tube that connected the leading edges with the keel, was firmly bolted in place. Those four tubes made the basic airframe of the glider, and were kept tightly in place by the noseplate and by bolting each intersection.

Satisfied that all bolts were tight, Jossele walked back to the front, set the nose on the ground, and verified the tension on the cables from the king post, rising vertically from the keel to act as a compression strut.

Cables ran from the top of the king post down to the noseplate, rear of the keel, and both leading edge tubes to prevent the tubes from flexing beyond their breaking point from negative loads, or forces that worked downward on top of the glider. The cables also kept the tension by pulling in the opposite direction from another array of cables under the glider.

Lastly, Jossele checked the most easily recognized portion of a hang glider: the sail. Made of several panels of Dacron cloth sewn together, it was supported by thin aluminum ribs along the entire width of the glider to give the sail the necessary shape for optimum stability, maximum lift, and reduced drag.

Despite common misconception, the seemingly weakest part of the hang glider was definitely not the sail. As a matter of fact, it constituted the strongest during flight, and on this moonless night Jossele counted on his strong sail to reach the landing site safely in spite of the strong winds.

Jossele checked the altimeter strapped to his right arm. Ten thousand feet. Not so high that they would need oxygen on their long glide down, but high enough to provide a comfortable safety margin to make it to the target zone twenty miles away, even in the event of a strong downdraft, which, based on the way the Hercules rocked its wings, seemed likely.

Satisfied that he had correctly assembled the glider, Jossele Dani secured a nylon backpack to the keel. It housed a portable satellite communication radio with encoded frequencies to reach Mossad operatives in any region of the globe. The equipment would be useless to anyone but Jossele, who knew the twenty-character password required to gain access to the system.

He gazed back and briefly eyed the two members of his team who would jump along with him during the first pass. One of them was Ken-Dror. Due to space constraints, only three gliders had their wings unfolded at a time.

The light over the ramp turned yellow.

"Strap your harness to the glider. We're jumping in one minute!" shouted Ken-Dror.

Jossele got under the glider, secured the cables coming from the back of his harness to the glider, and lifted the crossbar—the triangular tubular structure that hung from the keel's center point. He fastened a set of lightweight night vision goggles in place and briefly turned them on to verify functionality. The world appeared in shades of green. He turned them off and let them hang from his neck. He wouldn't need them until the final phase of the glide.

He felt the deceleration of the Hercules the moment the engines idled and the flaps lowered. The pilot eased the C-130 into a slow flight to minimize the windblast on the taut but relatively fragile gliders.

In order for the glider to create the necessary lift to maintain flight, a certain amount of air had to travel across the upper and lower surface of the aerodynamically shaped Dacron sail at around thirty to forty knots.

Any higher than that and the glider would be exposed to a stress larger than it was designed to handle. Any lower than that and there was the risk of a stall, or loss of the Dacron wing to provide lift, which would result in the glider plummeting to the ground in a spin. Since *Hashomer* was going to jump off the rear ramp, the initial windblast would come from behind the glider instead of the front, a situation that would cause the glider to flip in midair, resulting in the possible collapse of the wings from the ensuing stress.

To minimize the reverse windblast and its devastating effects, the Hercules's pilot idled the engines. That decreased the slipstream near the fuselage and across Jossele's initial flight path, but the craft as a whole continued traveling forward at over one hundred knots, more than enough to disintegrate the glider. The forward speed had to be reduced, and the only way to do it was through a stall.

Jossele felt the Hercules starting a shallow climb to bleed airspeed and enter a stall. He leaned back a bit to compensate for the angled floor as the rear ramp lowered.

"Ready!"

The craft achieved a twenty-degree angle of climb. Jossele stared into a sea of darkness beyond the gargantuan opening thirty feet away. He shifted his gaze to the light above the entrance. It was still yellow, and it would remain like that until ten seconds before the Hercules reached a full stall, when its forward airspeed would be momentarily reduced to twenty knots.

Twenty knots. That's how fast he would have to run toward the back of the plane to even out the relative velocities and trick the glider's wings into thinking that he was just jumping off a cliff from a standstill.

Green. The light had turned green, and even before his mind had a chance to register it his legs were already moving. He kicked hard and leaned forward, keeping the glider's nose almost parallel with the floor while mentally counting the seconds. Ten seconds for a stall, another two or three while the craft was suspended in midair, and then the Hercules's nose would drop, swinging the tail up. Jossele's worst fear was to be caught over the ramp as it flung upward, swatting him and the glider against the empennage.

And so he ran. In the five seconds since he jerked forward, his legs already burned from the powerful strides as the twenty-foot-wide opening got closer. It looked like an open mouth waiting to swallow him into an ocean of darkness.

Two more kicks and he reached the ramp, and the engine noise increased tenfold, blasting against his eardrums. The deafening noise seemed as intimidating as the lack of control he experienced after he took four more steps and the ramp wasn't there any longer. The Hercules wasn't there any longer, and his glider had entered a left spin. He was spiraling toward the Aegean Sea.

A spin? How can that be?

Jossele felt certain that he had achieved at least fifteen or even twenty knots by the time he'd jumped. Had he jumped too fast, before the Hercules's speed decreased to a minimum? Or had his senses fooled him into believing he had made the run in the prescribed time? What if he'd taken more than ten seconds? But then he would have seen the tail come up . . . *damn!* He glanced at his altimeter. Ninety-five hundred feet. He was dropping too fast, but that meant he now had forward airspeed at his disposal.

With both hands holding the center of the control bar, Jossele pushed his body back until the bar reached his chest while moving his hips to the right. These moves had the effect of lifting the nose and forcing the glider into a right turn to counter the left spin.

Level flight.

After alining his hips with the glider's centerline and reducing the forward pressure on the crossbar so that it returned to its neutral position six inches below his stomach, Jossele breathed easier and checked his altimeter once more. Ninety-four hundred feet. Still within the safety range, but he was going to have to watch it from now on. The target was twenty miles away, the minimum safe distance that Ken-Dror had determined to prevent the men on the mountaintop villa from hearing the Hercules's engines.

He briefly scanned the skies for the small red-and-green anticollision lights mounted on the right and left wingtips of each glider, but saw nothing. He decided that he might have dropped too much during the initial jump and the other two gliders could be as much as a mile away from him by now. With the anticollision lights' intensity set for recognition at just under fifty feet or less, he doubted he'd see anyone, but that really didn't matter much to Jossele. Each hang glider was capable of independently reaching the rendezvous point, one thousand feet above the target. This independence of operation required the three instruments mounted on the right side of the crossbar.

The first two, mounted side by side, were a simple compass for reference and an artificial horizon to prevent spatial disorientation and vertigo. The third instrument, fastened above the first two, however, was the most critical of the three. It was an Automatic Direction Finder receiver unit, which, as Jossele had learned just a month ago, was the simplest night navigation instrument ever devised. It consisted of a radio unit that, once tuned in to the frequency of an ADF transmitter, would cause the ADF needle of the bearing indicator to turn toward the source of the transmission in much the same way as the needle of a compass points to magnetic north. The bearing indicator was nothing more than a fixed 360-degree azimuth ring and a needle, with zero representing the glider's nose.

Jossele turned on the radio and tuned it to the frequency of the transmitter that Khalela had taken with her the night before. The ADF needle swung to life in the direction of the homing signal, and Jossele shifted his weight in that direction while pushing the control bar in the opposite direction. He watched the ADF needle turn until it lined up on zero. The glider's nose now pointed directly toward the ADF source.

Jossele released the control bar momentarily to let the well-balanced craft achieve its neutral point, which by definition would give him the best glide angle. In the case of *Hashomer*'s gliders, they were each designed with a glide angle of fifteen to one, meaning that for each fifteen feet of horizontal movement the glider sank by one foot. The mathematics from then on were simple. With Jossele currently flying at ninety-two hundred feet, his current glide angle would provide him with almost twenty-six miles of forward motion before he ran aground. With the target eighteen miles away and closing, that would leave him with some altitude to meet the rest of the team and coordinate a landing attack.

A gust of wind suddenly banked his craft by almost thirty degrees. Jossele automatically grabbed the crossbar and countered by leaning his weight into it to force the wing back down before the relatively strong wind flipped him. With the crossbar pushed almost all the way to the opposite side, Jossele kept the wing from banking further, but was unable to get back to level flight for nearly a minute, until the crosswind died down.

That was close, he decided, fully aware that he had been lucky to grab the crossbar and react before the wind could turn him upside down.

He centered the crossbar but did not release it. He didn't want to get caught with his hands off the bar again. Besides, he already had a good feeling where the bar's neutral position was, and verified this by checking his sink rate, which was glued to 110 feet per minute.

He turned his wrist and checked the altimeter. Five minutes had elapsed and he had already dropped eight hundred feet. A quick mental calculation and Jossele decided that all things considered, he was making good progress. . . .

Another gust. This one from the rear . . . *Jesus!*

The glider's tail suddenly lifted and, in a blur, Jossele saw the artificial horizon telling him the nose was pointed straight down toward the Aegean Sea. The sink rate indicator swung off the scale.

Firmly holding the crossbar, he pushed himself away from it until the bar was almost level with his neck, forcing most of his weight toward the rear of the glider. The move had the desired effect, and the nose once more hoisted above the horizon, but at the price of losing three hundred feet in twenty seconds.

He checked the ADF needle, adjusted heading, and continued to battle the winds as the Greek coast loomed over the dark horizon.

Back at the tree line bordering the well-manicured lawn, Khalela used her night vision binoculars to spot the first glider directly overhead, as it sailed

across the top of the clearing at about eight hundred feet. A minute later
she spotted a second, and then a third. Within five minutes there were
more than a dozen gliders circling the top of the mountain, like giant
vampires in search of prey.

She turned her attention to the eight guards spread around the clearing.
None of them showed any sign of alarm. The night and the sound of the
wind as it swept through the grounds hid the descending team.

Putting the goggles back on and grabbing the silenced Uzi, Khalela
checked her watch before lining up the first sentry in her sights. But she did
not fire. There was no need until the team approached the ground, when
Colonel Ken-Dror would give the order by firing first from his glider.

Turning her goggled face to the stars, Khalela felt her pulse quickening
as the gliders dropped below three hundred feet and the first guard
dropped to the ground from the silent bullets of Ken-Dror's automatic.

Khalela fired. Another guard collapsed. She switched targets, but
before she could fire, the sentry in her sights also went down, victim of
another gliding gun. One guard opened fire, the report thundering across
the clearing, warning everyone inside, as well as the Greek soldiers down
the road.

Damn!

Rapidly switching targets as the first glider reached the lawn, Khalela
took out two more guards before alarms blared in the mansion. Large
floodlights came on at the perimeter of the grounds, bathing Khalela, as
well as five members of *Hashomer,* with bright yellow light.

"The road!" screamed one of the landing men as he freed himself of his
harness, removed his helmet, picked up his weapon, and raced toward
Khalela, who had already left the protection of the woods and covered the
grounds with the Uzi. "Let's protect the road!"

A thin man with messy brown hair and a long face approached her. She
recognized Jossele Dani.

"It's already booby-trapped," responded the female Mossad operative
as she guided her superior toward the gravel road. A backward glance at
the compound showed her a dozen armed men racing inside the mansion.

"The military station is just over a mile down that road. I set up the
trap just as we practiced."

Without responding, Jossele followed her for another five hundred
yards, where Khalela cut inside the woods.

"There," she said, pointing to the tree with the molded HEP and the
grenade. "That should delay them."

"Good, Khalela. Very good," Jossele said, giving her a soft pat on the
shoulder.

In another five minutes a truck loomed around the turn. She recognized the shape of a transport truck, quickly followed by three others,
along with one open Jeep.

Khalela followed the lead truck as it noisily approached the trap. The truck slowed down momentarily as the Jeep drove up to its side, making Khalela hold her breath in fear and disappointment that the driver had spotted the trap. The thought of failure struck her with chilling force. If the soldiers made it up the hill, it would be all over for Ken-Dror's men. With the transport choppers still twenty minutes away, a perfectly planned operation was about to turn into a disaster. She relaxed as both the truck and Jeep accelerated once more.

A dazing flash, followed by a thunderous explosion, sent a brief wave of elation through her body. The tall pine fell over the truck and the Jeep as drivers and soldiers rushed outside, only to be engulfed by the flames following the trail of gas that ended under the truck. A few more seconds and both vehicles exploded, drowning the cries of pain and anguish of the burning men. A second detonation dwarfed the first as the truck's fuel tank went off in a rapidly expanding fireball that engulfed the three other trucks.

Feeling the intense heat from the inferno she had created one hundred feet away, Khalela watched it all in silence. Her light green eyes, which crowned the high cheekbones of her olive-colored skin, narrowed as her mind superimposed the maimed bodies of her loved ones, all killed by Arabs.

Khalela felt no shame in what she'd just done. She had buried such feelings along with her family. She had liberated herself from the fear of death, the fear of pain that hovered over those who still had something to lose if captured. No one could take anything else away from her that she had not already lost to those Arabs troops that had swept through her village in southern Israel long ago.

"Let's head back to the clearing," said Jossele, as he pointed to the mansion.

Khalela gave her work one final glance, with cold eyes, and followed her superior up the road.

"How was your glide?" she asked, while checking both sides of the road and keeping the Uzi ready at all times.

Jossele's long face turned to her. He wasn't smiling. "Next time I climb and you glide."

Khalela smiled.

Less than ten minutes had passed since Jossele had landed, and Ken-Dror already had the area under control. In fact, by the time Khalela and Jossele reached the front steps of the mansion, Ken-Dror was coming out through a set of French doors.

"I'm afraid we're too late," the stocky commander said. "They have moved the cargo."

Jossele stopped halfway up the steps. "What?"

"Your data is two days old, my friend," Ken-Dror responded, grabbing a half-smoked pack of cigarettes and a lighter from a side pocket. He pulled a wrinkled cigarette with his lips, lit the flame, and took a long draw. "You were right about this place, though. Those Iraqi bastards had quite an operation going here. They had already preassembled the components for three bombs. Bad news is that the hardware has been moved."

"Dammit!" said Jossele, as he stared at Ken-Dror in sheer disbelief.

Khalela was confused. The same Greek informant who had told her about the mountaintop estate, temporarily leased to international arms dealer Marcos Eduardo Dominguez, had also told her that the Iraqis were not planning to move their cargo for another week.

"I don't understand how it—" Khalela began to say.

"Most likely a change of orders," interrupted Jossele with a shrug, before turning to Ken-Dror. "But the hardware, Colonel. How do you know—"

"My men are questioning two Iraqi scientists we managed to capture alive. The rest had cracked cyanide capsules by the time we got to them. The scientists have already told them about the hardware, and right before I came outside one of them said that it is being taken to Lisbon."

"Lisbon? Why Lisbon?" asked Jossele, interested not in the way in which Ken-Dror had managed to extract such vital information so quickly, but in the information itself. Like the Mossad, the *Hashomer* was highly skilled at drawing out the truth from its victims. Jossele, who had passed the Mossad's gruesome interrogation clinics, devised to prepare operatives in case they got captured alive, often wondered how he would stand up to a real interrogation by a brutal intelligence agency like Iraq's *Mukhabarat*. His professional side told him he would succeed in keeping Israel's secrets from falling in the hands of the enemy, just as his father had over thirty years ago, when Jossele Dani was barely five years old. A colonel with the Israeli Defense Forces, Gideon Dani had been captured alive by the Egyptians a week before the Six-Day War. Two younger Israeli officers, who were also captured with Colonel Dani and were later rescued by an IDF commando unit, witnessed the bravery displayed by the elder Dani, who revealed nothing to the Arabs in spite of the razors they drove into his eyes, the fingers they severed one by one, and the castration that resulted in his death. Nothing the Arabs did to Gideon Dani made him give out the secrets of his country's defense. Jossele didn't remember his father, but he had seen him in his dreams as a courageous and elegant IDF officer, and in his nightmares as a disfigured man about to be castrated.

"They are being moved to Lisbon for transportation to America," said Ken-Dror. "The two Iraqis also claim that this site held only part of the hardware Marcos bought from the Russians. The rest is on its way to Iraq."

"We must warn the Americans," Khalela suddenly said.

Jossele turned to Khalela, whose long, black hair swirled in the evening breeze. A single Sikorsky Sea King helicopter was coming directly from Israel. The Sea King flew the seven-hundred-mile journey with a single air-to-air refueling north of the Island of Crete. The helicopter would also refuel on the return leg. "I will set up a meeting with my superiors as soon as we get back to Israel. They'll have to get the prime minister involved in this."

"That will take too long. I can reach America in less than twenty-four hours. I can be on a flight out of Athens in a few hours. We owe them this information right away, Jossele. Had it not been for the Americans bombing Allahbad, Tel Aviv would have been ashes by now."

Jossele Dani slowly nodded. "What do you have in mind?"

"Kevin Dalton, the Navy pilot who saved my life in Iraq and flew the mission to destroy Allahbad, is now working for the CIA. I will contact him."

Jossele put a hand on Khalela's right shoulder. "How do you know this Kevin Dalton will help you?"

"He and I . . . he did not only save my life. We . . . Had things been different in my life, we would be together now. Besides, he already knows I am Mossad. He trusts me, and he will know what to do with the information."

"How will you reach him?"

It took Khalela one minute to explain her plan of reaching Dalton at his secluded home in northern Virginia.

Once more Jossele turned to face the Aegean Sea. "Very well," he said. "Contact Dalton as soon as you can. I will use the satellite radio to alert our people in Portugal and Spain right away. I will get a team deployed in Lisbon within the hour. As soon as we reach Israel I will set up a meeting with my superiors." Jossele walked to his hang glider and removed the nylon backpack housing the satellite communications gear.

Bracing herself, Khalela Yishaid turned around and faced the cool wind. Memories of a man she'd once loved loomed in her mind. A year had gone by since she had last seen Kevin Dalton in a hospital room in Riyadh, following his daring and highly successful raid on Allahbad. Over the past year she had secretly used her connections in the intelligence world to learn about Kevin's whereabouts in America.

It took Jossele just a few minutes to make contact with Mossad operatives in Spain and Portugal. By that time, most of Ken-Dror's team had gathered in the middle of the clearing.

"Take care of yourself," Jossele said, as he donned the nylon backpack and began to walk backward while facing Khalela.

"I will make contact after I reach America," Khalela said, lifting a hand and waving at Jossele before heading for the edge of the cliff. The power raft would take her to a prearranged section of beach ten miles to the north, where her local contact, a Greek officer on the Mossad's payroll, would pick her up and drive her to Athens. All Khalela needed was the passport and the currency sewn inside the lining of her light jacket.

She disappeared inside the forest and reached the spot where she had left the climbing rope. The wind had gained strength, swirling her hair, and she briefly checked the knot securing the rope to the tree trunk. She began her descent, reaching the bottom in under a minute.

Khalela pushed the raft away from shore and climbed aboard. The Zodiac boat, powered by a small outboard, began to make its way up the irregular coastline of southern Greece.

Twenty minutes had passed since Jossele Dani, using a set of infrared field binoculars, saw the Zodiac disappear around a bend in the coastline. The small raft appeared to be doing close to fifteen knots.

He now listened to the nearing beat of helicopter blades breaking the still of the night. The Sea King had been delayed because of an unexpected head wind south of Crete. But at last it had arrived. For the last fifteen minutes the group had grown restless. Over forty minutes had passed since the initial strike, and everyone feared that was definitely long enough for the Greek military to figure out what had happened and send reinforcements.

As the helicopter approached, Jossele saw a streak of light arc toward the Sea King, now hovering at two hundred feet over the group.

In the second that it took his mind to realize what it was, the missile struck the descending chopper right above the exhaust nozzles of the twin turbines, cracking the main rotor shaft. Without a pivot point, the sixty-two-foot rotor spun out of control, tilting to the right as the Sikorsky began to drop. One of the rotor blades sliced through the center fuselage, cutting right into the main fuel tank.

A crimson ball of flames stabbed the night as the Sea King exploded just a hundred feet over the mansion, showering the clearing with burning debris. Rapid fire suddenly erupted from the far section of forest, mowing down many of Ken-Dror's men in seconds.

The scorching wreck crashed on the lawn fifty feet from Jossele with a thundering roar and a blinding sheet of orange-and–red-gold fire.

Echoing high above the reverberating guns, Ken-Dror's voice crashed over the Israeli team. "GET DOWN! GET DOWN!" the seasoned colonel screamed, as he brought his Uzi around.

Jossele Dani, who had reacted fast enough by jumping away from the group and rolling on the lawn, now lay on the grass just twenty feet from Ken-Dror, elbows planted on the ground, Uzi pointed at the enemy hiding in the forest, the small nylon backpack strapped to his back.

"Greek reinforcements!" Ken-Dror shouted over the noise of the machine guns that continued to decimate the Israeli team pinned down on the cool grass.

The smoke from the burning chopper danced in the wind sweeping across the clearing. Momentarily filled with a mix of surprise and fear, Jossele watched Ken-Dror getting up to coordinate a proper retreat into the woods sixty yards behind them.

Firing his Uzi into the distant muzzle flashes, the colonel began to walk backward. "To the woods! To the woods!" he shouted, as the grass and dirt exploded around them and near-misses screamed like wasps from hell.

"Christ, Colonel!" shouted Jossele. "Get down!"

The IDF commander kept his footing while reloading and firing another burst at waist level. Enemy firing temporarily subsided. Ken-Dror had gotten some of them.

"Back, men! Back!" commanded Ken-Dror.

The Israelis, on elbows and knees, and while firing into the tree line, began to follow their leader, who stood ramrod-straight as enemy fire gained momentum once more. Bullets screeched past them, tearing at the forest behind them, turning it into a cloud of bark, broken branches, and leaves.

"Dammit, Colonel! Get down!" screamed Jossele again as he shoved his skinned elbows against the ground to crawl back, his hands clutching the Uzi he fired in single-shot mode at the still-hidden enemy.

The Israeli colonel responded by throwing the empty Uzi on the ground and unholstering a 9mm pistol. Flipping the safety, the colonel extended his right arm and fired at the tree line. His team approached the forest, now just forty yards away.

As Jossele blasted another dozen rounds at the invisible enemy, Ken-Dror pressed a button on his pistol and dropped his empty magazine. He reached into his belt, pulled out a fresh one, and jammed it into the Colt's steel magazine well. He cocked it, chambered a round, and fired thrice more as he took another step back.

Just then gunfire broke out behind them.

Cross fire!

The thought had barely entered Jossele's mind when Ken-Dror fell victim to a spray of rounds exiting through his bursting chest. Jossele rolled away from him and cut loose a few rounds in the direction of the new muzzle flashes along the edge of the forest behind them.

The first figures emerged from the near tree line, a dozen men dressed in the light brown uniform of the Greek Army.

Two of Ken-Dror's men opened fire on the soldiers. Three Greeks fell before the rest hit the ground and fired back, taking out both Israelis.

Jossele didn't have much time. The soldiers crawling toward them thirty yards away would overrun the half dozen Israelis still alive in less than thirty seconds.

Reaching for the nylon backpack, he pulled out the miniature equipment, extended the foot-in-diameter parabolic antenna, and began to enter his password. He had to reach Tel Aviv and report.

The ground to his left exploded, showering him with dirt and grass. The next blast tore apart his radio, the plastic debris stinging his face and neck.

"Aghh!"

Bringing both hands to his bleeding face, Jossele Dani tried to roll away, but a brown boot stopped his momentum. Another boot swung toward his stomach.

The blow left him gasping for air as tears filled his eyes. His mind registered blurry figures around him, Greek soldiers. One of them kicked Jossele behind the right ear and everything faded away.

HIROSHIMA, JAPAN.

Security personnel outnumbered foreign dignitaries in the crowded reception room. Flags from many countries hung from cathedral ceilings as tall windows on both sides of the hall admitted the soft glow of a setting sun. The delicate clatter of silverware on china plates mixed with the hum of dinner conversation.

In a VIP suite overlooking the reception room, where in another few minutes the head of the Japanese delegation was scheduled to make the opening address to the forum on worldwide nuclear nonproliferation, President Bill Clinton held a private meeting with United Nations Secretary-General Adolfo Montoya de Córdova. A short Argentine in an iron gray suit, de Córdova sat placidly at the dinner table drinking red wine. Deep lines surrounded his coal black eyes as he lifted his gaze from the crowd below to President Clinton. A soft hand with manicured nails brought a wineglass to a pair of thin lips.

The secretary-general looked from behind a pair of horn-rimmed glasses with a concerned look. The American president had just spent the last half hour discussing the matter of Saddam Hussein with him.

"If Iraq is indeed in violation of the nonproliferation treaty, we must not waste time. This information must be presented to the Security Council immediately for a vote," the secretary-general said with the British accent he had developed while studying at Oxford over a quarter century before.

Sitting across the small conference table, President Clinton regarded the Argentine. A slow nod of Clinton's head and Montoya de Córdova leaned back, his long face relaxing a bit before saying, "There should not be a problem deploying a multinational force to augment your troops." The Argentine removed his glasses, breathed on them, and polished them with the end of a white cloth napkin.

Clinton grimaced at the thought of another confrontation with Saddam Hussein. The same questions that had flooded his mind a year ago now returned. According to Robert Bourdeaux, the Russian Mafia had acquired the nuclear hardware over two months ago. The president and his advisers had already assumed the worst: the hardware had gone from the Russians to Marcos Dominguez's network and on to Iraq. President Clinton feared that Saddam could even have some warheads already assembled somewhere in Iraq. And there was, of course, the possibility of previous shipments that the CIA didn't know about.

And, as before, the question was where? Where did Saddam hide his nuclear weapons?

"We must exercise caution. He is behaving just as he did a year ago," said Clinton, as the Japanese delegation entered the room and the crowd slowly began to take their seats. "He is sending troops south to cause trouble, just as he did when he already had missiles assembled at Allahbad."

The seasoned Argentine diplomat, winner of the prior year's Nobel Peace Prize, locked eyes with the American chief executive. "I do realize we must be cautious, but we must also be firm with Saddam."

Clinton nodded. "That is correct, sir. We must be firm, and we must send him a message immediately."

"A message?" the secretary-general asked. "What kind of message?"

"An ultimatum to stop his advance toward Kuwait and Saudi Arabia and to pull his troops back. Before my plane landed, I received calls from both Arab governments, and they expressed serious concerns about Saddam's latest actions in the region. The government of Kuwait is particularly nervous about this, for obvious reasons."

Checking his watch, the secretary-general looked back at Clinton and said, "The other members will be here within the hour. I propose calling an emergency meeting and voting on the issue immediately."

Clinton also checked his watch. Within another hour, after convincing the other members of the Security Council of the imminent threat those troops south of Baghdad presented to Kuwait and Saudi Arabia, Clinton planned to issue his ultimatum to Saddam Hussein.

The crowd broke into a welcoming applause for the leader of the Japanese delegation, Dr. Hosuku Miyuki, a survivor of the Hiroshima blast.

President Clinton silently looked at an old man thirty feet below walking up to the podium. The entire right side of Dr. Hosuku Miyuki's face had been burned beyond recognition by the heat flash that carbonized Hiroshima on August 6, 1945, when the eminent doctor had been but an eleven-year-old boy.

President Clinton put on the headphones next to him and looked at Montoya de Córdova, who kept his headphones on his lap.

"I speak fluent Japanese," said the Argentine.

Clinton adjusted the volume of his set as the interpreter began to translate Miyuki's words.

"At exactly two seconds past eight-sixteen in the morning of August 6,

1945, an entire society was laid waste to its very core. I witnessed the obliteration of thousands of men, women, and children. The destruction was sudden and thorough. Hotels, businesses, homes, automobiles, government offices, trees, dogs, birds, hospitals, temples, trains, theaters . . . *everything* was vaporized by the atom bomb.

"My face felt on fire, and I trembled when I realized that it indeed had just been on fire. Black smoke and a repulsive stench of burned flesh emanated from my left cheek. The pain was appalling . . . I began to believe that all human beings on earth had been killed, and only I was left behind in an eerie world of death . . . I walked past the only standing buildings, skeletons of steel and crumbling concrete. I approached the river to drink and I saw the faces of monsters reflected from the water dyed red with blood. The banks of the river were covered with the dead. People had come to the shore and plunged their heads in to drink and in that position they had died. Men and women, old and young, soldiers and civilians lay there with not a hair left on their heads, the broken skin of their burned faces stained bright red with blood, their bodies swollen and covered with flies and roaches. Yes, flies and roaches. Somehow the bugs had survived. Somehow."

Miyuki paused briefly to let the words sink in before continuing.

"In a single second I lost my family, my friends, my city. In that brief moment of time, everything I held dear simply vaporized in front of my young, naive eyes. *Everything.* This weapon does not leave anything behind. It begins to take human life away in the first fraction of a second, and it continues to take it years—and even decades—after the explosion. From leukemia to breast cancer, thousands of radiation victims from Hiroshima and Nagasaki have perished and continue to perish every year in our country."

Miyuki paused. Clinton briefly glanced at the Iraqi delegation, three diplomats sitting in the third row from the front. One of them wrote on a piece of paper while the other two listened to the speech.

Fucking hypocrites.

Clinton turned back to Miyuki.

"I saw people dreadfully burned; the skin on their bodies had peeled off. Underneath, their wet and mushy flesh became food for rats, flies, roaches, and maggots. Froth oozed from the noses and mouths of the dead. To prevent the spread of disease, we piled the corpses in huge mountains, doused them with oil, and set them ablaze. Some people, who were not dead but merely unconscious, found themselves burning and came running out!"

The powerful speech went on for another fifteen minutes. President Clinton clung to every word. The mind-numbing statistics echoed in his mind. Over 100,000 dead and 130,000 wounded had been the count after the first month! Nearly 140,000 had died by the end of 1945, and 200,000 by the end of 1950. Around 70,000 of the 76,000 buildings in Hiroshima were destroyed.

A hand on his chin, a look of worry on his face, the American chief executive tried to grasp the magnitude of the destruction. *Two hundred thousand dead! And all because of just one bomb. One bomb!*

Clinton slowly shook his head in sheer disbelief. When put in perspective, the twenty-kiloton bomb that destroyed Hiroshima was but a mere firecracker compared to the thermonuclear warheads packed inside a Trident missile.

As a standing ovation met the end of Miyuki's speech, Clinton's thoughts returned to the President's Daily Brief and his conversation with the secretaries of state and defense.

The president, eyes glaring with an anger he knew he would have to control, swore to use every power available to him to strip the Iraqi leader of his warheads.

BETHESDA, MARYLAND.

Kate Marston jumped into Robert Bourdeaux's arms the moment he walked in the door holding a bottle of white zinfandel.

"You're early," she whispered, while covering his mouth with hers and giving Bourdeaux a wet kiss.

The deputy director for operations embraced her light body and closed his eyes as the taste of her filled him, his free hand caressing the wet cinnamon hair that smelled like peaches and fell gently over her shoulders. Fine lines of age, always hidden in public by the use of well-applied makeup, moved over her face as she gave him a puzzled look. "You're never early, darling. Something wrong?"

"Nope. Just missed you too much, I guess."

"Liar." Gently pushing him away, Kate inspected Bourdeaux, who wore a dark overcoat over his work suit. In contrast, Kate Marston was naked under her black robe, her shapely legs showing below the silk cloth bordering her upper thighs.

"Well, no sense in me getting all dressed up now," she said, her brown eyes amusingly admonishing a delighted Robert Bourdeaux. "You, on the other hand, are wearing too much," she said, and pointed him to the stairs while she took the bottle of wine from his hands, gave him a soft kiss on the cheek and a pat on his behind, and headed back into the kitchen of the small town house. "Go up there and change, lover boy. I need to finish cooking our meal."

Spare furniture, mostly antiques, decorated the small living room. An Oriental rug covered a section of the hardwood floors between the single sofa in the living room and the dining room, where Bourdeaux saw two placings of white china and sparkling silverware under a dimmed chandelier. The smell of blackened mahimahi made his stomach grumble, the smell of peaches from that cinnamon hair made him feel like a teenager all over again.

Kate's bedroom was actually the largest room in the house, covering the entire second floor, save for an old-fashioned bathroom with an antique claw-foot tub and a pedestal sink. The toilet was new, and so was the ceramic tile, over which Robert Bourdeaux walked as he removed his coat, suit, and tie, before rolling the white sleeves of his shirt halfway up his forearms. Kicking off his shoes, the DDO walked back down the stairs and found the china plates already filled with half-inch-thick mahimahi steaks.

Bourdeaux sneaked inside the kitchen and quietly approached Kate from behind while she worked on a greasy pan in the sink. Abruptly, he hugged her.

"Aghh!"

"Got ya," he said, and kissed the back of her neck.

"Don't forget I have a weapon in my hands!" she warned, lifting the soapy frying pan with her left hand.

"You win. I'll gracefully retreat into the dining room."

Bourdeaux left her by the sink and sat at the table, but he didn't touch a thing. He waited until Kate finished a few minutes later and joined him. He filled their wineglasses with zinfandel.

"To you," he said. "For making me the happiest man on this planet."

Kate Marston smiled and brought her glass toward his. The rims touched and Bourdeaux saw a glint of sadness in her eyes. It didn't last long. Her warm glance quickly returned as they drank.

As he cut into the fish, he wondered if she still missed her husband.

Bob, you asshole! Of course she does! She was married to the same man for almost fifteen years and you're wondering if she still misses him?

"How was your day, honey?"

Bourdeaux looked up from his plate with a mouthful of mahimahi. He chewed it fast, swallowed with the help of some wine, and said, "Things are heating up. We think Saddam's on the move again."

He could relax with Kate. As secretary to Director of Central Intelligence Joseph Goldberg, Kate Marston not only had a security clearance as high as any CIA officer's, but she also had the inside scoop on internal affairs and operations at the Agency—mostly from having to type the director's memos and meeting minutes.

Kate nodded. "I've noticed Mr. Goldberg's been very short-tempered in the past couple of days."

"Yep," Bourdeaux said, as he drained his glass and poured himself some more. "We have plenty to worry about these days."

"I hope it doesn't last too long. I like you in bed with me. I had to hug a pillow in your place last night."

Bourdeaux grinned. "Must have been a big pillow."

"Oh, you men!"

Bourdeaux grinned even more and took another bite of fish. It was delicious. After swallowing with a few sips of zinfandel, he said, "With a meal like this, I promise you to be here every night."

"Yeah, right."

Bourdeaux sensed her frustration and stood. In a sense he understood the way she felt. After so many years of marriage, Kate was used to having a man with her in bed every night, and during the past few months Bourdeaux had awakened that feeling again. That, plus the fact that they were both getting up in age, was definitely shifting the priorities of the attractive Kate Marston.

"Come," he said. "You seem tense. I'll help you clean up later."

She took his hand and they walked upstairs. They undressed each other in silence with the lights off and crawled under the white sheets.

They kissed, the taste of wine and blackened fish alive in her mouth. Kate embraced him, her fingers massaging his lower back. Bourdeaux felt her warm, clean body pressed against his and closed his eyes in silent pleasure. Slowly, Kate's hands moved up his back, her fingers digging into the flesh below his shoulders.

Bourdeaux moved on top and slipped inside Kate easily, feeling her body relax and move with his, quietly at first, and then with a soft moan after every thrust.

Minutes later they lay side by side, their eyes locked, a smile of satisfaction painted across her face, her hair partially covering the side of her face.

"This is how I like you to be, Robert: with me in bed."

Bourdeaux put a hand to her face and stroked the hair gently out of the way. "I wish I could stay here with you every second of the day, but I can't. Too many people depend on me."

"Why don't we just quit and run away one day? You know, just disappear, the two of us. No forwarding address."

Bourdeaux laughed. "You're serious, aren't you?"

"I'm tired of this life, Robert. In a few years I'll be fifty. You're past fifty yourself. When does it stop? When do we get to call it quits and start enjoying life? And I mean more than just little moments like these at the end of a busy day."

Bourdeaux rolled on his back and rested his head on his pillow. Putting both hands behind his back, he stared at the slow-moving ceiling fan. "I wish I could answer that, Kate. I honestly do, but how can we quit when we have madmen like Saddam Hussein trying to build a nuclear Iraq? I mean, the bastard is at it again. He never learned his lesson from Allahbad. Christ! He never really got the message from Desert Storm!"

Kate moved over and rested her head on his shoulder while sliding a leg over his, the fingers of her right hand caressing the hairs on his chest. "I didn't mean to upset you, darling. I just want you all to myself, I guess. Call me selfish, call me whatever you like. I just want to be with you."

"I know. I know," Bourdeaux responded.

They lay there in silence for some time, immersed in their own thoughts. Then Bourdeaux felt a hand reaching down for his groin as her lips found his. He slid his body over hers and they made love again. Afterward they fell asleep.

4

THE MUKHABARAT

Men loved darkness rather than light, because their deeds were evil.
— Matthew 7:13

BAGHDAD, IRAQ.

Saddam Hussein sat in the rear of a bulletproof Mercedes-Benz limousine as it cruised through downtown Baghdad. The streets were nearly empty in the predawn hours as the caravan of five black automobiles and three armored vehicles brought a tired and very irritable Saddam, along with his army of bodyguards, to the outskirts of the city.

In his hands, the Iraqi tyrant held a faxed report from Damascus, delivered to him five hours before. The news was not satisfactory. His operation in Greece had met near-disaster less than twenty-four hours ago, when a team of Israeli commandos had raided the secret facility in Greece. Fortunately, the hardware had already been moved to Lisbon, where one of Saddam's most trusted men was preparing to board a ship to America. Marcos Dominguez had already made the necessary arrangements to get the hardware to a safe house in the state of Louisiana. The rest of the hardware, which Marcos had secured from the Soltnevo Group in Moscow, was on its way to Turkey. From there, Marcos Dominguez's men would fly it across the border into a secret assembly location outside the city of Tikrit, one hundred miles north of Baghdad, where Jafar Dhia Jafar, Saddam Hussein's top nuclear scientist, was already hard at work assembling a bomb from a shipment received two months ago.

A new shipment of nuclear hardware was due to change hands between the Soltnevo Group and Marcos's team within the next twenty-four hours. This new shipment would go directly to the safe house outside Tikrit.

The Jews who had dared attack Saddam's assembling facility in Greece had paid for their actions with their lives. The bribed Greek forces had managed to counterattack and eliminate all but one of the Israelis, as they were waiting to be picked up by a transport helicopter. The Greeks had managed to capture a member of the Israeli team and hand him over to the *Mukhabarat,* the Iraqi intelligence service.

From a remote airstrip in southern Greece, his men had flown the *Kurf,* or infidel, to Baghdad via Lebanon and Syria. After a day of interrogation, the Jew had begun to break down, and he had confessed that the Israeli team had interrogated two Iraqi scientists captured alive and it now knew about Saddam's plans. The infidel had also confessed that the Mossad had sent an operative to America to warn the CIA of the nearing nuclear threat.

Closing his eyes and gently pressing the tips of his thumb and index finger against his eyelids, the Iraqi president silently cursed these Israelis he could not control, but whom he was determined to eliminate.

The caravan came to a stop in front of a ten-foot-tall fence surrounding a white stone building a mile outside the Iraqi capital. The automatic gates opened and the caravan proceeded inside, where a dozen armed guards patrolled the arid grounds, German shepherds walking by their sides.

Saddam's Mercedes halted by the concrete steps leading to a pair of large metal doors at the front of the building. Armed guards leaped out of the vehicles and created a human wall around the Iraqi president, who left the dark automobile and walked up the steps.

A tall, bearded man wearing the uniform of the *Mukhabarat*—a pair of light brown pants, a long-sleeved shirt, and a thick black leather belt, from which an empty holster hung—pushed open the double doors and welcomed his leader. No one but Saddam's bodyguards was allowed to carry firearms when meeting with the Iraqi president. Those who disobeyed paid for their mistake with their own lives. Saddam's bodyguards had orders to shoot any man who approached him carrying a weapon.

"Ahlan wa sahlan, Great One," said Colonel Ali Karrubi, district chief of the *Mukhabarat,* as the president approached him.

Weary and nauseous from lack of sleep, Saddam Hussein didn't bother to return the greeting. The leader of Iraq simply stared at the bearded face of one of the most decorated heroes from the war with Iran. During the mid-eighties, Colonel Karrubi, then a captain in the Republican Guard, had been responsible for gassing more than one thousand Iranian soldiers outside Dehloran, a small Iranian city near the border with Iraq. Karrubi, with only a dozen tanks and less than one hundred soldiers under his command, had kept an Iranian deployment of over five thousand troops and seventy tanks from crossing the border until reinforcements arrived two days later. In Saddam Hussein's opinion Karrubi represented the ideal Iraqi warrior, and he personally had assigned the recently promoted colonel to this district to oversee the security of the citizens of Baghdad.

But even his admiration for this seasoned warrior did not overcome the gloom and hatred Saddam Hussein felt for the captured *Kurf* on this cool morning in central Iraq. Much effort and sacrifice had gone into the careful crafting of his network in Greece, as well as coordinating his people in America to work together with Marcos Dominguez's network, with the

Russian Mafia, and with Syrian President Assad's New Islamist International. The Iraqi president was determined not to let the Mossad interfere with his operations again.

"Where is the *Kurf?*" asked Saddam Hussein, his eyes now scanning the grounds of the district's *Mukhabarat* interrogation quarters. Saddam had ordered the construction of this and several other interrogation posts during the early eighties as a way to coordinate interrogations of captured Iranian soldiers during the nine-year-long war with that country. The same posts were used again during the aftermath of the Gulf War to debrief captured Kurdish rebels, and Saddam Hussein now used the interrogation centers to break anyone who opposed his vision of the new Islamic world order.

"We are close to breaking the infidel, Great One!" responded Karrubi, as he stepped aside and held one of the metal doors open for his leader.

Saddam Hussein went inside. The murky interior, combined with the coppery smell of blood, burned flesh, and ammonia, pushed the Iraqi president deeper into depression as his dark eyes gazed around the spacious front room. Soiled concrete floors met plain, windowless stone walls, which supported a ceiling made of reinforced concrete. A few fluorescents, hanging at the ends of long electric cords, bathed the rectangular room with gray light. To Saddam Hussein's immediate right and left were long corridors. A small courtyard in the middle of the building was visible through the partially opened door directly ahead of the Iraqi leader.

Colonel Karrubi pointed to their left, and Saddam Hussein began to walk in that direction with the colonel by his side and a dozen armed bodyguards trailing him. Doors to either side of the corridor connected to separate interrogation cells. The colonel stopped halfway down the corridor, in front of a dusty wooden door.

"He is in here, Great One," said Karrubi. "We have interrogated him for over twenty-four hours now."

Saddam Hussein pressed his lips in a slight frown. Karrubi was letting him know in advance that the sight inside the interrogation cell would not be a pretty one. The *Mukhabarat's* methods of interrogation ranked among the most barbaric but effective in the world.

Motioning Karrubi to open the door, Saddam steeled himself. The smell of blood and burned flesh he had detected when entering the building now filled the Iraqi president as he inhaled. It was mixed with the strong body odor emanating from the uniformed interrogator, a bald man with a powerful chest, huge arms, and large, hairy hands. Drenched in sweat, the soldier, right hand holding a white-hot butcher's knife, slowly turned around and froze at the sight of Saddam.

"It's all right, Sergeant," said Colonel Karrubi. "Our leader is here to personally oversee the interrogation."

"An honor, Great One," said the bald sergeant with a slight bow, which

Saddam Hussein did not return. Saddam's eyes had already found the naked Jew, strapped to the interrogation table with leather straps around his chest, waist, thighs, ankles, shoulders, wrists, neck, and forehead. A red cloth stuffed into his mouth prevented anything but a moan from escaping his lips, but the contorted eyes staring wildly around the room displayed unmistakable pain and fear.

Saddam pointed to the plastic bag covering the infidel's feet.

"We smeared syrup on his feet and let the ants inside the bag do the rest. We tied it shut at the ankles to keep the ants from crawling elsewhere. That will come later," said Colonel Karrubi.

"What have you learned from this *Kurf?*" asked Saddam Hussein, also noticing the rivers of salt traversing the infidel's legs, where the *Mukhabarat* had peeled off most of the skin. Like the ants slowly eating the flesh of the infidel's feet, the salt on exposed wounds was another way of providing the subject with a steady level of pain, a mere platform from which Karrubi operated by increasing the pain and slowly letting it come back down to this level.

"The infidel is a Mossad operative by the name of Jossele Dani," responded Colonel Karrubi, motioning his sergeant to continue interrogating the Jew. "He admits that he participated in the raid in Greece, but claims he does not know the details of the messenger sent to warn the Americans."

The interrogator brought the scorching knife right in front of the Jossele's wide open eyes, before slowly moving it over to his prisoner's left hand, which was already missing the thumb, index and middle fingers. The fingernails of the remaining fingers had long since been removed.

Without hesitation the sergeant pressed the knife against the olive skin of the ring finger, instantly severing it. The hot knife also cauterized the sizzling, smoking wound to prevent unnecessary blood loss. The idea behind it was a simple one: inflict maximum pain without killing the subject.

The moans intensified as the Jew went rigid for several seconds, then convulsed against the leather straps and finally went limp. The sergeant put the steel edge of the knife over the red-hot coil of a portable stove next to the wooden table and leaned down to pick up a bucket of water. Splashing the Jew's face and slapping him twice brought the prisoner back to consciousness.

"How is the Mossad planning to contact the Americans?" asked the Iraqi president.

Karrubi pointed at the interrogator, who removed the red cloth from the Jew's mouth. Jossele coughed several times and swallowed hard. With one of his massive hands grabbing the prisoner's genitals and squeezing, the sergeant put his face just inches from the Jew's, sweat dripping down the interrogator's face and onto Jossele.

"Where, *Kurf?* Where is the connection? Speak up, or by Allah I shall crush them!"

Jossele Dani could not see beyond a few inches from his face. The Arab's perspiration burned his eyes, temporarily blinding him. But for a brief moment he thought he had seen Saddam Hussein in the room. Perhaps it was the overwhelming pain, which had taken total control of his body for what seemed like an eternity. Jossele did not know how long he had been interrogated, but the little sanity left in him prayed for death. He could not hold off the details about Khalela's mission to America much longer. The river of pain inflicted on him had already cracked the dam of his self-control, forcing him to release information he thought he would take to his grave. But the pain. Oh, dear Lord! The ants feeding on his feet, the salt on his leg wounds . . . The pain had been so intense, and the interrogator would not let Jossele pass out from it either. It was hell. It was unbearable. And it would not stop. He could not understand how his father had taken the pain, how he had endured this brutal torture and still kept the secrets locked inside his head.

"Aghh . . . no . . . please . . ." Jossele heard himself say as his body trembled not only from pain, but also from the fear of living too long. *Is this what you felt, father? Did you wish to die? Did you—*

The sergeant tightened his powerful grip. The crippling pain streaked up Jossele's body, reaching every inch of his body. He tensed, jaws shut tight, fists pulling with all his might against the restraining leather straps, legs kicking and head jerking, but it was to no avail. Jossele let out a hair-curling scream, which the interrogator cut short by clamping his free hand over Jossele's mouth. Slowly releasing the pressure on the groin, the *Mukhabarat* interrogator spoke again.

"Where, *Kurf?* Where is the connection?"

Jossele could barely hear the question. His body felt alien, distant, removed. *Am I already dead? Did my wish get granted?* The pain from his groin hovered somewhere in the black hole into which he had suddenly jumped, a place that seemed far away from the reality of his life. But he was not dead, not yet. As the interrogator removed the hand over Jossele's mouth, the stunned Mossad operative heard the question once again.

"Where, *Kurf?* Where?"

"Aghh . . . Vir . . . Virginia . . . in Virginia."

Horrified at his own words, Jossele forced himself to shut his mouth. He could not speak another word. He could not let them break him all the way. His father's broken body loomed in his mind. The Egyptians drove razors into his eyeballs, cut off his fingers, castrated him. But he did not utter a single word, did not reveal one drop of intelligence to the enemy. *Resist, Jossele! Resist!*

As his final thoughts of defiance clung to the outer walls of his mind, desperately hoping to keep his thoughts from surfacing, Jossele felt the pressure in his groin again, this time, however, it was augmented by the same scorching knife that had already severed so many of his fingers.

Oh, Dear God! He is going to cut them off! No, please. No!

With the burning smell of his own pubic hair filling his lungs, the possibility of castration burst through any feelings of contempt that remained in him.

"What exactly will happen in Virginia?" the voice came.

Jossele's ultimate fear overran the final stand. The vision of his courageous father faded away, and the words began to flow out of Jossele's quivering lips, slowly at first, and then with increased intensity. His only hope was for a quick death upon delivering the information his captors requested, including not only the revelation of the Mossad team Jossele himself had deployed to Lisbon from the Greek hilltop, but also everything Jossele knew about Khalela's plans to meet with Kevin Dalton in Virginia. A terrified Jossele knew the implications of his words. People would die because of his weakness, because of his inability to withstand the pain. But he couldn't take it any longer. It simply had to stop. Ashamed as he was about his own human weakness, Jossele begged his captors for a bullet in the head after finishing his confession.

Saddam Hussein listened without interruption at the words coming from the infidel's quivering mouth. The *Mukhabarat* knew indeed how to break a man. But the information the Jew had just revealed would not be enough to stop the torturing process. Saddam Hussein had to be certain that the man spoke the truth, and so he ordered the bald sergeant to continue the interrogation to see if during a delirious moment the prisoner contradicted his story. This process would continue until the Jew died, but by that time Saddam Hussein would be back in Baghdad, where he would make the necessary arrangements to get word of this important revelation to the Iraqi courier in Lisbon and also to Skeikh Imman al-Barakah in New Jersey. The sheikh was one of many spiritual leaders of Islam in the United States. He was also one of Saddam Hussein's many agents in America. Saddam would order the sheikh to eliminate the Mossad messenger, but not the American hero Kevin Dalton. Saddam wanted the American pilot, who was responsible for the destruction of Allahbad, to die a slow death.

Leaving the *Kurf* to his destiny at the skillful hands of the *Mukhabarat,* the Iraqi president stepped outside the stinking building and into the plush comfort of his limousine, where he reached for the cellular phone and called his foreign minister.

Four hours later the veteran minister released a statement to the press in response to an ultimatum issued by President Bill Clinton five hours earlier from Hiroshima in regard to the troops Saddam had deployed south of Baghdad. The Iraqi government claimed that the troops were engaged in nothing more than a military drill. The prepared statement, recited in both Arabic and English by the minister in his four-minute press conference, had been carefully written by a special team of the *Mukhabarat*. The English version, which Saddam Hussein knew would be replayed all around the world by CNN, carried a special message for Sheikh Imman al-Barakah and for the Iraqi courier in Lisbon, both of whom had been instructed to listen to any official statement issued by the Iraqi government.

Saddam smiled at the simplicity and effectiveness of his communications channel. While the Americans spent billions monitoring foreign communications and satellite transmissions, Saddam Hussein used CNN to send messages to his operatives around the world. With time, the original method had been refined to the point that *Mukhabarat* scribes could encode multiple messages within the same press release. Each field operative, working with a different letter decoder, would extract a unique message.

JERSEY CITY, NEW JERSEY.

In a private prayer room in his Jersey City mosque, Sheikh Imman al-Barakah pressed the play button on the VCR's remote control. The image of the Iraqi prime minister issuing a statement to the press came alive on the TV screen.

The sheikh began to write the message on a piece of paper, making certain to include every word. He had to replay the video five more times before he got the entire message down.

After turning off the TV and the VCR, the sheikh copied onto a separate piece of paper every word in the message that started with the letter B. He counted twenty-four of them. These constituted the letters of his personal message.

After erasing all of the leading Bs, he proceeded to map each remaining letter into its corresponding decoded letter according to a set of rules he had committed to memory a long time ago.

Moments later, the message Saddam had wanted delivered to the sheikh appeared on the piece of paper. The sheikh silently thanked Allah and Saddam Hussein for the opportunity to fight for the rights of Islam. The message told the sheikh how to find Kevin Dalton, the infidel who had destroyed Allahbad. A Mossad operative by the name of Khalela would contact Kevin at his home in Virginia and inform him of the nuclear hardware headed for America.

Four hours later, Sheikh Imman al-Barakah stood in front of five young followers, five lost souls who knelt by his feet as he read to them a section of the Koran. Three were Egyptians and two were Lebanese, arriving in this country years before to earn a higher education in an American college. At the time of their arrival their hearts had been clean of the evil spirits of the West. They were all Muslims, worshipers of Allah, followers of the Prophet Muhammad. But a few years inside the garden of the Great Satan had corrupted their souls. The evil American society had stained their sacred spirits with American whores, American whiskey, and American movies. Now Sheikh Imman al-Barakah faced the difficult task of purging their suffering souls of the evil that lived in them, for only then would they be worthy of becoming true soldiers of Allah, true martyrs of Islam.

A slightly overweight man just under five feet in height, Sheikh Imman al-Barakah had a long, unkempt salt-and-pepper beard, thick horn-rimmed glasses, and a prominent, veiny nose. Well into his sixties, the Iraqi sheikh had been instrumental in the creation of a new wave of Islamic soldiers, true warriors of Allah, loyal to the teachings of Muhammad, and willing to die for the future of Islam as defined by Saddam Hussein.

Heads bowed, the five men, all in their early twenties, kept their eyes closed as Sheikh Imman al-Barakah extended his right hand over them while holding the Holy Book with his left.

"Fear not, my lost children," said the sheikh, as his eyes focused on the yellowish pages of the leather-bound copy of the Koran. For this session he had selected an appropriate *surah,* or chapter: *Al-takathur,* meaning "worldly gain."

"Your hearts are taken up with worldly gain from the cradle to the grave," said the sheikh, his right hand now touching the heads of his children. "But you shall know! Indeed, if you knew the truth with certainty, you would see the fire of Hell. You would see it with your very eyes. Then, on that day you shall be questioned about your joys."

Closing the book, the sheikh now extended both hands over his followers. "You have heard it from the book of Allah, my children. Reject the evils of the West! Reject the worldly gains of this society! Reject the children of the Great Satan! For only then shall you be free from sin, free to join our holy crusade against the evil that threatens the very existence of Islam, the very essence of our lives!"

Taking a step back, opening the Koran, and switching to a new *surah* titled *Al-dhariyat,* meaning "the winds," Sheikh Imman al-Barakah read aloud, "We are sent forth to a wicked nation, so that we may bring down on them a shower of clay stones marked by Allah for the destruction of the sinful. We let loose on them a blighting wind, which pounded into dust all that it swept before it. None but the perverse turn away from the true faith. Perish the liars, who dwell in darkness and are heedless of the life to come!"

Closing the Koran, the old sheikh added, "Rise, my children. Rise to the power of Allah!"

All five stood and inhaled deeply, their eyes displaying the inner fire that now burned in their souls, the fire of Allah.

"Do you reject the evils of the West?"

"We reject!" responded the five in unison.

"Do you reject the whores, the liquor, and the movies?"

"We reject!"

"Do you make now a lifelong commitment to serve Allah and the Islamic movement?"

"Yes, we commit!"

Looking at the three Egyptians, all of whom were terrorists who had fought with the *Mujahideen* in Afghanistan, the sheikh said to them, "Go, my children. Go to your mission in Florida. Go and become martyrs of Islam, for that is the only way to redemption. Always remember who you are, remember the words of the Prophet Muhammad, the words of Allah."

The three Egyptians bowed, turned around, and left the room. The other two dropped to their knees and reached for the sheikh's feet. These two Lebanese students had seen plenty of combat in Beirut before coming to America. They were excellent assets to the sheikh, and the old Iraqi planned to use those skills to fulfill another facet of Saddam Hussein's plan.

"How long, Holy One? How long before peace shall fill my heart once more?" said one of them, a stocky man with a thick dark beard, while the other wept, using the sheikh's robe to dry his eyes.

Leaning down and gently helping the crying men to their feet, Sheikh Imman al-Barakah said, "Now, my children. Now I shall show you the way to full redemption for your past sins. Just like your Egyptian brothers, who have departed to meet their destiny, now your chance has come to prove yourself worthy of Allah's kingdom. It is now that Allah calls upon you."

With that, another man entered the room. An Iraqi, one much older, who had worked for the sheikh since the mosque's dedication two years ago.

He bowed once and said, "Holy One, the mission must start immediately. The infidel American pilot must face the wrath of Allah."

"You speak the language of light and truth, my child," Sheikh Imman al-Barakah said. "With you I leave these two children of Allah, these two lost sheep who have returned to our flock. Show them the only way to redemption."

"I shall, Holy One. I shall."

After giving the Lebanese pair a final blessing, the sheikh left the praying room and walked to a small room in the rear of the mosque, where a beautiful Syrian girl dressed in high heels, a tight leather miniskirt, and a thin white blouse sat on an old and stained tan sofa.

"Rise, Child of Allah," the sheikh said to the sixteen-year-old girl. Awkwardly getting to her feet while lowering her gaze, the dark-skinned native of Damascus braced herself as Sheikh Imman al-Barakah approached her. She was the only daughter of a Syrian general caught spying for the Israelis. President Hafez Assad had ordered the general and his family executed, except for her. The New Islamist International had a far more practical plan for the beautiful virgin than putting a bullet in her head. She was a coveted asset, which the sheikh planned to use wisely to fulfill Saddam's plans.

"Fear me not, child, for I mean no harm to you."

Crying, the girl turned her round brown eyes to the old sheikh, her legs shaking out of fear and also from the high heels she had never worn before. "Please, Holy One. Please help me. I do not wish to be shamed with these garments of the West."

"And you shall not, my child. I despise the sacrilegious clothes that I have been forced to make you wear. My heart mourns at the sight of the satanic makeup covering your angelic face. But tonight you shall undo the curse brought upon you by the acts of your father. Tonight you shall regain the blessings of Allah."

With that, the sheikh called for one of his vehicles. The nervous girl was escorted by two large black men into the rear of the sedan, which sped away a few seconds later.

Across the street from the mosque stood an old two-story apartment building. In one of the units on the first floor, an FBI special agent watched and photographed everyone going in and coming out of the mosque. Ever since the World Trade Center fiasco, every single mosque in New York and New Jersey had been under surveillance by order of the director of the FBI.

The agent used the zoom of his Nikon camera to focus on the face of the girl sitting in the rear seat of a white sedan that had just left the mosque. He also snapped a picture of the license plate of the sedan as it drove down the street. Fifteen minutes earlier, he had snapped the photos of three young Arabs leaving the mosque together in a taxicab. Five minutes later, he had photographed another pair of Arabs as they walked away from the mosque and disappeared around the corner. In the previous minute he had consumed fifteen frames on the two large blacks flanking the beautiful girl as they left the mosque and got in the sedan.

In another three hours, another agent would come and work the night shift. The departing agent would take his film and bring it to the FBI Analysis Laboratory, where it would be processed, and the faces in every frame would be digitized and stored in a data bank, along with information on the time and place of the sighting. In a single twenty-four-hour period, the large computer system in the basement of the J. Edgar Hoover Building in downtown Washington, D.C., would process over one thousand digitized faces from all the surveillance teams deployed to cover mosques and businesses belonging to suspect Arabs. A percentage of the images would find a match in the data banks, and the file of the match would be opened and updated with the new information. If there was no match, a new file would be created with the digitized image and the accompanying information, making the database one of the most precious tools in the hands of the FBI for catching terrorists.

BETHESDA, MARYLAND.

Kate Marston arrived at her town house thirty minutes after five in the afternoon. She parked her Honda in front of her house, picked up her mail, and walked toward her front door while browsing through a mail order catalogue. She unlocked her door and walked inside. There was much to be done before Robert Bourdeaux arrived at seven. This time the DDO would take her out to dinner and the opera. She only had ninety minutes to shower, blow-dry her hair, put on makeup, and get dressed. She had to hurry.

She closed and locked the door and headed for the kitchen to turn on the lights, but she noticed the overheads were already on. She also detected the smell of cigarette smoke.

"Dobry vyechir, Katrina Aleksandra Markarova. You seem to be in a hurry. *Da?"*

Kate dropped the mail and spun around, dread filling her. Sitting on the sofa was a Ukrainian man by the name of Viktor Kozlov, one of many hired guns working for the Russian Mafia in America. A cigarette hung off the corner of his mouth. It moved as he smiled.

Kate braced herself. She remembered the last time she had seen the man with the broad shoulders, the square face, and the bad cough. Viktor Kozlov had raped her for refusing to cooperate with the Russian Mafia in this country.

"I made a deal with all of you a year ago," Kate responded, struggling to keep her voice from cracking. An intense fire burned her insides at the sight of this man. "You swore to leave me alone if I worked for you for six months. I kept my end of this deal and submitted my last report six months ago. I am not involved anymore!"

The large Ukrainian stood, coughed once, and pulled hard on the cigarette. "You can never leave the *Komitat Gosudarstvennoi Bezopasnosti,* Katrina Aleksandra. Don't you remember?"

"The *Komitat* does not exist anymore!" barked Kate. "It is dead! Finished!"

Viktor smiled and walked toward her. Kate took a step back toward the wall. "Not when it comes to you, my dear Katrina Aleksandra. The state paid for your education and your life in this country. It is time you paid them back."

"Lies! Those are all a bunch of lies! You and the others in Atlantic City . . . they are . . . they are using me to gain wealth! I didn't want to join them! I just want be left alone!"

The Ukrainian pushed her against the wall separating the living room from the kitchen.

"Pashol von!" she exclaimed. "Go away, please!"

Viktor smiled even more. "So, you do remember, Katrina. You do remember how to speak *parosske,* just as you remember the time I fucked you. *Da?"*

Turning her face away from him, Kate began to sob. "Please, go away. I did what you asked of me. I provided you with what you needed for six months. That was the deal!"

Viktor Kozlov pressed himself against her, his groin rubbing against her small pelvis.

"Tell me how much the CIA knows about the contraband of nuclear weapons!"

"Please. I can't!"

Viktor put his hairy, sailor hands on her skirt and ripped it cleanly off her. Another swift move and her panties followed. Now his hands rubbed against her.

"Oh, God! No, please!" she begged, without fighting him for fear that he might beat her just as he did the last time.

" 'God,' Katrina? *You* are saying, *'God?' "* the Ukrainian said, while pushing her up against the wall and separating her thighs. "God does not exist, or have you forgotten your communism? Now tell me, old whore! Tell me or I shall fuck you again!"

Kate Marston swallowed hard and began to speak, telling Viktor everything she knew about the recent information gathered by Donald Bane in Moscow, and also about the officer's plans to travel to Serpuchov to track the next shipment.

"Where do the Americans think the hardware is going?"

"Iraq . . . the hardware is going to Iraq . . . now, please! Go away!"

Slowly, the Ukrainian moved away from her. "You have done well, Katrina Aleksandra. The *Komitat* will be grateful for this information."

"I . . . I just want . . . to be left alone," she said, falling on the hardwood floors, hugging her legs.

Viktor lit another cigarette, inspecting the former KGB agent with distaste while blasting away in Russian. "You live in a world of fantasy, Katrina. This is not your country. You were once like the rest of us, but then you turned soft, emotional, fell in love with that dead American husband of yours. Didn't you learn your lesson a year ago when we killed him? Do you want us to kill Robert Bourdeaux as well? Do your work for us, and we will take care of you. Turn your back on us, and we will make your life a living hell. We are the legacy of the KGB, Katrina. You do not get to walk away from the *Komitat* just because our country is now run by fools! *We* are the *Komitat*. We created you, and we still own you."

The Ukrainian drew once more from the cigarette, threw it on the floor, and crushed it with a shoe.

"Good-bye, Katrina Aleksandra. And remember, the *Komitat* is always watching you. Do not do anything you might regret later. We will contact you in a few days and you better have more information for us, or . . ." Viktor rubbed his groin before turning around and walking out the door.

Kate Marston lay crying on the floor, with her arms wrapped around her knees. But by the time Robert Bourdeaux rang the bell at seven o'clock, she had managed to change into an evening dress and fix her hair as best as she could. By then, the tracks of her tears had been covered with heavy makeup. She remained fairly quiet during dinner, letting Bourdeaux do most of the talking, although she knew he sensed something was wrong. But Kate always had the excuse of her dead husband for situations when she didn't feel like talking, and she used it tonight, when Bourdeaux asked her what was wrong during one of the intermissions at the opera.

Her heart screamed simply to tell the truth and make the nightmare end. Whatever happened after she talked could not be any worse than her current life of deception and fear. Crossing the Russian Mafia, however, could have deadly consequences not just for her, but also for Robert Bourdeaux.

Kate loved Bourdeaux too much to risk it. She chose to continue with the lie while she tried to think of a way out of her predicament.

LISBON, PORTUGAL.

Mukhabarat Colonel Kemal Ramallah listened to the words spoken not by the Portuguese anchor of the local television station, but to the English words of the Iraqi foreign minister as he issued a formal response to President Clinton's ultimatum.

Most of the people in the crowded bar, which catered to sailors from all over the world, were not even watching the large screen behind the counter. Many had been at sea for months and drank heavily in the company of local whores. They could not care less about a public statement made by some Arab.

But Kemal listened carefully, intently. His mind, trained to memorize such messages with amazing ease, recorded every word starting with the letter L. Without the use of any paper, the *Mukhabarat* colonel then translated the message in his mind.

His eyes glinted with anger the moment he understood. The Mossad was after his cargo. Israeli operatives had been sent to intercept the hardware before it left Lisbon.

Paranoid eyes now slowly scanned the crowded bar, one of many lining a street a block away from the docks, where the Iraqi officer had already arranged for transportation to America aboard an Italian merchant vessel. Slowly, Kemal got up from the barstool and made his way to the exit.

The cool air carried the smell of the sea. Kemal inhaled deeply and shoved both hands in the side pockets of his brown trousers as he walked down the poorly lit street. At one o'clock in the morning many drunk sailors already slept it off on the streets around the docks. Kemal had to walk around two of them passed out on a dirty sidewalk next to large metal bins filled with garbage.

He walked for thirty minutes, stopping at four other bars, checking for tails. Satisfied that no one followed him, Kemal turned the corner and reached the docks in another minute. His vessel, the *Vesuvius,* was docked a couple of hundred feet away. Bright floodlights on the bow, midship, and stern illuminated the crew as they worked to load the final crates on board.

More cork, canned fish, and wine for the infidels, thought Kemal, as he approached the ship.

The vessel already carried enough Italian handmade tile to floor a thousand American homes, enough French wine to fill a large swimming pool, and the finest woods and textiles from Spain. Now the greedy Americans would also get the best produce from Portugal.

In spite of the recent revelation, Kemal couldn't help his feeling of hatred for the Americans momentarily overcome the paranoia that had been injected by the message from the Iraqi foreign minister. While his people starved because of U.N.-imposed economic sanctions, the American pigs enjoyed the best products the world had to offer.

Why Allah? Why must the infidels rejoice with the fruits of this earth while your people eat like dogs?

Suddenly, the words from the Koran echoed in his mind, reminding Kemal of his true mission in life.

The unbelievers among the People of the Book and the pagans shall burn forever in the fire of Hell. But of all creatures, those that embrace the Faith and do good works are the noblest. Their reward, in their Lord's presence, shall be the gardens of Eden, gardens watered by running streams, where they shall dwell forever.

Guilt overwhelmed him, not only for questioning his Master, but also for letting his feelings get in the way of the mission. In his hands he carried the enormous responsibility of delivering a powerful message to the same Americans who had killed his family in the War of 1991. His country depended on him to succeed. Saddam had put his trust in Kemal Ramallah to overcome whatever obstacles came in the way of turning New York City and Washington, D.C., into ashes.

Reaching the gangway connecting the weathered docks to the ship's main deck, Kemal slowly turned around and scanned the docks one final time. He saw nothing out of the ordinary. Just a bunch of drunken sailors catching whores. Slowly, Kemal made his way up the gangway and into the ship that would take him to America.

Three blocks away, a pair of inebriated sailors staggered over the cobblestone sidewalk. Vomit and wine stained their blue uniforms as they reached the docks.

The sailors leaned on a wall while making obscene gestures with their hands to a local prostitute walking by in a white miniskirt and black blouse. The Portuguese woman gave the pair a glimpse and walked even faster. The sailors laughed and howled as their eyes gravitated from the whore to the man walking up the gangway of the *Vesuvius.*

The sailors had seen the man come out of a bar and nearly trip on them as they pretended to sleep on the sidewalk.

They both had seen the face, which matched the face of the Arab man local Mossad contacts had seen walking the Portuguese docks looking for transportation to the United States.

Ever since Jossele Dani had called in from Greece to warn local Mossad operatives about the runaway nuclear hardware, several Israeli agents, their bribed local officials, and local contacts had been on the move at the Lisbon airport and the docks. It took this small army just over a day to find the Iraqi, but not his cargo. The man was definitely a professional, always checking his back, always walking in circles, never revealing the actual location of the hardware.

Now they had seen him boarding the Italian vessel. In less than five minutes the word would be out among the ranks of the Mossad agents operating in Portugal. The Iraqi messenger had been found.

5

IRINA

How art thou fallen from Heaven, O Lucifer, son of the morning!
—Isaiah 14:12

ATLANTIC CITY, NEW JERSEY.

The air inside the large club was heavy and the smell of smoke and beer filled Irina Bukovski's lungs as she pushed her way to the rear of the crowded bar in Atlantic City. Viktor Kozlov, pretending to work as a bartender while running security in the place, smiled and waved at Irina from behind the bar. A cigarette hung off the corner of his mouth.

Wearing a tight leather miniskirt and a gold blouse buttoned down the middle of her chest, Irina nodded as she elbowed a large American in the ribs to force him out of her way, making him spill his drink as she cruised by.

"You bitch!" he screamed, as he tried to go after the thin and pale woman with the short auburn hair and dark lipstick and eye shadow. Before he could take a step toward her, the Ukrainian reached from behind the bar and grabbed the American's right shoulder with a hairy hand.

"You do not wish to mess with her, my friend! She will cut off your balls!" he shouted above the noise of the crowd and the ear-piercing rock music.

Momentarily immobilized by the huge clamp on his shoulder, the American hesitated for a few moments and calmed down.

A minute later Irina finally reached the back of her club's main room, where two black men, their bulging biceps stretching the fabric of their sport coats, respectfully nodded as they let her through. A short hall with three doors on either side faced her. She went inside the first one on her right, walking into the large private office she used to run not just the profitable club but also her three-year-old underground network in the coastal city.

A product of the old Soviet system, which had taught her to hate

America for as long as she could remember, Irina Bukovski had been taken from her parents—a farmer couple charged with treason against the system for failing to meet their grain quotas—at the age of seven by the KGB. The naive but strikingly beautiful young girl had been trained to become an instrument of socialism. She belonged to the state. The state provided for her, and in return she had to obey without question. Forced sex with senior KGB officials at the age of fifteen followed by two abortions and a hysterectomy by the time she was seventeen had removed all remnants of affection from her heart. And that was exactly what the KGB had wanted to do: create a coldhearted, yet highly seductive machine to spy for the benefit of the Rodina. Innocent and angelic on the outside, Irina became a secretary at the American Embassy in Moscow, where she worked on young Marines and lonely diplomats. Once she even befriended a closet-lesbian U.S. Navy attaché. For years she spied for the Rodina, enjoying privileges denied to most Russians. From the best dental care, food, and clothing, to paid vacations in Paris and Rome, Irina grew attached to her deceptive but glamorous life, until the collapse of the Soviet Union, after which she found herself an outcast among her people. Looked down upon by everyone that knew what she had done for the KGB, Irina used her looks and skills to marry a U.S. Marine and move to Connecticut, where she divorced the young American a year later, but not before receiving her permanent residency. Irina had no plans to go back and face a tough life in the decaying post-Soviet economy. Unlike Russia, America held opportunities. The country was soft and ripe for Irina's kind. The Americans were far too predictable and easy to manipulate and intimidate.

Running a hand through her recently dyed hair, Irina turned her triangular face to a man who had betrayed her. With her strides long and confident, she slowly approached him, her high heels clicking over the tile floor, a pair of blue eyes taking in the bruised man held up by another pair of black Muslims as big as the ones guarding the private hallway. The Muslims were part of her arrangement with Sheikh Imman al-Barakah up in Jersey City. Through the old sheikh, Saddam Hussein provided her with able bodies and intelligence to protect her network. In return, the sheikh received a percentage of Irina's very profitable businesses, which included prostitution rings, gambling, and drug sales in New Jersey, and rapidly expanding into New York, Pennsylvania, and Delaware as her connections with the Medellin Cartel grew.

Her arrangement with Saddam reduced the amount of capital the Iraqi leader had to send to America through secret bank accounts and money-laundering schemes, two activities closely monitored by the FBI and the CIA to capture terrorists operating inside the United States.

Irina gave the dazed traitor a kiss on the cheek, her tongue softly rubbing a purplish patch of skin.

"You really thought you could steal from me? Yes?" she asked one of her top drug dealers in Philadelphia, a professor at the University of Pennsylvania, who had been caught while trying to run away with twenty kilos of cocaine following a large deal with the cartel. "You disappoint me."

The thirty-seven-year-old American mumbled something incoherent. His jaw had been broken by one of the brutes holding him by the shoulders.

Irina looked at the guards. "Cut his throat and throw him in the river."

Both men slowly nodded.

"The girl arrived from Jersey City? Yes?" Irina asked.

"She is in the bedroom," one of the Muslims observed.

"What about my client?"

"In the waiting room next door," the same Muslim responded.

"Is the video equipment ready?" Irina asked.

"Yes."

Irina walked over to the next room.

The white wall-to-wall carpet met off-white walls decorated with two long mirrors and several framed black-and-white prints of nude male and female models posing in balletlike stances. A black-lacquered round bed with satin sheets stood in the center of the room, below a large mirror covering most of the ceiling. Two antique chairs on the far side of the room and a love seat next to the door rounded out the room's sparse furnishings. Irina saw the Syrian virgin sitting on the sofa. Sheikh Imman al-Barakah had promised her to Irina to assist in her upcoming support of Saddam Hussein's most important mission.

The information Viktor Kozlov had extracted from Katrina Marka-rova told Irina that the Americans had learned much about the nuclear hardware–smuggling operation. Luckily for Saddam and his plan, it appeared as if the CIA suspected that the hardware was being taken to Iraq and not to the United States. Irina had also learned about the CIA operative Donald Bane and his plan to crack the smuggling ring. She had immediately used her connections in the Russian Embassy in Washington to relay a message to Moscow. The information quickly made it to the Soltnevo Group. Bane had to be terminated. Irina had also used the same channel to give Baghdad an update on the situation. This latter message had made it to the Iraqi capital via Moscow, Athens, Damascus, and, finally, Baghdad.

The Syrian girl stood, her captivating brown eyes slowly gravitating toward Irina. The smooth skin of her face reminded Irina of herself, before life had hardened her. A part of her felt quite jealous of the youth radiating from the Syrian. Not even the most expensive makeup, which Irina regularly imported from Paris, could make her skin look like that.

Approaching her, Irina reached for the girl's blouse and unbuttoned it, letting it fall to the floor. The girl quickly covered herself. Irina motioned her to turn around, and she unzipped the girl's miniskirt before taking a few steps back to inspect her.

Irina smiled. *Perfect.*

"Get dressed and wait here."

Before the girl could respond, Irina went into the next room, where a well-dressed American business executive smoked a cigar while he waited.

"About time somebody showed up!" the American, a slightly over-weight man in his fifties with large arms and a round face, protested, while throwing the cigar against the carpet and crushing it with a shiny black shoe. "Have you any idea how much my time is worth?"

"My apologies. But I can assure you that your wait will be worthwhile. Yes?"

The American shook his head. "It better be. I'm paying top dollar for this. Where is she?"

Irina noticed the anxious eyes of the aging executive, whose hands trembled in anticipation. She smiled inwardly. All of her special clients always exhibited such behavior right before Irina made their ultimate fantasy come true.

"She is waiting in the next room," the Russian woman responded.

"She better be a virgin," the American warned, as he headed for the door. "I'll be able to tell if she's not, you know. And if she ain't, our deal's off."

"Do not worry," Irina responded in a calm voice. She needed this obnoxious man, who happened to own a large flight school at the local airport. The aircraft inventory under his name included a large helicopter, which played a key role in fulfilling Saddam Hussein's plans. "Everything will be as promised."

Irina watched him go inside the bedroom and lock the door. She immediately went into her office, where Viktor Kozlov already waited for her. The Muslims had taken the college professor out of the building.

Viktor sat facing the large framed painting on the right side of Irina's desk, the fingers of his left hand working the knobs and switches of a small control panel built right below the painting.

The Russian woman walked behind Viktor as the Ukrainian dimmed the lights. The painting slid to the right, exposing a clear view of the bedroom through a one-way mirror.

The executive had already ripped off the virgin's blouse and was working on the miniskirt when Viktor flipped the switches to record the event.

"More insurance, Irina?" asked Viktor, without taking his eyes off the scene in the bedroom.

Irina did not respond. His eyes were fixed on the American as he forced the naked girl's back against the bed, tears rolling out of her eyes.

"La' minfadlak. No, please," the Syrian virgin pleaded.

"Shut the fuck up, bitch!" responded the American, slapping her across the face before lowering his pants.

"You belong to me now," muttered Irina as she watched the rape. Her mind replayed the day she had lost her own virginity to her KGB trainer. Just like the American pig who was now trying to enter the Syrian virgin, the KGB brute had forced himself inside Irina while her vagina was still dry, nearly ripping her in half. She had bled for hours afterward and had to be hospitalized.

The Syrian girl let go a loud scream the moment the American finally succeeded.

"We got him, Viktor. He is married, has three children, two grandchildren, and is a prominent member of Atlantic City society. He is *mine.* Send him a copy in a confidential envelope to his office tomorrow, along with instructions on when and where we will need his Sikorsky," Irina said, as she patted the Ukrainian's shoulder.

"Yes, Irina," he responded, while constantly making camera adjustments. The Ukrainian had personally set up the video system in the next room, with cameras hidden behind two walls and in the ceiling. Three small television monitors on Irina's desk displayed crisp black-and-white images of the rape scene.

The business executive had just become the latest acquisition of the Russian Mafia in America.

OUTSIDE OF SERPUCHOV, RUSSIA.

CIA Officer Donald Bane shivered as he slowly froze in the pitch-black woods west of Serpuchov, a city south of Moscow. He had been on that spot for nearly three hours now, and he didn't know how much longer he could hold out before hypothermia set in.

The first party had arrived an hour ago, right before sundown: four Russian soldiers hauling a dozen large boxes in the bed of a rusted Army truck. So far the information in Krasilov's papers was accurate.

Chain-smoking, sipping vodka, and talking about the whores they would be able to screw after receiving payment for the contents inside the boxes, the Russians stood by the side of the road a hundred feet away from Bane, who kept a good eye on them, thanks to the powerful night goggles the Moscow Station chief had given him. Their voices, amplified by the small parabolic antenna set up by Bane's feet, came clear through the headphones he wore.

The second party, the one Bane suspected to be connected to the Soltnevo Group, had not arrived yet. The longer it took for the Russian mobsters to come forth and trade with the soldiers, the wearier Bane became.

The swinging branches of towering pine trees and the growing intensity with which snowflakes now fell told Bane that things there were definitely heading the wrong way. Not only would his monitoring gear cease to operate as the snowstorm gathered strength and the temperature continued to drop, but the shots of vodka he had taken before leaving his Skoda, hidden in a ditch a half mile away, were wearing off. The gusts of wind chilled him to the bone.

I'm freezing my ass off!

Bane rubbed his gloved hands together and watched the winding road as three pairs of headlights slowly moved toward the flashlights of the Russian soldiers.

About fucking time!

Removing the night goggles, which Bane let hang loose from his neck, the CIA officer reached down for a white backpack he had taken with him and extracted a powerful Nikon fitted with a night vision telescopic lens. His hands fumbled with the camera for several seconds, and Bane decided he could not operate it with his gloves on. Taking them off, however, turned into a painful experience as his fingers quickly lost their elasticity to the harsh cold.

Bane began snapping photos of license plates and the faces of the soldiers and the three men that emerged from three large gray vans. A suitcase was exchanged for the boxes, which all the men on the road had to help move one at a time from the truck to the vans.

Donald Bane's fears came true as his mind translated the Russian spoken by the seven figures. Two of the civilians belonged to the Soltnevo Group, the third did not. He kept warning the others, including the soldiers, to be careful with the warheads or Marcos would come here himself and kill them. The other two civilians told him that the Soltnevo Group could buy Marcos several times over, and that if it weren't for the Russian Mafia, Marcos would never be able to get the shipment out of Russia tonight. The argument kept going back and forth between the civilians while the soldiers kept quiet and helped the loud trio pack all the boxes inside the vans.

That was it. The hardware was nuclear, the first buyer was the Soltnevo Group, the broker was Marcos Dominguez, and the end user had to be Saddam Hussein, Marcos's preferred customer.

Just as Krasilov's papers had suggested.

What Bane lacked was information on exactly when, where, and how the shipment was scheduled to leave the country. Based on the number of boxes, Bane estimated that this shipment was almost four times the size of the one described in the documents he'd found on the Ukrainian general. If the mix of hardware in this shipment was close to the one detailed in Krasilov's papers, Bane guessed that between the two shipments Saddam could assemble at least twenty small warheads, each as strong as the one that leveled Hiroshima.

Now I need to know how in the hell they plan to get this shipment out of Russia.

Fighting off the impulse to haul ass toward his car immediately, not just to report this finding to Langley but also to keep from freezing to death, Bane finished the roll of film, which the Moscow Station would use in conjunction with key members of the Moscow Police under direct orders from President Boris Yeltsin to crack the smuggling operation.

The camera automatically rewound the film as Bane trembled from the rapidly dropping temperatures and increased winds. He couldn't wait to reach his Sko—

Two shots cracked the night in half, the sound waves dislodging several pounds of snow accumulated on the branches of the tall pine above Bane.

The impact made him collapse and drop the camera.

Shit. The film, Don! Get the fucking film!

With zero visibility, save for the nearing beams of light from the soldiers' flashlights, Bane grabbed the camera, removed the film, and got up from the pile of snow, which covered the rest of his surveillance equipment. Another gunshot, followed by the sound of a near-miss, rang in his ears long after the round exploded in the pine.

Shoving the film in a coat pocket, he moved to the left, quickly realizing the cold was already retarding his movements. Reaching for the night goggles, Bane realized they were not there. They must have fallen off when the snow hit him. *Damn!*

With visibility increasing to around twenty feet as his eyes adjusted to the night, Bane saw the snow explode to his left, then to his right. This time he heard no sounds. Someone with a suppressed weapon had joined the first shooter.

Feeling like a duck in a shooting gallery, Bane wondered if he would be able to prevail in this cold for long.

Another shot, and Bane took cover behind the trunk of a pine. Pressed against the frozen bark, he looked over his right shoulder. The vans sped away as all four soldiers went after him, dark figures carrying long rifles with spotting halogens attached to the muzzles, their running silhouettes illuminated by the headlights of the departing vans.

Donald Bane closed his eyes, forcing his professional side to take control. Four against one, and the one was about to go into hypothermia. But he had a chance as long as he kept thinking. Four against one. Four against one. There was only one way to survive this, and that was for Bane to reverse the trap and take them all out.

Three shots came in rapid succession, all striking the pine. *Reverse the trap. Reverse the fucking trap!* The phrase repeated in his head over and over. He had to make the hunter the prey and the prey the hunter. But doing so against these odds challenged even the experienced dinosaur in Donald Bane.

Snow clinging to the sides of his face, Bane began to move quickly in the opposite direction from the four figures, roughly thirty feet behind, barely visible in the night. He stopped after putting another thirty feet of forest between them. The wind gathered speed, stinging his eyes.

Instinctively, Bane dropped to the snow-covered ground and reached for the Sig Sauer automatic, flipped the safety and cocked it. His skin froze to the cold metal. He remained still, almost buried in the snow as the foursome approached, the wind hissing through the trees, the glow from the road backlighting their nearing silhouettes.

The smell of gunpowder mixed with that of evergreens. Bane had to move quickly or risk losing to the cold weather. Frostbite would set in soon. But not yet. This would be his only chance to fire back, before his index finger lost the elasticity it would need to pull the trigger. The figures kept coming, halogen spotters searching for him. White beams of light crisscrossed over the snow and trees. The origin of the closest beam lined up with the sights of the weapon Bane clutched in front of him, elbows planted on the ground, snow reaching his shoulders and wrists.

His arms and legs shockingly cold, hands stiff, and fingers losing sensation, Donald Bane fired once, twice. The leading figure arched back. The other three leveled their weapons at him.

With snow and bark exploding around him, Bane rolled away from his hiding place before breaking into a run, the Sig firmly gripped in his right hand. He was about to reach a cluster of trees—

One, two, three bullets grazed past him and exploded in a cloud of bark as they struck a pine tree to his right. Their zooming sound rang in his ears as Bane cut left and kept on running for another hundred feet, the noise behind him growing louder. The trees to both sides of him turned into a solid wall as his boots kicked the snow . . . *the snow!*

Only then he realized that no matter how fast he tried to get away, the remaining guns would merely follow his tracks. Sooner or later they would catch up with him. The woods darkened as Bane left his hunters' high-intensity searchlights behind. But he didn't care. The darkness would protect him. The woods would shield him against the bullets of those soldiers only if he could stop leaving a trail in the snow.

He continued to run, but this time he searched for a break in the snow-covered woods. Perhaps . . . *a frozen ravine!*

That was it. With three more shots cracking through the frigid air, Bane raced past the frozen underbrush that led to a ten-foot-wide ravine. He could hear water flowing under the ice, and there was no way for him to tell how thick the layer was, but he had to take a chance. The guns were closing in on him, the beams forking through the woods.

Bane jumped on the ice and tried to run but slipped and fell face first. The blow stung and momentarily disoriented him. He felt a warm trickle of blood running down his forehead. For a few seconds everything appeared blurry.

Bane struggled to his feet and, instead of running, lunged forward and slid down on his belly for a few dozen feet until his momentum stopped. He reached the opposite side of the ravine and managed to grab a branch. He pulled himself up and was about to step on the snow by the edge, but stopped in time. Instead, Bane held on to a higher branch and swung his shivering body a few feet away, landed on his back, and rolled behind a tree as his pursuers reached the ravine. Bane saw three search beams.

He looked for his Sig . . . *my Sig!* The last time he had it was when he'd fallen on the—

"I think you dropped this!"

Bane saw one of the soldiers raise his Sig Sauer in the air while turning a full circle on the ice, obviously not knowing which direction Bane had taken.

"Come out and you will be spared! Resist and you will be shot like a dog!" the soldier shouted in Russian.

In spite of the cold, Bane wiggled his body into the snow, taking time to cover his legs and back. His arms were numb, his fingers swollen. The cold had made it into his body and quickly stripped him of life-supporting heat. If his temperature dropped any lower, Bane feared he would lose consciousness.

"Very well, then. Have it your way!" said another soldier.

The Russians split three ways. Two went back to the opposite side of the ravine while the third entered the forest twenty feet from where Bane hid. Slowly, Bane reached down to his right leg and curled his numbed fingers around the black handle of a ten-inch steel blade. The pain from his fingers as he forced them to clutch the handle hurt more than the wound on his forehead.

He narrowed his eyes as the Russian, wearing a bulky black coat that dropped to his knees, turned in his direction. The muzzle of the machine gun held by the soldier pointed at Bane. He remained pressed against the ground as the man scanned the forest in front of him with the weapon before taking two more steps toward Bane.

The cold began to cloud Bane's judgment, making him forget the threat behind the nearing beam of light while he stared in envy at the thick coat his hunter wore. He quickly forced his mind back to the moment and prayed that the snow over his legs and back was thick enough to disguise his presence. It appeared that way, because the gunman, after taking two more steps, turned his back on Bane.

With the Russian now less than six feet away, Bane hesitated about attacking. Would his achingly cold body move swiftly enough to reach his hunter before he turned around? Bane didn't know, but he felt certain of one thing: if he didn't move quickly, he would freeze to death. He had to make his muscles work to get his circulation flowing.

His hunter remained still, thin white clouds rising off his face as he breathed. The weapon pointed away from Bane, the search beam moving across the woods.

Bane took in the cold air once, exhaled, and breathed it again as he inched his legs forward to see how they would respond. They moved. Bane inhaled one last time, recoiled, and lunged.

The soldier must have heard him, because halfway through the attack he began to turn around, but it was too late. Bane kept the blade aimed for the chest and drove it in hard. Both men landed by the edge of the frozen ravine. Because of the heavy coat the Russian wore, the blade had barely gone inside his chest.

Their eyes locked. The Russian's lips parted, and Bane could smell his breath. The gunmen no doubt had had a few drinks to warm their cores before rushing into the woods after him.

"Napoma—"

Pinning him down on the snow, Bane jammed his numb right hand against the Russian's mouth as he tightened his grip around the young soldier's neck.

"Where? *Gdye? Gdye?"* Bane said over the noise of the wind and the rustling of tree branches. "Where is the shipment going?" Bane testily lifted his hands off the Russian's mouth.

"Dyshat . . . I can't breathe . . ."

"Tell me! Where!"

"Sheremetyevo . . . the airport," the soldier said in between gasps of air.

The airport! Of course! With the connections the Soltnevo Group had in Russia, particularly in Moscow, why not use those contacts to get the stuff out the fastest way possible.

"When? How?" Bane asked as he heard the nearing voices of the other two soldiers heading back this way.

"Napomash! Napomash!" screamed the young soldier before Bane got a chance to jam his hand back over the quivering mouth, and the Russian bit it hard. ❖

Out of choices, Bane palm-struck the knife's handle. The blade cut deeper into the Russian's body until the handle met the man's coat. The Russian shuddered, letting go of Bane's hand. His eyes rolled to the back of his head as he finally went limp. Bane knew that his hand should be hurting from the deep bite marks, but it didn't. He had lost sensation below the wrist.

Angry for not being able to extract more information from the soldier, Bane stood and dragged the limp body away from the ravine. The anger slowly faded as the wind tore away his body heat at a staggering rate. His lips trembled and his pockmarked cheeks twitched out of control. He couldn't feel his feet inside the frozen boots. Bane needed protection quickly before he froze, before the cold seeped deeper into him. His fingers, swollen and numb, didn't feel like a part of his body any longer, and neither did his ears, nose, and feet.

He leaned the dead man against a tree and pulled out his knife. The jagged edge cut a wider track on its way out, jetting blood over Bane's legs. He ignored it, set the bloody knife on the side, and undid the straps of the man's heavy woolen jacket. He removed it and quickly put it on. Next he slung the machine gun and—

"Mikhail? Mikhail?"

Bane's head snapped left. The other two were already back on the ravine. Bane got caught in plain view kneeling in the snow. One of the Russians looked straight at Bane and waved for a moment before realizing what had happened and leveling the machine gun in Bane's direction.

Leaving his knife behind, Bane jumped away as the slow rattle of the Russian weapon crackled through the woods and was followed by multiple explosions of snow. He got to his feet and reached a thick cluster of trees. The firing subsided. His back crashed hard against the trunk of a wide pine and, breathing heavily, he clutched the dead soldier's machine gun and glanced over his left shoulder. Gunfire erupted once more, shaving the bark off the tree.

Son of a bitch!

His face stung from the flying bark, blood dripped down his cheeks. The gusts intensified, obscuring his hunters. Trying to control his quivering hands, Bane dropped to the ground, rolled away, and opened fire in the Russians' general direction. Both ran for cover, giving Bane enough time to reach a fallen log.

Pawing through the snow on his belly, Bane spread both legs and set the muzzle over the log, and waited. Minutes went by. Bane kept the gun trained on the trees protecting the gunmen. The wind slapped his face, stung his eyes. The cold metal of the gun stuck to his hands. He felt caked with ice and snow, became appalled by the pain in his joints, flashed back to the hot and humid days of his last summer in Virginia, longed for the warmth of the sun, for the—

A whistle of wind pulled him away from his fantasy. His temperature continued to drop and the woolen jacket wasn't helping. Enough heat had already escaped his body to keep him from getting warm again. Bane understood what that meant: His body was falling deeper into hypothermia.

One of the Russians ran to an adjacent tree. As cold as he was, Bane managed to line him up and fired. The figure dropped in the snow.

The last Russian now ran, a bulky shape crossing his field of view thirty feet away. Bane fired and missed. He tried to fire once more but couldn't. He pursed his lips and forced his index finger against the trigger, but it wouldn't move. It was frozen stiff!

Bane found it harder and harder to breathe now. Every gulp of air that entered his lungs felt like a hard, cold hammer squashing his chest and forcing the last remnants of heat out of his exhausted body. His vision became foggy, cloudy. Mustering every ounce of strength left in him, the seasoned CIA officer lunged at the nearing shadowy figure, the ice-cold muzzle of the automatic aimed at the Russian's stomach.

The sound of a rapid expulsion of air coincided with a white cloud blowing out of the soldier's mouth as Bane drove the muzzle deep into the hunter.

As the soldier bent over in pain, Bane jumped over him and sat on the man's large chest, Bane's legs pinning the Russian's arms in the snow.

"Where is the shipment going? Where? *Gdye? Gdye?*" he asked, trying to cross-check his information.

"*Pa . . . pashol von!*" The Russian stared back at Bane defiantly.

Bane slapped him hard. "Tell me or I'll rip your eyeballs out!" the CIA officer shouted in Russian.

The man remained silent, a trickle of blood coming out of a busted upper lip. Bane pressed a thumb against the Russian's right eye and began to apply pressure.

"*Oy! . . . Nyet! Nyet!* Stop!"

"Tell me! Tell me now!" Bane pressed harder against the eyeball.

"Shere . . . Sheremetyevo Airport! In one hour! Please, stop! Stop! My eye!"

"Where in the airport? Where! *Gdye?*" Bane kept the pressure on the eyeball.

"The south terminal! By the south terminal, I said! Please!"

Bane relaxed the pressure as he asked, "Where is the shipment being taken?"

"I do not know this. I swear it!"

Bane thought about it for a moment as the brief rush of adrenaline from the fight began to wear off.

Suddenly, something grabbed him from behind and pulled him back. It was the Russian's feet! The sneaky bastard was trying to grab Bane with his feet.

Freeing himself from the leg lock, Bane grabbed the automatic rifle and struck the Russian at the base of the neck with the weapon's wooden butt. The soldier went limp.

Silence, broken by a gust of hissing wind and Bane's irregular breathing. The snow mixed with the white condensed air lifting off his nostrils as he exhaled heavily. The brief combat had temporarily restored his circulation, giving the boost of energy he would need to reach the warmth of the soldiers' truck. His Skoda was too far away. He would get it after he had warmed up.

Certain that he would find a bottle of vodka in that truck, Bane used the halogen spotter attached to his weapon to guide him out of the dark woods, reaching the frozen overgrowth at the edge of the road a few minutes later. Staggering to the truck fifty feet away, the CIA officer opened the passenger side door and crawled inside the old vehicle. The smell of cigarette smoke struck him hard, but in a way he welcomed it, for it was warmer than the frigid air outside.

He smiled when his fingers grabbed a half-empty bottle of a clear liquid. Taking a swig, Bane shivered. His body reacted to the hard liquor, sensing its life-giving energy, and instantly demanded more. Taking a few more sips, Donald Bane spent another ten minutes inside the truck before walking back to his Skoda, which he used to drive to the spot by the road where he had lost his surveillance equipment. Spending ten minutes pawing through the snow, Bane recovered everything, including the night vision goggles, before heading back to Moscow, wondering if he would get there in time to intercept the shipment. Based on the way the snow fell over the road, Bane somehow doubted it, and to make matters worse, he couldn't get a dial tone on the mobile telephone built in between the front bucket seats of the Czechoslovakian car.

Fucking country! Nothing ever works!

Pressing on the accelerator as the warm air coming through the dash's vent holes replenished his core, Donald Bane kept his eyes on the winding road as he headed back to Moscow.

CIA HEADQUARTERS. LANGLEY, VIRGINIA.

Robert Bourdeaux read the flash report on his screen, a look of concern on his face. His operative had just had a close call near Serpuchov, and the paranoid in Bourdeaux feared the worst: somehow, someone had leaked Donald Bane's presence in those woods.

Getting up while rolling the sleeves of his white shirt up to his elbows, Bourdeaux walked to his small refrigerator, grabbed a bottle of mineral water, twisted the cap, and took a swig, briefly closing his eyes as he swallowed.

Walking to the windows behind his desk, the DDO looked at the line of cars exiting Langley through the main gate. He checked his watch. It was quitting time, but not for him. The stack of reports and forms awaiting his signature told Bourdeaux that he would definitely have to cancel Kate this evening. He had a long night ahead of him.

His mind drifted back to Donald Bane. Bourdeaux could not understand how the soldiers spotted Bane from over a hundred feet away in the middle of the night, during a snowstorm, and without any night vision gear.

There's gotta be a leak.

Bourdeaux shook his head. Perhaps that also explained why the meeting with Krasilov had gone so badly, with Bane narrowly escaping alive.

At first, Bourdeaux had written it off as Krasilov's carelessness. The DDO felt that the old Ukrainian general had been followed, but now Bourdeaux began to feel a bit different. This second incident had just opened the door to the possibility of someone close to Bourdeaux leaking the info out of the sanctuary of the CIA.

He brought a finger to his right temple while closing his eyes and taking another sip of water.

Swell. Just the kind of shit I wanted to have to deal with now.

Realizing the possibility of a mole within the Agency was the easy part. Catching the son of a bitch was the task that had driven many previous CIA officers to near-madness. Moles with access to the kind of information that might compromise the lives of field operatives usually had worked at the Agency for some time and hidden themselves very well. Plucking them out, Bourdeaux knew, could not be done overnight.

Finishing the bottle of mineral water and throwing it in the wastebasket next to his desk, Bourdeaux removed his tie and unbuttoned his collar.

Time to get busy.

The deputy director of operations dived into his five-inch-thick stack of work. However, as he cruised through report after report, in the back of his mind he looked for clues, for subtle signs, for any hint that might get him closer to the mole that seemed to have surfaced for the sole purpose of ruining this very critical operation.

6

MARTYRDOM

It is the cause and not the death that makes the martyr.
—Napoleon

NORTHERN VIRGINIA.

The redbrick house stood in the center of the large oval clearing. Peaceful and secluded, it overlooked a dry ravine bordering a tree line of pines two hundred feet away. The waters of the Shenandoah River flowed peacefully on the other side of the small patch of forest facing the front of the house. An unpaved road connecting the house to the main road two miles away was pothole-filled and muddy—the main reason for the two-year-old white Ford Explorer, with oversize tires, parked in front of the house.

Kevin Dalton's arms burned as he hauled two large buckets filled with white mortar to the side of his forty-year-old house. Beams of early morning sunlight shone through a single large opening in the low layer of cotton white cumulus clouds, casting a vivid orange glow along the edge of the woods. A whistle of wind caressed Kevin's tanned face, swirling thin black hair over a wide forehead and partially covering drooping brown eyes. Kevin welcomed the soft breeze as he set down the buckets next to a pile of red bricks and sighed in relief while massaging his arms and shoulders.

At six feet in height and 185 pounds, Kevin kept the solid stomach and muscular but lean arms and legs of his high school varsity basketball days. A slender, slightly arched nose ran down the middle of his boyish face. A pair of full lips, their ends slightly curving down with the soft sadness that matched his slanted eyes, crowned a good and strong chin.

Taking a step back while wiping off a film of sweat on his face with a sleeve of his brown cotton shirt, the Central Intelligence Agency operations officer looked contemptuously at a project that could very well take him the entire weekend to complete. Last week's storm had broken loose a large branch of the old oak shading the west side of his house, taking down with it a good section of the living room wall. After two days of clearing the mess, Kevin was finally ready to start bricking, a job which at that moment he preferred to have someone else do while he went fishing down the Shenandoah, just as he'd done on most weekend mornings during the past four months. But he couldn't afford to hire someone. He had poured his life savings into purchasing the small house and five acres of riverside Virginia real estate around it. His modest CIA salary left him barely enough money to live on after paying property taxes. But he preferred living this way, even if it meant skipping a meal or two to make ends meet, rather than living in the city.

The sound of jet engines broke his train of thought. A pair of F-15s from Andrews Air Force Base flew in formation overhead. Kevin watched their white contrails as they cruised on an easterly heading at around five thousand feet.

A deep sense of sadness descended over Kevin Dalton. Images of his high-speed ejection from a crippled F-14 Tomcat filled his mind. Just the mere thought of that agonizing moment sent a wave of pain through Kevin's spine, which had been compressed by a quarter of an inch during his ejection, permanently ruining his chance of ever flying again. Further spinal compression could turn him into a paraplegic.

Frowning, Kevin shook his head and began to turn his attention back to the bricks and mortar when an alarm went off in his head. Eyes half-closed, he slowly shifted his gaze back toward the tree line facing the side of the house and saw the glint of glass flashing in the morning sun's orange glow.

Binoculars!

Kevin felt a knot in his stomach as the reality of someone stalking him sank in. That someone had definitely gotten over the barbed wire fence he had erected to keep all unwanted visitors from entering his sanctuary. Yet the glint was there. A definite amateur stalker—no professional would ever use a set of binoculars from that position at this time of the day.

Recently trained instincts took over. Slowly, casually, he walked back into the house, closing the door before rushing across the foyer. Pounding steps on the tiled floor echoed in his ears with the same intensity as his thundering heartbeat.

Kevin hadn't been in the intelligence business long enough to create any enemies. On the other hand, thanks to a CNN special report that had aired a month after the destruction of Allahbad, Kevin Dalton's face wound up plastered on the front page of every major newspaper around the world as one of the heroes behind the destruction of Allahbad, instantly turning nineteen million Iraqis into his mortal enemies. But even if it was an Iraqi out there, how had he found Kevin? The CIA kept a microfilm version of his dossier in a special vault in the basement of the old CIA building in Langley in case of emergency. Otherwise, only Robert Bourdeaux, who had hired Kevin after Kevin's early retirement from the Navy, knew his exact whereabouts.

Cruising through the living room and going into the kitchen, Kevin pulled a Beretta 92F pistol from a drawer next to the refrigerator. Long, thin fingers moved over the steel alloy frame of the 9mm weapon, releasing the safety and chambering a round, before curling around the black handle.

Through living room windows facing the backyard, Kevin scanned the tree line looking for signs of another stalker, but found none. Just tall pines. Fully aware that what he saw could have also been the telescope of a sniper rifle, Kevin Dalton breathed deeply while tightening the grip on the 92F until his clammy hand turned white.

One final scan of the tree line facing him, and, using the house as shield from the stalker, Kevin went out the back door, running a straight line for the woods.

The sound of a gunshot whipped across the clearing. The ground to his right exploded in a small cloud of dirt and grass.

Heart hammering inside his chest, nostrils flaring with every gulp of cool air, feet kicking the soft ground and eyes watering in the wind, the young CIA officer cut left, only to miss a second shot by inches.

Jesus!

Another shot. Another miss. The shots were coming from his far right, but he didn't have the time to look and search for the telltale muzzle flashes. His mind screamed a single word: *RUN!*

Reaching the edge of the woods in twenty seconds, Kevin zigzagged around the first dozen trees until his senses told him he had put enough forest between himself and the exposed clearing.

Breathing heavily, he pressed the back of his soaked cotton shirt against the trunk of a pine and, clutching the Beretta with both hands— just as he had been taught by his CIA trainers—he dropped to a crouch and listened for any sounds that didn't belong in the woods. Voices, crunched leaves, the rustle of branches, metallic noises, anything that would tell him if his attacker was approaching him. But the wind, hissing through the forest, masked all other sounds.

Kevin knew he had to move fast. There were at least two gunmen after him—the one he had spotted in the tree line facing the front of his house, and the second one, who had taken three shots at him from the edge of the clearing facing the left side of the house.

Warily, he stood up, back still pressed against the pine. Looking over his left shoulder, he scanned the terrain ahead, where he had walked many times during his late afternoon strolls, after putting in a full day at Langley. But on this cool and windy morning the woods had suddenly taken on a menacing look. His skin shivered at the thought of a high-speed round carving a hole the size of a fist in his chest. He had to be cautious, take all possible precautions, anticipate his enemy's next move.

Priorities. Selecting a tree ten feet away, Kevin quickly ran to it, backing up against the harsh bark at the last second, Beretta clutched with both hands over his right shoulder, chin digging into his left shoulder, brown eyes sweeping the area, searching for the enemy and selecting a new tree.

Moving slowly from tree to tree, Kevin followed a path that veered down to the left side of the clearing, close to the tree line, approaching the position where he estimated the shots had originated. His advance was a calculated one, selecting each tree far in advance, close enough to minimize exposure to a sniper bullet, yet far enough to close the gap on the gun quickly.

A minute later his back stung from scratching against the trunks. He stopped, rubbed his free hand against his back, and felt bloody flesh underneath torn cotton fabric.

Approaching the edge of the woods, Kevin dropped to the ground and crawled through the light underbrush bordering the dry ravine, elbows and knees burning, Beretta firmly held in his left hand. Eyes, like dark holes in his tanned face, swiveled in every direction until they found their target: the silhouette of a tall, stocky man holding a sniper rifle twenty feet ahead, moving away from him and back into the forest.

Quietly, Kevin got up and went after him, closing the gap in another minute, positioning himself directly behind the shadow.

The sniper stopped and started to turn around, a bearded man with brown skin, black hair, and thick brows over a pair of dark eyes, which swiftly looked in Kevin's direction.

Kevin recoiled and lunged, shoving the Beretta's muzzle deep into the man's abdomen while driving his left knee into the man's testicles. The sniper tried to scream, but all Kevin heard was a fast expulsion of air. Holding his groin while gagging, the sniper fell on his side, releasing the rifle. Kevin grabbed it as it hit the ground and threw it aside before jumping on top of the sniper and pressing the Beretta's muzzle against the man's creased forehead.

"Who are you?"

The bearded man, eyes out of focus, opened and closed his mouth, trying to get some air into his collapsed lungs.

Kevin thrust the palm of his right hand into the man's sternum.

"Who are you? What in the heck are you—"

"Fi amman . . . Allah . . ."

Kevin, left hand still pressing the Beretta's muzzle against the sniper's brown forehead, felt a sudden shiver as his mind slowly translated the sniper's Arabic words: *I'm in the protection of Allah.*

Who is this man? he asked himself as he grabbed the man's dark wool sweater with his right hand while keeping the Beretta firmly dug into the forehead. Kevin pulled him up and brought up the bearded face to within inches of him. Feeling the man's rancid breath, Kevin asked again, "Who are you?"

The man didn't respond but, instead, gazed deeply into Kevin's eyes as another alarm went off in Kevin's head. Kevin had been warned by his CIA trainers about that look. It was accompanied by the man's final words: *"Allamdu li Allah!"*

Praise be to Allah.

Kevin tried to jam his hand into the man's closing jaws, but he was too late. The sniper shut his mouth and went into instant convulsions. With the smell of almonds filling the air around them, the former Navy officer pulled back the Beretta, lifting it up and over his left shoulder, muzzle pointed at the skies.

Cyanide.

He barely finished that thought when a spark, accompanied by a sharp jolt in his left hand, forced him to let go of the automatic pistol. Another shot, and Kevin noticed a small object imbedding itself into the bark of the tree to his close left.

A dart! Someone was trying to take him alive.

His eyes searched the pine needle–covered terrain for the Beretta, but the wind had picked up strength, swirling the pine needles and burying his weapon.

Another shot cracked above the hissing wind, and another dart shot past him and landed on a pine to his right. Kevin dropped to the ground and went into a roll. Pine needles, trees, and patches of cloudy sky visible through the forest canopy filled his field of view as his body tumbled over the cushioned, wind-torn surface.

Smashing his right shoulder against a trunk, Kevin twisted his body around the tree and, kicking his legs, sprinted toward a cluster of closely spaced pines ten feet away, reaching them in seconds.

Darkness suddenly engulfed Kevin Dalton. With his left hand trembling from the dart that must have struck the Beretta he'd clutched thirty seconds before, and his skinned back burning from the perspiration soaking his shredded cotton shirt, Kevin dropped to a crouch and moved another thirty feet into the woods. The same wind that had hidden his Beretta now covered his tracks.

Knowing it would be just a matter of time before the second gun landed a dart on him, Kevin decided to change the rules of this game. Using his right hand, he removed the stainless steel Seiko hugging his left wrist, quickly set the alarm to go off in five minutes, and left it hanging from a branch at head level.

Cutting left, he made a wide semicircle to position himself directly behind the second gun, carefully blending his own sounds with those of the wind, all the while silently thanking his tough CIA trainers for providing him with the skills that were allowing him to defend himself this morning.

He stopped cold the moment he heard a branch snap. With his eyes half-closed, he estimated the noise had come from roughly forty feet straight ahead. Still in a crouch, he went directly toward it.

Another snap.

He noticed the dark shape of a man thirty feet ahead moving away from him. An automatic rifle held in both hands scanned the forest in front of the sniper.

Kevin closed in, and the man stopped briefly. Kevin did the same, holding his breath, wishing he still had the Beretta. A film of sweat accumulated on his forehead and neck. Kevin measured his enemy: a short, wide man wearing dark trousers and sweater like the first sniper, with the addition of a black baseball cap turned backward. The trousers flapped in the wind. He estimated the sniper was within twenty feet of the Seiko, which was due to go off at any moment.

Kevin proceeded silently as soon as the man continued forward, taking a step when he took a step, pausing when he paused. Slowly, foot after agonizing foot, he managed to close the gap to about seven feet and waited.

The low-decibel, high-pitched sound from Kevin's wristwatch alarm invaded the natural sounds of the forest, making the sniper turn his attention to the woods to his immediate right.

Shaping both hands into knife hands, Kevin lunged and pointed them toward the base of the sniper's neck. The man must have heard him because he instinctively turned sideways, missing Kevin's flesh-and-bone blades by an inch. A pair of green, deep-set eyes under heavy black brows stared back at him in the forest's gloomy light.

The man counterattacked, grabbing Kevin's left wrist and pulling him forward. Before Kevin could react, the man drove his right knee into Kevin's groin.

The crippling pain made Kevin tremble as he fell on his back. Just as the man leveled the rifle at Kevin, the CIA officer watched a dark shadow cruise through the forest at great speed and crash against the sniper, who let go of the rifle on impact. Both figures rolled on the soft ground, half-disappearing beneath the foot-high cloud of swirling pine needles as a perplexed Kevin looked on.

Slowly rising to a crouch while still weakened from the blow, Kevin watched the sniper overpower the other man, who wore a black jumpsuit and hood. The sniper shoved the hooded man against a tree, the hood crashing hard against the bark. The slim figure went limp.

But that was all the time Kevin needed to recover. Grabbing the sniper's rifle, Kevin pointed it at the bearded man.

"Stay where you are!" Kevin shouted, his body still recovering from the blow to his groin.

The sniper remained still, eyes never leaving Kevin's, the thick lips of his large mouth shaping into a broad grin, showing Kevin an upper row of gold-capped teeth.

Kevin, hands holding the rifle, left index finger lightly pressed against the trigger, simply stared at the defiant face. The man looked at the sky while whispering words the CIA officer could not understand, but whose meaning was clear.

"No! Wait!" Kevin screamed, but, once again, he was too late.

The sniper shut his jaw and his eyes rolled to the back of his head while his body jerked for a few seconds before going limp.

Damned fanatics!

Although Kevin wanted to check the bodies for clues, his training told him that the dead snipers and the guy who had banged his head against the tree weren't going anywhere. He would have ample time to check the bodies after making sure the area was safe.

Pulling the sniper's sidearm, a Colt .45 automatic, from a Velcro-secured waist holster, Kevin checked the ammunition clip, flipped the safety, and cocked it, loading a round in the chamber. Clutching the blue steel weapon with both hands over his left shoulder, for the next fifteen minutes Kevin swept the rest of his property but found nothing. Satisfied that he was temporarily safe, he returned to the spot where he had left the body of the second sniper and the other fellow, who had apparently been on Kevin's side during the short hand-to-hand combat.

Kevin warily gave the sniper another look before checking for a pulse. There was none. He approached the hooded man . . . or was it a woman? A closer look at this helpful stranger dressed in black revealed a pair of long legs, a thin waist, and the clear outline of breasts.

Slowly, Kevin Dalton reached down and felt for a pulse. *Weak, but it's still there.* He then pulled up the dark cotton hood and froze.

Kevin stared in sheer disbelief at the face of Khalela Yishaid, and, for the first time in the past thirty minutes, his hands began to tremble.

CIA HEADQUARTERS. LANGLEY, VIRGINIA.

Robert Bourdeaux left his office in a hurry. He had just finished calling an EMS helicopter after receiving Kevin Dalton's call. The chopper was already on the way to Kevin's place in Virginia, and it would bring Kevin and Khalela to the Georgetown University Hospital.

Khalela? This is insane!

The deputy director of operations shook his head in disbelief.

"Khalela Yishaid . . . Christ, what in the world is going on," he mumbled, as he walked past his secretary and headed down the hall.

"Mr. Bourdeaux? Mr. Bourdeaux?" his secretary said from behind her desk.

"Cancel all my appointments!" he shouted as he disappeared around the corner, reaching his car a minute later.

This was the third breach of security in the past few days. *First Krasilov is compromised, then Bane is almost taken out in Serpuchov, and now this?*

Flooring it, Bourdeaux left Langley and turned onto the Georgetown Pike, heading for Washington, D.C. He reached into a side pocket and pulled out a pack of Motrin. Popping three tablets in his mouth and downing them without water, Bourdeaux rubbed his right temple as his mind searched for an explanation.

JERSEY CITY, NEW JERSEY.

Sheikh Imman al-Barakah closed his eyes upon hearing the bad news. It had not been Allah's will that the American Kevin Dalton fall hostage to the *Jihad*. But the sheikh worked for a man who could not tolerate failure—regardless if it was the will of Allah or not. Today Sheikh Imman al-Barakah had failed Saddam Hussein. Not only was the American still alive, but according to one of Marcos Dominguez's sources inside George-town University Hospital, the Israeli messenger, a woman by the name of Khalela, was also alive. Fortunately for the sheikh, the word from the hospital was that the woman had a serious concussion. Based on the conversation between the American Kevin Dalton, who had refused to leave Khalela's side, and a nameless man who arrived in the company of four armed bodyguards, Khalela had not warned the Americans yet.

It was because of this crucial fact that Sheikh Imman al-Barakah knew that Saddam Hussein would spare his life. But knowing that his luck would take a turn for the worse the moment the Jew woman came around, the sheikh had already made the necessary arrangements with the Iranian owner of a dry-cleaning service to have one of his vans stolen.

Saddam's messenger is coming, the sheikh thought, while praying to Allah that his plan would work. The unbelievers had to be terminated to clear the way for the messenger, whose ship would arrive in three more days.

THE *VESUVIUS*.

Ten-foot waves slapped the hull of the Italian merchant vessel, engulfing the bow with clouds of foam and thick mist. Forks of lightning streaked across the dark sky, igniting the Atlantic's wind-torn surface with strobo-scopic flashes of white light. Ankle-deep water ran over the main deck as the ship disappeared in another explosion of water against metal, before stubbornly emerging over the waves, refusing to surrender to its much stronger adversary.

Lightning gleamed through the thick rain. A gunshot mixed with the sound of thunder. The round missed the Mossad operative racing toward the stern of the large vessel, his hands grabbing the railing separating him from the angry sea.

Another shot whipped through the night as the ship plunged into a rising wave, the report piercing the howling of the wind, the hissing of the rain. The operative fell to his knees under the impact of the hollow-point round. A flash of lightning showed *Mukhabarat* Colonel Kemal Ramallah bracing himself in the cabin door, a Makarov automatic clutched in his right hand.

The Iraqi colonel fired again, and the wounded man brought both hands to his face. The raging swells pounding the hull drowned his agonized cry. Staggering to his feet, hands blindly groping for the railing, blood covering his face, the Mossad operative desperately tried to move away from his hunter.

A fourth shot lifted him off his feet, flipping him in midair and over the railing, just as the vessel plunged into a wall of surging waves.

Wearing a heavy bright orange raincoat, Kemal stepped away from the dimly lit cabin, cold rain soaking his brown hair and seeping down his neck and back.

Cautiously, one hand holding the automatic and the other gripping the railing, he scanned the deck through the relentless spray of the sea. The ship's bow lurched into another wave, disappearing beneath a cloud of white foam. Kemal leaned over the railing, searching for his victim on the boiling surface, but he saw nothing but black swells.

Returning to the comfort of the cabin, Kemal closed the door and locked it, shutting the storm out. He shoved the automatic in the small of his back and held on to walls and built-in furniture as he reached the stairway leading to a narrow and murky hallway one level below.

A minute later he pulled out a key and unlocked the door to his cabin. A single light bulb swinging from the end of a coiled cord cast a yellow glow in the room. A bunk bed, a small desk, and a built-in metallic sink had been the only amenities the Italian captain had provided his unusual guest for the one-time fee to take him to America. Kemal had to work like the rest of the crew to pay for his meals, but his struggle wouldn't be a long one.

Kemal rubbed a hand over his two-day stubble as he quickly entered the five-digit code of his battery-operated motion detector security system—a small black box with a keypad attached to a thin, cylindrical canister of cyanide gas. The system was Kemal's way of protecting his valuable cargo, which consisted of a wooden box two feet in length and width and almost as tall as Kemal, housing the Russian nuclear hardware, which Saddam Hussein had paid so much money to acquire and preassemble, in radiation-proof containers. He had to be careful. The Jews had almost caught up with the hardware in Greece, and they probably would have intercepted it by now, had it not been for the warning he received from Baghdad right before boarding this vessel: Mossad operatives were after him and his cargo.

Two days ago Kemal had eliminated one Mossad operative thanks to this deadly security system. The curious Jew had broken into Kemal's cabin during working hours. The security system had automatically released a small fraction of the lethal gas. Death for the infidel had come instantly. After wrapping fifty pounds of steel chain around the Jew's chest, Kemal had thrown him overboard that same night, while the vessel sailed two hundred miles off the coast of Lisbon.

Now a second man was dead. Although the *Mukhabarat* colonel felt certain that no one had witnessed the shooting owing to the storm and the late hour, the Italian captain would grow suspicious nonetheless, and might want to turn back and let Italian authorities conduct an investigation.

Kemal pulled out the Makarov, released the ammunition clip, and used the towel over the sink to dry the weapon. He would take it apart and clean it and oil it thoroughly. The automatic was his life, his control, his ticket to America. The Italian captain would not turn back. The *Mukhabarat* colonel was prepared to hold the Makarov to the captain's head for the remainder of the trip if necessary.

Moscow, Russia.

Donald Bane stood outside the door of a small dacha by the shores of the Moscow River, two miles south of the Russian capital. Tired and sore from nearly freezing to death a few hours before, the CIA officer signaled the two junior operatives standing with their weapons drawn to either side of him. The rookies had met him at the airport an hour before, when Bane called the Moscow Station for reinforcements. He had learned from an underpaid night clerk working in a commercial hangar at Sheremetyevo Airport that the clerk's superior, a man by the name of Mikhail Petrosky, had personally handled the loading of many unmarked boxes into a private jet with an unknown destination. This information Bane had extracted after waving a one-hundred-dollar bill in front of the clerk's widening eyes. Another hundred told Bane that Petrosky was in the Soltnevo Group's payroll, and a final hundred permanently sealed the clerk's mouth.

Three hundred bucks. As Bane drew the new pistol, a 9mm Beretta that one of the rookies had given him, the seasoned officer shook his head. He remembered a time when he would have gotten the exact same information for a third of the money. *Fucking Russians are getting too damned greedy!*

Donald Bane kicked in the door and stormed inside the one-bedroom, wooden structure. The rookies followed him.

A high-pitched shriek from a reddish-skinned woman with heavy Oriental features drilled Bane's eardrums as she pulled the covers over her exposed breasts.

A Mongolian hooker.

Bane looked past her and trained the Beretta on the pale naked body of a man running for the rear window.

"*Astanaveetsa!*" the seasoned CIA officer shouted.

The man stopped.

"Hands over your head and turn around slowly, Ivan. Don't make any sudden moves or there'll be pieces of you scattered from here to Siberia."

The woman kept on screaming.

"Shut up, you whore!" Bane snapped.

"The whore does not speak *parosske,*" said Mikhail Petrosky, his back still to Bane.

"Then you make her shut the fuck up!"

Petrosky turned around and slapped her across the face with the back of his right hand.

The woman lowered her voice to a quiet sob. After motioning the other two officers to cover the outside of the dacha, Bane inspected Petrosky, a lean man, probably not older than forty.

"Looks like I came at the perfect moment, Ivan. Get back in bed." Bane took a few steps forward. Petrosky crawled back in bed.

"Covers all the way down to your feet, Ivan."

Petrosky yanked the covers from the woman's trembling hands and pushed them down to the foot of the bed. The woman instinctively covered her breasts with her forearms.

Petrosky looked at him defiantly. The short Russian placed his left hand over the woman's torso and rubbed it. The Mongolian whore quietly shuddered. "Want some, *Amerikansky?* It is very soft, *da?* I can get you her or any woman you want in this town. Even little girls and boys if that is—"

Bane leaned over the bed and struck Petrosky across the face with the Beretta's muzzle.

"Aghh!" Petrosky rolled off the bed with both hands on his face. Slowly sitting up on the wooden floor, the Russian took a deep breath, his burning glare on Bane. "What you want with me, *Amerikansky?*"

"The word out there is that you helped someone pack up a number of boxes onto a plane an hour ago."

Petrosky shrugged. "So? That is what I do. I run a commercial hangar!"

Bane approached him from the left and kicked him in the ribs.

Petrosky rolled on the floor, holding his side.

"You better watch your answers, Ivan. Do you want another?" Bane swung his leg back.

"*Nyet!* Enough! Go ahead and kill me if that is what you wish. I will never cross my people for an *Amerikansky!*"

Bane smiled. "I won't kill you, Ivan. I will, however, give you a cheap sex change operation."

"What are you talking . . ."

Bane lowered the Beretta, pointing straight at Petrosky's groin.

"*Zhdat!* Wait! You can't do that. *Nyet! Zhdat! Zhdat!*"

Bane cocked the automatic. "It's too late for that, Ivan. Today is the first day of the rest of your life. No more whores for you." His finger caressed the trigger.

"*Nyet!* No, please!" Fear showed on the Russian's face.

Donald Bane stopped and stared into Petrosky's wide-open eyes. The curtain of defiance had dropped away, exposing Petrosky's true feeling of terror at Bane's intentions.

"I'm listening, Ivan. It better be good." He pointed the automatic to the pine floor.

Petrosky inhaled and exhaled. "I'm only a helper, *Amerikansky*. I coordinate flights for certain people with good connections in Moscow. Some men approached me a week ago and asked me to do this job for them. The payoff would be big, yes? I said, sure, why not? I got them a plane and a pilot for a day, and they gave me one thousand American dollars."

"Where was the plane headed to?"

"I do not know this."

"Wrong answer, Ivan. You *do* know." Bane pointed the automatic back at Petrosky's groin.

"I'm telling you the truth! They just asked me to do that and—"

"Like I said, Ivan . . ." Bane's finger caressed the trigger once more.

"All right, all right. They were headed for Turkey, across the Black Sea."

Bane frowned. "Where in Turkey?"

"Istanbul."

Ten minutes later, Bane and his two CIA backups locked Petrosky and the woman in the rear of the Skoda and headed back to Moscow, arriving almost at sunrise at the American Embassy.

Having called ahead on the mobile phone, which had suddenly decided to come back to life, several Marines waited for Bane and his companions the moment the two-car caravan crossed the gates.

Bane followed one of the CIA rookies to the office of the Moscow Station chief while the Marines took Petrosky and the whore to a pair of rooms in the basement.

After spending ten minutes with the Station chief and getting on the horn with Langley to give Robert Bourdeaux a brief update, Donald Bane walked inside a ten-by-ten room in the basement of the building. He was fuming. Bourdeaux had insisted that Bane see this case all the way through, even if that meant getting on a plane to Istanbul.

Mikhail Petrosky quickly got to his feet, crossed his arms, and stared back at the CIA officer. "I have told you everything you wanted to know, *Amerikansky*. What else do you want?"

Bane ignored him, turned to the guard and nodded. The guard stepped inside. He had a rope in his hands.

"What is this?" Petrosky began to say as he took a few steps back. "I have rights, *Amerikansky*. I want to see a Russian official." His back hit the wall.

"Take it easy, Ivan," Bane said. "We just want some information from you."

"I've already told you—"

Bane punched him hard in the stomach. Petrosky bent in half and rolled on the concrete floor, gasping for air. Bane and the guard picked him up and laid him on the floor facedown. The guard tied Petrosky's hands behind his back while Bane worked on his feet. Bane turned him over.

"Listen to me, Ivan. I smuggled you into our embassy. Nobody knows that you're here, and to tell you the truth, nobody seems to be giving a shit where you are. I'm the law in this embassy, and I'm telling you that if you lied to me about Istanbul, you'll never see your polluted Rodina again."

Petrosky's face ashened. "I did not lie to you, *Amerikansky!*" he insisted.

Bane smiled. "All right, Ivan. In that case you shouldn't have anything to worry about."

A questioning look came to Petrosky's eyes. "What do you mean?"

Bane pulled out a small bag from his shirt pocket. He took out two hypodermics and two small vials.

"What is this?"

"Truth serum, Ivan."

Raw fear conquered Petrosky's facial muscles. "I have told you the truth!"

"That's exactly what I intend to find out. If you were lying to me, I'll find out, and after you tell me everything I need to know, I'll pump a little extra dose in you and turn you into an evergreen." Without another word, Bane held the vial filled with sodium pentothal powder up in the air.

"Please, don't—"

Bane looked at the large Marine and then tilted his head in the direction of Petrosky. The soldier walked over to the bed, leaned over, and unbuckled Petrosky's pants.

"Hey, hey! What you think you are—"

Bane punched him once in the face. Not very hard, just enough to get his attention. "Not another word, Ivan."

As a trickle of blood ran down Petrosky's chin from a busted lip, the guard lowered the Russian's pants while Bane mixed the sodium pentothal powder with water and filled one of the hypodermics. The second he filled with the contents of the other vial, Dexedrine.

First Bane injected half the sodium pentothal solution into Petrosky's femoral artery and waited a few moments. The heavy barbiturate had the desired effect. Petrosky's body relaxed. Bane kept the second syringe, filled with Dexedrine, next to the bed. He would inject small amounts of the strong amphetamine every time Petrosky started to fade away under the influence of the barbiturate. Bane could now keep the Russian in a state of semiconsciousness—the state where Petrosky would be most susceptible to telling the truth—for an extended period of time. He turned to the guard.

"Have you ever seen a chemical interrogation before?"

"No, sir."

Bane smiled. "Bring the tape recorder and the maps."

Thirty minutes later Bane wiped the sweat off his forehead with the sleeve of his cotton shirt. "He'll sleep for a day or two. Untie him and give him something to eat when he comes around. I've already made arrangements with the chief to hold him and the woman indefinitely."

Bane grabbed the maps and left the room. He had a long day and a long flight ahead of him.

7

SPECULATION

Man's most valuable trait is a judicious sense of what not to believe.
— Euripides

GEORGETOWN UNIVERSITY HOSPITAL. WASHINGTON, D.C.

Kevin Dalton paced the small private room on the second floor of the hospital, where the medical emergency team had brought Khalela the day before. Even after a full twenty-four hours to think through this bizarre incident, Kevin still couldn't figure out the reason Khalela had so suddenly rushed back into his life. What was so important that it had forced the Mossad operative—assuming she still worked for the Mossad—to make the trip across the globe? Protection? Had she come across information that led her to believe that his life was in danger? Her perfect timing certainly tended to support that theory. But was there something else? And how did the Iraqis find him? How did they figure out where he lived? It didn't take very long for Kevin Dalton to come to the conclusion that Saddam Hussein had ordered this attack.

Stopping at the foot of Khalela's bed, the former Navy officer stared at a face he had never thought he would see again. Her mere presence, combined with the kidnapping attempt, told Kevin Dalton he was in serious trouble, and unless he could alter the rules of the game, the enemy would strike again.

Operating with limited information made changing the rules quite challenging, of course. But it also gave Kevin something to occupy his mind until Khalela came around and explained this mess to him.

Sitting at the edge of the bed, Kevin put a hand to her cheek. She felt very warm.

Kevin rang for the nurse, and thirty seconds later a petite woman in her late thirties with shoulder-length brown hair walked in the door. "Yes, sir?" she said in a heavy Hispanic accent.

Kevin read the name GUZMAN clearly displayed on the name tag of her white uniform. He had seen the day shift nurse several times since his arrival. Nurse Peggy Guzman apparently ranked among the best in the hospital, and she had been immediately assigned to this room. She definitely looked better and behaved much more politely than the older nurse that took over at night.

"She's running a fever again," said Kevin as Nurse Guzman pulled out an electronic thermometer and took her temperature.

The nurse slowly shook her head. "Ninety-eight point six," she said. "Exactly as it should be."

Kevin frowned. "Maybe I'm the one who's too cold."

Nurse Guzman approached Kevin and placed a hand on his cheek. Kevin looked into her eyes.

"You are very cold, sir. When was the last time you slept?"

"It's been a little while, I guess."

Nurse Guzman gave Kevin a motherly look, almost as if she had decided Kevin couldn't look out for his own health. "What about food, sir?"

"Just some snacks. Haven't really moved since we got here."

Nurse Guzman's brown eyes opened wide. "You mean you haven't slept or eaten a good meal since you got here yesterday morning? That isn't good, sir."

Kevin slowly nodded. "I just can't get myself to leave her alone."

She checked her watch. "Well, sir, it might not be my place to say it, but you better get some rest before we have to put you in the next room. Exhaustion can lead to many complications."

Kevin didn't feel like being lectured, but the little nurse was right. During his CIA training, his instructors had forced him to go without sleep for almost three days. By the end of the third day he nearly had to be hospitalized from exhaustion. He became quite ill, vomiting everything he ate and beginning to hallucinate.

"Go home and rest, sir. We'll keep a good eye on her. Besides, there are always four men outside her room."

Robert Bourdeaux, who had spent a few hours with Kevin right after Khalela and he arrived at the hospital via an EMS helicopter, had gotten immediate presidential approval for three teams of four FBI agents to guard Khalela around the clock. But just like Kevin, the DDO had failed to help solve this puzzle and had left the hospital after giving Kevin instructions about contacting him the moment Khalela came around.

Kevin stared in the distance for a few moments. A hot shower, a good meal, and a few hours' sleep sounded great. But his eyes slowly gravitated back to Khalela. The only reason Kevin stood here today was because of her. Khalela Yishaid had saved Kevin's life in Iraq, when she rescued him from converging Iraqi search teams following his ejection from a crippled Tomcat. And the same Khalela had just prevented his kidnapping, even at the cost of risking her own life in the process.

Looking back at Nurse Guzman, Kevin said, "I think I'll stay a little longer. But thanks for being concerned."

"I'll send you something from the cafeteria, sir." The nurse smiled at him before leaving the room.

Kevin Dalton returned to Khalela's side, his immediate problem popping back up in his mind. *How did Saddam track me down?*

Only the Office of Security had access to his dossier, kept under a cryptonym in a safe containing microfilm dossiers of all other operations officers. A file, locked in a safe by the Directorate of Operations, listed the cryptonyms along with the actual names of all active and retired operations officers. Each office within the Directorate of Operations, as well as offices within the other three directorates of the CIA—Science and Technology, Intelligence, and Administration—maintained similar files to match the names of all their former employees with the dossiers kept by the Office of Security. In order for someone to know where Kevin lived, that person would have to have access to both the dossier and the deciphering file, which meant obtaining permission from the deputy director for operations, Robert Bourdeaux, and from the deputy director for administration. In addition the chief of the Office of Security would personally have to give out the specific information to the requester.

That's three high-ranking CIA officials, Kevin reflected, while softly touching Khalela's cheek with a finger. The smooth olive skin of the Mossad operative felt just as it had a year ago, during their brief but passionate time together.

Kevin saw her just as she had stood in front of him in that Kurdish village in Iraq. Kevin felt her embrace, the soothing words that had caressed away the pain, the anger, the supersonic nightmares. It had been a rapture Kevin Dalton prayed would never end, for it had removed him from the futility of his situation, from the anger and the frustration of getting shot down over Iraq while trying to avenge the death of his commander at the hands of an Iraqi ace. Khalela had taken it all away, she had drained his suffering while filling Kevin with the hope and determination that had pushed him to make a final flight to Allahbad, destroying not only the compound, but also his physical ability ever to fly a jet again.

At least he had survived, unlike his unlucky backseater, Lieutenant Chico Delgado, who perished during the ejection when his parachute failed to deploy.

How ironic, Kevin thought, looking around the room. It was at this hospital that Kevin had spent several hours every week for three months undergoing the physical therapy that now allowed him to do just about anything he wished, except fly jets.

His thoughts drifted to Saddam Hussein. Had the Iraqi leader actually bought a CIA officer? One who could have pulled off something liked this? What other explanation existed? Kevin told no one of his whereabouts after joining the Agency. Not even his closest Navy pals knew where he had gone. He also had left no paper trail for someone like Saddam to follow. Kevin did all of his financial transactions at the CIA credit union's downtown Washington branch, where his checks were automatically deposited every two weeks. He paid for everything in cash or by using a VISA card from the same credit union.

It doesn't make sense! Yet, not only did Saddam find him, but also the Mossad.

Christ.

Frustrated, he stood and walked to the window, wearily peering at the beautiful view of the city.

Dusk in the nation's capital.

The bloodred sun blazed right above the city skyline, throwing off shafts of yellow and burnt orange against the scattered cumulus, staining them with the same dazzling hues that bathed the distant Washington Monument.

Kevin remembered those colored clouds as seen through the clear canopy of an F-14. At least inside his fighter he knew who the enemy was. He knew when it would attack, and he knew how to defend himself and counterattack. The CIA had also provided him with such basic tools— tools which had saved his life the day before. But in the Navy he'd had a sanctuary: his carrier. At the end of a mission he knew he would be safe within the protection of the carrier and its escorts. Only while flying a sortie did he have to worry about the enemy.

Not anymore. In his new occupation the enemy could strike anywhere at any time. Kevin no longer had the luxury of a sanctuary, a safe haven where he could relax.

The crimson ball began to drop below the city, casting meandering, somewhat sinister, shadows over the street six floors below. A mercury streetlight kicked on, its lavender flickering slowly steadying while turning brighter. Neon signs came to life. Other streetlights joined the first, their light diffusing across endless blocks. The headlights of the evening traffic crisscrossed at the intersection of busy avenues.

Night in the nation's capital.

Kevin Dalton gave Khalela another glance before lying down on the small green sofa next to the bed and closing his exhausted eyes.

Ten minutes later, Peggy Guzman drove her car, a ten-year-old faded green Buick, out of the hospital parking garage and to a nearby apartment complex, where she walked to the unit she had been instructed to approach at exactly this time of the evening.

She knocked once on the white-painted door and a female voice boomed from inside. "It is not locked. *Entra, mujer. Entra!*"

The nurse's hands trembled as she turned the knob and pushed the door open, dearly hoping to see her three-year-old Roberto inside.

"Close the door, *pendeja*," the voice said.

The nurse immediately shut the door while trying to adjust her eyes to the murky interior. The overheads were off. *"¿Robertico? ¿Robertico? Are you here, my angel?"* the nurse said, praying to her *Diosito Lindo* that her only child would answer, but instead, her plea was met by a hard laugh.

"Do you really think I would have brought him here, *puta?* Do you think I'm a *pendeja* like you?"

"Please, *señora.* I just want to see him."

The woman sitting in the corner of the dark room, her face shielded by the shadows, crossed her legs. "The information, *puta.* Give it to me. What happened today in the hospital?"

In tears, Nurse Guzman began to speak, relating in the following twenty minutes everything that had taken place at Georgetown University Hospital that day. When she finished, the mysterious woman uncrossed her legs, a high heel tapping the tiled floor.

"Go, *puta.* Go back to your house and report to work at the hospital in the morning, as usual."

"But . . . my *Robertico.* When will I—"

"I said, go! *Ahora, andele!* Or you'll never see the *pendejito* again."

Quietly sobbing, the nurse turned to leave.

"Remember, *pendeja.* Not a word of this to anyone or it is *adios, Robertico. ¿Comprendes?"*

Nurse Guzman briefly turned to face the woman who had taken the person she loved most in this world away from her the day before. *"Sí, yo comprendo."*

Norma Dominguez waited until the nurse had driven away before leaving the apartment. The tall, fair-skinned Chilean woman, Marcos Dominguez's only sister, walked across the parking lot, got into a shiny Miata, and drove to the nearest gas station, where she approached a pay phone and placed a long-distance call to a number in New Jersey she had committed to memory two days ago.

"Black Youth of America," came the pleasant voice of the receptionist of one of the newest nonprofit organizations in the United States, catering to the needs of the teenage black.

"Extension four four four," said Norma.

"Just a moment."

The line rang three times.

"Your code?" asked the voice at the other end, a man with an Egyptian accent.

"La hermana."

"One moment."

The static that came on the line told Norma that the conversation would be taped from this point on.

"Your message?" the Egyptian man asked.

"Khalela Yishaid is still unconscious," she said slowly into the receiver, and she spent just over five minutes relating the facts of what went on at the hospital. The line went silent for several seconds.

"Your recommendation?" said the Egyptian.

"Proceed with plan. We are running out of time."

"Understood," finally came the reply before the line went dead.

Norma Dominguez returned to her black Miata and got in, slowly checking under the seat to verify that her loaded Uzi was still safely Velcroed to the seat's springs. She hated her current assignment, particularly because it had involved the kidnapping of a child. Norma liked children, but monitoring Khalela's room took precedence, and this had been the only way Norma could devise on such short notice to ensure the free and safe flow of the information vital to the success of Saddam Hussein's plans. Her love for children told her that the nurse would never do or say anything that would endanger the life of little Roberto Guzman.

THE VESUVIUS.

The yellow gleam of burning tanks and armored transports diffused across the evening sky, high above the desert. Roaring sounds of war swept across the battlefield. His right arm hung useless at his side. Broken, perhaps worse. His blackened face, swollen and bruised from bouncing inside the scorching helicopter after absorbing a direct hit from the advancing coalition forces, turned to this moonless sky, praying to Allah for his family, for his wife, for his two young boys.

The smell of gasoline fumes, burning rubber, and gunpowder filled the air as the pilot dragged his broken body over the cool sand, stained with the reddish fire spewing out of a graveyard of twisted machines of war. Inch after agonizing inch he crawled, away from the madness he had witnessed, his mind overcoming the searing pain of his burns. He was the only survivor, the only warrior spared from the surface-to-air missiles that had destroyed his entire helicopter unit after American tank-killer aircraft had fired on his helicopter south of Basra.

Now he staggered north, back toward Basra, his hometown, the city he had been commanded to defend against the blasphemous coalition forces.

A stiff wind blew clouds of dark smoke past the hill where he walked and down the arid plains that extended to the Persian Gulf. Leaving the charred corpses of his comrades behind, the lonely pilot ignored the distant flickering of artillery fire splattering streaks of crimson light across the horizon. He had to reach Basra before the city perished under the steel tracks of American armor.

Hours went by while he covered the distance, and by the time he reached the city he realized some buildings had collapsed over the streets. He reached his block and faced the rubble that had been his home. His family lived on the second floor of the small building. Walking on the sidewalk, he climbed on top of the mound of rubble and began to paw through the debris while praying that he would not find them. Perhaps they had heard the noise and fled. Perhaps they managed to leave the building in time.

Minutes passed; tears rolled down his face as he used his one good arm to move rock, brick, and wood aside. His muscles burned and his head throbbed, but it did not matter. He had to know. He needed to know. An overwhelming sense of despair suddenly filled his senses the moment he spotted his wife's body under a wooden panel. His sons were next to her. They wore their sleeping garments. Still hopeful, he knelt next to his wife, but froze when something didn't look right. His wife lay on her stomach but her eyes stared up to the dark sky, her head twisted at a repulsive angle.

Reaching inside his soul to pull the strength he desperately needed to remain calm, he walked over to his sons, their bodies facedown, but apparently intact. He turned the first one over . . . his face and chest were gone! He let go and leaned to the side, controlled the first convulsion, but the second reached his mouth. He couldn't even tell which of his sons that was! His body tensed and he let it all out. A third convulsion came and went, quickly followed by a fourth; this time only a dry heave.

The warrior straightened up, breathed deeply, walked over to his second son and turned him over. His body was not maimed, but the purple hue of the flesh around the neck told him everything he needed to know.

Dropping to his knees and letting go one loud scream of anger, frustration, and pain, he burst into tears again. The Americans had taken his loved ones. It was the Americans. It was the Americans.

Kemal Ramallah jerked in his sleep and woke up, his face moist with sweat, his hands trembling, his heart hammering inside his chest. Although a few years had passed since that dreadful night in 1991, when Iraq lost the war to the American-led coalition, the nightmare of a much greater loss still haunted him. To this day he could still feel the smothering pain of seeing his loved ones crushed in the rubble, killed under the stomping boots of the evil Americans.

Sitting at the edge of his bunk, Kemal rubbed his face with both hands. The stained sheet covering his waist and thighs bordered a thick scar that traversed his abdomen. A second scar ran the length of his right arm. A muscular man with emerald green eyes wide and shiny, a well-kept beard, and a fine nose, Kemal Ramallah would be called handsome by most. A pink scar across his right temple, although quite noticeable, added a dimension of ruggedness to his persona.

Getting up and walking across the small cabin to the tiny sink, Kemal closed his eyes and splashed cold water on his face, temporarily washing away the madness of his previous life. Kemal Ramallah was Iraqi by birth. His parents, however, were not Iraqis. They were Palestinians. Emigrating from Palestine in 1948, after the Jews established their state in his ancestors' Holy Land, Kemal's parents settled in Basra. Kemal was born that same year.

Turning off the water, Kemal dried off his face and stared into the shiny stainless steel mirror over the sink. His forty-four years of age had definitely taken a toll on Kemal's once lean and strong body. Although the beard on his face, without a trace of gray thanks to hair coloring, made him look younger than his years, his eyes gave him away. Deep lines of age surrounded a pair of intelligent eyes, which tended to widen when he grimaced. Kemal had done a lot of grimacing in his turbulent life, particularly after losing his parents to an Iranian 155mm artillery shell during the Iran-Iraq war of the eighties.

A look of hatred came over his face. Pressing both fists against the rusted sink while leaning forward, his face only inches from the mirror as he stared into his own pupils, Kemal Ramallah remembered the pain but savored its sting, for it filled him with the strength he needed to carry on his holy work against the children of the Great Satan. He was the chosen one, the instrument of Saddam Hussein. A life of suffering was the foundation of his inner fire, of his commitment, of his perserverance and patience. As much as he mourned the loss of everyone he had ever loved, Kemal Ramallah needed that pain to make him one with his destiny, with his mission in America.

America. Bastards!

His breath began to fog the mirror, clouding his reflection, lowering a white veil in front of his eyes as he rested his forehead against the glass, his knuckles still pressed against the old sink. Americans were nothing but a handful of fearful pigs, living in their secluded little world of luxury while passing judgment on the rest of humanity: Whom shall we bomb today? Which country should we use to show the rest of the world that America is still a superpower?

And in Kemal Ramallah's mind that was exactly the way the White House made its decisions on the use of force. If a new Pentagon budget would head for Congress in a week, bombing a "troublemaker" somewhere in the world was the politically correct thing to do in order to show the American people, and their congressmen and senators, the importance of a strong military force—regardless of the consequences of the bombing. If President Bill Clinton began to fall behind in the polls, the bombing of a helpless nation under a fabricated pretext would put the American Commander in Chief back in front, never mind what pain it caused to the innocent people on the receiving end of that Tomahawk missile or laser-guided bomb.

But now Saddam Hussein had turned the tables on the soft, fat Americans and their high technology. This time around it would be Kemal's people who would get to watch on CNN the terror inflicted on Americans in their own land, just like that glorious day at the World Trade

Center. This time around Saddam had made the right alliances to maximize the use of his network in America. This time around the Russian Mafia in America and Marcos Dominguez's network would join forces with Saddam and the New Islamist International to ensure success.

A smile flashed across Kemal's face in that foggy mirror. He could see the white gleam of his teeth beneath his black beard. He could smell his foul breath as he exhaled with his mouth open.

You Americans don't know the meaning of terror. Oh, but in the name of Allah, you will know. You will know.

Kemal Ramallah shook his head as he stepped away from the sink and began to dress. His Makarov tucked in his pants and covered with a large T-shirt, the Iraqi closed and locked the door to his cabin after arming the motion sensor protecting his cargo. A brief scan of the long corridor, and he headed for the stairs. The captain had asked him to stop by his office prior to reporting for work in the kitchen this morning.

A few minutes later, Kemal reached the captain's cabin and knocked twice on the metal door before going inside. The cabin's interior, gloomy and cold with cigarette smoke lining the ceiling, was twice the size of Kemal's. Walls of peeling green paint over rusting metal housed a set of bunk beds, a desk, two chairs, and a small sink and toilet. Unlike the rest of the crew aboard the *Vesuvius,* Captain Paolo Fiori, a man as large and wide as Kemal, but much younger and sporting a bushy, unkempt beard and thick black hair, did not have to share a toilet. The only time the captain needed to use one of the ship's four large bathrooms was when he had to shower. Based on the body odor emanating from this man as he pointed to a chair across his desk, Kemal decided that the captain did not shower much.

Wearing a dark woolen sweater with a turtleneck that disappeared in the thick beard, Paolo Fiori sat behind his desk. In his hands was a report he waved at Kemal, a half-smoked cigarette hanging from the corner of his mouth. An army of crushed butts crowded a blue, metallic ashtray on the right side of the desk. A mug of steaming coffee on a hot plate stood next to the ashtray. Even the smell of cigarette smoke and coffee could not disguise Fiori's strong scent.

"Buon giorno, mio passeggero," Fiori said.

"Buon giorno, Capitane."

"Two crew members are missing," Fiori said in Italian, a language Kemal had learned to master as part of his language studies at Oxford many years earlier, before joining Iraq's Air Force and the *Mukhabarat.*

Shrugging, Kemal said, "I have been keeping to myself, *Capitane.* I have minimized contact with your crew. You and I have an agreement for transportation with no questions asked. I have been working in the kitchen as agreed. I know nothing else beyond that."

The Italian captain, eyes narrowing as he shot Kemal a suspicious glance, said, "We heard on the radio that a man washed ashore near

Lisbon this morning. Our office in Rome has faxed us a copy of the newspaper article." Fiori pulled out a folded sheet from the pocket of the black jumpsuit he wore, and he handed it to the Iraqi.

Taking it in his large hands, Kemal eyed the faxed sheet and recognized the photo of the Jew he had shot two nights ago, after Kemal had found him trying to break into the radio room during the storm.

"I don't recall the face, *Capitane.*"

The skipper slowly shook his head. "I make this trip to America once a month, and I always use the same crew," Fiori said, the cigarette moving up and down on the corner of his mouth as he spoke. "This time three strangers came on board looking for secret transportation to America. You and this dead man are two of them. The third one is missing. His body still has not turned up. I'm afraid I'm going to have to turn back immediately, and let the authorities back in Lisbon investigate this problem, *capisce?*"

Kemal Ramallah regarded the captain, whose stern face conveyed much more than his words. He obviously suspected Kemal and would see to it that Portuguese authorities carried out a full investigation. The captain took a long draw and exhaled in Kemal's direction. The former Iraqi Air Force pilot wondered if he had made the right decision by taking a totally new route to reach America instead of one of the established channels, which in Kemal's opinion always ran a high risk of being compromised by the CIA or the FBI. Not wishing to gamble losing his precious cargo to the Americans, Kemal had made the call to select a clean vessel and bribe the captain. There was nothing the Americans had on the *Vesuvius,* and he had hoped to get to America without raising any suspicions from the crew. He would have succeeded, had it not been for the two Mossad Jews who also joined the crew, ruining Kemal's plans of keeping a low profile during the trip.

"But we're almost there," said Kemal, aware that in another two days they would reach Florida, where the vessel was scheduled to deliver a large shipment of ceramic tile.

"My decision is final," said Captain Fiori, studying the Iraqi through the wreathing smoke. "I can't continue under such circumstances, regardless of our agreement." The captain pulled on the cigarette, crushed the butt on the side of the metallic desk, and set it at the top of the pile on the ashtray.

Kemal took a step forward. "But the money! *Il denaro! Dieci mille dollaros!* You gave me your word to get me to America in under a week."

Fiori stood, leveling his stare with Kemal's while slowly blowing out the smoke before saying, "You don't understand, *mio passeggero.* I've just called my first mate to my quarters. I will order him to turn the vessel around and head back for Lisbon immediately."

Kemal thought this one out quite carefully, under the scorching glance of Captain Paolo Fiori, who remained standing, hands on his waist.

There was a knock on the door.

"Avanti!" Fiori yelled, while reaching into a pocket in his dark green pants and pulling out a half-empty pack of cigarettes and a plastic lighter.

Kemal slowly stepped to the side of the desk as the cabin door opened.

"You called, *Capitane?"* asked a short, wiry man with a black mustache as impressive as his long nose. Large, round, brown eyes in purplish sockets gravitated to Kemal and back to the skipper. The Iraqi recognized the skipper's mate, Gigio Rositti, who was second-in-command of the vessel and also doubled as the medic for the crew. Fiori had split Kemal's ten-thousand-dollar fee seventy-thirty with this man. No one else aboard the vessel knew of the trio's secret arrangement.

"Gigio," Paolo Fiori said as he lit another cigarette, "I'm afraid I have bad news for the crew. We're turning back to Lisbon *immediatamente."*

"Immediatamente, Capitane?" asked Rositti, who also wore a turtle-neck sweater. It looked a few sizes too large, hanging from his bony shoulders.

Kemal's entire future hinged on the next few seconds. Do nothing and he ended up in a Portuguese jail, awaiting trial after the port authorities ran a full investigation and searched the vessel, inevitably finding his cargo.

Pushing Rositti away from the door and reaching behind his back to pull out the Makarov, Kemal Ramallah shut the door and leveled the weapon at the startled duo.

"Non si muova!" shouted Kemal.

It took a few seconds for the seasoned Paolo Fiori to react. And he did, pounding hairy fists on the metallic surface of the desk. The coffee mug jumped an inch above the desk and landed on its side, the contents spilling over the faxed sheet of paper and the ashtray.

"How dare you pull that gun on me, *farabutto!"* Fiori screamed, punching the air in front of him with a back fist, the new cigarette hanging in the corner of his mouth. "I am the captain of this vessel!" he shouted, pointing to himself.

"Silenzio! Rimanete dove siete!" commanded Kemal.

"Put that gun away or I'll have you thrown in a cell until we reach Lisbon!" protested Fiori.

Standing next to the bunk beds, Kemal simply moved his gaze back and forth between the angered Fiori and the frightened Rositti, whose already large eyes glinted with terror as they focused on the pistol's muzzle.

Defiantly, Fiori turned to his first mate. "I gave you a direct order, Gigio. Relay my commands to the bridge and call the authorities."

Visibly shaken, Rositti mumbled something incoherent without taking his eyes off the gun.

"Dammit, sailor!" Fiori snapped, moving a step toward Rositti, on the other side of the desk from where Kemal stood. "He is not going to fire! He'll have to kill all of us! Now do as I say. *Adesso!"*

Rositti remained frozen; only his gaze moved between Fiori and the Makarov.

"Adesso, Gigio! Now, dammit! Go and relay my order!" Fiori shouted, while pushing a stiff Rositti toward the door.

Kemal had had enough. "Move back, *Capitane.* Get back on your chair and be quiet."

"And what if I don't?" asked a crazed Paolo Fiori, the adrenaline boost making him a difficult hostage for Kemal Ramallah, who saw only one way to handle this situation before it got out of hand.

"Rositti," said the *Mukhabarat* colonel, "you have just been promoted to the rank of captain."

The words made Fiori's eyes narrow, and he suddenly froze when he understood, his mouth opening wide, the lit cigarette falling onto the spilled coffee on his desk, its burning end briefly sizzling before the brown liquid put it out. Hands in front of him with the palms facing Kemal, Paolo Fiori began to speak, but Kemal no longer cared to hear his words.

Using his free hand, Kemal grabbed a small pillow from the lower bunk, quickly pressed it around the weapon, and fired once into the middle of Fiori's chest.

The muffled report sounded more like a hard stomp than a gunshot. The round lifted Fiori off his feet and threw him up against a wall already stained with his own blood. Falling on his side behind the desk, Fiori made no other motion. The hole in his back was large enough for a fist.

"Madre mia! Dio mio!" Rositti just stood there, his hand shaking as he made the sign of the cross before turning his bony, ramshackle frame to Kemal Ramallah, a despairing mask covering his emaciated face. *"Per favore, signore. Mio moglie! Mio bambinos!"*

"You have two options," the *Mukhabarat* colonel said. "You either do exactly as I say, or I will shoot you where you stand, and you can kiss your *moglie* and *bambinos arrivederci, capisce?"*

"Si, signore," responded Rositti, nodding rapidly.

"Very well, then. If you take me to America, I will let you and your crew live. Otherwise, I will execute you one by one until I find someone who is willing to take orders from me."

Rositti breathed deeply, his eyes moving from the gun to Fiori and back to the gun. "I will do as you say, *signore."*

Kemal smiled. "I want you to inform the crew that the captain is sick with a very contagious case of the flu, and he has passed command of the vessel to you. I also want you to tell them that you have confined the captain to his quarters for the remainder of the trip, and that only you can deliver his meals. No one else is to enter his cabin or he might risk taking the virus with him and spreading it to the rest of the crew. Tell them you had two immunization shots, and you chose to immunize us both. The rest of the crew is at risk if exposed. Are we clear so far?"

The Italian mate quickly agreed. Kemal continued, the Makarov always pointed at Rositti's chest.

"From now on, you and I will go everywhere together. You will spend most of your time down here, unless there is an emergency, in which case I will accompany you to the bridge. Otherwise, I'll expect you to issue your commanding orders from this cabin. If you do this, and you follow all my orders, in two more days I will be out of your life, and I won't care if you tell the whole world how I hijacked this vessel and forced you to do this. Are you still with me?"

The newly appointed captain of the *Vesuvius* compressed his lips while nodding. As the initial shock faded, the sailor in him began to accept his new situation. "I will help you, *signore,*" Rositti finally said. "I will do exactly as you say. But please, spare my life and that of my crew. I know every man aboard and, like myself, they have families."

Kemal Ramallah nodded. "Do as I say and no one else will be hurt. I promise that."

With that, Kemal stepped aside as Rositti dragged Fiori's body to the lower bunk, where he covered him up to his neck, before he took the towel above the sink and began cleaning the blood on the wall.

Kemal sighed in relief. Maybe, just maybe, he might still have a chance of making it to America in one piece.

TIKRIT. ONE HUNDRED MILES NORTH OF BAGHDAD, IRAQ.

In a white stone structure built into the side of a rocky hill outside Tikrit, Jafar Dhia Jafar, Iraq's top nuclear scientist, removed the jacket of his Armani suit and rolled up the sleeves of his white shirt.

On the center of the table in front of Jafar lay the heart of the project: a one-kilogram sphere of the very precious uranium 235, the rare isotope of the common uranium 238 after it has been enriched through a process that Iraq had been unable to develop because its enrichment facilities kept getting destroyed by the enemies of Islam. The Russians had been the ones who enriched the uranium in the sphere Jafar had already enclosed inside a nuclear reflector or tamper device, a hollow sphere of a very dense material, in this case a gold-graphite alloy, designed to minimize the amount of uranium required to achieve a chain reaction. This minimum amount of uranium was known as the critical mass.

One of two MIT graduates assisting Jafar worked the keyboard of a notebook computer, running a spreadsheet that calculated the minimum impact velocity required to strike the neutron initiator at the center of the uranium sphere. The initiator was a small beryllium core, designed to release a single neutron into the uranium mass when impacted with enough force by a small slug of enriched uranium fired at the initiator from a very close distance. The released neutron would collide with a uranium 235 atom, splitting it in half and releasing a large amount of energy in the form of heat and light, and also two more neutrons, which would then collide with other uranium atoms, releasing more energy and more neutrons. Some neutrons had a tendency to escape without colliding with any uranium atoms, reducing the efficiency of the bomb. That was the reason for the nuclear reflector, which bounced the drifting neutrons back into the core and forced them to participate in the fission reaction. According to Jafar's calculations, this bomb would equal twenty thousand tons of TNT, quite similar to the one that leveled Hiroshima. This fact was no coincidence. Jafar Dhia Jafar based his work largely on the public notes of Dr. J. Robert Oppenheimer and Dr. Robert Serber, two of the top scientists running the Manhattan Project at Los Alamos during the forties.

"Muzzle velocity?" asked Jafar, as he screwed a fifteen-inch-long steel tube to the beryllium initiator in the center of the assembly. This was a very critical stage, particularly because he had already inserted the beryllium initiator in the center of the uranium sphere, and he had enclosed it with the nuclear reflector. He had, in fact, achieved critical mass, and all he needed for an atomic explosion was a way to excite the beryllium initiator to release a single neutron into the uranium core. The rest would work just as in the complex mathematical formulas scribbled on the white boards covering much of the wall space in the assembly room.

The MIT graduate looked up from the monochrome screen and said, "One thousand fifteen feet per second."

Jafar immediately walked to an adjacent table, where he took an empty .357 Magnum shell and filled it with the precise amount of gunpowder by weight to achieve that exact muzzle velocity using a uranium 235 slug shaped like a bullet, which Jafar attached to the shell with a regular loading press.

Connecting the other end of the steel pipe to a modified pistol, Jafar loaded the round in the chamber and glanced into the faces of his two pupils.

"A pull of this trigger will destroy everything within six thousand feet."

Lifting his holy work with both arms, Jafar felt the forty-pound assembly and smiled, which he seldom did, and which caused his pupils also to smile. Iraq had once again entered the nuclear arena.

"Inshallah!"

ATLANTIC CITY, NEW JERSEY.

Irina Bukovski sat at the bar with a glass of warm vodka in her hands. She drank alone in the empty club. Alone with the image of herself in the mirror behind the bar. Not even Viktor was there. The large Ukrainian slept in one of the rooms in the rear.

She brought the glass to her lips and took a sip of the drink that brought back such terrible memories. She closed her eyes as the vodka warmed her throat, visions of her violent past rapidly filling her mind.

The *Komitat Gosudarstvennoi Bezopasnosti.* The KGB.

Irina Bukovski saw herself running. She ran as fast as her young legs would go. She ran across the street from the old KGB building and down the crowded avenue, passing rows and rows of street vendors and parked automobiles. Her bare feet splashed the melting snow as she took in lungfuls of freezing air to keep up the furious pace. She had to get away, had to lose the animals who not only had gotten her pregnant, but now wanted to take her unborn baby away from her.

This is my child! she had cried just ten minutes before, as the *Komitat*'s doctor and his assistant had arrived at her room carrying the tools that would reach deep inside her and extract the living baby in her womb, barely two months old.

"Padazhditye!" shouted one of her KGB pursuers. "Stop! Stop now!"

Irina could not, would not. They would not take her baby away!

A hand grabbed her from behind as she reached the edge of Gorky Park. Under the curious look of dozens of pedestrians, three KGB officials dragged her kicking and screaming like a crazed animal into a waiting limousine. Twenty minutes later, back in her room, the KGB doctor performed the forced abortion while several of her superiors, including the one who had gotten her pregnant, enjoyed the show smoking cigars and drinking vodka, while making bets on the sex of the fetus.

"How many does that make for you, Giorgi?" asked one of the KGB *officers to another as the doctor used cold instruments to spread open Irina's vagina and make some room for his tools.*

"Seven, my friend," the other KGB officer had responded, raising his *vodka glass to the spread-eagled Irina. "Seven pregnancies," he repeated, slapping Irina's naked thigh while the doctor reached in between her legs.*

The flow of vodka had continued during the entire procedure. Even as they wheeled her away to another room, under the applause of her demented audience, the KGB officers kept on drinking and smoking cigars.

Vodka.

Irina opened her eyes and stared into her own reflection once more. That child would have been around eighteen years of age this year, and her second child, whom she had lost to the same doctor the year after, would have been seventeen.

The hysterectomy had come then, during her second abortion, because of an infection. The *Komitat*'s doctor had crudely performed that procedure with dirty instruments, nearly killing her. Only the skills of a top Moscow surgeon, working under strict instructions from the chief of the KGB, had saved her from the infection.

Her love and affection had also left her body that same afternoon, while the surgeon removed a part of her that could never be replaced with anything the KGB had to offer. But that was precisely the reason for this torture. Just six months later, Irina participated in her first undercover operation as a secretary at the American Embassy.

"Irina?"

Setting the glass on the counter, the Russian woman turned around.

Viktor Kozlov stood there rubbing his eyes and yawning.

Facing the mirror once more and bringing the edge of the glass to her lips, Irina said, "The American pig enjoyed his video. Yes?"

Viktor lifted a hinged section of the counter, walked behind the bar, and also poured himself some vodka, no ice.

"He cried, like the others, and begged for mercy," Viktor answered, after downing half the glass in one gulp.

Irina smiled while staring into her own blue eyes and took a sip. "Mercy. Yes? Did he read the instructions?"

Now Viktor smiled. His square-set jaw rose a notch as a look of dark amusement covered his face. He reached for a pack of cigarettes and some matches, lighting one up for himself and another for Irina.

"He even offered to fly the helicopter himself," he said, passing one cigarette to his superior.

Drawing hard on the Marlboro, Irina cocked her head at him, her eyes dancing in amazement at the way she could gain absolute control over these naive Americans.

"Everything is coming together," Viktor added.

Nodding as her plan to rendezvous with the Iraqi messenger quickly materialized, the former Russian agent stared at the burning end of the cigarette she held between the index and middle fingers of her left hand, black-painted long fingernails pointed at the ceiling. Time was running out for the Americans. Soon Irina would become richer than her wildest dreams. She just needed to execute her plan.

"Is the sheikh's team on the way?"

"They will be in position in another twelve hours."

"Let's hope they are as good as the old Arab claims they are. Yes?"

A look of concern hardened the Ukrainian's face. "I trust no one but our kind."

"They will succeed," the Russian woman said. "They better succeed."

8

THE REPUBLICAN GUARD

For wide is the gate, and broad is the way, that leadeth to destruction.
—Matthew 7:13

EARTH ORBIT. THREE HUNDRED TWENTY-NINE MILES OVER THE MIDDLE EAST.

The cylindrically shaped, KH-12 orbital reconnaissance satellite circled the earth in an elliptical orbit. As it approached its apogee with an inclination of ninety-six degrees, a tiny amount of hydrazine and liquid oxygen from the integral propellant and oxidizer tanks was released to a single attitude control vernier rocket, which fired in a small hypergolic reaction to rotate two of its five high-resolution cameras toward the current priority target, which had been programmed from the ground an orbit before.

The thirty-thousand-pound satellite began rotating clockwise for three seconds before sensors told its electronic brain that the selected cameras were in position. The powerful microprocessor issued a new set of commands, and another vernier fired in the opposite direction to counter the rotation and stabilize the position of the search-and-find cameras, which rapidly began to adjust their powerful multispectral lenses to achieve a resolution of six inches while scanning a surface area of two square miles each.

The moment the area of interest—a fifty-square-mile patch of desert south of An Nasiriya, one hundred miles from the border with Kuwait— was reached, the cameras worked in parallel, snapping side-by-side shots that were exposed in batch sequence to a focal plane made of millions of microscopic photoelectric cells. They digitized the image and transferred it to the satellite's central processing unit, where another piece of digital hardware enhanced it to compensate for temperature variations and atmospheric haze effects before transmitting the images to Earth via a dedicated data link. By the time the first set of "real-time" photos reached the earth, the cameras had already shifted to the next two-square-mile grid and the computer photographing sequence, which took less than a twentieth of a second per frame, started again—shooting, digitizing, enhancing, transmitting, refocusing, and shooting once more. That was the primary task of the advanced KH-12, and it was by all means one of the best, most reliable pieces of orbital hardware the United States had on hand for reconnaissance.

The KH-12 dashed over the area of interest in under ten seconds, but by that time the cameras aboard the sixty-four-foot-long satellite had completed their task and over two hundred images had been transmitted to the data banks of the CIA's National Photographic Interpretation Center in Washington, D.C.

LANGLEY, VIRGINIA.

Robert Bourdeaux cruised west on the Georgetown Pike as he drove to the CIA headquarters after spending a very depressing morning at the NPIC. His analysts had showed him that the two divisions of Republican Guards, which amounted to around forty thousand troops, continued to drive south at a rate that would bring them to the border with Kuwait in another forty-eight hours.

Bourdeaux's fingers tightened around the black leather–wrapped steering wheel as he thought of the relatively small American force stationed in Kuwait. Although Clinton had armed the deployment with state-of-the-art weaponry, and the Army also had the full backing of the *Kennedy* carrier force in the Persian Gulf, the Marines' Hornets in Kuwait, and the Air Force planes at Salman Assad, if Saddam Hussein decided to strike, Bourdeaux felt the situation could turn quite critical. To complicate matters further, the nuclear hardware Bane had witnessed changing hands north of Moscow was definitely heading for Turkey—according to the information Bane had extracted from a Russian named Mikhail Petrosky. This meant the warheads were on their way to Saddam Hussein across the border. To top it all off, KH-12 shots over Baghdad indicated that additional Republican Guard divisions were being deployed around the city—almost one hundred thousand men—leading Bourdeaux to believe that the Iraqis were preparing to protect Baghdad from a large invading force.

Bourdeaux turned off the Georgetown Pike and rode along Dolley Madison Boulevard, going northwest until he saw the sign that said, CIA NEXT RIGHT. The sign had been taken down back in the sixties at the insistence of Robert F. Kennedy, then attorney general, in a silly effort to pretend that the large CIA headquarters didn't exist. In reality, every pilot flying to National Airport used the building as a checkpoint. The sign had been reinstated in 1973 by CIA Director James Schlesinger.

Robert Bourdeaux stayed in the left lane, keeping his speed below the posted 25 mph limit. A double chain-link fence, fitted with a vibration alarm sensor and topped with barbed wire, surrounded the compound.

Driving up to an employee-only post, equipped with an intercom and closed-circuit TV camera, Bourdeaux rolled down the window and flashed his CIA ID to a guard with white hair and a white mustache, wearing a broad-brimmed hat. After eyeing the ID and the sticker on Bourdeaux's windshield, the guard waved him through. Bourdeaux continued to the main gate twenty-five feet up the road, where he presented his ID to a guard inside a concrete-and-glass structure. The guard, a large blond man with blue eyes in his mid-twenties, also wearing a broad-brimmed hat, checked his ID before letting him go inside the compound.

Langley.

Although the name was commonly used to describe the Agency's location, in reality it did not exist. The CIA headquarters was officially located in McLean, Virginia. Langley was a small village founded sometime in the nineteenth century that eventually merged with nearby McLean in 1910. Yet, because the CIA was built in the area once called Langley, everyone to this day still referred to the Agency's location as Langley. Even the Agency itself was commonly called Langley.

Bourdeaux parked in the VIP parking lot in front of the Agency's original building, near a number of magnolia and tulip trees. He got out of his car and walked toward the building's main entrance, fifteen glass doors that led to a lobby floored with gray-and-white marble.

He checked his watch as he walked into the lobby. By the left wall stood a statue of William Donovan, the director of the Office of Strategic Services, the forerunner of the CIA. On the right wall hung the memorial to fallen CIA officers, consisting of fifty-five gold stars arranged in rows of thirteen stars, except for the top row, which had fourteen stars, and the bottom row, which only had three stars. Each star represented a CIA officer killed in the line of duty. The American flag stood to the left of the array of stars, and a flag with the seal of the CIA to the right.

Bourdeaux looked at the last star on the bottom row, added to the memorial during a short ceremony held only three days before. Officer Harvey Lee had perished while trying to provide his nation with vital information concerning its security.

Shaking away the sadness that suddenly filled him, Bourdeaux took an elevator to the seventh floor, walked down a long corridor, and reached the double glass doors leading to Director of Central Intelligence Joseph Goldberg's reception room. Kate Marston sat behind a glass desktop resting on two black marble pedestals.

"Morning," Bourdeaux said, walking up to her desk. They were alone in the reception room.

"Hello, Robert," replied Kate. "I missed you last night."

Bourdeaux put a hand on hers. "I'm really sorry. I promise to make it up to you tonight."

"Looking forward to it," she said.

Bourdeaux smiled.

Kate also smiled, picked up a black telephone, and pressed a single digit.

"Mr. Goldberg? . . . Yes, sir. He's here . . . Yes, sir." She hung up and looked at Bourdeaux. "He'll see you now."

Heavy automatic doors, layered with sheets of steel and Kevlar, slowly swung open. Bourdeaux gave her a wink and went in.

It took Bourdeaux's eyes a few seconds to adjust to the murky interior of the dark wood–paneled room. Aside from the two table lamps flanking a tan sofa on the right wall, the glowing sunlight bordering the edges of the drawn curtains behind the DCI's desk, directly in front of Bourdeaux, provided all the illumination in the room.

The director of Central Intelligence sat behind the desk. His long, bony face, flecked and wrinkled with age, turned in Bourdeaux's direction. A pair of piercing black eyes in sunken purple sockets blinked slowly over the spectacles. The fingers of his right hand fiddled with a burgundy Mont Blanc fountain pen.

"Come in, Bob," Goldberg said in a low, rheumy voice, while pointing to one of three chairs in front of his desk.

"Morning, sir."

Slowly, Bourdeaux sat down. Folding one hand over the other in his lap, he melted his gaze with Goldberg's grave stare. The end of the DCI's wiry lips curved down.

"I hope you didn't keep Kate out too late last night. She looks a little tired this morning."

Bourdeaux grinned, but inside he felt uneasy. Goldberg had never approved of the relationship but had learned to accept it, particularly because Kate put up with Goldberg's abusive managerial style, and also because Bourdeaux was the finest DDO the Agency had seen in years.

"We should get the call any moment. Looks like Saddam's latest actions are catching the president's eye," continued Goldberg, before Bourdeaux got a chance to respond to the first comment.

"It's a mess, sir," said Bourdeaux, keeping it professional. "Did the NPIC call you?"

Goldberg nodded as he used the pen to point to a manila envelope. "Got the photos five minutes ago. This is turning into a very serious situa—"

The phone rang, and Goldberg pressed the speaker button.

"Good morning, Mr. President," said Goldberg.

"Hi, Joe. I just got the PDB and the photos from Bourdeaux. Is he there with you?"

Goldberg looked at Bourdeaux as he said, "Yes, Mr. President. He's right here."

"Bob?"

Bourdeaux leaned forward on the chair, his eyes focused on the black speaker box. "Hello, Mr. President."

"Hi, Bob. Listen, I need to know how much time we have before the Iraqis reach the border."

"Those troops are advancing south very fast, sir. In my estimation, they should reach Kuwait in less than forty-eight hours."

The line went silent for a few seconds.

"I have already sent Saddam Hussein an ultimatum," Clinton's voice crackled through the speaker. "If his troops don't turn around by midnight tomorrow night, Washington time, we will launch an air strike against the two divisions of Republican Guard troops. I'm leaving Hiroshima within the hour and will be back in Washington this evening. We have already put a plan in place to use the F-18 Hornets of the Block Twelve from the Marines' El Toro, California, air station. They are currently running bombing exercises in Kuwait and Saudi Arabia in preparation. The *Kennedy* will provide cover. We'll keep the F-15s at Salman Assad on standby in case we need them. The Pentagon assures me we won't. The Hornets should be able to handle this. The Kuwaiti government is also backing the Marines with their own F-18s."

Bourdeaux slowly shook his head. This was very serious, but the repercussions of this strike could be devastating, particularly since Saddam was once again in the nuclear bomb business.

"This morning's PDB showed no updates on the smuggling ring situation. Any news there, Bob?" asked the president.

Bourdeaux rubbed a finger against his right temple and closed his eyes as he spoke, telling Clinton exactly what Bane had conveyed in his flash report several hours ago. A new shipment was on the way to Saddam, and Donald Bane was following its trail, which had taken him to Istanbul, Turkey. Bourdeaux felt quite certain the hardware was heading for Iraq.

The line went silent again. Bourdeaux and Goldberg exchanged glances.

"We must intercept the warheads before they make it to Iraq," Clinton said.

"We're working on it, Mr. President," responded Goldberg. "But we have to be very careful how we approach this, sir. There is a significant level of corruption in the Turkish government. We suspect that a number of high-ranking Turkish officials are on Marcos's payroll. If we let the Turks in on this, I'm afraid we're going to compromise our operatives and lose the hardware. I have my best man on the job, and he is currently teaming up with one of our most trusted agents in Istanbul."

Again, there was silence on the line for a few seconds as President Clinton digested the news.

"You're doing the right thing, Joe. Keep me informed as the situation develops."

"Yes, sir."

"What is your take on the one hundred thousand troops clustering around Baghdad?" asked Clinton.

Goldberg leaned back, tapping one end of the Mont Blanc pen against a temple while staring at Bourdeaux. "Difficult question to answer, Mr. President. We feel he might be playing it cautious, overprotecting Baghdad, his center of operations. But that's just a guess, sir. Too early to tell."

"What about the U.N. inspection team, Mr. President?" asked Bourdeaux. "Shouldn't we pull them out before the deadline, just in case?"

"I've already worked out that issue with the U.N. secretary-general," responded Clinton. "The inspection team is leaving this afternoon."

Bourdeaux nodded.

"Gentlemen, I will have a breakfast meeting in the Oval Office tomorrow morning at five-thirty. The secretaries of the state and defense, and the director of the FBI will also be there. Please make yourselves available to go over our strategy on this one. I want you to come prepared with issues, problems, options, and anything else you can think of that will allow for a solid response to this situation. Based on Bob's reports, there's a chance that Saddam has already assembled some warheads. We must play this out very carefully."

"Yes, sir," was the unanimous response before the line went dead. Bourdeaux leaned back in his chair and closed his eyes.

AL JABER AIR BASE, KUWAIT.

Marine Aviator Lieutenant Colonel Diane Towers welcomed the cold and dry morning air as she filled her lungs while jogging on the dusty road surrounding the base. The crimson ball of the sun loomed above the sand dunes, staining the sapphire sky with streaks of orange and yellow, casting a red-gold glow over the large air base on the outskirts of Kuwait City. The peace and beauty of a desert sunrise was the main reason why Diane always woke up this early. She wanted it all to herself.

Her Nike running shoes kicked the gravel at the edge of a road built back in the spring of 1991, during the aftermath of the Desert Storm victory.

As she picked up her pace to make it back to the base in time for breakfast, Diane Towers wished she were home, back at the Marines' El Toro, California, air station. After spending a year fighting alongside the poorly coordinated U.N. Security Forces deployed to northern Iraq to enforce the no-fly zone, the thirty-eight-year-old commanding officer was ready to go home. But orders were orders, and as a third-generation

Marine, Diane knew how to follow them to the letter without ever letting her personal feelings surface.

Like her father and her grandfather, Diane was above all a Marine. Diane belonged to a special breed of warriors, the elite of the elite. Using a World War II rifle, an M-16, or an advanced F/A-18D Hornet made no difference when a leatherneck came to the crossroads. Those were merely the tools of a professional, the mechanical artifacts used to achieve an end. The value was in the soldier behind the hardware, in the warrior clutching an automatic weapon or a control stick. The value was in the Marine living up to a code of honor.

So when Saddam Hussein began to create trouble in the region, when diplomacy failed to contain the lust for power of the Iraqi tyrant, when Kuwaiti leaders pushed the panic button and urged the world to come to their rescue and prevent another August 1990, the United States government sent its finest warriors and their flying machines to the rescue.

The Marines had landed.

Diane stopped as she reached the top of a small hill overlooking her base. A sense of pride filled her. The line of Hornets looked menacing and beautiful at the same time. Those were her birds, her squadron, her responsibility. Beyond those Hornets were the Kuwaiti Hornets, all twenty of them. Across the base, a group of twenty-four A-10 Warthogs from the 23rd Wing at Pope Air Force Base had arrived during the night. The Warthogs had been scheduled for war exercises in conjunction with Diane's and the Kuwaiti's Hornets at noon.

She ran a hand through her soaked, short brown hair. A five-foot-ten woman, Diane gave the impression of someone who worked out regularly. Her firm stomach and slim but muscular arms and legs were the result of a life with the Marine Corps.

Brushing off the perspiration accumulating on her lean cheeks and above her upper lip, Diane turned her gaze toward the northeast, toward the border with Iraq.

Here we go again.

Slowly shaking her head, Diane swore to do everything within her power to make sure this time would be the last time the United States would have to deal with Saddam Hussein. Like most Americans, Diane was simply tired of this game, tired of slapping the tyrant's hand instead of finishing him off.

This time will be different.

BAGHDAD, IRAQ.

Dressed in his usual fatigues and black beret, Saddam Hussein sat at the head of the long table in the Presidential Palace. To his right sat Jafar Dhia Jafar, who had just informed the Iraqi leader that Sheikh Imman al-Barakah, Marcos, and the Russians had their people in place. The assembly team, operating out of a safe house in southern Louisiana, were awaiting the delivery of the preassembled hardware.

The Iraqi leader felt quite confident this morning. According to CNN, an American air strike was imminent if the advancing Iraqi troops did not turn around by midnight tomorrow tonight.

"The American president is reacting just as you predicted, Great One," said Jafar, as he sipped from a cup of hot tea.

"That is the only way he feels he can control me, and I will now use that predictability against him. This meager deployment of expendable troops will keep him focused on the wrong issue while the warheads are assembled and delivered to Washington and New York."

"What about the U.N. inspection team?" Jafar asked.

"I will use them as human shields," Saddam said. An hour before, Saddam had ordered the *Mukhabarat* to round up all inspectors and take them to the front lines of the advancing army. "It is what the American president would expect me to do. Has your scientist made it to the front lines yet?"

Jafar nodded. "He arrived three hours ago."

"Is he prepared to do it at a moment's notice?"

"Yes, Great One. It will happen just as you have requested. He was sworn to total secrecy, and he will sacrifice himself for our cause. The Americans will look like the infidels they are."

Soon, Saddam Hussein thought as he made a fist with his right hand. *Soon my messenger will reach America. Soon the infidels will experience the kind of suffering that will be written in the history books as my greatest achievement for the Muslim cause.*

THE *VESUVIUS.*

One hundred miles northeast of Miami, the *Vesuvius* continued its westward course under a scorching midday sun. After just one day the crew had begun wondering about the health of Captain Paolo Fiori, and whether or not they should radio Nassau to get a chopper to the ship and airlift him to a hospital. Gigio Rositti, the acting captain, had delayed issuing such an order under the claim that the captain was just down with a highly contagious flu virus and was restricted to his quarters.

On the bridge, 9mm Makarov tucked under a T-shirt, Kemal Ramallah watched Rositti's every move as the lanky Italian with the huge black mustache issued command after command to steer the ship precisely as required by the U.S. coastal authorities. Paolo Fiori's rotting corpse still lay on his bed. Kemal kept the door of Fiori's cabin locked at all times, not just to prevent a member of the crew from entering, but also to keep the stench from spreading through the ship's lower levels. Even Kemal himself, who had witnessed so much horror and death in his life, found it borderline nauseating.

For Kemal, the situation had actually gone better than anticipated. With the exception of two members of the crew who had inquired about the health of the captain, in the past day there had been little excitement aboard the Italian vessel, and that suited Kemal just fine.

Aside from himself and Rositti, three other men stood on the bridge, one at the wheel of the ship and the others at a large control panel filled with gauges, dials, buttons, switches, and levers. The only instrument Kemal cared about was the compass, which showed their continued course toward his upcoming rendezvous. The bridge itself was only about fifteen feet square, with windows facing the bow and the stern, and doors on the sides. A flickering fluorescent bulb added a stroboscopic rhythm to the slow sway of the ship as it cruised through the rough sea. The Nassau Weather Center had announced mild winds with scattered showers all night and late into the morning. The visibility from up here actually amazed Kemal, who could not believe that no one had seen him kill the second Mossad operative a few nights before.

With Rositti handling the navigation through these waters, Kemal relaxed a bit. Seven more hours and he would reach his destination. He had contacted Irina Bukovski three hours earlier. The necessary arrangements to pick him up before the *Vesuvius* reached Miami Beach were already in place.

Two sailors dressed in orange jumpsuits and sneakers walked onto the bridge. Rositti immediately snapped at them. The bridge was off-limits to all personnel, except for those working. Kemal recognized the pair as the same men who'd inquired about Paolo Fiori's health the day before.

"Get back to your stations, men!" Rositti barked, pointing back to the door they had just came through.

"But, sir," one of them said, an unkempt beard masking two rows of yellow teeth. *"Capitane* Fiori won't answer his door."

"I thought I gave you strict instructions not to disturb *il capitane!"* Rositti snapped. "Those were my orders, *capisce?"*

"The crew is worried, sir. And he is not answering," the same bearded man responded with a shrug.

Rositti looked toward Kemal, who said, "I spoke with *il capitane* this morning, when I served him his breakfast. I assure you he is going to be fine."

The large bearded man and his equally corpulent companion didn't seem to buy that answer.

"We wish to see *il capitane,* sir," the bearded man said to Rositti, ignoring Kemal.

The former Iraqi pilot realized this was not going anywhere, and he decided to take the initiative. "Perhaps we should take them to see *Capitane* Fiori," Kemal said to Rositti, who turned his head toward the Iraqi, the round eyes on his bony face widening with surprise.

Now Kemal had finally gotten the two sailors' full attention. "So he is fine then?" asked the bearded man's companion, a large man with a blond mustache that competed with Rositti's.

"Certainly," said Kemal, pushing out his lower lip while raising his brows. "Let's see if he's awake."

Kemal began to walk toward one of the side doors and Rositti quickly caught up with him before telling the bridge crew, "Hold course until I get back."

With the two sailors following a few feet behind, Kemal and Rositti headed downstairs, reaching the captain's cabin a minute later. Rositti pulled out a key and unlocked the door while Kemal waved the sailors toward the door, waited until they went in, and pulled out the Makarov.

The large Italians froze the moment they took a whiff of the rotting corpse, sprawled on the lower bunk, a pool of dried blood covered the green metallic floor by the foot of the bunk. White feathers from the blown pillow Kemal had used as a silencer covered the desk, chairs and floors.

"Il capitane!" the bearded man screamed at the sight of Captain Paolo Fiori's grayish face, his dead, glassy eyes staring at the ceiling, his mouth wide open, a trickle of dried blood lining his bearded chin.

"You two keep it quiet! *Silenzio!*" snapped Kemal, while shutting the cabin's door and locking it.

The sailors turned around, stunned looks painted across their weathered faces. Rositti stood aside, near the bunk where Fiori lay.

"Tu!" said the bearded man, stabbing a finger toward Kemal. *"Tu sei responsabile, figlio di puta!"*

Kemal didn't move an eyelid, simply staring back at the sailor with a contemptuous glance. *"No si muova,* either one of you, or I will kill you," the *Mukhabarat* colonel called out while moving toward the second bunk bed and taking a small pillow. "Rositti?"

"Yes?"

"Please inform the crew that we now have an epidemic on board, and this section is under quarantine. There are three diagnosed cases, Captain Fiori and these two *farabutos."*

The bearded man and the blond looked at each other and then at Kemal. "You can't do this! We will call the authorities!"

"You wanted to meet with *il capitane?"* asked Kemal in a serious tone of voice, his eyes filled with dark amusement. "Now you will get your chance."

The bearded man looked at Rositti, at the blond, and back at Kemal, who brought the pillow over the Makarov and fired once. Again, the pillow absorbed most of the report, bathing the bearded man with white feathers as a 9mm round ripped his chest open. He was dead by the time he hit the floor. Turning over to the shocked blond, Kemal fired again. The second sailor fell over the first under the terrified eye of Gigio Rositti, who stepped back into a corner and began making the sign of the cross and whispering words Kemal couldn't understand and probably didn't care about.

Pulling a small folded map from a back pocket, the *Mukhabarat* colonel unfolded a section and showed it to the perplexed Rositti. "How many sailors do you need to get this ship to this spot," he asked, a hairy index finger pointing to the waters fifty miles off the coast of southern Florida.

"Ah . . . just two, including myself."

"How many crew members do you have."

"Thirteen . . . no, eleven. Eleven as of now."

"Let's gather everyone but the sailor you need in the bridge."

"What are we going to do with the other sailors?" Rositti asked, his round eyes glinting with terror.

"Do not worry. I will not kill them unless they give me a reason. I just want to lock them up until after I'm off this ship. What you do after I leave is not of my concern."

With that the two of them headed back upstairs. Kemal checked his watch. Soon he would reach the rendezvous point. He could only hope that Irina Bukovski would come up with a good enough diversion to keep the U.S. Coast Guard from ruining his mission.

JERSEY CITY, NEW JERSEY.

The air inside the mosque was heavy and stale. Planks of stained oak flooring ran the entire length of the main prayer room, meeting the marble by the entrance with an inch-wide brass strip. Sunlight forked inside the room through a crack between light gray curtains on the right. Dressed in a white robe and brown leather sandals, Sheikh Imman al-Barakah stood in the middle of the room, both hands extended over a kneeling group of two Iraqis and three Lebanese men, five expendables sent to him from the New Islamist International. Bathed in a soft, yellow glow from spotlights hanging from the white cathedral ceiling, the old sheikh gave the group a final blessing before they left for a mission that would grant them eternal life.

"I sense your fear, children of Allah," said the short and slightly overweight sheikh, his lips hidden in the unkempt beard, the yellow glare reflecting on his bald head and thick horn-rimmed glasses. "But fear not. You are the chosen ones. Today is the day to atone for your sins. Today is the day Allah will remove the evil that lives in your souls. The infidels must perish. The liars must perish. The enemy of Islam must perish. The righteous ones will prevail only by defeating the infidels, who shall perish in the flames of hell while you bathe in the cool waters of the gardens of paradise."

The sheikh paused momentarily before motioning the group to stand.

"Children of Allah, children of Allah! Open your eyes to the truth of your Master! In your hands rests the power to set your souls free."

The group held hands and began to pray out loud. "Allah is good! Allah is right! Perish the liars! Perish the infidels! Perish the children of the Great Satan! *Inshallah!"*

A final blessing and the group left the mosque. Sheikh al-Barakah watched them drive away to their destiny at Georgetown University Hospital. He checked his watch. Irina's plan to rendezvous with the Iraqi courier was already in motion. The sheikh prayed to Allah that his expendables would not fail him in Florida. Their holy mission was crucial to create the needed diversion at the precise moment.

GEORGETOWN UNIVERSITY HOSPITAL, WASHINGTON, D.C.

Nurse Peggy Guzman checked the large clock on the white wall to her left as she carried a tray with four cups of coffee to the four FBI agents standing by Khalela Yishaid's door down the hall. She looked terrible. The little makeup she wore could not conceal the bags under her bloodshot eyes. Inside, she felt even worse. Nothing could go wrong. She had to act as if nothing was wrong. The life of her son depended on that.

Giving the agents a slight grin, Nurse Guzman said, "Good afternoon, gentlemen."

All four agents responded in unison. "Afternoon, ma'am."

"I hope this helps you stay awake," she said, painting an innocent look across her eyes.

Three of the four agents grabbed a cup. The fourth one, a young blond kid, shook his head. "Thanks, but I don't drink coffee."

"Yeah," said the oldest agent in the group, a slightly overweight man with an all-gray head of hair. He always acted as if he were the leader of the FBI team. "Ray here's into all that health stuff. Ain't that right, Ray?"

The blond kid just shrugged.

Peggy Guzman handed the kid the cup. "I hate to waste it. If you don't drink it, perhaps one of your friends might."

Without another word, Nurse Guzman headed for the parking garage, just as she had been instructed by the mysterious *señora,* who had also told her that her son would be delivered to her within the next hour. A minute later she got inside her Buick, parked two levels below the hospital's lobby. She had been ordered to remain in her vehicle until the child was brought to her.

Ten minutes later, a Nissan Sentra with tinted windows drove down to the parking garage below the Georgetown University Hospital's lobby. The dark gray vehicle parked in the tight space between a pickup truck and a concrete pillar, one row of cars behind Nurse Guzman's Buick. Another vehicle, a white van, pulled up behind the Sentra.

After setting the hand brake, the driver of the Sentra got out and locked the doors. One hundred pounds of Semtex, a Czechoslovakian plastic explosive, laced with hair-thin, gold-plated nickel wire, loaded in specially designed cardboard boxes, and carefully stacked in the trunk and rear seat of the car, had been connected to a triggering device made out of a pressure switch underneath the Sentra. The pressure switch consisted of two copper contacts separated an inch vertically by a heavy coil. The moment the driver set the hand brake, the pressure switch was lowered over the concrete floor such that the lower contact remained about two inches above the floor with the tires fully inflated. The second copper contact remained just an inch above the first.

Reaching into a pocket and pulling out an ice pick, the driver poked a small hole into each of the Sentra's tires and was rewarded by a low hissing sound. In his estimation, it would take roughly two to three minutes for the tires to deflate, time he would need to get into the waiting van and drive away from the building. Although the timing device seemed quite crude when compared to a digital timer, it certainly had not only the advantage of simplicity—a definite plus when dealing with expendables—but once started, the process was basically irreversible.

The Sentra's driver stepped inside the van, plucked a three-year-old Hispanic boy out of the car, and set him on his feet facing the green Buick.

"¿Mami? ¿Mami?" said the youngster.

"Tu mami esta aya. Andale, Robertico," the driver said, pointing to the green Buick, before closing the door. The van sped away, leaving the building in under a minute.

Exactly two minutes and twenty seconds later, as Peggy Guzman opened the door and embraced her Robertico, the lower copper contact touched the floor. The pressure of the dropping vehicle encountered the heavy steel coil separating the contacts, and fifteen seconds later they touched, closing the circuit. A pair of thick wires connected to the Sentra's battery sent a river of electrical current to the three miles' worth of wire lacing the Semtex.

Peggy Guzman's last earthly sight was the brown eyes of her beautiful Robertico, before the flames swallowed them both.

The blast struck the ten-foot-diameter concrete pillar with a force great enough to crack it, causing part of the ceiling to collapse, and bringing down with it a section of the floor above. The explosion, although powerful enough to shake this wing of the hospital, did not make it collapse. But the destruction of the hospital was hardly the mission of the Lebanese team deployed under the direct orders of Sheikh Imman al-Barakah at the request of Norma Dominguez. This was just a diversion, merely the means to create the havoc needed for the nearing NII termination team.

Kevin Dalton jolted up from the sofa, where he had been sleeping for the past few hours.

"What in the hell was that?" he said, while rubbing the sleep out of his eyes and reaching for the Beretta automatic Robert Bourdeaux had given him the day before.

Glancing at the still-unconscious Khalela Yishaid, Kevin raced across the room and opened the door, finding to his surprise that only one of the FBI agents assigned to protect Khalela stood outside. The agent looked as if he had graduated from high school yesterday.

"What happened?" asked Kevin to the young FBI agent, a well-built blond kid dressed in a dark gray suit.

"Fuck if I know. Bastards leave me by myself for a moment and all hell breaks loose," he said nervously as fire alarms blared across the floor and nurses and orderlies, using wheelchairs, began to evacuate some of the less-critical patients.

"Where are the others?"

"Got the shits. Told them not to drink that coffee. Stuff's bad for you. All three are in the toilet down the hall."

"Bad coffee? What are you talking about?" Kevin shook his head in disbelief. These guys were supposed to be pros. Just as he was about to respond, a nurse walked by wheeling an old man.

"What's happening? What was that blast?" asked Kevin.

"We're not sure, sir. It sounded like an explosion," said the nurse, a petite, fair-skinned brunette, in a calm tone as she briefly slowed down. "Security just called our floor and told us not to panic. Whatever it was, it doesn't look like it affected this floor. We're just moving the less-critical patients to the top floor." The nurse continued down the hall and disappeared around the corner.

An explosion?

Just as he considered the implications, the electricity went off. Yellow emergency lights quickly replaced the darkness as some patients began to scream in fear, but the seasoned team of nurses and orderlies brought the situation under control. Still, the hallway and the nurses' station suddenly took on an eerie look, making Kevin Dalton feel quite uneasy about his situation. *Three agents suddenly go down because of bad coffee, followed by an explosion?*

Turning to the young FBI agent, Kevin said, "What's your name?"

"Ray," the agent responded.

"All right, Ray. I got a bad feeling about this. Why don't you see if you can call your pals on that radio and then give me a hand here." Kevin looked around him and saw a middle-aged nurse walking in his direction. A pink-and-white face with round brown eyes glared with a mix of surprise and fear. Kevin flashed his CIA ID and waved her over. He needed to get these people off the hallway immediately.

Just as the staff of Georgetown University Hospital reacted to the explosion, one of several fire trucks made its way to a side entrance. Three men dressed in the uniform of the Washington, D.C. Fire Department left the blaring vehicle and raced inside.

The leader of the group ran up the emergency stairs first, followed by the others. Several nurses, doctors, and orderlies came down. The smell of burning rubber and plasterboard filled the air.

"Get out of here!" screamed the leader. "Run out of the building and stay out!"

Reaching the sixth floor in under a minute, the leader kicked the thick fire door and faced a long, empty hall.

Where is everyone? The leader narrowed suspicious eyes at the thought. The sheikh's contact in the hospital was supposed to have disabled the agents protecting the room. *But where are the nurses? The patients?* The commotion of the first two floors was apparently not shared by the upper floors after the hospital's speaker system announced that the damage had been limited to the garage and the first two floors. Still, he had expected to see *someone* in the hallway or at the nurses' station.

The leader breathed deeply and headed down the hall. Empty or not, he still had a mission to accomplish. He raced down the hall, his eyes searching for the room number.

Room 607.

The leader stopped and glanced at the large white numbers on the light oak door. Pulling an Uzi, he waited until his group had caught up, before bursting through the door and pressing the trigger. The staccato gunfire thundered inside the small room as he sprayed it at waist level. White stuffing from the mattress and pillows clouded the room, mixing with sporadic explosions of plasterboard and wood, and the sparks from rounds striking the stainless steel bed frame.

The leader stopped firing.

Empty! By Allah, the room is empty!

The seconds of silence that followed made no sense, only serving to compound his growing suspicion that something had gone terribly wrong. Why was the hall empty? And why weren't his men shouting at the crowd of people that should have appeared in the hallway the moment the gunfire started? Confused, he went back to the hall.

"Freeze, asshole!"

The leader could not believe his eyes. His team lay on the floor facedown! They had been captured by two American agents, one of whom pressed the muzzle of a gun to the back of his head.

"My brothers and I are not afraid to die, infidels! We shall rejoice in Allah's gardens today!" the leader shouted in English with a heavy Lebanese accent. He no longer cared to hide his country of origin. At that moment the two Arabs on the floor went into convulsions, just as he cracked the cyanide capsule the sheikh had given him earlier that day.

"Inshallah!" he shouted, as he shut his jaw tight and colors suddenly exploded in his brain before everything went dark.

Kevin Dalton let the Arab fall to the floor while grabbing the Uzi, which he passed to Ray. Unable to reach the other three agents, Kevin had chosen to wheel Khalela's bed to an empty room down the hall, all the while flashing his CIA ID and ordering everyone to their rooms, nurses included. Hiding in the room across the hall from where Khalela was supposed to be, Kevin and Ray had surprised the two Arabs covering the one that had gone inside Khalela's room. It had been a classic textbook operation, and Kevin Dalton thanked his lucky stars—and his CIA trainers—that nothing had gone wrong.

Norma Dominguez had arrived at the hospital thirty minutes before the explosion. She had given Nurse Guzman her final instructions, which included heading for the parking garage after delivering coffee to the FBI agents. Norma had waited for the termination team to carry out the termination order. Now she could not leave the place without ensuring that Khalela Yishaid was dead. But she had to hurry. Two of Marcos's helicopters would land at the hospital's helipad in another five minutes to pick her up along with the termination team and take them away from this place.

One hand clutching the Uzi under the white cloth covering the surgical instruments cart she pushed, Norma Dominguez turned the corner and rapidly moved up the hall. She wore the uniform of a dead nurse from one floor above.

The Chilean woman saw Kevin Dalton and four FBI agents conferring by the nurses' station. Although she had observed the last-minute room shuffle Kevin Dalton had orchestrated, she had been unable to warn the termination team, which now lay dead next to the agents. It was entirely up to her to prevent Khalela Yishaid from warning the Americans. In a way she wished she had done this herself from the beginning, instead of working with the Arabs, but Marcos had insisted that she limit her involvement to intelligence gathering and leave the dirty work to the Arabs.

Mierda!

Kevin Dalton didn't know why he decided to turn around and look down the hall, toward the room where he had wheeled Khalela five minutes before. When he did, he noticed a tall woman rapidly approaching the room from the other end of the hall while pushing a cart covered with a white cloth. Something bothered Kevin. Perhaps it was the way she walked, or the speed at which she pushed the instrument cart. But something just didn't feel right about her.

"Do you know that nurse?" Kevin asked the same middle-aged nurse that had helped him clear the hallway.

The nurse looked in the direction of the oncoming woman, now just a dozen feet from Khalela's room.

"Never seen her before," she replied.

"You!" Kevin screamed at the woman pushing the cart, causing a dozen heads to turn in his direction. "Stop where you stand!"

The woman pulled out an Uzi, an action that prompted Kevin and Ray to draw their weapons.

"Everyone down!" screamed Kevin and Ray in unison as they hit the floor and rolled behind the counter by the nurse's station. The other three agents, still nauseated from the drug in the coffee, took a few extra seconds to react to the commotion.

Running backward while opening fire, the woman cut down one of the FBI agents. Two nurses and a few patients were also hit before the rest of the people in the halls disappeared through the nearest door.

The armed woman turned the corner, screams and shouts replacing the gunfire that still rang in Kevin's ears.

Weapon drawn and followed by Ray, Kevin reached the end of the hall and peeked around the corner. He caught a glimpse of the woman disappearing through the fire door leading to the emergency stairs. The screams and the smell of gunpowder filled him with rage. He had to get that woman.

"Let's go!" he screamed as he kicked the sterile floors with all his might, taking in lungfuls of air as he raced after her, his ears barely discerning Ray's footsteps behind his own.

"Move! Move! Move!" Kevin barked when a nurse and two patients emerged through a door. "CIA! Get out of the way!"

Zigzagging around the startled trio, Kevin and Ray reached the stairs. Kevin kicked open the door and went through, the Beretta firmly held in front of him sweeping the dark stairways, the dim yellowish light of the emergency lighting system casting an eerie glare on the concrete steps.

They heard a metallic noise coming from above, the clanking of the fake nurse's weapon against the iron railing.

"She's heading up?" asked Ray.

"The fucking helipad!" screamed Kevin, remembering how the emergency rescue team had flown Khalela and him from his rural Virginia property to this hospital. "She's going for the helipad!"

Ray instantly spoke into his lapel microphone. "Get a chopper to the hospital. Suspect is headed for the helipad. Repeat, suspect is headed for the helipad."

Without waiting for a response, Ray took the lead and darted up the steps, his Colt .45 clutched in both hands over his right shoulder. Gunfire briefly erupted from above, but not inside the building. Someone had opened fire on the roof. Kevin's heart quickly redlined as his burning legs tried to catch up with the agile Ray. Almost a full minute later Ray reached the gray door marked TO HELIPAD in large white letters.

The door led to the small covered patio of a security checkpoint. Both guards behind the counter had been shot dead. Cruising through the checkpoint, Kevin and Ray faced a long paved walkway that disappeared around a large water tank. Across from the water tank were a number of wood crates stacked by a large white brick wall. The helipad was on the other side of the large tank.

The late afternoon sun made him squint. Kevin broke into a run, the breeze swirling his hair, just as the low whopping sound of helicopters echoed off the tall walls of the water tank.

The moment he reached the other side, Kevin watched two dark shapes flying right above the city. They grew in size as fast as the noise from their rotors reverberated against his eardrums. One broke left, in a direct course toward the Hispanic woman, who had already reached the helipad. The second turned to Kevin and Ray, who had gotten caught in plain view. At that moment another helicopter entered the scene, the letters POLICE painted in blue over its shiny white paint.

While the first helicopter hovered over the woman, the second turned to intercept the police chopper, and at a distance of one hundred feet, two door gunmen with machine guns opened fire on the police craft.

"Jesus Christ!" screamed Ray.

Kevin Dalton stopped cold at the sound of the machine guns spraying the side of the white helicopter, which burst into flames and sank below the roof level. Seconds later Kevin heard the crash from the street below, followed by a cloud of dark smoke rising into the sky.

Now the muzzles turned to Kevin and Ray. Kevin began to run in the other direction as the thundering weapons unleashed a sizzling inferno of 7.62mm fire. The pavement exploded in clouds of black asphalt all around Kevin. He saw Ray go down with a scream. Kevin needed shelter, and he saw it a second later in the large wooden crates.

With Ray's bullet-riddled body sprawled on the hot tarmac, Kevin Dalton's whole self struggled to reach the crates under the deafening noise of the rotors and guns. The powerful downdraft of the dark craft hovering behind him like an apocalyptic beast, and the smell of gunfire filling the air brought him back in time. Before his mind flashed visions of Iraq, of a MiG-29, of Kurds being slaughtered along a shoreline, of his own high-speed ejection.

Black clouds of death erupted to his right just as Kevin cut left and went into a roll. Blue skies, exploding asphalt, the hovering chopper, and the Washington skyline filled his view as Kevin rolled over the hot roof, distancing himself from the spray of high-speed rounds spewed out by the machine guns. His back stung, reminding Kevin of the scratches he had inflicted on it a few days before outside his home.

He hit the crates hard with his shoulder. The pain streaked up his neck and down his arm as Kevin quickly hid on the other side, in the three feet of space between the wooden crates and the hospital's brick wall.

The former Navy pilot flipped the safety, cocked the weapon, and leveled it at the craft, just as it began to turn around to join the first.

He fired, the sound of his weapon drowned by the blasting rotor noise. He fired again, and again, and again, the recoil of the alloy pistol pounding against his wrist. Eleven times more he pulled the trigger, emptying the fifteen-shot magazine.

Kevin saw smoke coming out of the turbine above the cockpit. The helicopter began to rotate, seemingly out of control. The gunmen opened fire again.

The rounds pounded the crates, the brick wall, the asphalt, and went silent. The rotor noise increased as the pilot tried to gain altitude but failed. Like a wounded bird, the helicopter wavered in midair right before its tail rotor dipped into the top of the crates, showering Kevin with chopped wood, broken bricks, and a million splinters before the craft crashed on the asphalt, the rotor disintegrating upon striking the reinforced floor.

The earthshaking explosion preceded a thick column of orange flames reaching up to the sky. Black smoke from the burning craft coiled skyward, only to be washed away by the draft from the second helicopter, which immediately dashed over the city and was out of sight in a couple of minutes.

The smell of burned wood and rubber mixed with that of gunpowder. Rising to a deep crouch, the former naval aviator removed the empty ammunition clip and inserted another. Cocking the weapon, he peeked behind the crates to see if anyone from the chopper had managed to jump ship before it exploded. He saw no one.

Kevin heard nearing footsteps as the two surviving FBI agents, their eyes contorted with fear and surprise, reached Kevin.

"Jesus, you got one of the choppers," one of the agents said.

Kevin regarded the white-haired, slightly overweight agent. "Not soon enough, I'm afraid." Kevin pointed to the twisted, bleeding body of the fallen FBI agent on the paved walkway. "I didn't even know his last name."

As he returned to the sixth floor, Kevin watched the emergency personnel put the dead terrorists in black body bags while a few nurses wheeled the wounded to another floor. Cops and more FBI agents now filled the hallways.

"Fucking nurse," Kevin said to one of the agents who had been drugged by Nurse Peggy Guzman. "Go through the hospital records. Find out what they know about the little nurse."

Even though Kevin was CIA and not FBI, the events of the past few minutes had earned him the respect of the veteran agents.

"You got it," one of the Feds said as he headed for the nurses' station.

As the emergency personnel hauling black body bags disappeared behind the closing doors of the elevator, a nurse tapped Kevin Dalton on the shoulder.

"Sir?"

Kevin turned around and faced the same middle-aged nurse who had already helped Kevin Dalton twice today.

"Yes?"

"The woman, sir. The one you moved to the other room?"

"Yes?"

"She's awake and asking for you."

What? Rushing past the startled nurse, Kevin Dalton raced down the hall, under the curious stares of several policemen and orderlies. His mind went blank at the thought of seeing her eyes again. His mouth suddenly went dry, his heart quickened, and his rapid steps echoed down the sterile white corridor. Pushing the door to her room, Kevin slowed down and went inside.

The face, the eyes, the smile. It was all back in a second for Kevin Dalton.

"Hello, Kevin," she said in the deep, feminine voice that had always intrigued the former Navy lieutenant. "It is good to see you."

"Khalela! Thank God you're conscious!"

Sitting by the edge of the bed, Kevin put a hand to her face and she smiled. "How're you feeling?"

"Thirsty," she said, contemplating him with filmy, light green eyes. "And the top of my head feels on fire."

Kevin took a pitcher of water from the nightstand and poured her a half glass. Gently putting a hand behind her head, he brought the edge of the glass to her lips and let her take a few sips.

"Where am I? How did I get here?" she asked, while softly rubbing a hand over the top of her head. Although she had not bled, there was a large bruise, which caused the Mossad operative to wince and jerk her hand away.

Sitting down next to her, Kevin gave her a five-minute summary, leaving out the commotion of the last half hour. Her sleepiness faded to a frigid calculating expression. "How long have I been unconscious?"

"You've been out for two days now," he said, setting the glass back on the nightstand, and still not quite believing he was actually talking to her.

Staring in the distance, Khalela's full lips curved down. "That makes it a full week since the courier left Lisbon."

Half-dropping his eyelids at her, Kevin said, "Lisbon? What are you talking about?"

"That is why I came, Kevin. To warn you."

"About what?"

Khalela spoke for the next few minutes. Kevin listened to her words as his heart hammered inside his chest. The emotion of seeing her took a sudden backseat to the reality of her words, to the possibility of Saddam Hussein exporting nuclear terrorism to America.

"So that's what they wanted to prevent," Kevin said, getting up.

"Who is they?" Khalela asked as she tried to sit up in bed but failed. She was still too weak.

"You shouldn't do that," Kevin said. "That was a serious concussion you got. You need some time to regain your strength."

"You said someone was trying to prevent something. What?" She tried sitting up again, and again she failed. Her head landed back on the pillow.

"You really need to take it easy," he commented.

"Kevin, *who* was trying to prevent *what?*" she asked again, her eyebrows, a bit full for a woman, dropping over her inquisitive stare.

Reminding himself that he was dealing with a trained operative and not a child, Kevin Dalton's face turned somber as he sat back down and placed a hand over hers, giving it a soft lingering pressure. "Twenty minutes ago there was an explosion in the underground parking garage. Through the havoc it created, a hit team dressed as firefighters sneaked into the building, made it to this floor, and sprayed your room with 9mm rounds. It is obvious now that they were trying to prevent you from warning us about the nukes heading this way."

After looking around the room, Khalela gave Kevin a puzzled stare. "But this room is not . . ."

"I moved you to another room right after the explosion. I got suspicious when I found out that three of the four FBI agents guarding your door had suddenly gotten ill and were in the rest room."

Khalela took Kevin's hand to her lips and kissed it before saying, "Thank you."

"Actually, that makes us even again," responded the CIA officer. A year earlier, Khalela had saved Kevin's life by rescuing him from an Iraqi search party following his ejection from a wounded Tomcat. A few days later, Kevin had paid her back by rescuing her from an interrogation chamber inside Allahbad. They had just completed their second round.

"It is very good to see you again, Kevin," the Mossad operative said, her eyes flashing a sincerity that made Kevin wonder if there had been another reason for her being here today. This was the woman he loved, and regardless of how much time had gone by, she still meant as much to him now as she had during their short-lived adventure in southern Iraq.

Slowly, Kevin leaned down and embraced her, his eyes closing as he felt her body pressed against him, her hair caressing his face, her arms running the length of his back. No words were spoken. None were necessary. They both understood the situation and silently accepted it, just as they had long ago. Once again Khalela and Kevin found themselves in the center of a play directed by someone else; actors following a script written by a higher authority. But like a year earlier, both of them knew that the script could be changed, the play could be altered to achieve a different goal, to reach a new ending.

Kevin kissed her forehead before sitting back up, a thousand questions bombarding his mind. But just then Robert Bourdeaux walked into the room.

"You two all right? Christ, what a mess!"

Kevin went through the introductions.

Dressed in a plain white shirt and a pair of slacks, Bourdeaux said, "It's a pleasure to finally meet you, Khalela. For a long time I wondered if this guy here was just making you up."

Khalela tried sitting up once again. This time she succeeded, her strength slowly returning. "I am real, Mr. Bourdeaux, and so is the threat facing your nation. That is why I am here."

Bourdeaux looked at Kevin, who motioned his superior to take a seat. Hesitantly, dropping his bushy brows and giving Kevin a suspicious glare of brown eyes, Robert Bourdeaux sat on a white chair next to the bed. "Why do I know this is going to upset me?"

It took Kevin and Khalela just under ten minutes to bring the deputy director for operations up to date. By the time they finished, Bourdeaux was reaching into his pocket for a small pack of Motrin. With a mask of disbelief painted across his square face, the DDO said, "You got any water around here?"

Kevin took another glass from the nightstand and filled it halfway.

"We need to find this fucking courier," Bourdeaux said right before popping an orange caplet in his mouth and taking a swig. "Pardon the language."

Pulling her legs up to her chest under the covers and hugging them, Khalela licked her dry lips. "We sent two of our top operatives after the Iraqi courier in Lisbon. That was about a week ago. I lost touch with that operation when I decided to head here and warn you in case our people couldn't find and neutralize this courier."

"Sounds like we need to get you in contact with your folks," Bourdeaux said, while rubbing an index finger against his left temple.

"You need a sterile phone?" asked Kevin.

Khalela nodded, and thirty minutes later a dark-haired man dressed in a tan suit walked in the door hauling a black briefcase.

Without introducing himself, he set the briefcase on the bed by Khalela's feet, opened it, and handed her a cream-colored phone, one end of which was connected to a wire coiling into the portable unit.

A single nod toward Bourdeaux, still sitting on the chair massaging his temples, and the man was gone.

"That's a secure line," Bourdeaux said, briefly closing his eyes. "You can call anywhere in the world. Would you like us to leave the room?"

Khalela tossed her head at Bourdeaux, focusing her eyes on the DDO like a light beam. "It does not matter, does it? Any number I dial on this unit can never be used by the Mossad again."

Kevin, who still sat by her side, couldn't help but grin, while Bourdeaux simply shook his head.

The Mossad operative called a number in Rome, Italy, that she had long committed to memory, left a message in Hebrew, and hung up.

Bourdeaux stood and walked to the small window overlooking a street, which slowly returned to normal from the mess of an hour ago. Although this wing had already been declared safe, emergency teams continued to work on the damaged floors on the other side of the hospital, which had been directly above the explosion.

"How long before you get a response?" asked Kevin.

"It varies. It could be a minute or an hour. It depends."

"Depends on what?" asked Bourdeaux, still looking out the window.

"On factors that I'm not allowed to discuss with the CIA."

Bourdeaux turned around. "Exactly what do you mean by that? After all, it was the CIA that just saved you from turning into Swiss cheese."

"And I appreciate that, sir. But I cannot discuss any aspect of the internal operations of the Mossad with you or anyone not associated with my agency."

"All I want to know is how long before I know if your people intercepted this courier."

"I already answered that question," responded Khalela, the edge on her voice rapidly increasing.

"Time out, guys," Kevin said, as he jumped off the bed, walked around it, and got in between Bourdeaux and Khalela. "Look, she didn't have to come here and warn us at all, yet she did. She should be entitled to her privacy. I mean, look, this is a pretty awkward situation for all of us. The CIA and the Mossad are not the best of buddies, but perhaps we can make an allegiance of convenience against a common enemy if we learn to respect each other's ties with our own intelligence networks."

Bourdeaux slowly raised both hands, palms facing Khalela. "Look, Khalela, I just hope that you understand the situation we could be facing if this Iraqi manages to make it into the country. We're talking about the possibility of someone trying to blow up one or more of our cities with a nuke."

"We live with that fear everyday in Israel, Mr. Bourdeaux," responded Khalela. "Believe me, sir, I do understand *exactly* what you are feeling at this moment."

The room went silent.

Khalela, wearing a white hospital gown, looked at Kevin and said, "I need to use the rest room. Please help me get up."

Both Kevin and Bourdeaux helped her to her feet. Standing erect, the white gown falling gently down to her knees, Khalela leaned on both men as she took her first few steps. With confidence filling her, she let go of Bourdeaux and continued walking with Kevin to the small private bathroom next to the white chair where Bourdeaux had been sitting.

Stopping at the entrance, she told Kevin, "I think I can handle it from this point," before letting go of him and closing the door.

Kevin turned to his superior. "She really cares, sir. Otherwise she wouldn't be here."

Bourdeaux gave a single nod, to let Kevin know that the message had been received, before moving a finger back up to his left temple and rubbing. "Christ," the DDO said in a low voice. "I can't wait till the president hears this one. He's already considering striking Iraq if those troops don't stop moving south by midnight tomorrow night."

Kevin sat on the bed. He knew he should be exhausted, but the adrenaline from all the commotion, compounded with Khalela's revelation, kept him quite frosty. "What do you think's going to happen?"

"Hard to tell," Bourdeaux responded. "Clinton is not going to act impulsively. He'll probably stick to his original plan and then put the pressure on us and the Feds to intercept this courier."

Just then the mobile phone rang once. Kevin looked at Bourdeaux, who grabbed it from the bed and tried to answer it, but whoever had called had already hung up.

Khalela came out of the bathroom, and Kevin was already waiting to help her back to the bed, but Khalela shook her head. "I am feeling better. Thank you."

"The phone rang once," Bourdeaux commented.

Khalela nodded and sat sideways on the edge of the bed; the hospital gown inched up, exposing a pair of tan, shapely thighs. She reached for the phone, dialed a new number in Rome, and spoke a few words in Hebrew before listening for almost a minute. Kevin watched a sudden gloom shadowing her bony, triangular face.

"Well?" Bourdeaux said the moment she hung up. "What happened? Did your people intercept the courier?"

The Mossad messenger slowly shook her head. "I am afraid it is worse than that."

Bourdeaux briefly eyed Kevin before turning around and facing the window again, a finger glued to his left temple.

With his drooping brown eyes sizing up Khalela Yishaid, Kevin struggled to remain calm. Her dark hair falling over her shoulders, the Mossad operative stood, sliding slim hands over her hips to push down the hospital gown. "We lost contact with our two operatives four days ago. The body of one of them washed ashore three days ago near Lisbon. We believe the other one has also been compromised, otherwise he would have reported by now. We have also lost contact with the team that raided the mansion in Greece. The transport helicopter never made it back to Israel. We fear some members of the team, my superior included, might have been kidnapped by the *Mukhabarat,* broken during an interrogation, and told the Iraqis that I was headed over here to warn you. That would certainly explain the suicidal Arabs that attacked you at your house and the attack on the hospital. It would also explain why the Mossad operatives were compromised."

"Do you know the name of the ship, or its destination?" Kevin asked.

Khalela nodded. "The vessel's name is the *Vesuvius.* It is headed this way, but we do not know where."

"Christ," the DDO growled, his back still to them.

"What do we do now?" asked Kevin.

"Well," Bourdeaux said, turning around and looking at Kevin. "First thing's I gotta contact the White House and then the Coast Guard to see if we can find this ship. Hopefully we're not too late. Next, I need to get the Feds up to speed on this. Then, I'm going to make arrangements to move you both to a safe house. It's obvious that Saddam is after you two, and that puts everyone around you in danger since you are now targets."

"That's comforting to know," said Kevin, as Khalela simply stared into the distance. Kevin had seen that drawn, faraway look before, and he knew at that moment that Khalela would vanish soon. This messenger had completed her mission, and it was time for her to return to her own people.

Kevin Dalton silently cursed his profession.

NICE, SOUTHERN FRANCE.

The young Mossad operative slowly made his way to the rear of Le Charlot, Nice's oldest gay bar. Mostly young men crowded the long counter on the left side of the club, where four bartenders, dressed in black leather and sporting multicolor bandannas loosely hanging from their necks, efficiently mixed drinks and poured beer for the thirsty row of men sitting on the stools. Several danced in the cozy nook in the rear to the rhythm of an old Village People hit.

Thick cigarette smoke and the smell of whiskey and beer filled the Israeli, who wore a white T-shirt, tight black leather pants, black boots, and a Harley-Davidson jacket. He also wore a gold earring. His moussed hair, brushed straight back, revealed a long forehead. A two-day stubble over his boyish face gave him the good looks that had already caught the eye of at least a dozen men in the bar.

He slowed down the moment his blue eyes found what he sought. Next to a pair of sailors embraced in a lip lock at one end of the dance floor, the Mossad operative saw a man sitting by himself at a small table. In his right hand he held a cigarette. In his left a beer bottle. The man was alone this night. The Israeli quickly understood why. Mostly attractive young men filled the bar. The lonely man was not only middle-aged and balding, but he was quite unappealing. A nose too long and wide for his oval face almost looked like a connecting highway between a pair of thin lips and eyes set too close together.

The eyes gravitated to the Israeli as he walked right up to the table and took the man's hand.

"Would you like to get some fresh air tonight, *monsieur?*"

The comment and the unexpected physical contact took the man by surprise. But his mask of surprise quickly changed to a welcoming smile at the Israeli's good looks.

"Oui, oui," he quickly responded, getting to his feet and holding on to the Israeli's hand as they headed for the exit.

"I have a van," the Israeli explained as they walked outside. "There is plenty of room."

The older man filled his lungs with the night's cool air and reached for the Israeli in the middle of the parking lot, giving him a strong hug. The Mossad operative cringed as the man's lips brushed against his. He quickly pushed him away and said, "In there, *monsieur.* We can have some privacy in there."

The older man nodded, putting an arm around the Israeli as they walked side by side to the van.

The Mossad operative opened the side door and slid it back. At that moment, the barrel of an automatic rifle extended toward the older man, who looked at his young companion with shocked eyes. By that time the young Mossad operative held a small pistol in his hand.

"Get in," he ordered the older man. "You have information we need."

"But . . . but I no longer work for Marcos," he pleaded. "I have not worked for him in months."

The young operative shoved him inside the van and closed the door behind them. Almost immediately the driver pulled out of the parking lot and onto Rue St. François de Paul, turning left on Promenade des Anglais, Nice's seafront boulevard. Hotels lined one side of the Promenade; the beach and dozens of marinas covered the opposite side.

Boats and yachts of all shapes and sizes docked at piers from Nice to Monte Carlo. One of those yachts had been leased by Marcos Eduardo Dominguez over eight months ago for a month-long cruise of the Mediterranean. The aging homosexual in the rear of the van had been one of the guards Marcos had hired during that trip.

"Please," the gay man pleaded. "It was just a small job. I needed the money. I have nothing to do with his current operations or whereabouts."

"We want you to tell us exactly who visited Marcos during that month at sea," said the young Mossad operative matter-of-factly. "Or we will kill you slowly."

The gay man closed his eyes and began to speak. He told them about the visitors from Greece and Louisiana. He told them of the money exchanged for land leases, of the phone calls arriving at all hours of the day and night, of the mysterious day trips Marcos made by helicopter on the spur of the moment, returning late at night, sometimes alone, other times in the company of beautiful ladies, or businessmen, or both. He told them about the parties, about the naked women running around the ship, about the time when one of those lovely ladies had tried to unzip his own pants while the old guard guarded the yacht's stern, and he had refused. Marcos had witnessed the event and had given the guard a bonus for his dedication to the job, not realizing the real reason for the old guard's resistance to the sexual advances of a drunk and beautiful woman.

By the time the van reached a pier close to the border with Monaco, where the Mossad owned a yacht used as a mobile base of operations in the region, the former guard had already revealed more than the Israeli intelligence agency ever hoped to extract. But there would still be chemicals. The Mossad had to be certain.

FBI HEADQUARTERS, WASHINGTON, D.C.

Sitting behind his large desk, FBI Director Roman Palenski held on to the arms of his swivel chair, doing his best to contain the anger boiling up inside him. A madman armed with nuclear weapons aboard an Italian merchant vessel was heading this way, and for all he knew the bastard might already be inside the country.

An Arab nut in possession of a nuke inside America!

"Christ, Bourdeaux! Why in the hell did it take so damned long for your people to figure this out?"

Robert Bourdeaux let the comment go. He himself had gone through the same reaction after listening to Khalela an hour ago. But by now the Motrin had placated the pounding headache.

Instead, the DDO simply said, "I've already contacted the White House and the Coast Guard. A massive search of the waters off the coast of Florida is about to get rolling."

"Have you contacted the Department of Energy?"

Bourdeaux nodded. "I called Secretary O'Keel before leaving Langley. Like yourself, he got quite pissed on the phone."

"What's he going to do?"

"Start using one of the new Lacrosse satellites to try to find the radioactive material."

"I wouldn't hold my breath on that one," Palenski said.

"O'Keel claims the new Lacrosse has enough energy to penetrate buildings. In fact, the claim is that if we can narrow down the area of interest to just a few square miles, he can even achieve twenty to fifty feet of ground penetration, depending on the terrain."

Palenski remained skeptical, and Bourdeaux understood why. State-of-the-art surveillance equipment, particularly something as new as the Lacrosse II, never worked as specified.

"He's going to concentrate his search on the state of Florida," Bourdeaux added.

Palenski pinched the bridge of his nose while closing his eyes. "I hope to God somebody finds the damned hardware. How long has it been since the *Vesuvius* left Lisbon?"

"Just under a week."

"That's pretty close," Palenski said.

Bourdeaux didn't respond. He simply looked past the FBI director and gazed at the Washington skyline through the large windows behind Palenski.

BETHESDA, MARYLAND.

Kate Marston listened to the message Robert Bourdeaux had left on the answering machine. The DDO would not be coming for dinner this evening. He had to get ready for a breakfast meeting with President Clinton.

In a way Kate was glad Bourdeaux had canceled. Last night's incident had brought back the terrible memories of her early days in the KGB, when she was forced to have sex with her instructors. "Training," they had called it.

What a farce that was!

Katrina was amazed that the Soviet system had lasted as long as it did before collapsing. And when the Soviet Union did indeed come to an end, it had made her the happiest woman alive, because she had assumed that with the dissolution of the *Komitat Gosudarstvennoi Bezopasnosti* she would be free. The tentacles that had prevented her from leaving had been severed by the new Russia—or so Katrina Aleksandra Markarova had thought.

For four wonderful years she had actually been free, working her way up the same intelligence agency she had been planted to spy against, with a foolproof cover that could only be blown by an intelligence agency that no longer existed.

But her sense of freedom had ended a year ago, when Irina Bukovski had shown up at her doorstep. That had been the day when the nightmare started, when the Ukrainian brute that had visited yesterday raped her after Katrina had refused to cooperate. And just to make her point quite clear, Irina had killed Katrina's American husband.

Only her KGB training had prevented Katrina from going mad. She had forced herself to overcome the rape and the assassination of a man she had grown to love and respect over the years. Katrina had struck a deal with Irina: her freedom for any scrap of intelligence she could come across at the CIA for six months. But Irina had lied to her.

But the lies must end, she thought as she went upstairs and inserted a new audio cassette into the Sony system next to her bed. *No more lies. No more deception.*

She took a deep breath, steeling herself for her confession, before pressing the recording button on the stereo. Katrina's eyes filled with tears as she began to speak, first in the Midwestern accent she had worked so hard at perfecting, and then slowly switching to her native accent as her past came rushing back to her. The words that she spoke, words she had wanted to speak for a very long time, would be the last words Robert Bourdeaux would ever hear from her. Katrina knew she would have to disappear after delivering the tape to him. Bourdeaux would never accept her deception, her acts of treason. The DDO loved her, but he was also an American patriot, and neither Katrina nor anyone else would ever change that.

As the words flowed with greater ease, Katrina made sure to cover every single aspect of Irina's operation that she knew, including the club in Atlantic City and her dealings with the Arabs and with Marcos Eduardo Dominguez. Katrina knew there was much she didn't know about Irina Bukovski's affairs, but this would at least give Bourdeaux a lead to go after the Russian Mafia in this country. With luck, the Americans might end Irina's criminal network and in the process liberate Katrina from her ties to the past. With luck, Katrina would be able to start a new life in a faraway state, like California or Florida.

Although the thought of leaving Robert Bourdeaux tore her apart, the KGB operative in her managed to hang on to the pieces and keep them together long enough to survive this new chapter in the book of misery and death that was her life.

9

MESSENGERS

"Messengers," said Abraham, "what is your errand?" They replied: "We are sent forth to a wicked nation, so that we may bring down on them a shower of clay-stones marked by your Lord for the destruction of the sinful."

—The Koran 51:31

KENNEDY SPACE CENTER, FLORIDA.

They moved swiftly, quietly, with purpose under a moonless night on the east coast of Florida. Their advance was covered by the darkness engulfing the wide strip of beach near Launch Complex 39 Pad A, where the gleaming white orbiter stood perched over the concrete stand like a mythical bird of prey, its claws seizing a pair of solid rocket boosters and the huge external tank, its black beak pointed at the heavens. Bathed in light, the orbiter *Lightning* waited expectantly. The rotating service structure that shielded the orbiter against hail and high winds had rotated back to its fully retracted position, exposing the shuttle to the same breeze that cooled the film of sweat on the faces of the men walking near the shore.

All three were Muslims, loyal not to Saddam Hussein or Sheikh Imman al-Barakah but to Syrian President Hafez Assad and the New Islamist International. The leader of the group was Lebanese, and he walked in front. Since their arrival by powered raft five minutes earlier, he had killed two security guards with the knife strapped to his right leg. He knew that soon alarms would blare when the guards failed to report, but by then it would be too late.

The Lebanese looked up to the sky and briefly prayed for the strength and the skill to fire the Javelin shoulder-launched missile in his hands. The soldiers following him single file also carried Javelins and, like him, knew how to operate the British-made weapon with an accuracy worthy of the Royal Marines. They had all trained with the *Mujahideen* in Pakistan and fought in Afghanistan for many years before joining the New Islamist International, where they underwent further training before traveling to America to start new lives as taxi drivers. The NII had cared for them, given them the training, knowledge, and financial support needed to live in

America for two full years without arousing any suspicion from the FBI. Now that same NII had ordered them to follow the orders of the old sheikh, who had blessed their souls before sending them on a mission from which they would never return alive.

The Lebanese briefly eyed his weapon. Accuracy was not that important on this target. The huge rust orange external tank mated to *Lightning* would be hard to miss, especially with three missiles fired in rapid succession.

The trio stopped. They had gotten close enough. The range of their weapon was just over four thousand yards, making the external tank, a mere two thousand feet away, an easy target. Dropping to one knee, the Lebanese rested the unit on his right shoulder and trained the monocular sight on the center of the external tank.

It was T minus four hours. The colossal liquid hydrogen and liquid oxygen chambers of the external tank were already filled with the highly flammable fuel and oxidizer *Lightning* would need to reach orbit. But not tonight. Not if he carried out Allah's will. The famous American orbiter lay still, ripe, vulnerable, packed with enough liquid explosives to take out twenty city blocks in a fraction of a second, and all it needed was a fuse to start the irreversible combustion.

As his brothers knelt on either side of him, the Lebanese fired. The missile left the launching unit in a blaze, accelerating to twice the speed of sound in under a second. Flares fitted to the sides of the missile went off, allowing the sensor in the arming unit to acquire and bring the missile into the center of his field of view. Holding the external tank centered in his sights kept the twenty-six-pound missile dead on target. A radio link transmitted the guidance commands to the Javelin's control surfaces until it struck the thin shell of the colossal tank.

The explosion of the six-pound warhead seemed minute in relation to the massive size of the shuttle assembly, but bright flashes of orange light soon emerged through the small black cloud left by the fragmented warhead. A second explosion twenty feet below the first marked another hit by his team. The third Javelin struck the tank between the first two blasts.

In seconds the middle of the external tank came alive with small but rapidly expanding explosions of orange-and-red flames, of tongues of fire. The Lebanese began to walk backward as he prayed, anxious to meet his Creator in Paradise. Sheikh Imman al-Barakah had blessed this holy act of defiance against the infidels, this holy stance against the enemies of Islam.

"With gardens of delight the righteous shall be rewarded by our Lord!" the Lebanese screamed into the night, his hands extended to the heavens. "We swore a covenant with you, Lord—a covenant binding till the day of Resurrection!"

The crimson flames expanded farther up and down the external tank. Emergency alarms blared around the complex, right before the entire launchpad disappeared in a blindingly white explosion as a quarter of a million pounds of highly flammable liquid hydrogen reacted with a million pounds of liquid oxygen in less than one second, releasing an energy equivalent to that of a small thermonuclear warhead.

The intense heat evaporated the skin on the Lebanese's face in the same second that his mind came to realize his imminent death. His facial muscles fried to the bone as his boiling brain swelled inside the cranium. By the time the shock wave reached his position, propelling his body, and those of his companions, almost fifty feet back, the Lebanese's mortal remains had been reduced to a scorched mass of bone and smoldering flesh.

BAGHDAD, IRAQ.

Saddam Hussein al-Tikriti watched the CNN special news bulletin with a mix of joy and surprise. The blow had been far more powerful than anything Jafar Dhia Jafar could have anticipated, reducing not just the launchpad, but the entire launch complex to melted metal and blackened concrete. Even two hours after the explosion, firefighters could not get within a mile of the launchpad, and experts called it a total loss of the orbiter, its payload, and the launch complex. The crew had been fortunate not to have been scheduled to arrive at the launchpad until T minus one hour, but over three hundred NASA employees and general contractors had perished in the flames, largely because of the chain reaction the initial blast started with nearby fuel and oxidizer storage tanks. Although a full investigation of the explosion would not be possible until the chemical fire died out and a team of NASA inspectors could reach the launchpad area, a thirty-second clip from a CNN cameraman at the press stand two miles away clearly showed three bright objects striking the external tank in rapid succession seconds before the explosion. Apparently the CNN man had been testing his equipment in anticipation of the launch when he noticed the bright objects, but could not pan to their origin before the explosion swallowed the entire launch complex.

And all they'll find is just how vulnerable they can be, thought Saddam, certain that the inspectors would soon come to the conclusion that the so-called bright objects had originated from the shoulder-launched missiles of *Jihad* warriors in America.

Saddam Hussein's eyes rejoiced. A lot of American pride burned on that launchpad, a lot of American dreams and aspirations were going up in the black smoke whirling skyward from his holy work. The giant-screen TV in the video room of the Presidential Palace showed an aerial view of the fire while a NASA spokesman commented on the extent of the damage, calling it one of the largest terrorist acts of the century.

Still child's play.

But not for long. Soon Saddam Hussein would have the power of three nuclear warheads at his disposal inside America. Soon he would be able to unleash at will a firestorm larger than the inferno at Cape Kennedy, but in highly populated areas, like New York City and Washington, D.C. Soon his messenger would reach his destination.

THE *VESUVIUS*.

The Italian vessel plunged into a wall of seawater as it cruised through the rough Atlantic, splitting six- and seven-foot waves with the force of raw tonnage. Rapidly moving dark clouds covered the star-filled sky of just an hour past. Flashes of lightning streaked across the horizon, illuminating the vessel's bow through the light rain peppering the bridge's window-panes.

Gigio Rositti manned the wheel while another man navigated. Kemal Ramallah had rounded up every other crew member and confined them at gunpoint in a large cell three levels below. This close to his objective, the *Mukhabarat* colonel would not take any chances. During his last radio conversation with Irina Bukovski, they had confirmed the location of their rendezvous point, now only a few miles away from where the Italian ship cruised at nearly fifteen knots.

One hand clutching the Makarov and another holding on to one of dozens of metal pipes lining the seven-foot ceiling of the vessel's bridge, Kemal kept his gaze—and his weapon—trained on the duo steering the ship toward the culmination of the first phase of his mission. A nauseous stomach from lack of sleep and from the constant swaying of the ship clouded his senses. But Kemal fought it with all his might. He had come too long a way to get seasick now. He had spent his entire life devoting himself to fighting the enemies of Allah, the infidels who had killed his wife and two sons. Now it was his turn to inflict the ultimate blow against the West.

The sounds of a helicopter brought him back to the reality of the moment, the whistling wind gaining strength with every passing minute, the rain slowly turning thicker, the ship rocking with increasing intensity.

Walking to the radio, Kemal dialed a prearranged UHF frequency and, seated against the panel, brought the small, black microphone to his lips.

"*Izzay yak,* Irina. You're early," Kemal said.

"*The diversion worked better than anticipated!*" crackled the voice of Irina Bukovski over the radio static. "*No one cares about this vessel or our helicopter at this moment. Every American in Florida is either watching CNN or fighting the hell we have created in their land. Turn on your bow lights and cut your engines!*"

Putting down the microphone, Kemal smiled broadly. Everything was going according to plan. The smile quickly disappeared as he glanced at Rositti and shouted, "Turn on the bow lights and shut off the engines!"

Reaching for a small control panel to his right, Gigio Rositti threw two large switches. Floodlights, used to load and unload cargo at night, engulfed the entire bow of the vessel as Rositti shut off the engines. The chopper came into view, its landing lights dancing on the same waves pounding the *Vesuvius*'s hull. Red-and-green navigation lights flashing, the craft hovered twenty feet over the moving bow, the rotor's downwash swirling the flags by the edge of the main deck. A pale figure emerged through a side window.

Kemal smiled as he picked up a pair of field binoculars and briefly trained them on the helicopter, before setting them back down and grabbing the microphone. "Is that you, Irina?"

"Yes," came the response. *"I'm lowering a cable. Is the cargo ready?"*

"Secured and ready on the main deck as you instructed."

"Come and meet me then. We do not have much time," Irina said, before disappearing inside the chopper.

Kemal glanced at the thick cable, slowly being lowered over the heaving deck, before his gaze gravitated to the two Italians in the bridge. The *Mukhabarat* colonel had no more use for them, and he had no time to lock them up with the rest of the crew. Besides, Rositti knew too much about his operation.

Leveling the weapon at Rositti's navigator, Kemal fired once. The report, amplified by the metal-and-glass structure, drowned the single cry of the Italian sailor, who jerked forward as the round broke his back and exited through his chest, spraying the control panel with a red mist.

Rositti snapped his head toward the fallen sailor and back to Kemal. The smell of gunpowder hung in the air. Thin smoke coiled up from the Makarov's muzzle.

"Por favore, signore, have mercy. I have done everything you have requested. *Mi familia.* They need me, *signore,"* implored the thin Italian. His black eyes, contorted with shock, pleaded for the mercy absent in the Iraqi's cold stare.

Kemal thought of his own family, remembered how they had all died. His own boys, crushed like animals. No one had cared then. None of those pigs had shown a drop of mercy. No one but Kemal Ramallah had mourned their deaths, leaving him to face the rest of his life alone, to endure the pain alone.

"Mercy, Mr. Rositti?" Kemal responded, while gazing at the Italian sailor, but in his mind seeing his family's twisted bodies. "Mercy is a weakness in the hearts of fools." Kemal fired once into the Italian's face and left the bridge without feeling an ounce of remorse.

Outside, the drizzle had turned into a downpour and the winds gained strength, making the helicopter transfer difficult, but not impossible. His face splashed with rain, which seeped down his jacket and soaked his cotton shirt, Kemal raced to the main deck, where he strapped the cargo to the harness.

He signaled the hovering helicopter, and the cable began to lift the one-hundred-pound cargo. A minute later the cable was back down, and Kemal strapped himself to it. Feeling the powerful downdraft, which created a swirling cloud of mist and water around him, Kemal left the deck of the *Vesuvius.*

BATON ROUGE, LOUISIANA.

Dressed in a pair of dark slacks and a white silk shirt, Marcos Eduardo Dominguez walked out of his bedroom and onto the front balcony of his leased antebellum mansion, across the Mississippi River from Baton Rouge, Louisiana. Surrounded by vast fields of sugarcane and the legendary river, the mansion stood under the shade of huge oaks and magnolia trees.

A warm breeze swirled Marcos's brown hair as he took a sip from a cold bottle of Cerveza Regia. The evening had finally quieted down following heavy rains that had pounded the region. The distant horns of vessels and barges cruising up and down the river mixed with the sounds of trucks hauling sugarcane from the fields to the mills in the area and the light traffic from the city across the river.

The sounds were all very low, very subtle, slowly fading away as the whop-whop sound of an incoming helicopter grew in intensity. The powerful halogens of the incoming chopper stabbed the night as two Toyota trucks drove up to the large helipad on the south side of the plantation, where the international arms dealer kept three of his own helicopters disguised as crop dusters. The craft were always fully fueled and ready for a quick getaway, as were the three powerful motorboats docked by the shores of the Mississippi.

"Is it here, *hermano?*" asked Norma Dominguez as she walked outside the balcony, a cold Regia beer in her right hand. Norma was Marcos's only sister. They had grown up together in Valparaiso, Chile, a coastal city fifty miles west of Santiago, the capital.

Marcos smiled, smelling his sister's soft perfume. Her scent, combined with the taste of the beer in his hand, brought back wonderful memories of their teenage years, before politics and greed took over their souls. Norma, who had fought alongside the Marxist-Leninist guerrillas in Chile during the years following the overthrow of Marxist president Salvador Allende Gossens by right-wing army strongman Augusto Pinochet Ugarte in 1973, left Chile in 1976, after it became evident that Pinochet's government was there to stay. She went on to join the crusade of Peru's Shining Path rebels during the eighties and played a crucial role in helping Marcos escape a CIA trap in 1990.

Norma had been successful in devising the quick and safe way to extract the required information for the sheikh's termination team. But that was where the good news ended. The ill-fated assassination attempt of Kevin Dalton and Khalela Yishaid had Marcos quite concerned. Kevin

Dalton would have been an incredible present for Saddam Hussein, and the Mossad woman should never have been able to warn the Americans of the nuclear hardware that was now being carried from the helicopter to the trucks.

The transport helicopter left as quickly as it had arrived. The cargo, as well as the two passengers, headed toward the mansion in the trucks.

"Come," Marcos said. "Let's go meet our friends."

"You mean *your* friends," Norma responded. "That Russian *puta* has no business getting off that chopper. She has already been paid. What is she doing here? She will cross you the first chance she gets, just like she crossed me in Chile. She has no loyalty, *hermano.*"

Marcos turned around and cupped her face. "That Russian woman, *hermanita,* just caused over fifty million dollars to be transferred to one of our accounts in the Cayman Islands. She might have fucked you over back in Chile, but she is now on our side. She is a highly professional operative, and she never fails. Now, let's *go.*"

Marcos went back inside. The feud between Irina and his sister dated back to their post-Allende, revolutionary days in northern Chile, when Irina Bukovski, then a liaison between the KGB and the Chilean Marxist guerrillas fighting to regain control of the government, received orders from Moscow via Fidel Castro to terminate all support operations for the rebels, who faced an obvious lost cause. Irina was ordered to divert her attention to Central America, where the atmosphere was right for a revolution. Many of Norma's comrades were slaughtered by Pinochet's forces when Russian military support came to an abrupt stop in 1976.

Wearing a pair of jeans and a T-shirt, Norma tucked a tiny Walther PPK .380-caliber pistol in the small of her back, covering it with the T-shirt. Barefoot, she followed Marcos down the circular staircase and into the ample foyer. Flanked by four armed guards, his guests were already waiting for him.

Marcos smiled when he saw Irina Bukovski in the presence of a large Arab, who wore a determined look. The former KGB agent looked pitifully small next to the Arab or the bulky bodyguards, all of whom kept their machine guns ready but pointed down at the oak floors covering the entire first floor.

"It has been a very long time," Irina said in Russian to Marcos, ignoring Norma Dominguez. Irina's eyes filled with dark amusement as she extended a fine, pale hand to the world's most wanted black market arms dealer.

Marcos shook it, his gaze never leaving the face of the woman who had made the delivery possible. Her pointy chin, her crafty smile, and the firm grip were the same as when Irina had first introduced her KGB friends in the Soltnevo Group to Marcos back in 1990, when Marcos had just arrived in Europe with the few millions he had managed to save from the grip of the CIA.

Regardless of how much Norma hated Irina, Marcos could not show any sign of disenchantment for the Russian. He owed Irina as much as he owed Norma. Irina's ex-KGB contacts inside the Soltnevo Group had made the multiple transfers of Russian hardware into Marcos's European network possible. Irina had also engineered the brilliant diversion, the destruction of the American orbiter, needed to clear the way for her helicopter. Sheikh Imman al-Barakah had simply followed her plan.

As he released her hand, Marcos wondered if Kevin Dalton and Khalela Yishaid would be alive today had Irina been handling the termination mission instead of Norma and the old sheikh.

"It is good to see you again, Irina," Marcos finally responded in English.

Irina introduced Kemal Ramallah. Marcos smiled and pumped the Arab's hand. Norma gave Kemal a slight nod before putting an arm around her brother's back as she dropped her fine eyebrows at the pale Russian woman. "I was very sad to hear you wouldn't be staying long," Norma said, regarding Irina with a sarcastic look.

Marcos shot a sharp glance at Norma as Irina pulled out a pack of Virginia Slims and put one to her lips. One of the guards pulled out a matchbox and lit it. After winking at the tall and tanned guard, Irina drew heavily on the long cigarette and exhaled in Norma's direction. At Norma's burning glare, Irina cannily winked.

"When may I start the assembly?" asked Kemal Ramallah, getting down to business.

"Kemal is right," said Irina, taking another draw from the cigarette. "We mustn't waste any time."

"How long will it take?" asked Marcos, forcing his voice to remain professional while wondering if he had made a terrible mistake by letting these two women within sight of each other.

"One day per bomb. I have brought enough hardware for three small bombs, three large messages from Saddam Hussein to the Great Satan," responded Kemal matter-of-factly.

"What is the yield?"

"The first two are one hundred kilotons. Enough to level all of New York City and Washington, D.C. The third is only forty kilotons, but still quite devastating."

"What are Saddam's instructions?" asked Marcos.

The Iraqi terrorist looked at the bodyguards before shifting his gaze back to Marcos. "You and Irina can stay. Please order your guards and Norma outside. This information is too sensitive."

Marcos hesitated for a moment before motioning the foursome outside. One by one the guards walked outside to the front porch, leaving Marcos, Kemal, and the two women in the foyer.

Kemal pointed at Norma. "What about her?"

Marcos slowly shook his head. "Norma is my sister. I trust her with my own life. There is nothing she cannot hear."

Kemal eyed the tall Hispanic woman with an air of indifference. "Very well," he finally said after a few moments, his eyes back on Marcos. "My leader has requested that I deliver the first message directly to President Bill Clinton. He has asked specifically for Irina Bukovski to become the second messenger. She will go to New York City. The third messenger with the smaller bomb will go to Hope, Arkansas, the birthplace of the evil Clinton. Saddam has asked that you find a suitable messenger."

After a few seconds of biting his upper lip while staring in the distance, Marcos glanced at Norma, an empty smile flashing on his face, a mere agitation of his mouth muscles, which volunteered his sister for a new mission.

"Now, why don't you show Kemal to the room we have prepared for him, *hermanita,* while I show Irina around the plantation? Saddam has personally sent two of his soldiers to assist in the assembly. They have brought radiation-proof suits for use during the assembly," Marcos said.

Exhaling heavily, Norma motioned Kemal to follow her and began to walk away from the group. "Come," she said to the large Arab in a harsh tone. "I will show you to the assembly room behind the house." Kemal went after her.

"She sure knows how to hold a grudge," said Irina, before dragging at the last of her cigarette, which she used to light another.

"I'm paying you two more than enough to forget about your personal problems," said Marcos.

At Irina's frown, Marcos added, "I gave the same speech to Norma before you arrived. I will talk to her again later. We are all professionals. There is too much at stake here to let our personal differences get in the way of the job."

Irina pulled deeply on the half-smoked cigarette before throwing it on the oak floor and crushing it with a leather boot.

Marcos let it go and asked, "How well do you know this Kemal?"

The Russian woman hitched a shoulder. "Well enough."

"You did well tonight," he said.

"It's not over yet. I must contact Viktor and get a message ready for Saddam."

Marcos nodded.

The Russian woman put a hand to the back of her neck and rubbed. "Long night," she said, closing her eyes.

Marcos took her in with a warm, admiring glance. "You look tired. Would you like a drink? It was a long flight on that chopper. You must be thirsty."

She gave him a devilish smile. "You remember the last time we drank vodka? Yes?" Her eyes sparkled with a hint of immorality that reminded

Marcos of a dacha in the snowy hills outside of Moscow, where Irina and Marcos had spent an entire weekend in front of a fire drinking vodka and having the most memorable sex of his life.

Taking her hand, Marcos led her to the bar at the back of the living room, where Irina also found a telephone. Before she could relax with vodka and Marcos, she had a thirty-second chat with Viktor Kozlov. The messenger and his cargo had arrived.

NEW YORK CITY, NEW YORK.

Sitting behind her crowded desk, a phone solicitor working for the commercial ads division of *The New York Times* looked at the fax in her hands. It came from Atlantic City, a half-page advertisement for a very popular oceanfront club. For the past six months the owners of the club had been quite consistent in advertising once a week in the *Times.* Every Friday. To be included in the international issue of the paper. No exceptions. The ad, however, varied every time. The small map at the bottom of the ad, which gave directions to domestic and international tourists, never changed. Nor did the phone number and hours of operation. The verbiage describing the place, however, *always* changed, she noticed.

She found it odd, but, then again, she catered to quite a few number of odd businesses, all of which, like the large club in Atlantic City, consistently placed ads in the *Times* and paid their very expensive bills on time.

She pulled up last week's ad on the computer and edited it to reflect her customer's current request. Then she set it up to run in the morning edition, as usual.

ISTANBUL, TURKEY.

The air inside the crowded Kervansaray nightclub in downtown Istanbul was too thick to breathe. Donald Bane took in the smell of cigarette smoke, body sweat, and cheap perfume with a frown and a silent curse at his luck, which kept pushing him in the wrong direction from the onetime assignment to meet with Krasilov, collect the intelligence, pass it on to the Moscow Station, and head the hell back home in a hurry. Exactly why he had gotten so deeply involved in this mess Bane wasn't even certain. Bourdeaux had ordered him here, of course. Bane could have refused to come, yet he didn't. In fact, he didn't even argue with his superior. Harvey Lee's death had certainly played a part in Bane's decision. But if there was one reason why Bane stood here tonight, he would have bet a paycheck that it was because of the information he had collected from Krasilov.

As he made his way past the club's large center stage, where belly dancers took turns at robbing European, American, and Japanese tourists of their dollars, Donald Bane accepted the fact that he simply could not stand the thought of Saddam Hussein in possession of more nuclear weapons. This feeling alone fueled the true driving force behind his determination to strip the Iraqi tyrant of weapons that did not belong on this earth in the first place.

Long bars lined each of the four walls on the first floor, where bartenders poured everything from Russian vodka and American beer to *raki,* an eighty-seven-proof local drink made of distilled grapes with aniseed. Donald Bane currently clutched a cold Budweiser, which had cost him just over fifteen thousand Turkish lira—or about four bucks. His CIA contact, a historian who went by the name of André Boyabat, was already on his second glass of *raki,* which according to the former professor of the universities of Istanbul and Baghdad was the national drink of Turkey.

Dressed in a pair of black jeans, a red shirt, and a black leather jacket, André elbowed his way through the crowd. A man of medium height slightly on the heavy side, the fifty-year-old Turk twisted his thin lips into a smile as he looked over his shoulder at Bane while pointing to a table in the rear of the place. André's huge hooked nose crinkled as he grinned, flaring large elliptical nostrils.

Bane gave him a slight nod as he followed him to a corner table, squeezing past the sweaty bodies moving to the rhythm of the blaring music. André did not seem the historian type, and Bane wondered if the Turk was pulling his leg regarding his past life, before Robert Bourdeaux recruited him at a Baghdad university during the mid-eighties. André looked more like a boxer or a wrestler than a historian.

Bane took a sip of beer, the taste of which made him wish he were back in the good ol' U.S. of A. He simply missed the place and he cursed again the strange sequence of events that had landed him here. But it was all for a noble cause. The warheads were heading toward Iraq, and he simply had to stop the shipment, or at the very least know where it would end up so that the Air Force or the Navy could go in and erase the place from the map.

"*Iyi aksamlar,*" said a woman, as Bane walked by her. She sat by the bar, a tight, black miniskirt and a button-down silk blouse barely covering her well-tanned body.

Before Bane could say anything, André turned around, the hooked nose pointed straight at the woman. "Wrong whore, my friend. Come."

With a nod, Bane kept walking until André found what he was looking for: a gaunt brunette dressed in a pair of jeans and a shiny leather vest over a white T-shirt, long hair outlining her lean cheeks. She sat at a table with three other women. André walked up to them.

The woman recognized André, leaned over to one of her cheaply dressed friends, and whispered something in her ear. The second woman, another tan queen with red hair and dark eye shadow, looked at André, then at Bane, before smiling and giving them a slow female wink. Bane frowned.

"Iyi aksamlar," the brunette said as she lit up a cigarette. A pair of hollow cheeks nearly touched each other inside her mouth as she pulled on the smoke. *"Nasilsiniz?"* she added while exhaling through her nostrils, all the while keeping her bony arms close to her body, which forced her shoulders to rise to a permanent shrug.

André remained quiet. After a few moments, he nodded and smiled. The Turk rubbed his thumb over two fingers and motioned the woman to go outside. A finger toying with a strand of her own hair, the woman considered André's proposal before nodding and getting up.

Only then did Bane realize just how tall this woman was, almost an inch past Bane's six-foot-two. André barely made it to the large breasts that stuck straight out of her sunken chest. Long, anorexic legs in loose-fitting jeans began to move ahead of them toward the exit. Bane followed the pair outside, where the air was cold and felt good.

Bane breathed deeply and rubbed his eyes. He hated cigarette smoke. It not only gave him an instant sore throat, but it also irritated his eyes. During his last year of marriage his wife had picked up smoking just to aggravate him. The thought of her blowing smoke in his face made Bane hate the entire female gender.

Giving the CIA officer an odd little glance while her brown eyes traveled from his waist to his shoulder, the brunette turned to André and blasted away in Turkish.

They stayed at it for a minute, until André finally reached into his pocket and pulled out a one-hundred-dollar bill, waving it at her while pointing to both Bane and himself and speaking more Turkish.

The gaunt brunette regarded Bane again, lowered her gaze to his groin, turned back to André, and grabbed the money, shoving it inside a pocket in her jeans. André smiled and motioned her to the parking lot after patting her small buttocks once.

The whore glanced at Bane and said, "Me make you happy, American. You see. Happy."

Bane forced a smile to his face. *Swell.*

Since his wife had raked his ass through hot coals during their divorce five years before, Bane couldn't bring himself to think about the opposite sex, and the weathered brunette with the cheap makeup didn't alleviate his current contempt for women. But he had to play along. According to André, this one knew one of Marcos's guns in Istanbul, and rumor had it that she had spent the night with the guard, who apparently had been paid a thousand dollars for a three-hour job at Atatürk Airport, at just about the same time that a twin-engine jet from Moscow had landed there the day before.

They walked in silence for roughly six blocks, until they reached an old apartment complex, where Bane and André had paid the landlord a full month's rent for one of the top floor units facing the Sea of Marmara to the south.

Bane walked into the small apartment last, locking the door behind them. The place was in a shambles. The smell of mildew rose from the worn-out green carpet, which went along well with the badly stained tan sofa, the scratched coffee table, the broken armchair next to the table, the peeling off-white paint on the walls, and the dozen roaches that had stormed out of sight the moment André turned the lights on. But the place did have a great view out of the living room. The tranquil waters of the Sea of Marmara extended into the night sky.

As André got a bottle of cheap whiskey from a paper bag in the kitchen, the whore, sitting on the sofa, began to undress. She lowered her jeans and exposed a pair of skinny but well-tanned legs, the mere sight of which did awaken something inside Donald Bane. Concerned that he could get excited over this poor excuse for a woman, Bane watched in silence as the whore removed her T-shirt, exposing what had to be a silicone implant job on her skinny chest.

Wearing only a ridiculously small red panty, the woman caught Bane staring and pushed out her lips at him while opening her legs and planting her feet on the coffee table. "Like, American? Like?" she asked, opening and closing her legs while keeping her feet on the wooden surface of the table, her knees slightly touching the sofa when she opened them fully. The woman had an incredible stretch.

Bane didn't like what he was feeling. Perhaps he had been without it for so long that now his body reacted to any sight that resembled a woman, including this trash in front of him. But whatever it was that squirmed into action quickly faded away the moment André, with a smile on his face, walked up to the half-naked brunette and slapped her across the face with the back of his hand, lifting her lithe frame off the sofa and sending her bouncing over the coffee table. She landed over the worn upholstery, stunned, dazed, her long hair over her face. The whore brought a hand to her face, moving the hair out of the way while blinking rapidly, tears filling her brown eyes, legs sprawled sideways as her upper torso turned to face her attacker.

Exploding in a burst of Turkish with an imploring tone absent until now, the woman began to plead with André, who raised his hand to her again. The woman quickly buried her bruised face in her long, thin arms and began to cry, slowly shaking her head.

André looked at Bane. "Says she does not know. But I know she is protecting him."

"She must tell us where this guy is. He's the next link in the chain."

André nodded and cut loose with more Turkish. The woman lowered her arms. A large reddish spot on her right cheek began to turn dark. Sobbing, she spoke for about a minute. When she finished, André turned to Bane and said, "I have a name and an address. She says he is there now."

"How do we make sure she isn't lying?"

The historian returned to the kitchen and came back out seconds later holding a small shoe box. He set it on the coffee table in front of the sofa, where the whore now sat with her knees pressed together and her arms crossed over her breasts, a somber look across her face, the brown eyes now distant. Opening it, André pulled out a roll of duct tape and motioned her to turn around.

Slowly shaking her head while complying, the brunette didn't say a word as André bound her thin wrists behind her back, and then her ankles, before putting a piece of tape over her quivering lips.

Next he pulled out a small device with a digital timer. He looked at Bane. "A small bomb. I'll set it to go off in four hours. If she is lying and something happens to us, bye-bye whore."

Her eyes grew wide the moment André translated and set the device on the table, the small display facing her.

The whore began to make groaning noises under the tape, which André ripped off her mouth in one flesh-tearing move. The bleeding lips moved again, shooting a rapid fire of foreign words that made André smile. She only spoke for several seconds, before lowering her gaze, shaking her head, and crying.

"She gave me a new name and a new address."

"She will be killed for telling us this, right?"

André shrugged while crinkling his hooked nose and pressing his lips together. "Maybe. It all depends on how she acts if she is ever confronted by Marcos's henchmen. All she did was accept a hundred dollars from a Turk and his American tourist friend for sex. That is all everyone saw."

Leaving her to face the misery of her situation alone, Bane waited for André to put another piece of duct tape over her mouth before the two of them left the apartment.

"False bomb," André said as they headed for the Turk's automobile, an easy, knowing grin flashing over his pale face, the flaring nostrils breathing in the cold night air. "It works every time."

10

BILLY BLYTHE

To some generations much is given. Of others much is expected. This generation of American has a rendezvous with destiny.

—Franklin D. Roosevelt

For as long as he could remember, President Bill Clinton had stood up for what he believed was right, regardless of the consequences. Born to Virginia Cassidy Blythe on August 19, 1946, he learned from personal experience what it was like to live in a lower–middle-class family. His father had died in an auto accident four months before his birth, forcing the young family to live from one day to the next. But in spite of the economic hardship and the lack of a father, Billy Blythe learned at a very early age the basic values that would carry him one day all the way to the White House. Seeing his maternal grandfather, Eldrige Cassidy, who owned a small country store in a predominantly black neighborhood, extend credit to poor families who lacked money to buy food showed Billy Blythe how to be kind to all people, regardless of the color of their skin. But his grandfather also taught him how to stand against what was wrong. And what was wrong in Billy Blythe's early years was Roger Clinton, Sr., a car salesman Virginia Cassidy married when Billy was merely four years old. Roger Clinton, an alcoholic, occasionally beat Virginia and Billy after drinking. Although a calm and kind person when sober, Roger Clinton became violent when drunk. But the violence ended one day in 1960, when Billy Blythe, then fourteen years of age, broke down the door of his parents' room one night while they were having an encounter. Taking his mother and younger half brother by the hand, Billy Blythe took a stand against his abusive stepfather. Billy Blythe told him that if he wanted to hit them, he would have to go through him first. His stepfather never harmed them again and eventually stopped drinking.

The stand.

Sitting behind his desk in the Oval Office, President Bill Clinton made a tight fist as DDO Robert Bourdeaux and DCI Joseph Goldberg finished their briefing. The situation worsened with each passing minute. He not only faced the challenge of damming the river of nuclear hardware flowing from Russia to Iraq, but he also had the critical problem of an Iraqi courier having made it to America. The Coast Guard had found the *Vesuvius* drifting along the Florida coast with its crew either shot dead or trapped in cells. To top it all off, NASA was now certain that someone had fired shoulder-launched Javelin missiles at the shuttle. One smoldering launcher unit had been found on the beach, along with the carbonized remnants of three men. The FBI was currently trying to match dental records.

What a mess.

His eyes gravitating from a framed eight-by-ten of Hillary and Chelsea to his defense secretary, President Bill Clinton said, "What's the situation in the Gulf?"

The defense secretary, a grave look covering his oval-shaped face, cleared his throat. "The detachments of the Republican Guard are only eighty miles from the border with Kuwait and Saudi Arabia, sir. They've picked up the pace since we last spoke yesterday."

"What about our troops?"

"We now have a deployment of six thousand men and two hundred tanks. The C-5s are flying around the clock to bring in additional troops and equipment just in case. The *Kennedy* is flying practice missions in conjunction with the Marines in northern Saudi Arabia. The Strike Eagles at Salman Assad are ready to kick into action at a moment's notice. The tension is rocketing, and, to make matters worse, we have the U.N. inspection team issue."

At his subordinate's harsh tone of disenchantment, President Clinton rubbed his chin and leaned back on his swivel chair. Thirty minutes ago he had received a call from a distressed U.N. Secretary-General Adolfo Montoya de Córdova. The inspection team had been taken hostage and flown to the front lines of the advancing Iraqi army. Saddam Hussein was playing the human shield game again. Although the Security Council had already voted in favor of an air strike to protect Kuwait, Montoya de Córdova had nevertheless urged President Clinton to hold off any attacks on Iraq until after U.N. diplomats had an opportunity to discuss the terms of the team's release with Saddam Hussein.

Shaking his head at the naïveté sometimes displayed by the secretary-general, President Bill Clinton stood and faced the Armorlite windows behind his desk, a chalk-striped suit hanging elegantly from his broad shoulders. Hands behind his back, the president watched the early morning traffic on Pennsylvania Avenue and wondered how many times presidents had stood on this spot while thinking through critical issues of national or global importance, making decisions that would impact generations to come. Bush during Desert Storm, Reagan during the height of the Cold War, Carter during the hostage situation in Iran, Kennedy during the Cuban Missile Crisis, Truman during the final days of World

War II. They had all been leaders faced with tough decisions in tough times, and often while under heavy fire by media critics and opposition parties. But each president had looked deep inside himself and found the courage to make difficult and visionary decisions in the face of adversity.

Now it's my turn at the helm.

Turning around, Clinton's stare landed on Bourdeaux and Goldberg. "What is the CIA's assessment on the possibility that Saddam Hussein has assembled nuclear weapons?"

The two intelligence officers looked at each other before slowly shifting their eyes back to Clinton.

"There is a strong possibility that he has at least a few warheads ready somewhere, sir," said Goldberg, while lightly drumming the end of his burgundy Mont Blanc pen against the top of his left thigh.

"And that somewhere could be either Iraq or the United States, Mr. President," added Robert Bourdeaux. "According to Donald Bane, with the right technical expertise some of the hardware stolen could be quickly assembled into small fission bombs. We know part of the hardware has probably already made it into America. The balance went to Iraq. Bane is tracking another shipment. That's two that we're aware of. There is no telling how many more have made it out of Russia since we destroyed Allahbad a year ago. I believe that Saddam Hussein has direct control of at least one warhead somewhere, but might not use it until he can get more assembled."

Clinton regarded the CIA men with a serious, yet remote, glance. Although he heard their words, his mind was already considering the angles. Saddam Hussein was definitely playing the same game he had played a year ago. He was antagonizing Clinton, perhaps praying for an American strike against Iraq to give Saddam an excuse to use his nukes. But on the other hand, Saddam had never before needed an excuse to use nonconventional weapons against another country. The Iraqi tyrant had repeatedly used chemical weapons against Iran and the Kurds, and he probably would have used them against Israel if he had thought he could get away with it.

Convinced that Saddam would use the nuclear weapons the moment he got his hands on them, President Bill Clinton decided to maintain the midnight deadline he had given Saddam Hussein to call back the Republican Guard troops approaching the Kuwaiti border. If Saddam had the boldness to order troops south to threaten his neighbors while disregarding U.N. Security Council resolutions, Clinton would respond in the only language the Iraqi president appeared to understand. Clinton could not afford to back down.

The chief executive turned to his secretary of state. "Contact the secretary-general. Inform him that he has just under nineteen hours to get the inspection team away from the front lines. My ultimatum stays."

"The air strike could have adverse repercussions with some of our allies, Mr. President," the secretary of state said. "The inspection team is made out of representatives from several countries, including the United Sta—"

"I *know,"* said Clinton. "And it's *very* unfortunate, but we have to send Saddam a strong message. He tried to pull the same human shield stunt during Desert Storm. It didn't work then and it won't work now."

"Yes, Mr. President.

Clinton turned to Palenski, the tall and bald FBI director sporting a dark mustache and currently biting into a chocolate doughnut he had taken from the breakfast tray on the cocktail table between the sofas. "What's the situation on this end?"

Chewing fast and swallowing, Roman Palenski wiped his mouth and mustache with a white napkin before addressing his Commander in Chief.

"I have been briefed by the CIA, and my people are already running the domestic show with some assistance from the Agency, the Coast Guard, and the Department of Energy."

In situations involving international terrorists operating inside the United States, the FBI was supposed to be in charge, but the CIA had the responsibility of providing its sister agency with intelligence data collected from overseas operations that had an impact on the ongoing FBI domestic operations. This was new territory for both agencies, which had classically avoided cooperating with each other because they had a very basic institutional conflict of interest. The FBI's objective was to collect as much evidence as possible to obtain an indictment. In the process, however, sources of intelligence had to come forward and testify in court, making them useless for future investigations. The CIA, on the other hand, believed in protecting well-placed sources at all costs, particularly because some of those sources of intelligence, like the former Ukrainian agent General Vasili Krasilov, only came around once in a lifetime.

"Any clues from the *Vesuvius?"* the president asked Palenski.

Palenski reached for a cup of coffee on the table and took a sip. "None yet, Mr. President. Two men on the bridge were found shot dead, one in the head, the other in the back. Several others were found trapped inside a cell on the lower deck. They've been taken to a hospital in Miami Beach. My agents are currently debriefing them. I also have over one hundred agents running surveillance on a dozen suspect mosques in the New York and New Jersey area. We've also matched the faces of the two terrorists that attacked Mr. Dalton outside his house to two Lebanese students that frequented a New Jersey mosque run by Sheikh Imman al-Barakah. We have doubled the surveillance on the mosque and we're currently trying to match the faces of the terrorists involved in the assassination attempt on the Israeli woman. This is our first real break in this case, Mr. President, but we have to be careful and not act hastily. The sheikh is connected here with this mess, but we don't know how deeply. We have him under surveillance and we're hoping he'll lead us to the smuggled hardware. We've also deployed all the available agents in Florida, Georgia, and Alabama to search for the hardware."

The president turned to Bourdeaux, who was slowly shaking his head. "Bob? Do you have anything to add?"

"Oh, I agree with the director, sir. I was shaking my head at the magnitude of the problem we're facing here. This is all beginning to fit together. The messenger from the Mossad warned us that the Iraqi courier had left Lisbon aboard the *Vesuvius.* Now we find that same vessel drifting near our coast with the crew either dead or disabled. The courier is here, sir. The Iraqi has made it into this country with his cargo, and the hardware is being assembled somewhere as we speak."

"Any theories on where they might be assembling the warheads?" Clinton asked in a sepulchral voice.

"There is a possibility that they're somewhere in Florida or Alabama, but that's just speculation," responded Palenski in his booming voice. "In reality they could have moved the cargo to any location inside the U.S. If I were them, sir, I would try to find me a quiet little town in a very secluded area, far away from the madness of the cape."

Clinton turned to Secretary of Energy Patrick O'Keel. "What is your data showing?"

The tall, thin secretary with black hair and a well-trimmed mustache cleared his throat before addressing the chief executive. "My department is working together with the Nuclear Regulatory Commission, sir. So far we have concentrated the satellite surveillance in the state of Florida. We have a small army of interpreters combing through the images with additional help from the NPIC. So far we have found nothing out of the ordinary."

"Just what kind of resolution can you get from those images?"

"Well, Mr. President," O'Keel responded, "it boils down to a compromise between the level of sensitivity of our equipment versus the area covered. We're making the assumption that we're looking for at least a few kilograms of radioactive material. In their most sensitive mode of operation, the X ray, gamma ray, neutron, and energetic-particle detectors mounted in our satellites can detect as little as a few ounces inside a regular structure, like a brick or concrete building—given the right atmospheric conditions, of course. The problem is that with such a level of resolution it would take over a week to scan just the state of Florida. We have backed away from that level of resolution to increase the area covered each hour. That approach has its drawbacks, particularly if the terrorists have split the hardware and the amount of radioactive material at one location is less than a kilo. In general, though, I feel very strongly that we should be able to find the hardware, but we need a good starting point. Checking the entire country at a reasonable resolution will take months."

Clinton looked back at Bourdeaux and Goldberg. "Any chance of getting another hint from the Mossad? I could call the prime minister himself."

Goldberg shook his head. "The woman has told us everything she knows. We also received a request from the Israeli government to release the Mossad operative immediately. We're putting her on a plane back to Europe today. As far as calling the prime minister, go right ahead, but I doubt if it would do any good. The Mossad has already warned us of the threat. They won't go beyond that, sir. The Israelis are just too consumed with their own problems to worry about ours."

Clinton turned back toward the windows. Goldberg couldn't be any closer to the truth. The Israelis had faced this kind of problem from the day they claimed their independence. *Now the threat has come home and I must deal with it.* But in order to truly deal with it, the president knew that, in addition to directing the FBI and the DOE efforts at finding the Iraqi courier and the cargo, he had to attack the problem at the root. He had to stop the flow of nuclear hardware out of the former Soviet Republics. To that end, he had already purchased $500 million worth of excess weapons-grade uranium and plutonium from Russia to prevent it from falling into the wrong hands. Air Force C-5 Galaxy transports had hauled the hardware to the United States, where it would be properly disposed of in radiation-proof containers. In addition, Clinton had approved $1.2 billion to streamline the proper accounting and disposition of the nuclear hardware in Ukraine, Belarus, and Russia. Clinton had also sent a separate package to assist President Boris Yeltsin in his fight against organized crime, which was at the heart of the smuggling ring. But Clinton also had to deal with the hardware that had already made it out of Russia.

Outside, a wan orange light bathed the White House lawn. Men wearing overcoats and gloves patrolled the grounds. Tourists lined up outside the gates for the White House tours that would start in another three hours.

"What is the situation in Europe?" Clinton asked.

"Officer Donald Bane was in Istanbul, sir," replied Bourdeaux. "He and our top local agent are now tracking down the shipment to Tavtan, a city in south-central Turkey, about a hundred miles from the border with Iraq. Bane is carrying portable satellite communications equipment. I haven't received a report in a few hours. One is due to arrive at any moment."

The president remained silent for a few moments before turning his attention back to O'Keel. Clinton said, "The Iraqis obviously don't have the technology to make a twenty-megaton thermonuclear warhead. What size bomb do you feel they are capable of assembling?"

"I've discussed this with the chairman of the Nuclear Regulatory Commission. We both agree that if the papers Mr. Bane collected from his agent in Moscow are any indication of the type of hardware Saddam has acquired, it's entirely plausible that the Iraqis have assembled at least one or two bombs, each housing anywhere from one to three kilograms of plutonium. If it's assembled properly, and also if they enclose the plutonium with an adequate reflector, the bomb might yield anywhere between twenty and one hundred kilotons."

Clinton shook his head. The potential was enormous. "What kind of damage are we facing?"

"Let's take something in the middle of the range . . . say fifty kilotons. Let's also assume that a terrorist manages to detonate the bomb in the heart of this city, like at the intersection of Constitution and Pennsylvania . . . halfway between the White House and the Capitol. The radius of severe blast damage would be around twelve thousand feet, or about two miles, meaning every structure from the Arlington Memorial to the V.A. Hospital would be leveled. The Pentagon, the Lincoln Memorial, the White House, the Capitol, the museums, the Library of Congress, the National Gallery, the State Department, the Treasury Department, the Supreme Court . . . everything in this town would be vaporized in the first half second. The initial temperature of the heat flash would reach about seven thousand degrees, carbonizing everything in the same two-mile radius. At three miles out, all structures except for those with a strong steel and concrete frame would also be leveled from the shock wave or burned to the ground from the heat flash. At four miles out, which would encompass most of the District of Columbia plus half of Arlington and portions of Alexandria, all buildings with wooden frames will sustain severe structural damage and possibly also catch fire. At that distance, the heat flash will cause serious burns to any unprotected area of the human body."

Silence filled the Oval Office. O'Keel continued.

"I'm just scratching the surface, sir. There's also radiation effects to consider. Furthermore, if the bastard really wanted to maximize the damage, he might consider detonating the bomb at the lowest level in the Metro Center. Not only will the city be destroyed as I just described, but the entire Metro system would act as a gigantic blast tube, carrying the explosion way past the destruction on the surface. Remember that the Metro reaches Maryland and Virginia. Places as far away as Bethesda and Springfield will also be affected."

More silence followed O'Keel's words.

"In short, Washington, D.C., will cease to exist," said Clinton.

"I'm afraid so, Mr. President. And that's just fifty kilotons, about two and a half times the size of the one we dropped on Hiroshima. If this thing is larger, the damage will increase accordingly."

Taking a deep breath while feeling quite ill at the thought of an atom bomb going off inside the United States, President Bill Clinton silently cursed Saddam Hussein. It was now time to wait. Waiting, however, was one of the hardest things about being a president.

AL JABER AIR BASE, KUWAIT.

Lieutenant Colonel Diane Towers, helmet in hand and hoses hanging from the G suit and oxygen mask she wore over her flight suit, walked away from her Hornet after another practice mission. Her weapons systems officer in the backseat had remained with the plane, securing his ejection seat. Diane usually flew the F/A-18C, the single-seat version of the Hornets, but tomorrow's mission called for the "Deltas," two-seater F/A-18Ds. The Marine Corps had delivered twelve of the very expensive Deltas to support this particular mission.

Diane's face, lined with red marks from her oxygen mask, turned to the northern breeze sweeping across the base. Albeit warm, it felt refreshing, cooling down her overheated face.

"Howdy, ma'am."

Diane stopped between two rows of parked Hornets and turned to face her squadron's executive officer, Major John "Blue Jeans" Levi, a well-built Texan, thirty-three years of age, with brown skin and brown hair. Levi had been born and raised on a catfish farm in southern Texas, outside of Houston. Blue Jeans was the nickname he had been given for owning, aside from his flight suits and his dress uniform, nothing but Levi's, white T-shirts, and boots.

"How did you do out there earlier today, Blue Jeans?" asked Diane. The young major had flown practice sorties three hours before and was scheduled to go out again in another hour. Diane had staggered her practice missions in order to keep at least a dozen pilots and their fighters ready at all times while the rest of the group flew training exercises, along with two squadrons of Kuwaiti Hornets and USAF A-10 Warthogs. The Eagles at Salman Assad had been working on their own independent practice sorties. Overall control of all air forces, land-based and carrier-borne, rested in Central Command in Riyadh.

"Just peachy, ma'am," Levi answered, his left cheek inflated with chewing tobacco.

"Did you get nailed?"

Blue Jeans smiled broadly, showing Diane two rows of teeth slightly stained with the chewing tobacco. "No way, ma'am. I done roped me two Tomcats though."

"Two F-14s?"

"Yep. Them Navy boys are always flappin' their jaws on the squadron frequency. This mornin' they sure were mighty quiet after I nailed me two of 'em. Sneaked right up on their butts before they saw me."

"Well, congratulations."

"Thank you, ma'am."

Diane smiled at her second-in-command. To this day Levi had never called Diane by her rank. The lieutenant colonel had confronted him once with this, and Levi had simply replied that it went against the way he had been raised. Ladies were called ma'am and spoken to with respect. Period.

"You're welcome. Now, if you don't mind, I think I'm going to freshen up before my next sortie. The real thing's still scheduled for tomorrow." Diane began to walk toward her tent. Blue Jeans went after her.

"Ma'am?"

"Yes? What is it?"

"About the mission assignments for tomorrow?"

"Yes?"

"Well, I noticed that you've got me flyin' the second group."

Diane shrugged. "That's right. I'm leading the first strike. You're my second-in-command. I need you to lead the second strike team."

Levi shoved both hands into his back pockets, dropped his gaze, and slowly kicked the sand with his right boot. "By the time we get there I reckon the first team would have already taken care of ropin' and brandin' all of them Iraqis. I was surely hopin' to see me some real action."

"I'm sure there will be plenty of opportunity, Blue Jeans. But for tomorrow I need you to lead the second strike team."

"Yes, ma'am," he responded, looking down at the dusty ground.

"Anything else?"

"No, ma'am."

"Then I suggest you go and get ready for your sortie."

Diane turned around and left the cowboy standing by himself in between two Hornets with his hands in his pockets.

DULLES INTERNATIONAL AIRPORT. WASHINGTON, D.C.

As a river of humanity walked up and down the wide concourse, Kevin Dalton stood by an American Airlines gate with Khalela Yishaid. Roman Palenski and seven of his agents had escorted the couple, about to say their final farewells for the second time in their lives.

"So this is it again?" Kevin asked, while Khalela held his hand. The Feds had stepped away from the gate and stood in a group on the main concourse.

Dressed in a pair of stone-washed jeans and a starched white shirt, Khalela said, "Please understand. I have to go back. Saddam Hussein is assembling warheads in Iraq again. Our situation is as critical as—"

The final-boarding call came and Kevin cupped Khalela's face, giving her lips one long, passionate kiss, and for a moment it seemed as if he were back with her in that one night of love they had shared in a nameless village, before he'd finally been rescued by U.S. forces. Kevin remembered her face in the candlelit room, her body shivering under his, the smell of her filling every inch of his exhausted, bruised body. But the flashback ended when Khalela slowly pulled away from him, rubbing a long finger over his lips.

"Do not forget me, Kevin Dalton."

"That's hardly the problem here," he responded. "Will I ever see you again?"

The Mossad operative shook her head. "I do not know, Kevin. This is very difficult for me, too. Perhaps one day."

Perhaps one day. Kevin remembered those same words being spoken in a hospital in Riyadh long ago, and the same feeling of frustration and anger filled him now as it had then. He almost wished she had never come back into his life. In a year he had managed to remove the sting from the wound, which reopened the moment he pulled off that black hood from her head in the woods outside his house.

Khalela let go of his hand and began to walk backward toward the gate. "Do not forget me, Kevin Dalton," she repeated. "We will see each other again. I can feel it."

Kevin didn't respond. He simply shut his jaw, tightened his fists, and held back the tears while staring one final time into the green eyes of the woman he still loved. Every other woman he had ever known fell very short of the mark when compared to the tall operative now turning around and approaching the double doors leading to the wide-body DC-10.

Kevin slowly backed away from the gate.

"I take it you two know each other quite well?"

Kevin turned around and stared into Palenski's dark eyes. The director was sucking on a lollipop, its white stick poking out of the corner of his mouth.

Kevin nodded. "I think I need a cold beer."

Palenski smiled. "I'm headed back to work, but I'm going to keep three agents here until the plane leaves. If you want a ride back to the city, just let them know."

"Thanks, but I think I'm going to find me a bar in this place. Looks like this is your guys' ball from here on out."

Palenski nodded. "Hopefully we'll nail these bastards soon."

Kevin sighed. "Hopefully."

As Roman Palenski disappeared down the concourse flanked by four of his men, Kevin found a small bar, where he could keep the gate in sight, and ordered a beer. The three Feds chatted by the panoramic windows next to the gate. Kevin felt torn by feelings he thought he had learned to control, but which now had taken control of his life.

Dammit, Kev. You're a fucking professional! Get a grip!

Kevin put the cold mug to his lips and watched the gate on the other side of the concourse while a dozen faces crossed his field of view every second, but in his mind Kevin saw Khalela just as he had the first evening following his high-speed ejection. He remembered the perspiration-soaked white T-shirt tucked inside a pair of desert fatigues, the light green eyes studying him inside the moonlit room of the Kurdish hideout, the pain from his wounded leg, the smell of 'araq—the potent Kurdish liquor made from dates.

Memories from a year ago filled Kevin Dalton's mind as he ordered a second cold draft and took in a deep breath, deciding to stay there until the plane had pulled from the gate.

A blond flight attendant in the first-class section of the DC-10 approached Khalela Yishaid, who sat by herself staring at the terminal through the small window.

"I've been asked to give this to you," the flight attendant said, handing Khalela a large paper bag.

Questioning green eyes quickly focusing on the blonde, Khalela took the bag as the woman pointed to a nearby lavatory. "You don't have much time. We close the doors and leave the gate in another five minutes."

Khalela stood, went inside the lavatory, locked the door, and opened the bag. She found several hairpins, a wig that would turn her into a blonde, an American Airlines flight attendant uniform, a woman's Casio digital watch, a key to a locker, and a small note written in Hebrew.

Upon reading the note, the operative took two additional minutes to change clothes, pin up her hair, put on the wig, stuff the old clothes inside the bag, pocket the key, tear up the note and flush it down the toilet, and come back out, where the blond flight attendant waited for her. Handing her the bag, Khalela exited the plane.

With a mouthful of pretzels, Kevin Dalton was halfway through his second beer when he saw a blonde in an American Airlines uniform deplaning.

They must be about to pull away from the gate, he thought, downing the pretzels with a gulp of beer.

Keeping her head down, the woman quickly moved away from the gate, past the three FBI agents and down the concourse, her long, blond hair swinging across her back, well-defined muscles pumping against the light olive skin of her shapely legs—

An alarm went off in Kevin's mind. *It couldn't possibly . . . Jesus Christ!*

Kevin left a ten-dollar bill on the counter and headed after her.

"Hey, want a ride?" asked one of the Feds as Kevin walked past the trio.

Without stopping, Kevin gave him a casual shake of the head. "Feel like walking for a while. I'll catch a cab. Thanks."

After verifying that the Feds weren't following him, Kevin kept his distance as Khalela cruised through the crowded concourse and left the secured area through a pair of double doors. She briefly turned her head to the left, flashing Kevin the profile that brought a smile to his lips, followed by a frown. *What is going on? What in the world are you up to, Khalela?*

His training took over from there. He knew he had to be careful. As lovely as she was, the woman walking forty feet in front of him was a highly trained operative, who could vanish from sight in a moment. Kevin carefully followed her, never letting her out of his sight, yet remaining far enough back to hide in the crowd if she decided to check her back, which she did several times in the ten minutes it took her to reach a set of lockers at one end of the concourse.

Kevin stopped at a newspaper stand, picking up a magazine and bringing it up to his face, the slim figure in the dark uniform across the crowded concourse barely visible over the edge of the paper he flipped through without reading.

Khalela Yishaid felt certain she had not been followed. Apparently the trick had worked.

Her fingers now fumbled with the key to one of the orange lockers in front of her. She found the right number, inserted the key, turned it, and pulled open the door. Inside she found a small garment bag, which she took with her to an adjacent ladies' room.

Alone, inside one of the stalls, the Mossad operative opened the bag and inspected the contents. She found further instructions, a one-way Delta Airlines ticket to Atlanta, Georgia, with a connection to Baton Rouge, Louisiana, and a rental car reservation in Baton Rouge. She also found a map of southern Louisiana, highlighting certain roads in bright orange, a key to a locker at the Baton Rouge regional airport, a VISA card and Louisiana driver's license matching the name on the Delta ticket, a new wig, some makeup, and another change of clothes.

After checking the time of her new flight and going through a new transformation, Khalela stayed in the stall for another thirty minutes, quickly memorizing the lengthy instructions before she tore them up and flushed them.

Stuffing the uniform in the garment bag, she headed back outside.

Kevin Dalton came very close to giving himself away by almost walking away from the newspaper stand and approaching the entrance to the restroom. He had grown quite restless with each passing minute since Khalela had gone inside. His eyes had carefully inspected every woman that had gone in and come out of the rest room. So far logic told him Khalela was still inside, but what if he were wrong? Was there a back door? Or perhaps a back window leading somewhere? Was Khalela now miles away from him? Had the seasoned operative managed to fool the rookie? Should Kevin have informed the Feds of his discovery instead of playing it out alone?

Those questions crowded Kevin's mind just as his eyes spotted a tall, thin woman with shoulder-length red hair, dressed in a denim skirt, a maroon silk blouse, and penny loafers. From behind his newspaper, Kevin shook his head in disbelief. *She's a fucking chameleon!*

The game started again, continuing through crowded concourses, security checkpoints, endless gates, concession stands, gift shops, two more stops at rest rooms, where she switched back and forth between the uniform and the skirt and blouse outfit she wore when she finally arrived at a Delta Airlines gate just as a Delta clerk made the final-boarding call on the speaker system. The Boeing DC-10 would depart for Atlanta in another five minutes.

Atlanta?

After checking in at the gate under her new name, Khalela reached her seat in the rear of the plane, where she finally collapsed.

The plane pulled out of the gate fifteen minutes later and taxied to the runway. She checked her watch and replayed the instructions in her mind over and over again, until they became second nature.

Taking a deep breath of bitterness mixed with the excitement of the upcoming mission, her mind drifted back to Kevin. Rubbing a finger over her lips, the Mossad operative suddenly felt alone, empty, longing for the embrace of the American she felt unable to eliminate from her thoughts, the taste of him still alive in her mouth. Bracing herself at the thought of his body pressed against hers, Khalela felt tears reaching her eyes.

But it cannot be! Israel needs you!

But what about my needs? What about my life?

Life? Your life belongs to Israel! Your country has invested a fortune in you. You must pay them back!

And I have been paying back. What about all these years? All the missions? Isn't that enough?

Closing her eyes as a few tears rolled down her high cheekbones, Khalela remembered the missions, the injuries, the deaths. She recalled the victories as well as the defeats, the glory and the pain, the love and the emptiness; an emptiness that had started many years ago, when her parents and sister were killed by the Arabs, when the fear and anguish of what she had witnessed turned into anger and hatred, when the girl turned into a woman committed to serving her country and sparing other Israelis from the horror she had experienced. This was her destiny, her fate. This was the reason why she had been the only survivor in her kibbutz, the only one spared from the wave of death that had swept through her life before the Israeli army arrived and pushed the Arabs back across the border, unknowingly leaving a witness behind, a weeping young Khalela hiding in the rubble of what had been her home.

The flight attendants prepared for takeoff as the jet lined up on the runway. The engines wound up and the craft rolled off the tarmac thirty seconds later. Khalela Yishaid closed her eyes and slowly fell asleep.

REPUBLICAN GUARD DIVISIONS. SOUTHERN IRAQ.

Abu Habbash had waited for this day all his life. He knew he would embrace it when it finally came, and he did, thanking Allah, Saddam Hussein, and Jafar Dhia Jafar for the privilege of being the instrument of revenge against the Great Satan.

Abu Habbash's life belonged to the Ba'ath Party. He had given himself totally and unconditionally to Saddam's holy crusade after the day an American Tomahawk missile struck downtown Baghdad, killing his wife and unborn son.

Just hours before the deadline imposed by the evil Bill Clinton, Abu Habbash sat in the rear seat of a Jeep and gazed at the quarter moon, which bathed the tanks of the advancing Republican Army. He was not a handsome man. His hollow cheeks and sunken eyes seemed lost in his bony, weathered face. Abu Habbash, however, was a very intelligent man. After graduating with honors from the University of Madrid, Spain, he went on to complete his postgraduate work in nuclear physics in Munich, where he'd met Wadia, the daughter of a prosperous Syrian businessman. At the time, Wadia was pursuing her master's in chemistry. After marrying her and settling in the Iraqi capital, Abu Habbash began to work as a technical consultant for the Iraqi Nuclear Project at Osirak, which purchased a lot of Russian, German, Brazilian, and Chinese technology. But life quickly changed for Abu Habbash. During the war of 1991, a Tomahawk missile from an American war vessel killed Wadia, six months pregnant at the time.

Abu Habbash's eyes, as dark as the sky, focused on the plains that led to Kuwait and Saudi Arabia, where the Americans kept their expensive fighters. He hoped they would attack after Clinton's deadline, fulfilling his leader's prophecy.

Flanked by dozens of Russian-made T-72 tanks, all painted in a desert camouflage pattern, Abu Habbash checked the bomb assembled by Jafar Dhia Jafar himself. It had been an honor meeting the noted scientist and hero of the nuclear project, and he could only hope not to fail in the mission that would be his last.

"Is the helicopter ready?" Abu Habbash shouted over the noise of tanks and armored vehicles to the Republican Guard colonel sitting in front, next to the driver. The colonel had been assigned by Saddam to escort the scientist during the war exercise.

"Everything has been arranged!" responded the colonel, a bearded man who, like everyone else in this army, operated under the misconception that this was just a war exercise. Everyone except for Abu Habbash, that is. Because of the nature of his cargo, carefully packed inside a suitcase chained to his wrist, the middle-aged scientist knew the fate facing the soldiers Saddam Hussein had ordered south.

DELTA FLIGHT 1250.

"You're where?" crackled the voice of Robert Bourdeaux through the phone Kevin Dalton had just dialed after using a credit card to release it from the back of the first-class seat in front of him.

"Delta Flight One Two Five Oh heading for Atlanta," responded Kevin as he drank a tomato juice the flight attendant had brought him a minute ago. "Somehow, Khalela managed to change clothes, and she left the plane for Munich, changed clothes twice more, and boarded this plane a few minutes before it left. I barely made it."

"Are you out of your mind? Why didn't you tell the Feds that were with you? This is their turf."

"Because I didn't have time. I almost lost her as it was."

"What do you think she's up to?" asked Bourdeaux.

Kevin, who had used his CIA credentials to get Delta to hold the plane while he purchased a first-class ticket, had no earthly idea what the Mossad operative was up to, but he did feel certain that whatever it was, the CIA and the FBI would definitely benefit from the information he could collect.

"I'm not sure, but I intend to find out."

"Do you want me to contact the Atlanta Station?"

"No. Right now it's only me following her. If we put more people on this, we run a much larger risk of getting burned," Kevin responded. "I'll call you from Atlanta."

There was silence on the line. Kevin's mind was already made up about following Khalela, and he would do it with or without CIA sanction.

"Any chance she's already spotted you?"

"Doubt it. I also coerced Delta in telling me where she was sitting. She's way in the rear of the plane. I'm in first-class. That way I can deplane first and be ready to pursue the moment she comes out."

More silence on the line. Bourdeaux was obviously thinking this one through. When he finally spoke, he told Kevin exactly how to follow Khalela to minimize the chance of detection. She was a very seasoned operative, and Kevin, whether he liked it or not, was new at this game. The DDO spoke for another five minutes, and by the time Kevin hung up the phone and finished his tomato juice, the former naval aviator was wondering how in the hell he got himself into this mess.

SOUTHERN TURKEY.

Donald Bane raised his eyes and saw the predawn stars over Tatvan, a small city by Lake Van Golu in southern Turkey, ninety miles from the border with Iraq. It was the same crystalline sky he'd contemplated for countless nights while working night surveillance shifts during his FBI days. The stars reminded him of the smell of old pizza, body odor, and eavesdropping gear. They also reminded him of the earlier years of his marriage, when he had actually been in love with Jessica Bane, the woman he had grown to ignore and take for granted over time. Bane remembered the two of them sneaking up to the roof of their apartment complex in Idaho after spending the previous hour rolling under the blankets. The two of them, sharing a blanket, would gaze at the stars and talk about forever. But then he became too involved in his job. As a young agent he got assigned the shit hours, mostly nights and weekends, when Jessica, who worked as a secretary at a law firm, wanted to go out and enjoy life. *Soon,* Bane kept telling her. *Soon I'll build up seniority and get better hours.* But it never happened that way. The more involved Bane got at the FBI, the more hours he worked. By the time his ten-year anniversary with the Bureau came around, he was already spending most of the day and the night of every day on the job, and his wife dropped to a secondary plane of existence.

My Dear Donald: I am out of your life. Now you'll have all the time in the world to work with your spies and your agency. Jessica. Those had been the words written on a piece of yellow paper Bane had found next to the divorce papers in their apartment.

A tug on the arm pulled him out of the flashback. Bane glanced to his left. André Boyabat was lying on the ground next to him. They were on top of a small hill overlooking an abandoned airstrip two miles north of Tavtan, where the brunette's friend—after a little persuasion from André—had confessed that the shipment had been taken before being flown across the border. The guard, however, had also indicated that the plane would return to this dusty field at sunrise, after making its delivery somewhere in north-central Iraq. André's rusty four-wheel-drive Rover was safely parked a half mile behind. They had been here since midnight.

Donald Bane checked his watch. It was four o'clock in the morning, and he was beginning to feel the signs of exhaustion. He set down the Heckler & Koch MP5 submachine gun that André had given him earlier and rubbed his eyes.

I'm too old for this shit.

André had a Winchester Defender eight-shooter lying by his side. By now Bane had learned about the Turk's love for the twelve-gauge pump-action shotgun. Upon inspecting the weapon on the way from Istanbul, he understood why. The former professor of history had tons of firepower in his eight three-inch magnum shell #000 buckshot, the largest ever manufactured, each packing ten 0.36-inch pellets. Each pellet was just a dash smaller than that of a regular .38 Special slug. André had eighty of those at his immediate disposal.

"They are here," André said.

Bane raised his head a bit and, after giving a parked pickup truck on the other side of the runway a glance, closed his eyes and heard the faint engine noise. André had a fine ear. "You're right. It's here."

On their bellies, Bane and André crawled forward and down the hill until reaching a spot forty feet from a patch of dry grass that bordered the end of the short runway. Bane looked up once more. This time his eyes didn't focus on the stars but on the bright dual halogen lights strapped to the nose gear of what sounded like a twin-engine propeller craft. Bane remained still while the craft made a low and slow circle around the strip. Then he noticed the headlights of the truck suddenly blinking off and on. The craft rocked its wings and turned into a direct landing approach.

"All right, my friend. Come with me," André said, as Bane followed the craft all the way down. It cleared the truck by a dozen feet and gently touched down.

The plane struggled to come to a halt before the end of the runway, and it barely succeeded, stopping a mere fifty feet from the trees, and only thirty feet from where he stood in a crouch. Bane now understood the smuggling scheme. The plane was painted all white, except for the large red crosses on either side of the fuselage, under the wings, and over the wings.

Fucking Red Cross!

André got to his knees and trained the Winchester on the landing gear as the pilot began to make a U-turn. Bane heard the loud blast, followed by three others in rapid succession. A total of forty pellets left the hot muzzle with an initial velocity of thirteen hundred feet per second. At such close range, Bane estimated a pellet round dispersion area of no more than two feet in diameter. He was right. A large number of pellets crashed against the nose gear with enough energy to make it collapse. The nose dropped to the ground at the same time the propellers chopped the soil before the tips twisted inward.

Gunfire erupted from the other end of the grass runway as the truck gathered speed in Bane's direction. As André kept the Defender leveled at the pilot sitting behind the thin canopy Plexiglas, the CIA officer rolled away from the plane, the retracted stock of the MP5 jammed against his right armpit as he set the weapon's selection lever to full automatic fire and unloaded half his magazine on the incoming truck's windshield.

The weapon was indeed amazing. With minimum vibration, 9mm jacketed rounds left the MP5's muzzle and caused the pickup truck to waver out of control, turn sideways, and roll three times before it came to a stop, upside down, halfway up the runway, a thin cloud of dust boiling up around it.

André, weapon in front, slowly approached the twin-engine, shouting in Turkish.

The pilot remained seated. André sprang forward and crashed the Winchester's wooden butt against the Plexiglas windowpane. He created a six-inch hole and rapidly flipped the shotgun in midair and aimed it at the startled pilot.

It didn't take André very long to extract the information he needed from the bound pilot stretched across the Rover's rear seat. His wrists tied behind his back, his legs immobilized by André's weight as he sat on them, and André's stainless steel blade an inch in front of his left eye, the pilot quickly revealed anything and everything André wanted to know while Bane drove them to the border.

"Tikrit," said André after crawling to the front seat. Tikrit had been the destination of the cargo. It had been taken to a safe house built into the side of a hill a half mile from the small airfield outside the medium-size city located one hundred miles north of Baghdad. The pilot himself had helped carry the load in there.

"He claims they are doing the assembly in there, but knows nothing beyond that."

"Keep pushing him," said Bane.

André's thin lips curved up at the ends as his hooked nose crinkled and the nostrils grew in size. He laughed. "I will, my friend. I most certainly will. This was just the first round."

Tightening the grip around the steering wheel, Bane cursed his luck. Although he was making progress, this mission kept sucking him deeper and deeper into the core of the problem. And he couldn't walk away from it now. He was too involved to quit. In fact he couldn't quit. This was what he did best, and his instincts told him he was on the verge of a serious breakthrough.

"There is more," André said, rolling down his side window and letting the wind dry the perspiration on his square wall of forehead.

"More?"

"This was not the first trip he has made across the border. There were others."

"Damn. What kind of cargo?"

André put a hand on Bane's broad shoulders. "The same kind, my friend. The same kind of cargo. And because they have Red Cross credentials, U.N. forces have issued them a code to avoid getting shot down."

"Oh, Christ. You go figure, André," Bane said, hitting the steering wheel with the palm of his right hand. "Our boys in northern Iraq blew up a couple of our own choppers because they flew through the no-fly zone and forgot to turn on their IFF transmitters, yet they let Marcos bring in anything he wants into Iraq under the Red Cross flag. Damn and double-fucking-DAMN!"

Donald Bane stepped on the accelerator. The border with Iraq was just over two hours away. Somehow he had to get to Tikrit and verify the site before calling in the big guns to blow it off the map. Bane wished there were U.N. forces in the region, but Saddam's latest actions had prompted the quick evacuation of all U.N. forces back across the border into Turkey. Even if he could reach the small deployment of U.N. troops, it would not have done him any good. The U.S. forces assigned to the United Nations team had been redeployed to Kuwait by the Clinton administration.

Bane was alone on this one. All he had with him was the handy André Boyabat and the portable telecommunications equipment and eavesdropping gear Bourdeaux had arranged to have delivered to Bane upon his arrival in Istanbul. He had already used the communications equipment to contact Bourdeaux twice. Once after Istanbul, and again just before leaving Tavtan.

As the border with Iraq neared, Donald Bane mumbled a few obscenities, cursing his luck again. In a couple of hours he would be within the reach of the most sadistic son of a bitch on earth. He prayed that his wits would steer him out of trouble long enough to rid Saddam Hussein of his illegally purchased hardware.

11

FIELDS OF SUGARCANE

NEAR BATON ROUGE, LOUISIANA.

Under a blanket of stars, Khalela Yishaid left the rented gray Chevrolet Caprice hiding behind a cluster of trees off the road leading to the sugarcane plantation, which her Mossad superiors now believed belonged to Marcos Eduardo Dominguez, based on the information extracted from one of Marcos's guards in France.

Wearing a light brown, long-sleeved shirt, brown pants, hiking boots, and a pair of night vision goggles—not only to be able to see farther than an inch in front of her, but also to protect her eyes from the razor-sharp leaves of the immense field of sugarcane she had just entered—the Mossad operative moved slowly and silently in a deep crouch, twisting her body to avoid rustling the seven-foot-tall cane. She wore a brown headband to keep the perspiration out of her eyes and her long black hair out of her face.

Gray clouds now hid the stars that had covered the predawn skies over Baton Rouge, where she had arrived uneventfully and on schedule a few hours earlier, giving her ample time to get her new set of instructions from a locker at the Baton Rouge regional airport, rent a compact car, and grab a hamburger and fries on her way to the plantation across the Mississippi River from the state capital.

Checking her Casio, she picked up her pace. She had just under twenty-four hours to verify her superior's suspicions about Marcos. In the brown backpack she hauled was the equipment she would need either to confirm or deny the allegations of one of Marcos's bodyguards, captured and broken by her people in southern France.

Warm air streamed through the field as a soft breeze blew from the river, rustling the leaves around Khalela, who winced in pain as a dozen razor-sharp edges slashed the back of her neck and hands. Wishing she had worn a pair of gloves and a scarf, as ridiculous as it might have seemed in such warm and humid weather, Khalela plodded forward, beads of sweat now rolling down the sides of her face, down her neck, and over her breasts. The ground was muddy, especially the narrow irrigation ditches dug in between rows of tightly packed cane. The muck stuck to the bottom of her boots, slowing her advance.

An hour later she stopped at the edge of the cane field, next to a dozen huge trucks lined up on the side of a dusty road. Under the long branches of several oaks, the trucks' beds had been heaped with the sugarcane that had filled the cleared field on the other side of the unpaved road.

Breathing heavily, Khalela slowly sat on the moist ground and massaged her calves. A film of sweat covered her face. Removing the goggles, she wiped it off with a sleeve. Deep, red lines on her cheeks marked the rubber ends of the goggles that now hung loose from her neck. Moving a hand to the top of her head, she felt the bruise that had kept her unconscious for two days. It still hurt to the touch, but the sting of the day before was already gone. The bruise made her think of Kevin Dalton, a thought that she quickly discarded. She couldn't afford the distraction.

Putting the goggles back on, she reached behind her back and pulled out the suppressed Beretta 92F she had found next to the backpack in the locker at the Baton Rouge airport. Flipping the safety, she curled the fingers of her right hand around the stainless steel handle and scanned the road for another minute. Nothing showed through the palette of green hues as the goggles amplified the light filtering through the clouds and from the large house at the end of the unpaved road. Khalela knew she didn't really need to use the goggles, but with a mission of this importance she couldn't afford a mistake.

Remaining several feet inside the protective coverage of the cane field, Khalela moved toward the house, stopping every few feet to listen for sounds that didn't belong in the field. Footsteps, the rustle of leaves out of rhythm with the breeze that swirled her black hair, voices, metallic sounds.

Faint traces of light broke through the darkness, enhancing her vision. It would be morning soon, and Khalela pressed forward. She had to reach the house by dawn, collect her information, and get the hell out of there.

Fifteen minutes later she was in position. Khalela removed three devices from the backpack. The first one, shaped like a surveillance camera, was a state-of-the-art, low-energy, infrared laser gun with a spotting scope. She held it in her right hand while carefully extending a tripod neatly folded on its underside. She set the apparatus on the ground, facing the mansion. The second device was a square metallic box. She opened the top and unfolded a small antenna dish. There was a miniature control panel on the back side of the box. She oriented the antenna to face the large house and plugged the third device, a high-quality tape recorder, into the receiver unit in back of the square box. Finally, she activated the battery-operated eavesdropping equipment.

The laser gun responded with a barely audible hum as Khalela trained its narrow, bright green beam—visible in her night vision goggles but not to naked eyes—on the mansion's front porch. Using the spotting scope, she zoomed in and spotted the tiny green dot near the front steps. With her right hand moving the plastic adjusting wheels of the laser's tripod, Khalela watched the green dot move up the steps and onto the porch. She continued making fine adjustments until she positioned the laser beam on a glass panel on the center door of the first floor.

She removed a set of small Sony headphones from the bag, put them on, and plugged them into the receiver. Slowly she turned the tuning knob of the receiver to sync up to the frequency of the laser beam bouncing off the glass, which vibrated in response to the sound waves from the conversation inside the mansion. The receiver compared the frequency of the original laser beam with that of the returning beam. The difference— the conversation inside the mansion—was electronically amplified and, much like tuning a radio to a specific radio station, Khalela's fingers stopped rotating the tuning knob when she heard clear voices on the headphones.

She listened for a minute. Two guards held a conversation. Apparently one was complaining to the other about having to baby-sit Marcos while he screwed every woman he could get his hands on, including the Russian "babe" the arms dealer was bedding in one of the guest bedrooms upstairs.

Russian babe?

Khalela repositioned the laser beam on each of the second-storey windows facing the front of the mansion. She started on the leftmost window, paused to listen for about thirty seconds, and then moved on. She noticed a woman walking out to the front balcony, which ran the length of the second floor and faced the sugarcane field. Just then, Khalela heard voices coming from one of the windows. A man and a woman moaning.

Khalela smiled. She had found Marcos.

Marcos Eduardo Dominguez pulled away from Irina after their second round in the past two hours. His forty-nine years of age were definitely showing when attempting to please the insatiable sexual appetite of the former KGB operative.

"You really love her. Yes?" Irina asked, the white covers of the king-size bed dropping below her breast line as she reached for a pack of cigarettes and a box of matches.

Marcos, naked and walking toward the bathroom, slowly turned around, briefly catching his reflection on the large mirror behind the bed. He was gaining too much weight. The firm stomach of his youth was expanding into a gut he would have to address soon.

"Love who?"

"Who?" Irina said with a smile, before pulling on the cigarette. "Well, Norma. Yes? It shows, you know."

Marcos shrugged. "Of course I love her. She is my sister."

"Does she mind us together?"

"I have my needs. She understands."

Walking back to the bed, Marcos sat next to her, a hand going under the covers, touching a spot on her that made Irina close her eyes. "She understands and accepts what I do. That is why she is with me. Is that why you are with me?"

Breathing deeply, Irina opened her eyes and slowly shook her head. "I am here for the money. I am with you in this room for the sex. Yes?"

"Honest answer," he responded, keeping his fingers on her.

"I do not think you can afford to get me excited again," she said, fine eyebrows rising over her blue eyes as she nodded to his flaccid penis.

"You will be amazed at what I can afford."

"With what Saddam is probably paying you, I am sure you can afford anything you wish," she answered.

"And so can you," responded Marcos, the index and middle fingers of his right hand now venturing inside her.

With a slight gasp at the unexpected penetration, Irina slowly closed her eyes again. "I will be able to afford anything I want after I nuke New York."

Marcos abruptly pulled his hand away, making her shiver and brace herself, the cigarette now hanging off the corner of her mouth, a trail of smoke spiraling to the ceiling. "Have the Arabs finished?"

"Not yet. They have one assembled. The other two are close."

Marcos nodded as he peeked through the curtains, surprised to see his sister standing outside, facing the fields of sugarcane.

"With Kemal going to Washington and me to New York, who will go to Hope?"

"I will send Norma to Hope," Marcos said, while staring at Norma's rear end as she leaned over the railing.

Marcos returned to the bed and abruptly pulled the covers off her.

Smiling, Irina took him in with a lusty glance of amused blue eyes while pulling hard on the cigarette and exhaling in his direction. "You like what you see. Yes?"

Nodding, Marcos took the cigarette out of her mouth and pressed his groin against her face.

Norma Dominguez was angry. Since Irina's arrival at the plantation over twenty-four hours ago, Norma had seen little of her brother and the Russian. Under the pretext that he had to be hospitable to his Russian guest, whose contacts inside Russia had made Marcos more money than all his previous sales of conventional weapons, Marcos had spent every

breathing moment with Irina. If they were not touring the plantation, they
were swimming in the large pool behind the house, or drinking at the bar,
or . . .

He is fucking the puta!

Stomping a fist over the railing bordering the second floor balcony
overlooking the vast field of sugarcane that had not yet been cut, Norma
felt like emptying every damned round of that Walther PPK into the pale
body of the Russian bitch.

Dammit, Marcos! Can't you see she is nothing but a whore?

With sweet farmland odors filling her lungs, Norma pursed her lips.
She leaned her slim body against the railing, elbows planted on its top as
her round, brown eyes gazed across the large field, now stained with traces
of orange and yellow. The first beams of light forked over the horizon as a
breeze swayed the sugarcane in predictable, uniform patterns . . .

Norma bolted up, rubbed her eyes, and looked directly at the spot on
the field she had just been contemplating.

There!

She saw it again. Two . . . no, three hundred feet away, a section of
sugarcane did not move with the same rhythm as the rest. Someone was
approaching the mansion, someone who preferred to walk in a sea of
razor-sharp leaves rather than on the road that ran next to the field,
connecting the mansion to the main road.

Reaching for the PPK and also for the small radio in the rear pocket of
her jeans, Norma headed back inside the house. Racing down the steps
and out the front door, the Chilean woman motioned four armed guards
standing by the front steps to follow her, all the while keeping an index
finger over her lips.

The tanned and muscular bodyguards, three sporting Uzis hanging
loose from their broad shoulders and the fourth holding a sawed-off
shotgun, crowded around Norma.

"There is someone hiding in the field," she whispered, the PPK
clutched in her right hand. "You and you cover the road. I will go into the
field a hundred feet the other way and circle back. You two wait on this
side of the clearing." The guards ran off as Norma reached the edge of the
clearing and went in, instantly feeling at ease. The sugarcane reminded her
of the Chilean fields of tall grass where she had stalked and killed
Pinochet's soldiers.

With her shoulder-length black hair grazing the sharp leaves, the slim
guerrilla cruised swiftly and quietly, easily blending her sounds with the
rustling of leaves. She moved with the breeze, stopping when it died down,
and moving forward once more with the next gust. In this fashion she
covered fifty feet of uneven, muddy terrain, keeping her sneakers off the
narrow irrigation ditches and on the muddy, yet firmer, soil layered with
purplish roots.

She stopped with the wind, her ears listening, alert brown eyes gazing in all directions with the intensity that had kept her alive as a revolutionary in Chile and Peru. It had been years since she had moved through a field like this, yet the instincts were all there, fresh, alert, polished to perfection by years of living directly from the land, especially after the Russians left them in the merciless hands of Pinochet's death squads. But she had survived. She had outwitted even the most clever of enemies, just as she gained ground on the dark figure now barely visible thirty feet in front of her.

With the agility of a mountain cat, Norma Dominguez silently sprang forward, the PPK aimed at the back of her prey, who appeared to be out of its element. The figure seemed of medium build and medium height. Brown hair. Unarmed.

Twenty feet.

This close to her prey, Norma could afford to move a bit faster, particularly since the amateurish figure now fifteen feet ahead of her made enough noise for the both of them.

Ten feet.

Still unaware of her presence, the figure moved closer to the house, clumsily moving leaves with bloody hands. *The* pendejo *is using bare hands to push away sugarcane leaves!*

While using her slim body to move through the field like a snake, Norma narrowed the gap to six feet, recoiled one final time, and lunged. At the last possible second, the figure reacted, but it was too late.

Striking the base of the neck with just enough force to incapacitate for a few minutes, Norma watched the figure unceremoniously drop facedown over an irrigation ditch.

Briefly speaking on the radio, Norma knelt next to her victim and turned him over, the PPK trained on the muddy face of a man with very familiar features.

Impossible!

Wiping the mud off with her free hand, Norma Dominguez's eyes widened as she stared at the face of Kevin Dalton.

Khalela Yishaid had just gotten over the conversation she had heard inside one of the rooms on the front of the mansion, when she saw the guards entering the field of sugarcane. For a moment she wondered if they had seen her, but the guards had noisily cruised fifty feet behind her, obviously going after another target, or perhaps they were spot-checking the field for security reasons.

In any case, she could breathe easier again. She was within a hundred feet of the mansion's front steps and ready to leave. She had already packed up her gear. All she needed to do was get to her car and call a Mossad termination team, hiding in a merchant vessel cruising the Gulf of Mexico. The team would come in within forty-eight hours and terminate Marcos.

"I got him!" Khalela heard a woman scream about a hundred feet away, near the edge of the field, but down toward the other end of the mansion. "Get over here, now!"

She saw three guards suddenly appear from the opposite side. They looked like the same guards that had gone inside the clearing a moment before. Two of them carried Uzis, the third a sawed-off shotgun. A fourth guard, also carrying an Uzi, suddenly followed the other three.

Leaving her backpack hidden in an irrigation ditch, she moved closer to the edge of the field to get a better view of the commotion on the dusty clearing separating the field from the mansion. Khalela Yishaid watched the foursome being joined by two others. A woman wearing blue jeans and a white T-shirt pointed a gun into the back of a man, who stumbled as he walked away from the field. The man was dressed like . . . *Kevin!*

Stung by the vision of Kevin Dalton captured, Khalela sat back on the muddy field, her professional side suddenly overwhelmed by feelings she had hoped would never surface again. Suppressing her emotions, Khalela considered her options. She knew her best chance of rescuing him would be now, before he was taken away to some cell and guarded by a dozen armed men. Given the relationship between Marcos and Saddam, she feared that Kevin faced a gruesome fate.

"Go and tell Marcos that I have captured the *pendejo* Kevin Dalton!" Khalela heard the woman order.

Three of the guards went back into the house.

As Kevin was left with the woman and only one armed guard, Khalela decided the opportunity wouldn't get any better than this. Moving along the edge of the field, she made it to within fifteen feet of the trio.

Kevin stood in between the woman and the guard holding the shotgun, which he aimed at Kevin's chest. Rubbing the back of his neck, the former naval aviator briefly looked toward the field of cane. He seemed dazed, but Khalela decided he would probably come around with the commotion she was about to create.

Dropping to one knee, Khalela centered the woman in the Beretta's sights and fired, the bulky silencer responding with a low spitting sound.

"Aghh!" The woman arched back as a round struck her in the middle of the chest. As she fell, she also fired once, the muzzle pointed at the sky, the report cracking through the morning air like a whip.

Kevin snapped his head toward the fallen woman, now convulsing on the dusty ground as blood gushed out of her chest.

Before the guard could react, Khalela fired again. The guard dropped to his knees, the shotgun still in his hands. Quickly realizing what was happening, Kevin wrestled the shotgun away from him and looked toward the field, spotting Khalela emerging through the cane.

"Here! Catch!" he screamed, throwing the shotgun at her before reaching for the dead woman's pistol, a Walther PPK automatic.

"You stupid American!" Khalela screamed as she turned around and went back into the field. "What do you think you were doing following me here?"

The back of his head throbbing, Kevin Dalton didn't answer her before alarms began blaring across the plantation.

After quickly dressing, Marcos raced outside the mansion, where he froze the moment he spotted Norma's body sprawled on the ground by the edge of the cane field.

"*Hermanita!*" he screamed at the startled bodyguards. "Who did this? *¿Quien fue el pendejo?*"

"She found *el Gringo* Kevin Dalton hiding in the cane, *patrón,*" answered a tall guard.

"Dalton? Find him! Find the *pendejo!* Use the helicopters! He can't get away! Find him!"

As an army of guards ran in every direction, Marcos leaned down and lifted the body of Norma, tears of rage welling in his eyes.

He heard footsteps behind him and looked toward the mansion. Irina stood there, barefoot and wearing one of Marcos's robes, her dark red hair messy over her pale face. The bright blue eyes staring down at him showed a hint of compassion.

"Don't just stand there!" Marcos screamed. "Go and make sure the Arabs are all right! Then go and help find the *pendejo* who did this!"

Slowly turning around, the former KGB operative went back inside the mansion, a hundred thoughts running through her mind. Someone had found this hiding place. If her instincts were accurate, whoever had shot Norma was probably a scout, a probe, and if he got away, that meant this place would become compromised. Actually, it had become compromised the moment someone thought it suspicious enough to send a probe.

Running over the wood floors, Irina reached the rear of the house, went out to the pool area and toward the small room adjacent to the pool house.

Locked.

The door was locked.

"Kemal!" she screamed. "It is me, Irina. Let me in!"

The door slowly inched open, and as Irina crept in, a hand grabbed her wrist and pulled her in. The end of the robe was caught by the closing door, leaving her naked as the Arab dragged her inside the room.

In total darkness, and with the Arab's body odor filling every cubic inch of warm, stuffy air inside the room, Irina heard him whisper, "In the name of Allah! What is happening? I thought you said this place was secure."

With the Arab's hand clamping her thin wrist like a vise, and his foul breath sweeping across her face, Irina used her free hand to grab the Arab's testicles, squeezing hard. "Do not do this to me again. Now, back off!" she said, releasing the startled Iraqi.

The hand on her wrist was gone, and a moment later a light came on in the corner of the room, right above a table where, to her utter surprise, Irina saw three red backpacks standing next to three assembled units. The two on the right were about twice the size of the one on the left.

"The bombs," she said, her naked body pale in the room's light. "You have finished?"

Kemal, who did not wear a radiation-proof suit but only a pair of pants, ran a hand through his thick, black hair, which also covered most of his chest. "They are ready," he said, while his eyes traveled the length of her.

"Isn't it dangerous to be in here without a suit?" she asked, pointing to the opened radiation-proof containers that had housed the hardware."

"The bombs are already assembled," answered Kemal, lifting his gaze to hers. "The radiation is safely enclosed by the reflectors in the bombs."

"But, what about the place? It was exposed to the hardware during the assembly."

Kemal shrugged. "We are soldiers of Allah, Irina. Life on this earth exists only to serve our Lord."

"I was afraid you would say that," Irina said, shaking her head and beginning to walk toward the door. "Where are the two Lebanese students?"

"In the pool house, with orders to fire on any stranger approaching this room. What in the devil happened outside? I heard a shot and many screams."

"A probe. The safe house is compromised," she responded, reaching the door, freeing the robe, and putting it back on. "This place will be swarming with police and FBI agents in no time. Pack up your work. I will be right back."

She left the room and returned to the mansion just as the helicopters left the ground.

After five minutes cruising through the razor-sharp hell, Kevin heard the sound of rotor blades beating the air.

Helicopters!

"Wait. I hear choppers," he told Khalela, who briefly stopped. Soaked in perspiration, the Mossad operative closed her eyes and listened.

"We are in trouble," she said, opening her eyes and giving Kevin a concerned glance, her chest heaving as she breathed through her mouth. Kevin did likewise, his heart drumming inside his chest, his wound pounding the back of his head.

"There," he said, as he spotted three small choppers flying close to the mansion. They were the kind used as crop dusters.

While two helicopters hovered above the large field at roughly one hundred feet, the third one grazed the field about two hundred feet from their position. Four men dressed in black and carrying automatic weapons leaped out and disappeared in the cane. The helicopter then joined the other two.

"Come, Kevin. Move!"

Without waiting for an answer, Khalela lost herself deeper in the field of sugarcane with Kevin right behind her. On the other side of the field, beneath large oaks, a dozen trailers topped with sugarcane waited to be trucked to sugar mills. The workers were watching the commotion. Khalela moved in the trucks' general direction, her boots sinking in the soft, muddy soil, slowing her advance.

Razor-sharp leaves cut the skin of her hands as she used the shotgun to move the seven- and eight-foot-tall canes out of their way. The sound of mosquitoes buzzing in her ears mixed with the splashing of their shoes over the wavy terrain. Khalela glanced over her right shoulder to make sure Kevin was following her, before looking up. One helicopter hovered a hundred feet above them. It was guiding the termination team directly toward them.

If she continued to play by their rules she and Kevin would be dead in a matter of minutes, perhaps less. But if she could alter their game, turn it to her advantage, maybe they would have a chance.

She suddenly stopped and Kevin rammed into her, pushing them both into one of the foot-deep irrigation ditches between the rows of tightly packed sugarcane. On the ground, with Kevin lying next to her in the mud, Khalela could no longer see the helicopter overhead, which also meant the helicopter could not see her and could not guide the termination team to her position.

A smile flashed across her face. Actually, the helicopter would guide the termination team to the last position where Khalela and Kevin were seen, meaning right here.

Rising to a deep crouch, Khalela turned to Kevin.

"Can you walk a little longer?"

"Yeah," he said, blinking rapidly. "But I don't know how long I can keep this up. I'm feeling light-headed." The blow to his head, coupled with the race for safety, had taken a toll.

"All right. Do not stand straight, Kevin. Keep very low and follow me."

He nodded, clumps of mud and brown water covering his face and hair. They moved roughly thirty feet to the right of their position before squatting and waiting.

Helicopters now raced back and forth overhead, obviously looking for them. The men on foot approached their last position, one of them speaking loudly on the radio. Hands lacerated and stinging, Khalela signaled Kevin to sit and stay put. Kevin complied as Khalela dragged herself back toward the termination team, now standing still thirty feet away from her, apparently waiting for instructions before moving out.

Careful not to get any water inside the shotgun, Khalela rolled slowly in the mud, her body quickly melting into the surroundings. She could see the dark shapes moving in between small breaks in the sugarcane pattern, but Khalela doubted they could see her while she dragged herself like a snake, shotgun pressed against her chest, her elbows and knees propelling her forward.

Two had their weapons ready and continuously scanned the terrain around them. The other two seemed more concentrated on the radio and what the helicopters were finding.

Overconfidence.

Khalela had been in this business long enough to know what a deadly pitfall overconfidence could be. Underestimation of the enemy because of its position, or lack of numbers or firepower were sins field operatives paid for with their lives.

Slowly, inch after agonizing inch, the skin of her elbows grinding against the small rocks and debris mixed with the mud, her face and body naturally camouflaged, she closed the gap to ten feet.

Amateurs! Marcos seemed to be surrounded with overconfident, high-tech amateurs, men and women who had grown too attached to electronic gadgets, fancy radios, and other surveillance teams to do the thinking for them.

Leveling her weapon at the four figures standing almost over her, Khalela pressed the trigger twice.

Nearly passing out from the throbbing pain in the back of his neck, Kevin Dalton heard two loud blasts reverberating from the direction Khalela had gone, and immediately he thought the worst. He was now alone, and an inner voice told him that he would soon perish unless he moved quickly. He tried to stand but couldn't. The ache behind his neck also reached his right ear, affecting his balance and giving Kevin the headache of a lifetime.

Unable to escape, yet aware that he couldn't allow them to capture him alive, Kevin Dalton realized he would die. The termination team would close on him, and his inner voice told him he would end up in front of Saddam Hussein. He'd rather expose himself and be shot, depart this nightmare with the same abruptness with which he had entered it.

Kevin struggled and got up, wet mud clinging to his cheeks and neck. He would die on his feet; he would not be killed like a worm in this muddy hell that seemed to be his destiny. Chin up in the air, Kevin Dalton faced the incoming helicopters, defiantly looked at the silent muzzle flashes of the snipers hanging on to the sides of the craft.

Two dark craft dropped right above the sugarcane, cruising toward him, the guns of the sharpshooters alive with fire. Kevin closed his eyes, the sound of near-misses carrying him back to another place, to another time. He was running away from an incoming Iraqi MiG, away from the inferno of 30mm fire slicing through the middle of a Kurdish village with metal-ripping force. He remembered the Kurds, remembered Khalela screaming at him to hurry, felt the stinging pain from a wounded leg. It was all back in a moment as Kevin Dalton sensed death rapidly nearing. The fear, the agony, the horror of a violent death filled him as the MiG's rounds created a cloud of dust and debris around—

A pair of explosions ripped the morning in half.

Opening his eyes, Kevin saw the helicopter on the right tremble and tilt to the left, directly into the second chopper flying in tight formation. In the flicker of his eyelids both craft disappeared behind a sheet of orange flames, and a second later the shock wave pushed him back to the mud, where he lay dazed.

The third helicopter approached the crash site, but quickly flew away at the sound of another gunshot blasting against the lower section of the Plexiglas bubble.

A realization flashed in his mind, and it sent a wave of elation through him.

Kevin sat up while the third helicopter circled the area. This time he did not stand. He remained in a crouch, listening expectantly. His ears discerned the noise of the rotors from that of feet splashing over mud and water, shoving sugarcanes aside; the noise Khalela made as she reached him, still alive, still clutching the shotgun she had used to down the helicopters while he, unknowingly, had acted as bait.

She grinned, two rows of glistening teeth and lively light green eyes in a face blackened with mud. She had removed the long-sleeved shirt. The white T-shirt she wore underneath, soaked with brown water and mud, stuck to her breasts.

"Very good, Kevin. I got two of them. The third one came around, and I fired and hit it but it got away."

Khalela took his hand and rushed in the direction of the trailers as she told him of her plan. In the distance, they heard the shouts of additional searchers as they entered the cane.

The wind hardened the mud on his face, pulling on his cheeks and forehead. The back of his neck throbbed as he kept up with Khalela, who would not let go of him. Every step his sneakers sank in the mud, the effort to pull them back out slowly weakened him. Adrenaline rushing through his veins, Kevin maintained the rhythm, running in a crouch, his muscles burning, demanding more oxygen than his lungs could provide.

Khalela stopped, motioned for him to stay low, and then stood cautiously erect for a few seconds while turning in a full circle. Dropping back down, she pointed to their right, and off they went again, dashing over the mud and through seemingly endless rows and rows of sugarcane with greater ease, quickly learning to adjust to their surroundings. Again she stopped, inspected the area, and moved out again. Making such fine adjustments, like the captain of a submarine navigating among enemy destroyers with nothing but his periscope, Khalela guided them through the approaching termination team, running circles around them, at times going back over their own footsteps for a minute before cutting left onto a new trail. After a few more minutes, and with the sound of sirens blaring in the distance and mixing with the rotor noise of the hovering chopper, Khalela and Kevin finally reached the other side of the field and went under one of a dozen large trucks—their fifteen-foot-deep beds filled with muddy cane—lined up single file at the edge of the field, under the shade of large oaks.

Kevin looked around but saw no one. The workers had no doubt fled at the sound of gunfire. The trucks now shielded him and Khalela from the termination team, still hunting for them in the field. The solid canopy of branches and leaves protected them from the surviving helicopter. A stiff wind swept through the field from the approaching dark clouds, which blocked the sun.

Nearly out of breath, Kevin ran up and down the line of trucks, looking for the least-filled one. He found it almost at the front of the line and waved Khalela over. He pointed to a ladder on the side of the yellow truck. Khalela nodded and went up. He waited until she had reached the top before climbing up a dozen built-in steps and over the edge, landing on a bed of sugarcane, which missed reaching the sides of the steel bed by almost three feet. This gave Khalela and Kevin room to hide. They pawed through the cane, digging a hole large enough for the two of them.

Shouts in the distance made Kevin peek over the side of the truck. The termination team had left the field and now searched the grounds at the other end of the line of trucks.

The first drops of rain fell on the field. Lightning forked across the sky and thunder followed as a light drizzle cooled the land, but not where Khalela and Kevin were. It would take more than a drizzle to get through the thick canopy of the oaks.

Khalela went in first. Lying faceup at the bottom of the three-foot-deep hole, Kevin lowered himself over her, his back against her, and used his trembling hands to tip the stack of cane at the edge of the hole. A hundred pounds of sugarcane came crashing down on Kevin, who used his hands not to shield himself, but to hold on to the sides and prevent the weight of the cane plus his own body weight from crushing Khalela below him.

The silence that followed for the first few seconds was interrupted by the rhythmic spitting sound of suppressed automatic fire. Kevin felt Khalela's arms embracing him from behind and her face pressed against his upper back. Kevin didn't say a word. He understood the emotional roller coaster they were traveling. The feelings of fear, liberation, peace, anger, and happiness were woven in a circle of false reality for the men and women operating in the field. A feeling of concern also spread over Kevin at the realization of the termination team's tactics. He could only hope that they ran out of ammo or time before they reached their truck, but that wish did not match the cards dealt to Kevin this rainy afternoon.

As the storm gained strength, large water droplets began to hit the top of the pile. Kevin heard—and felt—a man climbing up the ladder, the metal-against-metal banging sound accompanying him was from the same muzzle of the gun that he pointed at the heap of sugarcane.

"Hurry up. Shoot the fucking cane!" a voice thundered outside.

Kevin moved Khalela's arms behind him, trying to align his body right over hers as the shooting started.

He closed his eyes as a cloud of yellow dust and debris preceded a searing pain from his right leg, instantly bringing back memories of an Iraqi helicopter firing on him by the shores of the Euphrates River after his ejection from the Tomcat.

Clamping his jaw shut, Kevin Dalton tightened his fists and took the punishment in the same silent, resigned way as the shield of cane above him. There was no place to run, no other place to hide.

The firing stopped. The sirens of emergency vehicles replaced the rotor noise.

Warm blood flowed freely out of Kevin's leg and onto Khalela, who embraced him once more, but this time not out of fear but out of gratitude and consolation.

"Hold on," she whispered. "You will be all right, Kevin. You will be all right."

The words, softly spoken in his ears, were as soothing for Kevin Dalton as her powerful embrace, which seemed to caress away the pain, the anger, the futility of his situation.

With his life flowing out of him he felt her hands lowering to his thigh. How she managed to move with so much weight over her he couldn't imagine, but her hands were on his bleeding wound now. The ripping of cloth preceded the pressure he felt around the base of the thigh as she applied a rudimentary tourniquet to stop the blood loss.

The rain intensified. Water fell freely over them, and Kevin Dalton welcomed it, even if it made him feel cold. Was it because of the water or the blood loss that he shivered? Slowly everything faded away, her soothing embrace making it all good, warm and comfortable.

"We must move immediately," complained Irina, standing next to Kemal and three red backpacks in the mansion's foyer. The two young Arabs who had helped Kemal stood to the side. She had already shouldered one of the two sixty-pound backpacks and decided she could handle the bomb that would level New York City.

Irina felt quite certain that Katrina Markarova had crossed her. *Perhaps she managed to make some kind of deal with Robert Bourdeaux and the other American pigs. Perhaps . . . that bitch!* Irina decided to deal with Katrina later. Right now they had to move quickly.

"This place is compromised," Irina continued. "Kemal is a pilot. He can fly us out of here."

Marcos, who had just ordered his men to hide inside the mansion and be ready to fight if the plantation manager failed to handle the police, slowly nodded. Although his mind was still cloudy and in shock from the death of Norma, he knew that Irina was right. Even if his manager could temporarily fool the arriving police cruisers and emergency vehicles by claiming that someone had tried to steal the crop dusters, the plantation would be swarming with Feds in no time. But Marcos couldn't leave just yet. It would take him and his men at least thirty minutes to sanitize the place. He had to make sure no clues were left behind for the FBI to follow. In his vault in the basement Marcos had documents that could be quite damaging to his cartel connections in Miami, Houston, and Medellin, Colombia. These were some of the people who had helped him tremendously during his post-Chilean days, when he had arrived in Europe and needed help to establish a new network of operations. These were the same friends who had helped him establish this and three other safe houses in the southern United States a year ago.

"All right. We need to separate in case one of us gets captured. You two take one warhead to New York. Use the last helicopter. I own a twin-engine airplane, which I keep in a leased hangar at a small field outside Lafayette, a city fifty miles east of here. The hangar is blue and it's right next to the main terminal building. These are the keys to the hangar and to the airplane. Now, go. I must stay and sanitize this place. My men and I will take the second warhead and leave on the speedboats," said Marcos.

Irina nodded. "Contact my people in Atlantic City after you reach safety. Viktor Kozlov will know what to do. He will deliver the bomb to one of my condos in Washington, where one of Saddam's expendables will be waiting to detonate the weapon."

"All right," responded Marcos.

"What about the third warhead, Marcos?" asked Irina.

Marcos dropped his gaze to the smallest backpack and, looking back at the thin Russian woman he had loved for the past day, simply said, "It won't be going to Hope, as Saddam requested. I need it to clean up after myself. I'm sure Saddam won't mind as long as it is used on an American city."

The sounds of police, fire trucks, and ambulances came and went. Khalela and Kevin remained buried in the pile of cane in almost-perfect silence. They both knew the risks of getting caught by Marcos's men. Words were not necessary now. They would talk later, when they reached safety. Meanwhile the only sound his ears could discern was that of her hands releasing the tourniquet to promote momentary blood flow to his wounded limb before applying pressure again.

The rain and the shivering had stopped now. Sunlight pierced through the cane pile, casting a yellow glow inside their hidden pocket of life.

Other voices came, and Kevin felt someone getting in the truck's cabin, shutting the door, and starting the engine.

They left the bumpy road behind and got on the smooth surface of the interstate.

"Which way are we headed?" Khalela asked.

"Most likely toward a sugarmill."

"How do you know that?"

"Trade secret. I can tell you but then I'll have to kill you."

"Dammit, Kevin! I am serious."

"We're in a truck packed with sugarcane, and it's sugar season," Kevin finally said. "We're probably headed for a sugarmill somewhere in the area."

His head and leg throbbing, Kevin finally dug himself out of the heap of cane and helped Khalela out. For fear of being spotted either by the truck driver or by another motorist, they remained below the line of sight of the truck's bed, the wind blowing in their faces, dislodging dried mud from their clothes and hair. Her torn T-shirt raised and flapped in the wind. The missing portion of the T-shirt Kevin wore around his thigh. Khalela rolled up the edges of the T-shirt and tied it right below her sternum.

Temperatures were up again. The short rain had only served to raise the humidity level. Wiping a film of perspiration off his muddy face, Kevin began to feel light-headed again. Inspecting his wound a bit more closely, he realized he was bleeding once more. At least the bullet had passed clean through the side of the leg, without touching the bone.

"Shit," Kevin said, "I need to cauterize it."

Khalela nodded, reaching into her pockets and pulling out a lighter and a switchblade. She sat next to him and gave him a consoling look.

"I hate to do this to you, Kevin," she said, lighting the flame and placing the side of the six-inch stainless steel blade over it.

Kevin watched in silence for another two minutes as she kept her body hunched over the flame to keep the wind from blowing it out while slowly turning the steel until he saw the center turn bright pink and a deep red glow appear at the edges. The lighter went off. Empty.

Khalela sat on his legs, right below the knees, to immobilize him. Her hair swirling in the wind, she handed Kevin a chunk of sugarcane, which he placed between his teeth. Its sweet taste contrasted with the pain about to be delivered by the blade Khalela brought within an inch of his flesh.

She pressed the side of the red-hot metal against the bleeding wound, and the searing pain broadcasting from his leg carried the power of a gigawatt station. Every single inch of his body tensed, his jaws clamping the chunk of sugarcane like a vise, his tight fists pounding like hammers against the cane, his convulsively twitching lids darkening his surroundings, his mind jumping away from the scorching reality of his life.

With the smell of burned flesh filling his nostrils, Kevin shivered as the pain streaked up his body. He felt it reach his mind, his soul. Khalela's face, the clouds dotting the afternoon sky, the bare metal walls of the bed of the truck—everything disappeared as he closed his eyes and kept pounding on the cane with tight fists. He tried to twist his body but Khalela's weight on his legs kept him in place. The blade continued to move up and down the side of the wound, and then it was gone.

Kevin just lay there, too weak and stunned to move, breathing in short sobbing gasps. He felt Khalela get off his legs and lay beside him. He couldn't talk, couldn't even think straight as the initial sting subsided, but the throbbing remained.

"Kevin? Kevin?"

No answer. He could hear her but could not bring his lips to move. His body would not respond.

"Kevin? Kevin, please answer me!"

Kevin didn't respond. The whole world began to spin around him. He had pushed his body beyond the brink. The blow to his neck, the stress, the blood loss, and the pain he had just endured taxed his body past his limit.

Everything around him reduced to a tunnel, and he saw Khalela's face at the end. Kevin Dalton fell unconscious.

THE MISSISSIPPI RIVER. SOUTH OF BATON ROUGE, LOUISIANA.

Marcos Eduardo Dominguez closed his eyes to the moist breeze caressing his tanned face and swirling his brown hair as the speedboat cruised down the Mississippi toward New Orleans. In his hands he held the bomb he swore would level Washington, D.C. In his heart he held evil thoughts of revenge against the American Kevin Dalton, who had murdered his sister Norma.

The boat leaped into the air as it used the wake of a large merchant vessel as a ramp, splashing down against the polluted river a second later. Marcos held on tight to the bomb as he sat next to one of his bodyguards in the back of the boat. Behind him was another boat. The other two cruised a mile upstream, far enough away to warn Marcos by radio if someone had sprung an ambush on them.

The late morning sky over southern Louisiana was partly cloudy this afternoon. Dark cumulus dotted the southern horizon, bringing with them the possibility of a midday shower.

"We will be there in two hours, *jefe,*" said one of his bodyguards sitting in the front, next to the guard steering the boat away from Baton Rouge. "Everything looks *muy bueno.* The team in front says all is clear."

Marcos barely acknowledged him. His mind was preoccupied with achieving revenge against the American Dalton. Up to this point the missions had been strictly business. Saddam Hussein had paid Marcos a considerable amount of money to deliver his weapons to America, and the Chilean arms dealer had done just that. The death of Norma, however, had not been in the plan. The American had put a bullet in his *hermanita,* and Marcos Dominguez swore not to rest another day until he had paid Kevin Dalton back in kind.

Clouds of foam and mist rose from the black waters splashing under the fiberglass boat. The cool spray washed away the heat of the day. Marcos kept his eyes closed and listened to the noise of the outboard engine mix with that of the water and the whistling of the wind.

12

FISSION

In my mind's eye, like a waking dream, I could still see the tongues of fire at
work on the bodies of men.

—Masuji Ibuse, Black Rain

SOUTHERN IRAQ.

Tranquil waters bathed in moonlight extended as far as U.S. Marine Corps
Lieutenant Colonel Diane Towers could see. The dark silhouettes of
scattered cirrus overhead dotted the night sky as Diane's F/A-18D Hornet
two-seater reached its cruising altitude of twenty-three thousand feet
shortly before turning to a northerly heading.

Menacing, yet aerodynamically beautiful, the titanium bird of prey
grazed the speed of sound thanks to its General Electric F404-400
augmented turbofans, which unleashed a combined twenty-seven thousand pounds of thrust. The Marine Corps had purchased the F/A-18D
specifically for its all-weather night attack sensor suite, which included a
special radar, a forward-looking infrared pod, a laser target designator,
and a cockpit design compatible with night vision goggles.

"Put on your goggles and arm your weapons, Keith," Diane said over
the intercom to her weapon systems officer, Captain Keith Wallace, sitting
in the backseat of the thirty-six-thousand pound jet.

"Coming on," Wallace responded.

Diane reached for the GEC Avionics "Cat's Eyes" night vision goggles
secured in a foam-filled compartment located near her right elbow in the
Hornet's forward cockpit. Using her right hand, she snapped the one-piece
NVG instrument into a bracket mounted on the front of her helmet,
positioned so that two small combiner lenses were suspended directly in
front of her eyes.

The Cat's Eyes presented Diane with a bright, green-tinted, two-
dimensional image of her surroundings without blocking her view of the
forward-looking infrared image projected on the Marconi Heads-up
Display, or on the three Kaiser CRT displays arranged in a V-pattern on
her control panel.

From this high altitude, Diane could see the waters of the Persian Gulf giving way to the Iraqi coastal plains. Normal traffic leading to Umm Qasr, an Iraqi port located in the southeastern section of the country, became clearly visible with the help of the goggles. But traffic going into the Iraqi port was of no interest to Diane on this cool and windy evening. The target of the Hornet's underwing stores was the front echelon of the Republican Guard divisions ten miles from the Kuwaiti border. Diane flew one of ten Hornets that had left Bahrain thirty minutes before. The second strike, headed by Major Blue Jeans Levi would not leave the base outside Kuwait City until Diane's team had completed their bombing runs.

"Target coming up. One seven zero at sixty," said Wallace from the rear.

Diane clicked the mike in response as she briefly glanced at the color map and verified her navigator's report before pulling back on the throttles and diving to two hundred feet while maintaining 420 knots.

"Moon's perfect tonight," said Wallace, commenting that their NVGs were getting enough illumination for proper mission operation thanks to the quarter moon. NVGs provided anywhere from 20/70 to 20/100 visual acuity depending on the moon phase, angle, and weather. Though not equal to human 20/20 day vision, NVGs allow night vision where the human eye does not perform.

"Yep." Diane smiled. She liked Keith Wallace, a native of New York City who had had to push himself above and beyond anyone else in his class to get his WSO certification in a world where, because of continuing military budget cuts, the Marine Corps could afford to be highly selective with its recruits for high-tech positions.

With the goggles restricting her vision to a small thirty-degree circular patch directly in front of her, Diane continuously moved her head from side to side, scanning her surroundings so as not to fixate on a particular object. Yet, with every sweep she had to overcome the NVG-induced loss of visual acuity and force herself to pick out unlit towers, oil-pumping stations, antennas, and other obstructions far ahead in her flight path.

Fighting the deadly combination of loss of peripheral vision, depth perception, and acuity, Diane concentrated on speed and altitude, including cross-checking the radar altimeter with every visual sweep. Owing to their lack of distance estimation capability, NVGs tend to seduce pilots to go lower for a clearer picture, leading some right into the ground. Her brain begged her to climb to one thousand feet and buy a little more margin for error, but the seasoned pilot in Diane knew that as long as she continued to move her head she would get a clear enough picture of the surroundings to maintain her current approach.

"Green Knight Four One Seven, Redeye."

Inside her oxygen mask Diane frowned. One of the AWACS—Airborne Warning and Control System—flying racetrack patterns over Saudi Arabia was trying to make contact with her. Along with the squadron of

Hornets, the squadron of A-10 Warthogs, and the Eagles in Salman Assad and aboard the *Kennedy,* the United States had provided the services of two AWACS, which housed state-of-the-art computers, radars, and communications equipment to monitor and control air activity in a three-hundred-mile radius. Dividing the southwestern section of Iraq into two sectors, the pair of AWACS electronically interrogated every aircraft within their range. If the code in the interrogated aircraft's Identification Friendly or Foe (IFF) system didn't match with any of the AWACS codes, the jet would be tagged as hostile and its coordinates passed to the *Kennedy*'s F-14 Tomcats or Salman Assad's F-15s.

Diane switched to the secure frequency and spoke into the voice-activated microphone inside her oxygen mask.

"Redeye, One Seven."

"One Seven, two bogeys. Three four zero, thirty miles, two thousand feet at two hundred knots, headin' zero niner zero. Looks like Hinds," the AWACS reported, informing Diane of two possible Russian-made attack helicopters in the region.

"Ah, roger, Redeye."

Diane switched back to intercom. "What do you think?"

"Think it's OK for now," responded Wallace. "They're just a couple of choppers and not after us. Let the Navy or the Air Force handle them. Stay on course."

"Will do." Diane switched back to the secure frequency. "Redeye, One Four. Call in Tomcats to intercept. Our mission priority is Alpha One."

"Alpha One confirmed. Will vector F-14s. Good shooting."

"Rog." Diane remained on the secured frequency to let the AWACS monitor her radio chatter during the bombing run.

"Target's just ahead. Three miles. We're red and free," said Wallace, informing Diane that the underwing ordnance was armed.

"Roger."

"Two miles."

Diane climbed slightly to clear a hill. The valley that followed was illuminated with the lights from the eastern flank of the advancing army, an ocean of T-72 tanks, personnel carriers, and other vehicles.

With the goggles automatically adjusting their light sensitivity to avoid blinding her, Diane began her one and only bombing run: a flight straight over this section of the five-mile-long line of Russian-made tanks, their crews and ammunition. Other Hornets, working different sections of the large deployment of forces, would follow Diane's initial strike. The Warthogs, with their 30mm cannons, would pound the southern flank, while Kuwaiti Hornets concentrated on the northern flank.

"Fifteen hundred feet to target," reported Wallace.

"Rad Alt at one-forty," she warned, setting the radar altimeter beacon to go off at 140 feet.

Dropping to a dangerous 150 feet to minimize her exposure to ground fire for the three seconds that it would take her to fly over the Iraqi line, Diane advanced the throttles until her airspeed read 650 knots.

"Range one thousand feet. Mark!"

With her heartbeat rocketing, Diane eased back the centerstick and popped up to two hundred feet. Her right hand grasped the throttle controls, ready to shove full power if any of the jet's aerial sensors detected a surface-to-air missile.

"Five hundred feet to target. The coast is clear. Four, three, two . . . bombs off!"

Feeling the Hornet jerk upward as twelve one-thousand-pound Cluster Bomb Units were released from the inner and outer underwing pylons at 0.15 second intervals to spread them out across the eastern flank of the Republican Guard, Diane shoved full power and began climbing and jinking to avoid being hit by a surface-to-air missile or antiaircraft artillery. The evasive maneuver resulted in several g's piling up on her.

The Hornet's G sensor, detecting the monumental pressure hammering her, rushed compressed air through the G hose connected to Diane's G suit—a pair of zippered pants with air bladders around her waist, thighs, and calves—to force blood back up to her head to keep her from losing consciousness.

With the pressure pounding her into her ejection seat, and feeling five times heavier than normal, Diane kept the rearward pressure on the center stick while looking back at her target, puzzled at the total lack of enemy fire.

. The CBUs glided over the Iraqi forces for another second before breaking up and releasing 202 97B bomblets each. Weighing 3.4 pounds and traveling at seven hundred knots, the bomblets descended over men and machines like an apocalyptic chastisement. A fraction of a second after the bomblets' downward-pointed shaped charges pierced through artillery armor, the small bombs' fragmentation steel cases detonated into rapidly expanding clouds of flesh-shredding steel particles engulfing the entire front line. Finally, the 97Bs' zirconium rings exploded 0.3 seconds later, creating a blanket of flames that took care of anything missed by the first two explosions.

Diane shook her head. No matter how many bomb runs she had done in her seven-year Marine career, the power of those submunitions never ceased to amaze her.

"Initial target destroyed. No secondary explosions," said Wallace as Diane pointed the nose south and headed home at six hundred knots.

"What? No secondaries?"

"Affirmative. Either their munitions didn't blow, or they weren't carrying any."

Alarms now blared in Diane's mind. This didn't feel right. Those Iraqis were headed south either to scare the Kuwaitis or to reclaim the country they once conquered in 1990. Either way, Diane expected them to carry a serious load of ammunition. Otherwise, why go through all the trouble of deploying such a large force of men and tanks? And why didn't they fire a single antiaircraft round at her Hornet?

"The rest of the team's going in for its bombing run. No enemy fire to report. The Warthogs and the Kuwaiti Hornets also haven't seen any secondaries. New heading—"

"One Seven, One Seven, Redeye."

Diane switched frequencies as her right eye narrowed suspiciously. It was one of the AWACS again. "Redeye, One Seven."

"One Seven, two bogeys. Heading One Four Six at eighty, angels two," the AWACS said, giving Diane a Bearing, Range, and Altitude report (BRA).

Wallace checked the information painted on the radar and reported it to Diane. The helicopters had remained at two thousand feet but had slowed down to 150 knots.

Five thousand pounds of fuel left. Diane had plenty of juice to make it back across the border to Kuwait, but not enough to engage for any period of time, even if it was with a couple of Hinds. The helicopters, however, did pose a serious threat to a diving Hornet during a bombing run if positioned close enough to loose a missile or a few rounds from its 23mm cannon. And this was exactly what Diane feared those Hinds were doing, providing some level of air cover for the advancing troops. But on the other hand, why hadn't any of the Iraqis fired at the Hornets or the Warthogs yet?

"Redeye, One Seven. Where are the Tomcats?"

"Had problems getting off the deck, One Seven. Catapult problems."

Diane exhaled. *Damn! Leave it to the Navy to screw it up!*

"Redeye, what about Salman Assad?" she asked.

"They won't get there in time to intercept. Warthogs are busy with the tanks in the southern flank. The Kuwaitis are still working the northern flank."

Rats. "Ah, roger, Redeye. One Seven turning to intercept."

"Confirmed."

"Track them, Keith," Diane said, after switching to the intercom and turning the Hornet back around.

Wallace activated the Hornet's pulse-Doppler radar controlling the Advanced Medium Range Air-to-Air Missiles attached to the outer pylons. The advanced radar locked both incoming bogeys and presented Wallace with a number of options to engage them.

"Got 'em in the bag. Range twenty miles," he finally reported.

Diane silently stared at the two green tracks on her radar screen, wondering what was going through the minds of those Iraqi pilots, who were apparently protecting an unarmed division of Republican Guards.

*   *   *

In the rear section of one of two Hind-D attack helicopters circling above the advancing army, Abu Habbash's ears rejoiced the moment the stroboscopic flashes three miles away confirmed the radio operator's warning: The Americans were attacking the front echelon of the tank divisions. His leaders had been correct. The Americans were very predictable, and engaging in such predictable behavior, they had secured Abu Habbash a place in Paradise.

His pulse quickening and his mouth dry, the Iraqi scientist mentally rehearsed the simple, yet crucial procedure Jafar Dhia Jafar had shown him two days before.

Opening the suitcase, Abu Habbash removed the gun attachment from the stainless steel tube connected to the main bomb assembly. Reaching into a side pocket, he pulled out a single .45-caliber round and brought it up to his face. He had stared at the uranium-tipped bullet many times since arriving at the front lines, and now it was time to load it in the pistol. This, however, he did with difficulty. The fingers of his hands trembled as he pushed the bullet inside the empty chamber. Abu Habbash did not know if it was fear or the simple anticipation of his journey to the gardens of Allah.

Reattaching the gun assembly to the stainless steel tube, Abu Habbash pulled the hammer with his thumb and gazed out of the helicopter's side window, his eyes taking in the crescent moon. The current altitude was perfect. It was the same altitude used when detonating the bomb over Hiroshima. Two thousand feet would maximize the blast damage, incinerating everyone within a two-thousand-foot radius, destroying all machinery and equipment within six thousand feet, and creating a cloud of radiation that would kill every living creature within eight thousand feet.

"Allamdu li Allah!" he shouted at the stars, before pulling the trigger.

With alarms and warning lights filling her cockpit, Diane Towers let go of the controls and quickly brought both gloved hands to her goggles to shield her eyes as the night turned into day from the brightest flash she'd seen in her life. Already the intense light had destroyed the electronic circuitry of the NVGs, rendering them useless.

Jesus! What in the world—

Then the thought hit her like a hard slap across the face, and the realization made her shiver with fear: The blinding flash had resulted from a nuclear explosion. The brightness of the fireball covered an area of the sky a few hundred times as large as the sun, delivering energy at a rate a thousand times that of sunlight.

"Oh, my God! We just nuked the Iraqis!" screamed Wallace.

"Shut your eyes, Keith! Don't look at the light!" she screamed as the Hornet, with both engines disabled, entered a reverse flat spin, but by that time the initial flash had ended.

"We got engine failure! My screens are roasted!" Wallace said. "Goggles off! Let's get the hell out of—"

"Don't eject!" commanded Diane, removing the goggles. "Don't eject or we'll be fried out there!"

Wallace did not respond. As the entire world spun out of control, Diane managed to get a glimpse of the rapidly developing fireball rising up to the sky just a couple of miles away, right over where the Republican Guard forces had been a few seconds before.

Mother of God! Did we do this?

The ball reached about a thousand feet high before cooling off, forming the familiar mushroom-shaped cloud with a column of smoke and dust. The fireball's initial thermal energy of seventy-seven hundred degrees Celsius covered an area of five hundred feet in the initial 0.3 seconds, rapidly expanding in diameter while cooling down. By the time it reached Diane's Hornet, the short exposure to such high heat in the form of ultraviolet, visible, and infrared light, caused the Hornet's titanium skin to heat up to one thousand degrees.

Diane was dropping fast. Her eyes glanced at the backup analog altimeter just as her searching hands found the ejection handles. Six thousand feet. She waited. She had no choice. With Ground Zero so close, Diane made the call to endure the increased cockpit temperature in order to survive the shock wave that would soon follow.

The heat flash gave way to a powerful wind that shoved the F/A-18D to starboard, almost as if Diane were executing a maximum-g turn. The windblast that engulfed her was a mere fraction of the one ton per square foot of pressure that had pounded the region surrounding GZ, where the fireball, heating the air to incandescence, had moved the surrounding air outward in all directions at an initial velocity over four times the speed of sound. Soon a second blast wave reached her position, coming from the opposite direction, as cool air rushed back toward GZ to fill the partial vacuum created by the explosion.

"Get ready to eject, Keith."

Silence.

"You with me, Keith? . . . Keith? . . . shit!"

With the mushroom still visible in the distance and cockpit temperatures reaching 130 degrees, Diane saw the earth come up to meet her and, at an altitude of just five hundred feet, she pulled the handle, ejecting Keith Wallace first and then herself.

The world seemed to catch fire around her as the clear canopy blew upward and she followed it under the power of the Martin-Baker ejection seat's solid propellant rocket, which shot her up to nine hundred feet as the Hornet burst in a ball of flames that reached out for her.

God, it's hot! her mind screamed, but her body couldn't do anything about it while strapped to the life-saving seat, shot upward like a cannonball. The windblast nearly crushed her chest, turned her upside down and to the side as she darted across the sky in a parabolic trajectory. Visions of flames, mushroom clouds, and stars flashed in front of her, but her eyes barely registered them as a deep sense of isolation drowned her, a sense of helplessness, of sadness . . . of fear.

A hard tug told her the parachute had safely deployed. The brutal windblast turned into a soft breeze, a cool breeze that seemed to caress away the pain, the anger, the shock of what she had just witnessed; the terrible vision of fire and destruction unlike anything she'd seen before.

And who did this? she asked herself. *Did we do it?* Could it be possible that the president had decided to send Saddam the ultimate warning? Or was it an accident? Did someone make a paramount mistake and load a Hornet with a nuclear-tipped bomb instead of conventional munitions? Diane couldn't buy that. A lot of high-ranking officers, all the way up to the president himself, would have had to sign off on even letting nuclear-tipped bombs be deployed with the Marines, much less actually loaded onto a Hornet.

But regardless of why or how it happened, the sad truth was that it *had* happened. A terrifying nightmare had unfolded itself in front of Diane's very own hazel eyes. Yellow fires billowed up in the distance. Explosions, like lightning flashes, illuminated the shaft of the dark mushroom menacing over what had been enemy tank divisions a minute ago.

But for Diane Towers, lieutenant colonel in the U.S. Marine Corps, the worst was yet to come. At that moment she was being bombarded by an invisible enemy: gamma rays. Although she couldn't see it, smell it, or feel it, the radioactivity that filled the air entered her 115-pound body every time she inhaled. Her flight suit offered quite a bit of protection by temporarily shielding her skin from the enriched uranium isotopes attacking all living cells, but even though she was now several miles away from the epicenter, in the few minutes it took her to reach the ground Diane was exposed to about three hundred rem, equivalent to thirty thousand ordinary chest X rays.

Her boots sank into the muddy soil, and she rolled to cushion the fall. The first thing that struck her as she sat up and began massaging her arms, which ached from the g's, was how warm the ground was. Actually, it was borderline hot.

Diane checked her body for any obvious injury, but found nothing, except for a general body soreness due to the ejection. She knew adrenaline lessened the effects of the windblast and the spinal compression from being shot out of the Hornet like a bullet. In another hour she would be really hurting. She staggered up and began to collect her parachute, but quickly gave up on the idea. After all, who was she going to try to hide the chute from?

She removed her helmet and brushed back her soaked, short brown hair with a gloved hand.

Diane scanned her surroundings. The distant fires cast a dim orange glow over the entire valley, allowing her to see that she had landed on what appeared to be a farm—or what was left of it: a collapsed stone house and windmill surrounded by blackened trees, some of which had fallen to the ground, their exposed roots sticking up in the air. A fence of some sort had stood between the windmill and a field of something, of which nothing but charred stubs remained. Steam boiled up from the small pond to the left of the house. . . .

She felt an intense urge to vomit as her nostrils filled with the smell of burned flesh. *Oh, Jesus!* She stopped breathing for a half minute as her logical side tried to cope with the reality of having witnessed a nuclear explosion.

You're a damned Marine, Diane! Start fucking acting like one!

Slowly, Diane managed to calm down. Her face sobered. She looked at the situation from as objective a standpoint as she could muster. Her survival training took over.

She flipped the PRC-112 handheld radio on, set it to Talk—two-way communications—and tried to reach the border or Wallace for about thirty seconds. She got no response. Diane had no idea if anyone could hear her. The PRC-112 seemed operational, but the atomic blast's electromagnetic pulse could have fried one of the radio's components. Sighing, she switched off the radio and strapped it back in a pouch of the gear vest she wore over her flight suit, where she also carried a Smith & Wesson Model 39 automatic pistol and two extra magazines.

From another pouch, Diane pulled out a Portable Global Positioning System (PGPS), a handheld unit with a two-by-three-inch liquid crystal display, capable of showing her position with respect to a superimposed map of southern Iraq with an accuracy of twenty feet. The PGPS was linked with twenty-two GPS satellites.

Zooming in to her location, Diane quickly determined that she was about eight and a half miles from the border with Kuwait.

A brief inspection of her survival kit revealed an assortment of essentials: a dozen aspirin, antidiarrhea medicine, Band-Aids, surgical tape, insect repellent, flares, signaling mirrors, a space blanket, and a compass, among other items. Strapped to her belt was a slim, plastic canteen holding eleven ounces of drinking water.

A glance at the compass and at the PGPS, and she began walking south, away from a man-made hell, and toward her people. She got as far as the broken-down fence surrounding the farm when she heard something behind her. A noise of some sort. It sounded more animal than human, yet it had come from someone slowly crawling in her direction. With the glowing city in the background, the person seemed dark, menacing, intriguing. Remembering that there were Iraqi soldiers in the region, Diane decided to take no chances and pulled the Model 39 free of the Velcro pouch, flipped the safety, and chambered a round. With her other hand she grabbed her flashlight and trained it on the shadowy shape.

Her hands began to tremble. The sight made her nauseous again.

The naked person—she couldn't tell the sex—had probably been exposed to the short but very intense flesh-scorching thermal flash. The result was the grossly burned soul reaching out for her. The skin, burned and inflamed, had become loose and dropped in flaps. Charred layers of flesh, burned hair, blistered lips, melted ears, and webbed hands filled Diane's eyes, touching her heart. Diane Towers thought she was going to pass out, but she managed to keep her composure.

Diane uncocked and holstered the weapon before kneeling down, and with her eyes filled, she held the trembling stranger in her arms and stared at the horribly disfigured face. Most of the hair was gone, and the eyes . . . the eyes seemed huge and dark and glassy . . . the eyelids were gone. The rest of the face was grossly blistered. Diane could hardly tell what was what. There was a lump in the center with two orifices where the nose had been, two short stubs on the sides for ears, badly inflamed lips. The rest . . . oh, God. The rest was unrecognizable.

"Mayya . . . mayya."

Water. The man spoke in Arabic, which Diane understood well after spending a year in northern Iraq as part of the U.N. security forces in the region.

Diane felt light-headed and fought it. According to her training, nuclear victims suffered from acute thirst within minutes of the explosion.

"Pain . . . pain . . . water . . . the pain . . ."

What can I do? All I've got is aspirin. What you need is morphine. Jesus Christ, this can't really be happening!

"Kill me . . . please."

Diane was breathing heavily again. A lump filled her throat. She wanted to save him, but felt impotent, incapable, lacking even the drugs to alleviate what looked like horrendous pain.

Diane prayed that the man, who now had gone into convulsions, would soon die, if anything out of sheer human mercy.

"Please . . . kill me," came the whisper again. Although she could barely hear it, Diane felt the foreign words grasping her most inner feelings.

"Kill me . . . pain . . . please . . ."

The voice didn't even sound human. It appeared distorted, muffled, as if spoken through a piece of cloth. The large glassy eyeballs continued to move in every direction. Diane reached for her Model 39 again and pressed the muzzle against the man's forehead, but she couldn't bring herself to pull the trigger. In her years with the Marines, Diane had dropped more bombs on more people than she cared to remember, yet she could not force her index finger to apply the necessary pressure to end a life that had really ceased to exist a few minutes before. *But that was the enemy,* she thought, trying to justify past actions. *This is a helpless human being!*

"Please . . . kill . . ."

"I can't . . . I can't," Diane heard herself say in Arabic as she broke into tears while holding the man against her.

"The pain . . . please. Please . . . do it . . . now. I'd do . . . it for you."

Diane closed her eyes briefly and reached down into her soul for the strength to do something her instincts told her was wrong, yet she had to do. If the situation were reversed, she would probably be making the same request.

She opened her eyes, stared into what was left of that stranger, and squeezed the trigger. The gun went off once. It was enough.

Slowly, Diane got up and walked away with the gun still in her right hand. She did not look back even once.

Diane Towers staggered south for twenty minutes, making emergency calls every five minutes, but so far she had made contact with no one. More and more she began to believe that her PRC-112 was broken. Diane also wondered what had happened to Keith Wallace. Had he made it in one piece? Wallace had not answered Diane right before ejection, although that could be attributed to a malfunctioning auxiliary intercom.

With the PGPS showing her the way to the border, Diane tried to come to terms with what she had seen. Even as she walked away from Ground Zero, she couldn't believe that it had actually happened. It all seemed to belong to some kind of bad dream. Yet, for all she wished the events in the past thirty minutes were figments of an imagination gone mad, reality told a different story. With a fury that robbed the life of most living things and reduced material objects to ashes, an atomic bomb had once again laid waste to human beings. Most of the Iraqi force had vanished without a trace. The dark storm clouds that had spread over a small island in the Far East long ago had returned, obliterating tens of thousands of people and projecting depths of misery as large as the mushroom cloud that still hovered over the vaporized Republican Guard divisions five miles away.

Diane checked her watch. She had been on the move for almost thirty minutes, making her way through the agricultural valley that led to the border with Kuwait, and still no sign from Wallace or a rescue helicop—

A crippling pain in her abdomen made her drop to the ground and bend over, into a fetal position.

Jesus!

Feeling as if her stomach was on fire, Diane breathed deeply, held it, and slowly exhaled. The pain disappeared as suddenly as it had come. Wearily, she sat up.

What in the hell was that?

She hadn't even finished that thought when her stomach forced her quickly eaten dinner up to her throat. Clenching her teeth, she managed to control the first convulsion, but failed on the next, bending over and vomiting. Eyes filled and body tensed, Diane let it all out until there was nothing but dry heaves.

Shaken and tired, Diane staggered up and wiped her mouth with the sleeve of her flight suit. In all her years flying with the Marines, Diane had thrown up only a handful of times—at the very beginning of her flight training—before her system developed an immunity to the rigors and disorientation maneuvers associated with tactical jet flying.

Oh, God. What's happening to me? Diane thought as she noticed something white swirling in the distance. For a moment she thought it could be nothing but the reflection of the moon over a water pond or lake, but soon she realized what she saw . . . *a parachute!*

She broke into a run, reaching the parachute in under a minute. Keith Wallace lay on his side tangled in the nylon lines. His parachute appeared to have opened fully. She couldn't explain why he was unconscious.

She knelt next to the helmeted WSO and checked for a pulse. She felt none. Her eyes drifted to the helmet. As she stared into her own reflection on Wallace's lowered green visor, Diane reached over to pull it up, and quickly realized that it was very hot to the touch.

Blinking twice, Diane pulled away, struggling to remain calm, her heart pounding again, her mouth dry.

Hot?

Then her logical side pieced it all together, and the revelation made her breathe in deeply, eyes closed, fists tightened. Slowly, she exhaled through her clenched jaw, almost as if purging herself from any emotional thought, forcing her mind to remain focused, logical, professional.

It was the angle, Diane. The fucking angle!

Diane Towers realized how lucky she had been, and how *unlucky* Wallace had been. The atomic heat flash had occurred as the Hornet spun out of control toward earth, scorching all exposed surfaces, including those inside the cockpit. Unfortunately for Captain Keith Wallace, because of the angle of the plane with respect to the heat flash during that crucial fraction of a second, his helmet had been exposed directly to the incinerating blast.

That had been the reason why her WSO had not responded right before ejection: he was already dead, or well on his way as his helmet suddenly turned into a high-temperature oven, roasting his brain.

For all her years in the military, all the nuclear weapons training, all the seminars about nuclear attack survival, Diane never imagined that the results would be so inhuman, so unforgiving, so downright unfair. Here she was, walking away from it all with no visible external damage, while Wallace, who had been within feet of her, lay dead.

The abdominal pain returned. Diane fell to her knees and bent over. Bile rushed to her throat and she didn't fight it, resigning herself to the fact that she had been nuked, but refusing to think of the long-term conse-

quences. The short exposure to radiation would not kill her today or
tomorrow, but the aviator felt certain that it would kill her someday.

A minute later, dazed and light-headed, Diane rubbed her temples as a
migraine began to pound her. She wiped the mud off her face before
reaching down into her survival kit, where she took three aspirin and
downed them with a gulp of water from her canteen, wondering as she
swallowed if she had just drunk radioactive water.

Oh, screw it! If I'm gonna die, I'm gonna—

Everything around her began to spin. Her vision tunneled. She fell on
her side.

Her eyelids feeling as if they weighed a thousand pounds each, Diane
Towers stared at billowing distant fires lining the menacing mushroom
cloud, but in her mind she saw the stars, saw the mountains, saw her
beloved California. She remembered the clean cool air, the towering trees,
the sparkling streams. A breeze smelling of wet leaves and earth blowing
down the mountains as sunlight shafted under cumulus clouds, lighting
the grasslands. It all flashed in front of her eyes, memories from a distant
past, visions of yesteryear, all so peaceful, so soothing, so full of life. But
then the clouds grew dark, the breeze turned into a stiff wind. A rumble of
thunder, and cold rain hissed down from the skies. A whoosh of raindrops
clashed against the windows as a sixteen-year-old girl stood next to her
mother while men in uniform folded an American flag into a perfect
triangle. The soldiers solemnly saluted their fallen brother in arms, one of
many Marines who had died a useless death while asleep at the hands of a
Muslim, ten thousand pounds of dynamite, and a stolen truck. One of
many "peacekeepers" thrown in the middle of a passion-filled conflict in a
land where everyone else was dying to leave. Milk-faced, naive American
boys crushed under mounds of concrete rubble and pillars of flame due to
their country's failure to realize that in Beirut no one was immune to the
political and military cross fire that ruled its streets.

And so the girl turned into a woman on that rainy day long ago.
Through bitter tears she waved farewell to the father she loved and
admired more than anything else in this world. Saying a silent good-bye at
the closed coffin that cradled everything she'd always wanted to be, Diane
Towers held on to her mother's hand and slowly walked away, vowing that
one day she would grow up to be a Marine and continue the tradition that
her father and her grandfather had started.

As the past faded into exhaustion, and the sound of a helicopter
approached from the distance, Diane Towers closed her eyes.

THE WHITE HOUSE, WASHINGTON, D.C.

President Bill Clinton wished someone would pinch him and wake him up
from the nightmare that was unfolding in front of his eyes. A nuclear
device had detonated just as the bombs from the third Hornet were

released over Republican Guard divisions. The results of the explosion were beginning to appear on CNN and the networks as field reporters stationed in Kuwait and Saudi Arabia quickly made it to the area. Mostly confusion and speculation filled the reports, but the general feeling not only across the United States, but also across the entire world, particularly after the widely televised press conference Saddam Hussein had held thirty minutes after the explosion, was that the United States had either made a terrible mistake by accidentally loading a nuclear device on the Hornet, or worse, that the Clinton administration had purposefully used a nuclear device to send Saddam Hussein a strong message. Whatever the reason, the world was in a state of shock as the first color images of the vast destruction of men and equipment began to fill the airwaves.

To make matters even worse, the Iraqi leader had also claimed that his troops had carried no live ammunition, only the blanks they intended to use in a war exercise the Clinton administration had apparently mistaken for an assault on Kuwait.

White House phones had rung nonstop since the story had broken an hour ago, and President Bill Clinton had yet to appear on television to address a very confused, surprised, and angered world. His aides had been holding back calls from the leaders of several nuclear powers, including China, Russia, England, France, and even Israel. Most countries of the world had already issued statements condemning the actions and demanding a full investigation.

Peace activists had already started organizing nationwide demonstrations, one of which had camped outside the White House twenty minutes ago. Signs requesting Clinton's immediate resignation dominated the scene. In the Middle East, the American flag–burning ritual was in full swing. From Teheran to Beirut and everywhere in between, the anti-American sentiment had reached a new high in the face of the nuclear explosion that had annihilated forty thousand Arabs in a single second.

His arms crossed, President Bill Clinton leaned against the edge of his desk with his eyes glaring at his subordinates. His secretaries of state and defense sat on one sofa, facing Director of Central Intelligence Joseph Goldberg and FBI Director Roman Palenski. Standing in the rear of the room were the Joint Chiefs of Staff and the secretary of energy.

"It is impossible for a mistake like this to happen, Mr. President," said the defense secretary, his bloodshot eyes meeting the president's gaze. "I had my people look at the ammunition inventory and, as expected, nothing unconventional shows at the Marines' field in Kuwait."

"Is it possible that in rushing supplies to the region several days ago something slipped through?" asked Clinton.

"I seriously doubt it, sir. We're in the process of going through the inventory list—and when I say we, I mean over six hundred clerks from twelve different bases—and everything so far is as it should be. I firmly believe this wasn't us, sir. Someone has planned this out quite carefully to put us in this situation."

Clinton extended his arms in front of him, palms facing up. "If not us, who then? Did the Israelis time this to loose a nuke on Saddam? Or did Saddam himself nuke his own troops?"

"Those are two possibilities, Mr. President," said DCI Joseph Goldberg in his raspy voice, the fingers of his right hand fidgeting with his burgundy pen. "The problem is that, although we could generate mounds of paperwork showing that we did not do it, the final proof—that is the physical evidence of what actually happened—was vaporized along with the Iraqi troops."

"And along with many of our own pilots, a dozen Hornets, and just as many Warthogs," added the defense secretary. "Only one pilot of the first-strike team survived the blast. Apparently she'll be all right. A rescue chopper found her twenty minutes ago. The rest of the first wave were all too low and too close to the area when the nuke went off."

"True and very unfortunate," replied Goldberg. "There is, however, a small possibility of shedding some light on this incident."

All eyes, the president's included, gravitated to the lanky Goldberg, who shoved the Mont Blanc in a coat pocket, interlaced his bony fingers, and set them below his chin, as if he were praying.

"Robert Bourdeaux has informed me that one of our KH-12s was over the region collecting real-time images of the air raid as it progressed. In fact, the air raid was timed such that we would have satellite coverage of the attack to quickly assess the damage and reprioritize primary and secondary targets for the second-strike team."

Goldberg paused to let that sink in before adding, "Bourdeaux is currently at the NPIC going over the digitized images downlinked ten minutes after the blast. This might help us figure out what happened."

"How long before we know anything?" asked Clinton.

"Within the next few hours, Mr. President," responded Goldberg.

Turning to his defense secretary, Clinton said, "What about the report from the AWACS crew monitoring the Hornet's and Warthogs' squadron frequency?"

Clearing his throat, the defense secretary looked in the distance while licking his lips before his gaze shifted to the president. "The initial reports seem to confirm Saddam Hussein's claim that his troops were not carrying live munitions, sir. The first-strike team reported no secondary explosions or antiaircraft fire."

Clinton closed his eyes and nodded.

The few seconds of silence were broken by the secretary of state. "Mr. President, if Saddam Hussein did indeed manage to get a bomb and use it to vaporize his own troops, the question would then be why? Why would he do such a thing? What is his goal? And one of the answers that immediately comes to mind is that he might be trying to discredit us in the eyes of the world when discussing nuclear nonproliferation, while at the same time further promoting his clandestine nuclear arms buildup. By sacrificing his own men—something he has done in the past at the blink of an eye—Saddam has gained a lot of sympathy, particularly within the Arab world."

"He has also done something else," added Goldberg. "Saddam has made us a bit more wary about using air strikes as the means of sending him a message. What if he has a few more of these devices already built, and he's simply waiting to blow up other sections of his own country the moment we launch another air strike?"

Clinton remained quiet as he thought of another possible explanation for Saddam's behavior: The Iraqi leader was ready to detonate an atomic bomb inside the United States but, fearing a powerful nuclear retaliation, Saddam had chosen to sacrifice many of his troops by staging an American nuclear strike on Iraq, thus hoping to preempt a retaliatory strike on a highly populated city, like Baghdad.

If this scenario reflected reality, then America faced the imminent and immediate danger of a nuclear strike. If Saddam was able to detonate a bomb with such accurate precision when the Hornets and Warthogs began their strike, then it was entirely possible that he could have managed to smuggle a nuclear weapon inside the United States already.

Looking at FBI Director Palenski, Clinton simply raised his brows.

Palenski ran a hand over his bald head. "I have every agent at my disposal tracking down every possible lead, Mr. President. In the past twenty-four hours we have arrested over one hundred suspects, mostly Muslims. Over half of them were in possession of a weapon or explosive. Many of them were followers of Sheikh Imman al-Barakah, the old Muslim running a mosque in New Jersey that was attended by the two Arabs who tried to kidnap Kevin Dalton outside his house. We have a warrant to arrest the sheikh, but we are holding back in the hope that he will lead us to the hardware. My resources, however, are thinning with every new case popping up. In the past hour alone we had reports of ten additional bombings nationwide, and we fear that's just the beginning. The Muslim population in this country is enraged, and they're fighting back, even if they kill themselves in the process, or get caught in the act. It doesn't seem to matter to them, Mr. President, as long as they can manage to succeed in a few instances."

Clinton slowly looked away. The situation was worsening across the country. Although local authorities had been sufficient to control the angered crowds in many cities, Clinton feared that he would have to call in the National Guard, or even the Army itself, fairly soon.

For a second he thought about boarding Air Force One and running his country from the air for the next few days, but quickly decided against it. Saddam Hussein wasn't about to muscle Clinton into changing the way he ran his country. On the practical side, however, Clinton owed it to the

American public to leave a strong leadership in place if indeed Washington, D.C., was blown off the map, but it had to be done subtly enough to avoid raising suspicions, which could send the entire country into a panic.

After much consideration, under the stare of his own staff, Clinton decided to send Al Gore around the country to speak on behalf of his administration immediately. He also ordered the secretary of state to head for New York City and address a special session of the United Nations Security Council. The defense secretary would remain in the Pentagon, Goldberg in Langley, and Palenski in Washington, except if Clinton called an emergency meeting. Finally, the president decided to send Hillary and Chelsea to Camp David.

After issuing these orders, Clinton asked his staff to leave the room. He wanted to gather his thoughts before the press conference he had scheduled in another four hours. He could only hope that at least the CIA would come through for him and give him some ammunition to soothe the anger sweeping across his nation, across the world.

BAGHDAD, IRAQ.

In his Presidential Palace, Saddam Hussein smiled as Jafar Dhia Jafar translated the words spoken by the CNN anchor on the large television screen. The annihilation of the troops had been practically total. A few units on the periphery of the nuclear blast did manage to survive the initial explosion, but many had died a few hours later from severe burns or radiation sickness, most of them while in the care of International Red Cross units and of the first U.N. relief convoy that had begun to arrive in the region around Ground Zero an hour ago. None of the arriving troops or medical personnel were American. In fact, none were either British, French, or Italian. The members of the Red Cross and the United Nations flowing into Iraq were mostly Pakistani, Spanish, Brazilian, Greek, and Turkish. The leaders of Libya, Chad, Sudan, Syria, Jordan, Egypt, and even Iran had already contacted Saddam with their most deepest sympathy, and medical relief planes were already on the way to assist the efforts of the International Red Cross.

"You have succeeded, Great One," said Jafar, as Saddam sat still on a leather couch while facing the predawn sky over Baghdad. "The entire world has turned against the Americans."

"For now," Saddam said, as he glanced at the television and saw images of the charred bodies of Republican Guard soldiers being loaded to waiting helicopters by Red Cross personnel wearing radiation-proof suits. "How close is the team with Marcos from first assembly?"

"The messenger arrived safely. He is in Louisiana with Marcos and the Russian woman. The bombs should be assembled in less than twenty-four hours," Jafar said, holding a copy of *The New York Times,* where coded messages, disguised as advertisements for a club in Atlantic City, provided

Saddam Hussein with weekly updates on his operations without the risk of the Americans intercepting a critical message that might jeopardize the entire operation. It took Jafar another minute to bring Saddam up to speed on the situation, including the recent problems with Sheikh Imman al-Barakah and the FBI surveillance of his New Jersey mosque.

Saddam leaned his head back and took a deep breath while scanning the outlines of buildings, the onion domes, but in his mind he saw another skyline in another city disappearing behind an explosion similar to the one that had consumed so many of his men. But in order to achieve this vision, Saddam had to maintain the wave of terrorism inside the United States to keep the Federal Bureau of Investigation busy enough to give Clinton a false sense of progress. This task had been made easier by the weapon he had detonated on his own troops. The enraged Muslim population in the United States needed little encouragement to carry out every conceivable terrorist strike against the evil Clinton.

Saddam also had to ensure that the man who knew just about every aspect of his U.S. operation did not fall into the hands of the FBI. Sheikh Imman al-Barakah was under FBI surveillance after it had become evident that many of the terrorist strikes carried out by expendables in the past forty-eight hours, particularly the bombing of the Georgetown University Hospital and the strike on the American space shuttle, led directly back to the old sheikh. Hiding in his New Jersey mosque while awaiting transportation out of the country, the marked sheikh posed a threat to Saddam's operation. But the Iraqi tyrant had already anticipated such problems and had given Marcos freedom of action to order the execution of anyone who might jeopardize the mission.

A knock on the door broke his train of thought. Saddam frowned at the intrusion. "Come!" he said in his booming voice.

Three generals walked in. They all wore masks of disbelief. The highest ranking was General Sa'dun Mustafa, commander of the Republican Guard. He looked like a commander: tall, well-built, tanned, a mustache similar to his leader's adorning his hawkish face, a permanent intense look in his brown eyes.

"Great One! Oh, Great One, what a dreadful moment this is for our country!" Mustafa said as he approached his leader. The general wore no sidearm, and neither did either of the other two generals. The eternally paranoid Iraqi leader lived in constant fear of assassination, even at the hand of his most trusted generals. In fact, Saddam trusted his bodyguards more because they had nothing to gain with his death and also because they all came from Tikrit, his home village a hundred miles north of Baghdad. General Mustafa, on the other hand, could easily become the new leader of Iraq. He had the full support of the Guard, and he was quite popular with the people. Because he had been born in Halabja, a predominantly Kurdish town, he had some appeal to the Kurdish masses. But the general had never shown a drop of disloyalty to Saddam. Just the opposite, Saddam had every reason to trust this intimidating man but chose not to. Mustafa had much to gain by Saddam's death, and one day Saddam planned to put a bullet through his face. But not yet. Saddam needed Mustafa to coordinate several Republican Guard units preparing for a new drive south.

The other two generals were young and predictable. They basically followed Mustafa's orders and posed no threat to the Iraqi leader. Both had been recently promoted to fill the shoes of older generals, whom Saddam himself had shot for failing to protect Allahbad.

Mustafa approached Saddam and bowed. "We lost many brothers tonight, Great One. It was a terrible loss. A terrible loss."

Saddam patted him on the shoulder. Mustafa took the loss very personally. Three of the colonels leading the now-vaporized divisions had been his own brothers.

"The infidels have murdered our people, Sa'dun," Saddam said. "They have created many orphans this night. They have inflicted a severe blow to our Muslim society, but we shall rise from the ashes. We shall strike back with renewed commitment. Nothing will prevent us from claiming our lost land of Kuwait. We shall persevere and succeed."

"Yes, Great One. Yes!"

The other generals remained quiet and kept a respectful distance. This was an emotional moment for all of them. Saddam could see it in their eyes, and he smiled internally while a mask of grief covered his face.

"You must go now, Sa'dun. You must go and prepare for the counterattack, prepare to avenge the deaths of our beloved Iraqis, prepare to make the enemy drown in rivers of their own blood!"

"Yes, oh yes, Great One. And drown they shall!"

With that, the generals turned and left Saddam and Jafar alone again. Saddam slowly shook his head and said, "Many sacrifices must be made before we can achieve our goal, Jafar. But unlike you and me, some of the men do not have the wisdom and the courage to do what is necessary to succeed. It falls into our hands to make the hardest decisions for the benefit of Iraq. For the benefit of Islam."

Jafar didn't respond. He simply continued to hold the copy of the *Times* in his hands while staring into Saddam's grave countenance.

SOUTHERN IRAQ.

Iraqi Colonel Muhammed Hassani flew in from the north, skimming the salt marshes that abruptly turned into a sea of sand as he crossed the border into Saudi Arabia, his MiG-23 dashing across the cool, predawn sky at just under the speed of sound.

Colonel Hassani, a forty-eight-year-old veteran of the Iraqi Air Force, loved to fly the MiG-23, a remarkable improvement from the MiG-21, an airplane that always brought back painful memories. A pair of plastic kneecaps had replaced Hassani's own, which the colonel had shattered while ejecting from a MiG-21 after losing a dogfight to an American Tomcat during the war of 1991. Because of his size, a section of both knees hadn't cleared the underside of the MiG's control panel and were smashed as Hassani shot out of the cockpit.

Hassani reviewed the information currently projected onto the Heads-up Display of his air superiority fighter. All systems read nominal. He glanced to both sides and verified that his flight squadron remained with him in the inverted V formation Hassani led. Satisfied, he spoke into his voice-activated headset. "Range to target thirty miles. Seven minutes, my brothers! Seven minutes before we avenge the inhuman attack of the infidels against our people!"

"Inshallah!" came the unified response over the squadron frequency as the MiGs got dangerously close to Salman Assad Air Base in Saudi Arabia, home to the majority of U.S. Air Force fighters in the region. The base also housed over twenty F-15s from the Saudi Arabian Air Force.

While checking the flight formation, Hassani also eyed the conditions of his wings. The air surfaces of all MiG-23s in his team had been treated with a new Chinese-made Radar Absorbent Material, quite similar to the one used on the American F-117 Stealth Fighter. Based on the lack of enemy fighters, Hassani guessed the RAM was doing its magical work.

"Turning to new heading. Mark one eight seven," Hassani said as his hand applied left pressure to the control stick.

Twenty miles.

SALMAN ASSAD AIR BASE.

A fuel truck made its way past two rows of F-15 fighters tied down on the tarmac. The night was quiet, peaceful, cold. The truck's driver, a Lebanese-born man who had spent his entire adulthood in Saudi Arabia after his family had been killed by the Jews in Beirut, kept the window rolled down, enjoying the refreshing breeze as his eyes kept watch for the guards he prayed would not be there. They usually weren't at this precise time of the morning, when the security personnel changed shifts. The Lebanese had spent several mornings watching the soldiers until he had their pattern down to a science. The truck that picked up the previous shift always led the truck hauling the new guards by around ten minutes.

Ten minutes is all I need, he thought as he continued to scan the tarmac. With the explosion in Iraq, he could not be too cautious. He had seen many airplanes take off soon after the news of the atomic blast reached the base. But that had been over three hours ago. The word at the hangars was that the commotion would pick up in the morning, when the first International Red Cross relief planes, airplanes from Riyadh and Oman, would stop to refuel before continuing to Iraq.

He reached the end of the row of Eagles, stopped the truck, got out, and walked around to the rear. A number of valves and gauges layered a control panel on the right side of the back of the truck, above the bumper. The driver pulled on a lever, pushed three buttons, and was instantly rewarded by a river of JP4 fuel flowing out of a hose on the side of the truck. A red light glowed over the panel, telling the driver of the dangerous mistake he had made by activating the fuel pump and opening the release valve without having connected the hose to a jet. An alarm was also supposed to sound at this time, but the driver had disabled it by disconnecting it from the truck's battery.

Getting back on the truck, the driver spent the next few minutes spraying the entire row of F-15s just as the air raid alarms blared across the base. The incoming Iraqi MiGs had finally been detected, but it would be too late.

A smile flashing across his bearded face, the Lebanese ran away from the truck before pulling out a pistol and firing repeatedly into the truck's fuel tank from a distance of one hundred feet.

The truck disappeared behind a sheet of flames that streaked across the tarmac, following the river of JP fuel and igniting the recently fueled Eagles just as an army of pilots left their hangars and ran to them.

Too late! It is too late, infidels! It is time to perish in the flames of hell!

Colonel Hassani watched the pyrotechnic display and smiled broadly as fighter after fighter went up in flames, the bleeding clouds reflecting the rhythmic flashes of orange and yellow and red-gold.

"Concentrate on the hangars!" screamed the colonel, as he flipped on his radar and watched a half dozen enemy planes already airborne converging on his squadron.

Pushing full throttle, Hassani kept his low-altitude approach toward the main buildings in the center of the large air base before pulling on the stick at the very last minute and releasing his entire load of cluster bombs.

With the g-forces hammering him into his ejection seat, Hassani watched the partly cloudy sky light up from the massive explosion below him, and a second later an even larger blast turned the night into day as the stored munitions inside the hangars detonated.

Without further thought, and using the night and the massive explosions as his getaway shield, the Iraqi colonel hugged the desert and headed back toward Iraq in full afterburner.

Forty minutes later Hassani brought his MiG to a full stop inside one of many bunkered hangars at Khalid Khassan Air Base ten miles north of Baghdad. He was exhausted. Tonight's mission had ended two days of planning, during which Hassani had only slept four hours. He removed his helmet and lifted the canopy.

A ground crew member rolled a ladder to the side of the Russian-made jet. Hassani removed his safety harness and jumped out of the cockpit, leaving his helmet on the flight seat.

"I want this plane refueled and rearmed in two hours!" he yelled as he jumped onto the oil-stained concrete floor. Hassani took the sudden pain that streaked up his reconstructed knees in silence. He had long since learned to accept it as a part of his life. It was this pain that pushed him to fight the Americans with utter resolve. It was this pain that made him volunteer for the most difficult of missions—and succeed. It was this pain that had made him conceive the plan to destroy Salman Assad.

Without looking back at his crew, Hassani walked outside the hangar, built into the side of the hill bordering the east side of the paved runway. He took a deep breath of the early morning's cool air and briefly inspected the six other single-jet hangars, where the remainder of his flight group had just taxied their craft. All of his jets had made it back except for one.

Still, the raid had been a complete victory for Iraq. Salman Assad and its sophisticated American fighters no longer posed a threat to his country.

Checking his watch, Hassani headed for the communication's tent. He had to call his superiors in Baghdad immediately and report the results of the bombing raid.

Ten minutes later, the seasoned colonel left the communications tent and caught a ride on a Jeep to his stone home on the outskirts of the base. His house, as well as the homes of five other pilots, stood in a row behind a tall sand dune that served as a natural shield in case the base came under attack.

From the Jeep's rear seat, the Iraqi colonel welcomed the breeze with closed eyes. His conversation with one of Saddam's top generals had gone quite well. It was easy to report good news, particularly when Hassani himself had been the one who suggested carrying out the strike while the smoke and debris from the nuclear detonation still hung high in the Mesopotamian sky. By destroying American fighter planes, Hassani and his squadron had saved Iraqi lives, had spared the women and children from the horror that his own family had to endure in January of 1993, when the Tomahawk missiles launched by order of outgoing President George Bush changed Hassani's life and that of his family forever.

Hassani thanked the driver as he got out and walked the thirty feet of gravel that separated the narrow road from the wooden entrance of his home, a palace by regional standards, yet a shack when compared to the house in downtown Baghdad where he had grown up and lived all his life until that horrid night in January of 1993.

Without knocking, Hassani pushed the heavy wooden door and immediately felt his gut filling with melting lead. The feeling hadn't changed since his three-year-old son Khalil had lost his right arm and eye to the flames that consumed their home in Baghdad. Khalil was now almost six years old, and his hatred for those who had robbed him of his right to a normal life only grew with time.

This was the sad truth that CNN would not show to the world. This was what American military experts called *collateral damage:* Iraqi children maimed by the weapons of destruction of a powerful nation fired against a weaker, less-sophisticated country. How easy it must have been for President Bush to make the phone call and order the strike! How easy it must have been for the U.S. Navy officers to convey those orders to the sailors manning the launch stations! How easy it must have been for those sailors to enter the launch codes and push the button that had sent that Tomahawk missile directly toward Hassani's family! CNN would vividly portray those missiles launching in slow motion, elegantly leaving their launching tubes and cruising across an indigo sky. CNN would display the massive explosions from a sanitized altitude while military experts concentrated not on the pain inflicted on the population, but on the surgical accuracy of the missile and on the negligible collateral damage. Everything on that screen seemed so clean, so unreal, so carefully mixed, baked, and served to satisfy the appetite of an American population who did not care to see or hear about the amputations, the scars, the burns, the agony, the suffering, the pain. Yet, the misery that followed a Tomahawk strike remained very much a part of its surviving victims for the remainder of their lives, long after American newspapers stopped printing stories on the strike, long after millions of Americans pressed the remote control buttons of their television sets and switched channels without giving the images of the exploding missiles a second thought.

But the tide would be reversed one day. Hassani firmly believed the Americans would soon experience a reversal of fortune of such magnitude that they would never again trivialize the damage inflicted upon another nation by their powerful weapons. And while the children of the Great Satan screamed with the same agony that so many Iraqis had experienced for so long, Hassani would reach for the remote control of his television set and calmly switch to another channel.

"Look, father! Look!" Khalil said as he played with his younger sister Jazmine, who had been spared the disfiguring wounds of his brother by being in the womb of her mother Samia at the time of the fire. Jazmine's face was the color of the sand at dawn, her eyes, light green in color, were as radiant as Samia's had once been. The little girl held a doll dressed in a red, blue, and white dress made from a toy American flag left behind by the American soldiers during the War of 1991. The girl held the doll in her right hand and was screaming as Khalil, holding a homemade wooden model of a MiG-23 in his left hand, approached the doll from the back.

"Bang, bang, bang! Die, infidel! Die!" Khalil shouted as he imitated the noise of jet engines and machine gun fire.

As the boy made his strafing pass, his three-year-old sister, well trained by the boy on how to react to this attack, dropped the doll facefirst on the stone floor and began to clap and jump with joy.

The Iraqi colonel picked up his children, one in each arm, and, ignoring the silent alarm blaring from his knees, painfully carried them to the kitchen, where Samia prepared the morning's meal.

With her back to him as she worked on a cutting board, slicing a small block of goat cheese, Hassani briefly admired her long, black hair, one of the few things that had escaped unscathed from the fire. The sight always brought back memories of what had once been a naturally beautiful woman. Not like the whores of the West, who needed the magic of expensive cosmetics to give themselves a face that had been Allah's gift to Samia Hassani. Now that beauty had been passed on to little Jazmine. The golden skin, the catlike green eyes, the fine lips, the pearl white teeth. The fire had taken it all away from Samia, leaving behind a face laced with scars, a pair of bloated lips that even the best surgeons in Baghdad and Damascus could not fix, and a nose that consisted of a pair of platinum tubes inserted in her disfigured nasal orifices to keep the canals to her lungs from closing. At least the doctors had been able to give her a pair of eyelids from a patch of undamaged skin on her right thigh. Only her dark hair had survived, by some miracle of Allah, at least leaving Hassani with one fragment of a physical beauty that was now past.

Samia turned around, and Hassani forced the same mask of pleased satisfaction he had learned to wear since the doctors removed the bandages from her face three months after the fire.

"I was worried," she said in the guttural, raspy voice of someone who had her vocal cords irreversibly damaged by an emergency tracheotomy. With her nose burned to a cinder and her bloated lips melted shut, the military medic that arrived at Hassani's house did the only thing he could do to keep Samia from asphyxiating. He had cut a hole in her throat and in the process robbed her of the deep, sensuous voice that had captivated Hassani from the very first day he laid eyes on her. But all of that now belonged to the past.

"It is all right, my love," he responded as he put the kids down, approached her, and pressed his lips against the scar tissue of her right cheek, his right hand softly running through her hair. "It is all right. We inflicted a big blow on the infidels this morning."

"I am glad you are all right. I always worry about . . . well, you know."

"I know. Just remember that the state will take care of all of you for the rest of your life should that happen."

She slowly closed her eyes and nodded before asking, "Are you hungry?"

"Very," Hassani responded, as his children led him to the rectangular wooden table next to a large window on the side of the kitchen. Early morning sunlight forked inside the room as Hassani sat at the head of the table, his back against the window. A narrow beam of sunshine landed on Samia as she turned around and approached the table carrying a tray filled with dates and goat cheese. She instantly turned her face away from the blinding light. For a moment, a very brief moment, her face glowed in the yellow light. The disfiguring scars suddenly disappeared and the golden skin of years past returned to her cheeks. Like a mirage in the desert, his wife's beautiful face briefly returned in the glowing sunlight diffusing across the room. Hassani savored the moment, for that was all it was: a brief moment in time when Allah gave the brave warrior the simple pleasure of looking through a window to the past.

The vision revitalized his heart, renewed his love for this strong woman, fueled his desire to keep on fighting the enemies of Islam.

As Samia sat next to him and Khalil said a short prayer, a tear escaped the corner of Hassani's right eye. The warrior was about to lift a finger and wipe it off, but his wife beat him to it.

"You must accept the present as Allah's gift to you, my love," she said, a hand running over his. "We are indeed blessed for the love we have, for the children we have."

Hassani stared into the eyes of his wife and did not notice the missing eyebrows, or the disfigured nose, or the bloated lips. Muhammed Hassani simply saw his Samia, saw her eyes, felt her hand caressing his.

As his family leisurely talked about the day's planned activities, Hassani silently ate his food.

National Photographic Interpretation Center. Washington, D.C.

Robert Bourdeaux hadn't heard from Kevin Dalton since he had last called in from a Delta flight heading toward Baton Rouge. He didn't know if Kevin had flown somewhere else after that or had remained in Louisiana. The longer it took for Kevin to report, the more worried Bourdeaux grew.

Bourdeaux had left a message with Goldberg about this issue before heading for the National Photographic Interpretation Center in downtown Washington, where the deputy director of Operations knew he would most likely spend the rest of the day. As he pushed away the small plastic box of half-eaten Chinese noodles he'd had for lunch, the former field operations officer leaned back on his chair at the head of the conference room, where one of the NPIC's top analysts had spent the last hour going over the sequence of satellite photographs that was slowly making Bourdeaux's tired but still frosty mind suspect that Saddam Hussein was behind this nuclear incident.

"This photograph here, sir," said the NPIC analyst, a red-haired, freckle-faced man in his early thirties, while pointing to the image on the large screen on the other side of the room. "This one shows what I was just talking about."

Leaning forward and planting both elbows on the laminate surface of the rectangular table, Bourdeaux motioned the analyst to go on. The image on the screen showed a three-square-mile area of desert thirty seconds before the blast. The image, taken using the KH-12's both visual and forward-looking infrared cameras—the former thanks to the quarter moon—had generated amazingly clear digital photographs of the area. Bourdeaux recognized the tank divisions of the soon-to-be-vaporized Iraqi army.

"These here," the analyst continued, using a pointer to circle two small dots on the top left-hand corner of the image, "are the two hostile contacts made by the AWACS a few minutes before the explosion. They're Hind-D attack helicopters, and at the time this photo was taken, they were approaching the rear of the Iraqi main echelon." The analyst pressed a button on the remote control unit in his hand and the screen changed to a blowback of the section he had circled a moment ago. The fuzzy shapes of two helicopters came into view.

"Yep," the analyst said, after taking another look at the choppers. "Hind-Ds for sure. See the turbine location with respect to the cabin and the rudder? And the short stub wings definitely give them away."

"All right. I'm with you," Bourdeaux said.

The analyst switched to another frame. "This is another blowback from the same frame I showed you earlier. See, by the time the choppers reached the rear of the Iraqi divisions, two Hornets had already made their bombing runs, and five others were going into theirs. In addition, the Warthogs were already engaging the tanks in the eastern flank. This here marks the bomb damage by the first Hornet."

Bourdeaux's trained eyes examined the long, narrow blackened streak of tanks and personnel carriers created by the munitions of a Hornet. A new frame appeared and the DDO saw the destruction created by the second Hornet, very similar to the first. Zooming back to the original frame, the analyst ran his pointer through the two black streaks on the image.

"Here are the destruction lines again. This one for the first Hornet and this one for the second. These circles over here are—"

"The damage done by the Warthogs," Bourdeaux interrupted.

"Ah, yes, sir. As you can see between the two Hornets and the A-10 Warthogs, they had annihilated close to five percent of the advancing army. The rest of the Hornets plus more pounding from the A-10s would have bagged a significant portion of the entire unit, but it didn't happen that way.

"What I'm about to show you is a series of photos taken at 0.1 second intervals right before and after the blast."

A new frame came up on the screen, again another shot of the entire Iraqi division.

"Here are the two Hinds, now moving much closer to the center of the advancing army. Over on this side is where the third Hornet was coming in for its bombing run," the red-haired analyst said, pointing to a location roughly a mile from the helicopters.

The next frame showed a small circle of light where the helicopters had been. The following three frames showed the circle of light expanding over the area, until the entire division was engulfed by it, including most of the American planes flying overhead.

Bourdeaux stood and walked around the table. "So, it's true then?" he asked, more to himself than to his subordinate, who returned to the frame showing the smallest circle.

"Looks like the fireball was roughly a hundred feet in diameter when the KH-12 snapped this shot," the analyst said, "probably right as the device was detonated aboard one of the helicopters. In another three-tenths of a second the blast had expanded to cover most of the area. Notice how the light faded in intensity as the circle expanded."

"Just as it should be in a nuclear blast," Bourdeaux added, before slowly walking back to his seat.

Once again Saddam Hussein had managed to get his hands on the bomb, which he had used to kill forty thousand of his own men, not only to make the United States look like a merciless tyrant in the eyes of the world, but also to preempt a retaliatory strike when Saddam detonated a bomb inside America.

Rubbing a finger against his right temple, the DDO reached the conclusion that unless the FBI and the Department of Energy somehow managed to stop the terrorists who had smuggled nuclear hardware into this country within the next few days, a nuclear device would be detonated in America. If Saddam used one to blow up his own troops, he certainly had to have at least one more assembled and ready to use inside this country.

Abruptly getting up, Bourdeaux looked at his analyst and said, "Get me color prints of these shots ASAP. I've got to brief Goldberg and the president immediately."

As he got ready to head back to Langley, a secretary peeked her head inside the conference room.

"Mr. Bourdeaux?"

Bourdeaux gave the short blonde a drop of his bushy eyebrows. "Yeah?"

"You have an emergency call on line three."

Pushing the blinking button on the phone in front of him, the deputy director for operations said, "Bourdeaux," and for the next minute he listened intently to the voice of Khalela Yishaid. Her instructions were precise, her voice firm in spite of the tale she quickly related to the seasoned, yet shocked DDO. *Marcos? Here? In Louisiana? Three bombs? Impossible!*

But he had to believe her. The last time she had called with such revealing information had resulted in the eventual destruction of Allahbad.

The line went dead, and Bourdeaux quickly got another outside line and dialed a number he knew from memory. It belonged to Roman Palenski, director of the Federal Bureau of Investigation. When he hung up with the director, he dialed Patrick O'Keel at the Department of Energy to get those Lacrosse satellites surveying Baton Rouge and vicinities instead of Florida. By the time he'd finished his five-minute conversation with the secretary of energy, the analyst handed Bourdeaux an eleven-by-fourteen brown manila envelope stuffed with the digitized images Bill Clinton would need during his upcoming presidential address.

Thirty minutes later Robert Bourdeaux walked inside Goldberg's reception room. Kate Marston quickly stood. She wore her hair tied up in a bun behind her head, giving her a mature, yet elegant, look.

"Robert, we have to talk about—"

Holding the manila envelope, the DDO slowly shook his head. "Not now, Kate. Sorry. I have to brief Goldberg and the president in five minutes."

While she stood behind her desk, Bourdeaux put a hand to her face. "Tonight," he said. "I'll try not to be too late. Please?"

Nodding while pressing the intercom button and telling Goldberg that Bourdeaux had arrived, Kate Marston sat back down. "We must talk tonight. It's very important."

Bourdeaux went inside the office and wouldn't come out for two hours. By that time, Kate Marston had already gone home.

LAFAYETTE, LOUISIANA.

For Kevin Dalton the nightmare returned with formidable force. The smell of gunpowder and jet engine exhausts mixed with the sound of screaming children and women. He was alone in the middle of the Iraqi village, the MiG-29 zooming over the desert, low, menacing, its cannons alive with 30mm fire. He heard Khalela scream, heard her shout over the noise of the incoming jet. She was already inside the underground tunnel used by the villagers to escape Saddam Hussein's sporadic attacks. Kevin began to run in her direction, but a field of sugarcane suddenly blocked his view. The sweet smell of the cane as it was blown apart by the MiG's explosive rounds filled him as he struggled to find Khalela. But all he could hear now were her words, softly spoken, before fading away as the blaring sound of a nearing helicopter made him tremble with fear, but not because of the possibility of death. Kevin trembled at the sight of Khalela boarding the chopper and leaving him again.

Kevin Dalton ran as fast as his aching legs would go, but the muddy terrain of the sugarcane field slowed him down. He had to reach her, had to stop her from leaving him again.

"No . . . please . . . don't . . ."

Khalela Yishaid bolted up from the couch next to the double bed in the truck stop motel room five miles east of Lafayette. The driver had made the stop for diesel forty minutes after Kevin had passed out, and as much as Khalela had tried to awaken him, Kevin would not come around. It had been up to her to figure a way to get them to a safe place. So when the truck driver went into the diner, Khalela, covered head to toe in black, dried mud, had cut her brown pants into shorts. Her legs were clean. She had turned her shirt inside out and retied it over her waist, and then had made it to a nearby ladies' room outside the huge gas station. In a few minutes, she had washed the mud off her hair, face, and arms, making herself somewhat presentable to the motel clerk, whom Khalela paid cash for a two-night stay. Then had been the hard part: getting Kevin down from the truck. Fortunately, after fueling the truck, the driver had parked it between two eighteen-wheelers, making the five-minute ordeal of moving Kevin to the edge of the truck before slowly lowering him feetfirst over the concrete parking lot much less conspicuous. All the moving had half-awakened him, and he was able to walk to their room while hanging on to her. Stripping him to his undershorts, she had wiped his face, arms, and legs, carefully cleaning the wound using wet towels. Leaving him snoring in bed, Khalela had spent another ten minutes trying to reach Robert Bourdeaux. After passing her intelligence findings to the deputy director for operations—something she did not to help the CIA, but because she knew Mossad forces would not be able to act fast enough to take out Marcos before he fled the plantation—Khalela had taken a long, hot shower. She also washed her clothes, letting them dry under the bathroom's heat lamp for nearly an hour, before dressing and walking to the large roadside restaurant and souvenir shop, where she bought five large T-shirts, a bag full of junk food and soft drinks, some rubbing alcohol, and several two-packs of extra-strength Tylenol. She had used the alcohol to clean the cauterized wound before tearing one of the white T-shirts to wrap his upper thigh.

Khalela approached Kevin, messy brown hair over his forehead, full lips murmuring something. She placed a hand on his forehead. No fever.

"Please . . . no . . . Khalela . . . Khalela . . ."

Khalela walked to the bathroom, wet a clean towel, returned to his side, and lightly pressed it against his forehead and cheeks, before lowering the rag to Kevin's neck and upper chest, her mind torn between her professional training, which told her to leave him here and head back to Tel Aviv immediately, and her emotional side, which simply wanted to get in bed with him and hold him.

She had purposely left out their current location during her short conversation with Bourdeaux. She needed time to think about her next move and did not relish the thought of twenty American agents knocking on their door and taking them to some sterile room in a remote safe house. This way she not only remained in control of her own destiny but also got a chance to spend some time alone with the man who had just placed his own body in front of her to protect her from the bullets of Marcos's henchmen.

"Khal . . . no . . . Khale . . . Khalela . . ."

Khalela Yishaid stared at Kevin. He was slowly coming around.

"Khalela . . ."

Kevin's eyes flickered open before closing again. He did that for another minute before murmuring her name again.

"Yes, Kevin. I am here," she responded, rubbing the rag over his forehead again.

"Here . . . where?"

"At a motel near Lafayette."

"How long?"

"It's almost one in the afternoon. You've been out for about three hours."

Three hours? He bolted up, startling Khalela. "I have to call Langley. The . . ."

He felt light-headed. He had gotten up too fast and collapsed back in bed, still weak from the blood loss and the stress.

"Easy," Khalela said. "You have gone through a lot. You need to rest now."

Breathing heavily, Kevin looked at the wet, black hair, the light olive skin, the light green eyes staring back with a condescending, motherly look, as if he were incapable of taking care of himself.

Briefly inspecting his body, he suddenly realized he only wore his underpants. "Did you . . ."

She nodded. "You were filthy, but do not worry. I kept my eyes closed . . . most of the time."

Kevin laughed briefly, his eyes looking at the wound on his leg. "I suppose you did this too?"

"Yes. I am used to working on that leg."

Kevin sighed. A year ago, when Kevin had been wounded in the same leg by an Iraqi search party, Khalela had also cleaned and dressed the wound. "How did we get here?"

Khalela smiled and spoke without interruption for a few minutes. By the time she finished, Kevin's inquisitive gaze had changed to one of admiration for this beautiful woman.

"Thank you for saving my life back at the plantation."

Her eyes brightened at the compliment. "I'm the one who is grateful, Kevin. But you must stop using your body as a shield."

His face sobered at the thought of the termination team. "What were you doing there?"

Khalela told him everything she knew, including the phone conversation with Bourdeaux.

"You talked to Bob? When?"

"About thirty minutes ago."

His drooping eyes staring in the distance, Kevin said, "One bomb is headed for New York City and the other for Washington, D.C.?"

"Yes. I could not understand the destination of the third, but I did hear them state clearly that they had only three."

"Only three?" Kevin shook his head in disbelief. "Dear God! What do we do now?"

His question was met with silence. Kevin grimaced. He hated this profession. Here he was, half-naked in a hotel room with the woman he loved, and the farthest thing from his mind was embracing her. Two bombs were on their way to two of the most important cities in America, and he didn't have the faintest idea how to stop them.

"What are we *really* facing here, Khalela?" he asked as he stood, keeping most of his weight on his left leg while testing the strength of his bandaged leg. Slowly, he began to walk to the bathroom, the motel's blue sheets falling to his feet.

Kevin glanced back at her, her slanted eyes on him, lips pressed together, pointy chin high in the air. She sat on the couch while briefly shifting her gaze to the clouds through a crack in the curtains.

"Please, Khalela. I need to know."

Crossing her arms and cocking her head at him, she finally spoke; her voice was cold, her tone of voice strong. "The Russians have infiltrated your society more than you could ever imagine. They are everywhere, Kevin, and what is worse, they have made allegiances of convenience with the Arabs and with South American drug kings. Saddam Hussein and Marcos Dominguez are part of the glue that holds this huge network together. That is why I was ordered to Louisiana, to confirm Marcos's presence at the plantation and order a Mossad termination team into action. The team would have quietly eliminated everyone in the plantation twenty-four hours later. But that all fell apart the moment you showed up and the commotion started. Marcos is no fool, Kevin. He is probably halfway to Europe by now, and the weapons are on their way to their targets. We missed our chance."

The consequences of his action ripped through Kevin Dalton just as those bullets from the helicopters had carved a trench across the field of sugarcane.

"My God. What have I done?" Kevin closed his eyes and turned away from her, his hands clasping the doorframe that led to the small bathroom.

"It is not your fault, Kevin. Our government owes you a great deal for what you did a year ago in Iraq. This is why I was allowed to come and warn you."

But Kevin Dalton wasn't listening to her words any longer. In his mind he saw suffering, saw destruction, saw the bright flash of incinerating death that would descend on his people at the hand of Saddam Hussein. His ears rang with the final scream of millions of Americans as the cloud of vaporizing hell engulfed them. His heartbeat skyrocketing and his hands trembling as they held on to the wood molding, Kevin felt weak again, his mind flashing the same message over and over. *I am responsible! I am responsible!*

His legs gave, and Kevin began to fall, but a pair of arms reached out for him, holding him, embracing him, taking him back to the bed he wished to crawl under. Kevin felt her nearness, sensed the comfort of her body pressed against his back as he rested his head on a pillow, her hands running the length of his chest, her lips softly kissing the large bruise behind his neck, a thigh slowly wedging between his legs.

In the darkness Khalela and Kevin were two shadowy shapes, visible only by the narrow beam of sunlight filtering through a crack in the curtains. But for Kevin Dalton, former naval aviator, the dark figure behind him was the source of life and hope that slowly replenished his pained, guilt-ridden conscience. She was back at his side, loving him, caressing him, telling him that it was all right, that they would make it through.

Kevin closed his eyes and let it all go as he rolled over to face her, and their lips met, softly at first, a mere brush. In an instant the taste of her brought back coveted memories. But this was today, now, here. The woman he loved was back, her body pressed against him, the heat of her passion radiating toward him, his hands caressing her lower back, pulling down her shorts, feeling the light olive skin he had missed so much.

Their bodies came together in the dark, partners in a rapture Kevin prayed would never end. Fine fingers caressed his back, pressed his skin, forced him against her, time after time, second after second, her legs wrapped around his, moving with the same rhythm that Kevin could no longer control. His mind drained of all thought as her firm, shivering body took it all away, the guilt, the physical pain, the uncertainty of tomorrow. Khalela absorbed Kevin Dalton, taking him to a world of wondrous sensation, a place where he wished to live forever. But he felt the end coming and fought it, refusing to give in. He wished he could remain like this, away from the realities of a world filled with hatred, with pain, with betrayal. But the end came, and Kevin abandoned himself to the spiraling climax, shuddering as she arched her hips to meet him one last time, to be with him fully during this final moment of passion, before slowly cupping his face and giving him a soft, lingering kiss.

"I missed you, Kevin Dalton," she said, before slowly rolling over and backing herself against him.

Kevin embraced her glistening body from behind just as his eyelids grew heavier and his mind cloudier. Slowly, one hand caressing the satiny planes of her stomach and another snuggled between her breasts, Kevin fell asleep.

OUTSIDE TIKRIT, NORTHERN IRAQ.

Under a crystalline blanket of stars, Donald Bane dragged himself plus his extra twenty pounds to the edge of the clearing on the side of the high cliff. It overlooked the safe house five hundred feet below, by the shores of the River Tigris, just outside Tikrit, exactly where the captured pilot had confessed it would be. He pressed the rubber ends of a pair of night vision field binoculars to his eyes while flipping the ON switch with an index finger.

Darkness gave way to a palette of green hues as the binoculars' image intensifier system enhanced the light reflected by very dimly illuminated objects. In a second, Bane clearly saw the stone structure where Saddam was alledgedly assembling nukes. The house, thirty feet wide by roughly ten deep before it disappeared into the side of the hill, only had one entrance, located in the front. The roof was covered with the same sand and rocks of the surrounding hills to make it less obvious from the air, certainly good enough to hide it from American spy satellites. Bane had seen three cars come and go. Two had been army Jeeps, the last an open truck. The place had been quiet since.

Shifting the binoculars to the right of the safe house, Bane focused on a pair of weathered army Jeeps and one truck, all hidden under a canopy painted desert brown. A dirt road running in front of the house disappeared in the darkness, leading directly to the city, roughly two miles away. *Tikrit.*

Setting the binoculars down, the CIA officer rubbed his eyes, yawned, and shivered. He was freezing his ass off while André Boyabat sat quietly near the front of their Rover four-wheel-drive vehicle, parked twenty feet away under a ledge. The Turk appeared to be immune to the weather and to the food that had already given Bane a mild case of diarrhea.

They had crossed into Iraq at a desolated spot south of Zakho, a border town. Using maps and a Global Positioning System handheld unit, they had arrived at this location two hours ago.

Bane was simply exhausted after the nonstop chase from Moscow . . . *how many days?*

He shook his head. Too many fucking days, and from the looks of it he wasn't about to get any rest anytime soon. Using the portable satellite communications gear, he had already contacted Bourdeaux and provided him with the coordinates of the place in case they wanted to blow it away before Bane confirmed the captured pilot's data with his surveillance gear, which so far had proved useless because everyone who had approached the place so far had kept his mouth shut. André's Arabic had not been put to the test yet, but when it was, Bane hoped it would be good enough to piece together—from the conversations Bane planned to record on the miniature tape recorder connected to the parabolic antenna by his side—the proof they needed to finally confirm the site and get the hell out of here.

As he brought the binoculars up to his eyes once again, Bane silently swore to stay in Iraq not one second longer than required to assure the elimination of Saddam's nuclear hardware. Then it was *adiós* to this shithole and back to the U.S.A.

Bane slightly nodded. *Only an asshole would be out here tonight, in the middle of no-fucking-where in freezing weather.*

Moving up the lapels of the cheap coat André had picked up for him at a bazaar by the border, Bane cursed the camel hair, which didn't keep him warm enough but gave him a rash around his neck. Reaching up with his right hand, he scratched behind his neck.

"What is wrong, my friend?" asked the thin-lipped André, taking out a lighter and a pack of cigarettes from a pocket in his leather jacket. He pulled a cigarette out with his lips and lit it, while keeping his free hand covering the lighter. Although he was not in plain view of the safe house a half mile below, he didn't want to risk someone spotting the glow in the darkness.

Rubbing his big hands close to his face while blowing warm air into them, Bane said, "I'm really too old to be doing this shit."

The Turk's brows arched over his dark eyes as he regarded the CIA officer with amused curiosity. "But this is our job, my friend. This is what we do."

"Wrong, pal. This is what I *used* to do, and believe me, I've done enough of it to last me twenty lifetimes. I'm tired of it."

Dragging at the cigarette, André Boyabat looked up at the twinkling stars of the Mesopotamian sky. "This is very peaceful."

"And very fucking cold."

André contemplated Donald Bane through the wreathing cigarette smoke. "Saddam Hussein was born down there, you know?"

"Who gives a shit? I just wanna get rid of his nukes, and I wouldn't mind also getting rid of the bastard if I could get my hands on him."

"That city is almost sacred to him," André continued, ignoring Bane's comment. "He holds it with such great affection, that most of his chieftains also come from Tikrit." The Turk pulled on the cigarette.

"Yo, André," Bane said, waving a hand at the Turk. "Save the history lesson for your students. I don't give a shit about Saddam and his past."

"But you see, that is the very reason why you Americans have been unable to defeat him."

That comment finally hooked Bane's attention. "What do you mean?"

Giving Bane a fatherly grin, the historian moved his hands in front of him as he spoke. "You must go beyond the caricature of 'the Butcher of

Baghdad' to understand how Saddam Hussein thinks. You must come here, to Tikrit, the place where it all started, and see the world through the same eyes that the young Saddam saw it back in the forties."

Bane slowly turned and gave the glowing city lining the dusky horizon a quick glance. "Doesn't look so special from over here. Just another city full of ragheads."

Shaking his head while taking his last drag, the Turk crushed the cigarette against a rock. "There is a lot of history in that city, my friend. Back in the year 1394, the Tartar hordes of Tamerlane swept across this land, butchering, raping, and looting. It is here, in Tikrit, that Tamerlane had his men build a pyramid with the skulls of his victims."

Bane cocked his head at the Turk historian. "A pyramid of skulls?"

"It is in all the history books, my friend. Look it up yourself. But the reason why Tamerlane chose Tikrit as the place to erect this monument of his evil ferocity was not accidental. You see, a small group of independent Arabs manned a formidable fortress here—in fact its remains are still here, higher up on this very mountain. These Tikritis had defied all invaders, including Tamerlane. So after the Mongol conqueror swept over the city and the fortress, he ordered his men to erect such a macabre monument to show the world how he dealt with those who dared challenge him.

"And even before Tamerlane's time, back in 1137, Tikrit was also the birthplace of Salah al-Din, or Saladin, as he is called in the West. Saladin was the legendary Kurd who defeated the Crusaders—particularly Richard the Lion-Hearted—and liberated Jerusalem from Christian rule. Do you see now why Saddam considers this place almost holy? The Tikritis have always been men of courage, or as you would say, 'men with guts.' These were people who defied even the largest and most powerful of enemies, regardless of the consequences. It was the Tikritis that defied Tamerlane, even at the price of dying what must have been horrifying deaths. It was Saladin who defied and defeated the powerful Crusaders. It was Saddam Hussein who defied all the armies of the world in 1991. Saddam sees the mere fact that he was born here as prophetic. He sees himself as the next Saladin, who must defeat the West, the Christians, to ensure the survival of the Muslim world."

"But that alone doesn't explain why the man's always trying to be such a pain in the ass," replied Bane. "These Tikritian ragheads were just trying to defend their homes from Tamerlane or the Crusaders. They weren't looking to start shit just for the hell of it, as Saddam did in '91."

"That is not totally true. You see, Saddam thinks the West is out to get him. He thinks Clinton, like Bush before him, is trying to have him assassinated, ousted from office. He views the West as another Tamerlane coming to destroy his land," André said. "In his mind he truly believes his home is being threatened. He wanted—and still wants—Kuwait because the small country would have given him significant control in the oil market, thereby making him more powerful and less likely to be threatened by his enemies.

"Now, this feeling of constant paranoia about the possibility of being assassinated not only by the West, but also by his most trusted officers, goes back to his childhood, to Tikrit. You see, Saddam's parents were quite poor. His father died before Saddam was born, and his mother, who could not support the orphan, left him in the care of her brother, Khairallah Talfah, a passionate Arab nationalist and army officer. Saddam's uncle became his role model during his formative years. Unfortunately, when Saddam was only six years old, Khairallah participated in an ill-fated uprising and was sentenced to jail for five years. Saddam was shipped back to his mother, who by that time had already married Hasan Ibrahim, a brother of Saddam's late father. They lived in al-Shawish, where Saddam was often mocked for being fatherless. Without friends, he was confined to a lonely existence. His stepfather amused himself by humiliating the young boy. Using an asphalt-covered stick, Hasan forced Saddam to dance and dodge the blows. He also sent Saddam to steal for him. Saddam got caught once and wound up spending some time at a juvenile detention center. These events had a traumatic effect on the young boy, forcing him to become totally self-reliant. By the time he returned to Tikrit at the age of eleven, shortly after Khairallah's release from prison, Saddam already felt the need to intimidate others to avoid being seen as prey again. Back in Tikrit, under the protection of Khairallah, Saddam enrolled in school and began to build up his self-esteem, but in his thoughts he always carried the fear of becoming a victim. Through his studies, Saddam became aware of the history behind this place, and he began to see himself as the savior of Islam in a world filled with Christians. In a way, you might think of Saddam Hussein as the son of two fathers. Hasan made him see the world as a hostile place, where everyone was out to get him, where he could trust no one. Hasan gave him the paranoia that has actually kept Saddam alive all these years. But his experience with Hasan alone would not have been enough to get Saddam to where he is today. The wealthy and well-connected Khairallah provided the avenue for Saddam Hussein to gain an education, to leave the peasant life in al-Shawish, move to Tikrit and eventually to Baghdad, where he joined the Ba'ath Party at the age of twenty. In Baghdad, his overriding insecurity and paranoia over being victimized propelled him to the very top of his party and eventually to the presidency. And it all started over there, in Tikrit."

Bane leaned back down, putting both hands behind his head as he looked straight up at the stars. "Sounds as if you admire the bastard. Maybe you ought to join this Ba'ath Party yourself. I still see him for the motherfucker he is. I wouldn't piss on the asshole if he was on fire."

"Make no mistake. I do not admire this man," André said in a harsh, yet low tone of voice.

Bane sat back up and looked at the Turk, whose nostrils expanded and contracted with every heavy breath. He was obviously upset at Bane's comment.

"You never asked me why I do what I do," said André.

Bane shrugged. "I usually make it my business to know what motivates my agents. But in your case, Bourdeaux said you were to be trusted. That was enough for me. I apologize for my remark, though. I just can't stand the bastard, and you painted him a little too human for my taste."

"I used to teach history at the university in Istanbul many years ago," André said, taking a deep breath while lifting his face to the sky. "One day, a visiting professor from Baghdad held a series of seminars on Iraqi history at our campus. Her name was Labha Qammadi, and it didn't take long for us to fall in love. I followed her to Baghdad, where we were married, and I began teaching at the university there. Labha also taught history there, but she also traveled to the countryside to teach the peasants. Then one day my Labha is taken away by the *Mukhabarat.* I asked why and no one would tell me. I go to the dean of history, and he tells me nothing. I go to the military, and they tell me nothing. I go to the Turkish embassy in Baghdad, and they tell me I must stop asking questions and concentrate on my teachings at the university or risk imprisonment for being associated with a supporter of the Kurdish resistance. *My Labha a Kurdish sympathizer?* I refused to believe such lies! I demanded to speak with the ambassador. It was then that I found out the truth from the Turkish ambassador in Baghdad. It turned out that in her travels my Labha made the mistake of visiting a few Kurdish villages and was labeled as a sympathizer. That was all the information the *Mukhabarat* needed to take her away and do horrible things to her."

André lowered his gaze, a tight fist pressed against his chin. "I never knew what became of my Labha. She simply vanished, and I was about to return to Turkey when Robert Bourdeaux approached me in 1988 at a historian's convention in Basra. It turned out that he knew quite a bit of Middle East history himself, and he used that as a cover to recruit spies for the CIA. With the knowledge that the *Mukhabarat* would torture me in unheard-of ways if caught, I started spying for the Americans soon after. You see, my friend, I had nothing to lose. Saddam, in his relentless paranoia to purge everyone that gave off even the smallest smell of trouble, had already taken away my reason for living. During the Gulf War, I stayed in Baghdad and provided your government with valuable insight on the situation here. Afterward, I went to your Camp Peary, in Virginia and—"

"You've been to The Farm?"

The Turk nodded. "I needed formal training to help me survive after I was labeled a spy by the *Mukhabarat,* following the closing days of the Gulf War. Somehow they figured out my scheme for contacting the Americans by the Saudi border and almost captured me. But I managed to escape south through the confusion that followed the end of the ground war. Bourdeaux made the necessary arrangements for my training, and then I was deployed to work underground in both Turkey and northern Iraq."

"That's quite a story," said Bane.

"It is my story, and it should tell you how I feel about Saddam Hussein."

"My apologies again, André," Bane said.

The Turk silently accepted them before lying down and closing his eyes. Bane could hear his steady breathing after a few minutes, wishing he could fall asleep as easily. But he could never get himself to do it while in the field. The fear of getting caught with his pants down taking a nap kept his eyelids fully open, his senses tuned to the surroundings, and his mind alert and frosty. But he could only keep this up for so long, and he felt he was reaching the end of the road here. Perhaps after André woke up, Bane might be able to sleep some, just as he had done after leaving Istanbul.

Looking back at the city in the distance, Bane thought about André's words. *A pyramid of skulls!* That seemed a bit too farfetched, *but given the right number of victims and the necessary evil and warped imagination to do it, who knows?*

Bane felt Saddam Hussein could do it. Closing his eyes, he pictured the Iraqi leader standing atop a mountain of American skulls. Nothing would give that tyrant more pleasure than having CNN broadcast such a sight to the entire world. If there was ever a drop of humanity mixed with the picture of Saddam Hussein in Bane's mind, it quickly evaporated as the Iraqi leader stood smiling and waving to a crowd of maddened Iraqis atop his mountain of skulls. And the thought suddenly struck Bane: Saddam Hussein was no Saladin. Saddam Hussein was a modern day Tamerlane. The Iraqi dictator was the ruthless murderer that the Tikritis themselves had defied; someone so evil that he ranked alongside Adolf Hitler and Joseph Stalin. Yet someone who had an apparent weakness: His love for Tikrit, his hometown.

As he pressed the binoculars against his eyes and looked not at the safe house but at the outskirts of the city, Bane wondered how he could use this weakness to get to Saddam Hussein.

André began to snore. Bane turned in his direction. The Turk lay on his back, under the Rover's bumper, his head propped up by a blanket. It struck Bane as quite ironic that the reason why André joined the espionage game was because he'd lost his wife, while Bane lost Jessica *because* he joined the espionage game. And as much as he wanted to hate Jessica for leaving him, Donald Bane knew he had no one to blame but himself. He had been the one who had blown the marriage. He had been the one who made her waste the best years of her life alone, waiting for him to come home. He had been the one who kept resisting having kids because kids would interfere with his work. He had been the one who had literally abandoned her night after night, weekend after weekend, until she finally called it quits. Until the day Bane returned home from a two-week surveillance job and found his apartment empty. She had taken everything, except for his clothes, an envelope stuffed with divorce papers on the kitchen counter, and a handwritten note.

Reaching for his wallet, Bane opened it and pulled out a folded, yellow piece of paper. He stared at the handwriting of the woman he had lost; he thought about the life he had thrown away to play the intelligence game.

Was it all worth it?

Bane usually avoided this question because he knew the answer all too well, and the realization that he had fucked up his life by losing the one good thing that had ever happened to him always resulted in tears filling his dark eyes.

As he thought of this, a cold gust of wind swept over the hillside, making Bane shiver and reach for the lapels of his cheap jacket. As he cursed his luck and scratched his neck, another voice came alive inside him, repeating the same phrase Bane had heard since given the assignment to meet with Krasilov: *I'm too old for this shit!*

13

SEMTEX

Thou shalt not hate thy brother in thy heart.
—The Bible, Leviticus 19:17

JERSEY CITY, NEW JERSEY.

In the early afternoon hours, a Chrysler minivan with dark-tinted windows slowly drove up to the front of Sheikh Imman al-Barakah's mosque. Two men stood guard inside the mosque and another in the two-story brick building. The sheikh, whose living quarters occupied over half of the reinforced basement under the mosque, was not there but on his way to Dulles International Airport—with a three-man FBI tail.

The minivan came to a stop in front of the brick building. After setting the hand brake, the driver stepped out into the street and locked the minivan's doors. He had done this once before at an underground parking garage not so long ago. Over six hundred pounds of Semtex, laced with gold-plated nickel wire, loaded in specially designed cardboard boxes, and carefully stacked in the rear of the van, had been connected to a triggering device made out of a pressure switch underneath the vehicle.

The driver pulled out an ice pick and quickly went around the van, puncturing a small hole in each tire. Fast-walking down the dark street, the driver hurried to turn the corner, just as a dozen FBI agents, who were running the day shift of the surveillance job on the suspect mosque, realized that they were looking at a possible car bomb. One of the sheikh's bodyguards, who happened to be looking out the window, also noticed the minivan and the driver's behavior before disappearing around the corner.

Thirty seconds later, the copper contacts closed. The earth-rumbling explosion shook Jersey City as the powerful shaped charge detonated, igniting into a massive fireball that pulverized every building within a hundred yards, including the mosque, the living quarters, and the apartment building where the FBI team operated. Over three hundred residents perished, including the FBI team and many of the sheikh's bodyguards.

* * *

Just five hours after the assault, while the police, the fire department, the FBI, and two dozen ambulances still worked the scene at the demolished mosque, a Delta Airlines maintenance crew member at La Guardia Airport in New York pulled a heavy aluminum cart down the aisle of a Boeing 727, scheduled for departure in forty-five minutes. His name tag said Pedro Sanchez, but that was not the name the tall, skinny native of Lebanon had been born under. Pedro Sanchez was the name under which he operated for the benefit of Saddam Hussein, who had pulled him out of the violent streets of Beirut five years ago and sent him to the United States, where he had been fed, clothed, and trained for the sole purpose of serving Saddam's version of an Islamic world.

Sanchez checked his watch and stopped halfway down the aisle, by Row 24. Looking behind him, he verified that he was alone. The cleanup crew had already left the plane, and Sanchez had been called in to fix a leaky faucet in one of the two aft lavatories. Another disciple of Saddam Hussein, traveling in this airplane from Boston, had purposely twisted the thin spout of the lavatory sink until it separated from the gasket, inducing a leak he had pointed out to the flight attendants prior to landing thirty minutes ago.

Leaning down, Sanchez removed a small leather bag left under Seat 24C by the same traveler from Boston. Since many of the passengers on this flight, which originated in Boston, with stops in New York City and Orlando, were ticketed all the way to Orlando, flight attendants expected to see carry-on luggage left in the plane as passengers went inside the terminal to stretch their legs while the maintenance crew looked into the "mechanical problem."

Sanchez set the bag on the floor and opened it. While looking toward the front of the plane to make sure no one saw him, Sanchez removed the battery cover of a Sony Walkman, pulled out the thin wires soldered to the AA batteries, and connected them to the exposed gold-plated nickel wire lacing three pounds of Semtex. The thin strips of plastic explosive were not only sandwiched between sheets of dark plastic lining the leather bag, but they were also wrapped with a cheesecloth material to keep the Semtex at its optimum humidity level.

Sanchez checked his watch again and turned on the Walkman, leaving the volume all the way down before closing the bag and setting it exactly where he had found it. Seat 24C had been paid for all the way to Orlando.

Sanchez fixed the leaky faucet in ten minutes and headed for the front of the plane just as two flight attendants, a gorgeous brunette and a middle-aged blonde, walked down the aisle.

"All set?" asked the blonde.

"Yes, *señorita,*" replied Sanchez in the Hispanic accent he had learned to fake to near-perfection, before moving to the front of the 727 and exiting through the service and maintenance entrance.

*   *   *

Thirty minutes later, Sheikh Imman al-Barakah sat on seat 23C of Delta Flight 847, headed for Orlando. He no longer wore a beard. His face, darkened with makeup to blend his pale cheeks with the rest of his tanned face, was wrinkled with age. Wearing a pair of loose slacks, a polo shirt, a baseball cap, and white sneakers, he looked like any other senior citizen on his way to Florida to escape the New England winter.

Buckling up and redirecting the overhead air vent to his face, the sheikh leaned his head against the headrest and closed his eyes. His mind was in turmoil over the commotion of the past few days. According to a message he received from Marcos, because of the increased FBI activity, Saddam Hussein had requested the sheikh to move south, to central Florida, where he could spend a few weeks in hiding before leaving the country. Saddam Hussein had a new assignment for the sheikh in Baghdad.

An FBI special agent took his seat in First Class, while his two assistants sat seven rows in front and eight rows behind the unsuspecting sheikh. A call had already been made to Palenski about the sheikh's sudden departure. The director had ordered surveillance teams in Orlando to get ready to tail the sheikh after he deplaned. There was a good chance that the sheikh would lead the FBI straight to the smuggled nuclear hardware.

The whine of the engines grew as the jet left the terminal and taxied to the runway. The 727 accelerated down the runway and took off. The barometric sensor housed inside the Walkman, made from a plastic disk which had been machined to form a hollow core, had a thin rubber membrane secured over the open end of the disk. Copper contacts had been inserted on the inside of the rubber membrane and all the way through the plastic disk. As Delta Flight 847 began to gain altitude, the change in air pressure inside the cabin slowly depressed the rubber membrane, bringing the two copper contacts closer together.

The moment the plane reached thirty thousand feet, enough pressure was applied to the rubber membrane to push the copper contacts together, closing the circuit, and allowing the flow of current from the two AA batteries to the triggering device, which took an additional thirty seconds to charge up before releasing a very short but intense voltage spike onto the gold-plated nickel wire lacing the Semtex.

Just as Sheikh Imman al-Barakah forced a yawn to clear up his ear canals from the steady change in air pressure inside the cabin, the Semtex detonated with metal-ripping force, engulfing the passengers in rows twenty through twenty-seven in a cloud of shrapnel from the disintegrating seat 24C. The rapidly expanding shock wave reached the 727's ceiling, exceeding the maximum rated stress of the aluminum skin of the Boeing design.

Although the initial blast was only strong enough to puncture a hole slightly larger than the size of a dime, the large pressure differential rapidly expanded the initial opening, much in the same way a puncture hole in the rubber skin of an inflated balloon expands as the balloon bursts.

But unlike a bursting balloon—and most fortunately for the majority of the passengers of Flight 847—the aluminum frame of the Boeing jet held the rapidly expanding hole to just over six feet in diameter before the air pressure reached equilibrium.

As oxygen masks automatically dropped from overhead compartments, a severely wounded but still alive Sheikh Imman al-Barakah, along with four other passengers and the brunette flight attendant, were sucked out of the plane before anyone could react. The blond flight attendant, who had been pushing a cocktail cart near Row 15, almost joined her coworker, had it not been for one of the FBI agents sitting in Row 17, who managed to grab her by the ankles and pull her down over his lap.

In the cockpit, alarms blared as the captain dropped the Boeing's nose and brought his jet below ten thousand feet while radioing Dulles, the closest airport, requesting an emergency landing, which he successfully executed five minutes later.

One at a time the passengers of Flight 847 slid down the inflatable escape slide and into the expert hands of Dulles's emergency evacuation personnel, who hauled noninjured passengers into a bus and the wounded into waiting ambulances for their short trip to Georgetown University Hospital or D.C. General.

As the initial commotion subsided and the cameras of the press left the scene trailing the bus and an army of ambulances, another team arrived inside three unmarked dark blue vans. Men and women dressed in blue slacks and sporting blue jackets with the words "FBI" written in white across their backs left the vehicles carrying dark suitcases. These were the world's foremost experts in bomb-construction technology. These were members of the FBI's Explosives Laboratory, and in less than twelve hours they would comb through the Boeing 727 and gather enough evidence to determine the way the bomb was constructed.

FBI HEADQUARTERS, WASHINGTON, D.C.

In his high-security suite at the J. Edgar Hoover Building, FBI Director Roman Palenski wondered why in the hell all this shit had to happen on his watch. His record had been pristine since becoming head of the Bureau six months ago, and he believed it was due to his management style, which gave field agents total freedom of action. Palenski had figured that the criminals already *had* total freedom of action. Restricting his agents' ability to fight back was essentially making them easy targets for the scum the FBI had to shovel out of the way to keep America peaceful.

But the reports arriving on his desk from all over the country showed a different story. There was chaos rapidly developing in the United States.

The growing number of terrorist attacks had sent the population into a frenzy, and Palenski, with all his agents focused on fighting this huge wave of terrorism resulting from the nuclear detonation in Iraq, felt impotent to do more than what he was already doing. To make matters worse, one of his best leads in the ongoing investigation had just gone up in smoke. Sheikh Imman al-Barakah had perished in the bombing aboard the Delta flight, and his mosque had been vaporized by another terrorist bomb, not only breaking the link in the chain that Palenski hoped would lead him to the nukes, but also adding a new level of complexity to this insane game: terrorists were apparently fighting terrorists on American soil, and the citizens of this country were getting caught in the cross fire. He had spent ten minutes on the phone listening to one of his foremost experts on the subject of the Arab terrorist mind, and the director had obtained a couple of theories that attempted to explain this new terrorist behavior. The first theory went along the path that terrorists, like the members of any other organized group, were quite territorial. When two different factions found themselves fighting on the same piece of land, there was a strong possibility that a conflict could develop. One group's actions could interfere with another group's planned missions, creating tension between the groups. This tension could escalate to open warfare between the groups for the purpose of gaining control of a territory, just like city gangs or Mafia rings. Another explanation employed the concept of expendability. The old sheikh had done his job, had trained and deployed soldiers as ordered by a higher authority, like Saddam Hussein, and now that the FBI was closing the noose around the sheikh, the higher authority thought it best to remove the link in the chain. The sheikh had been expendable and he had been removed. Period.

Palenski's tired eyes wandered around the suite, known inside the Bureau as mahogany row because of its wood paneling. As his mind struggled to find an answer, an explanation—something that might help his team crack down on the smugglers—his eyes simply moved from bookshelf to bookshelf.

He sighed. Whatever the explanation, one thing was for certain: the dam was bursting, and all it needed was a final blow to send the nation into anarchy. He had made this clear to President Clinton, who put the armed forces on immediate alert in case he had to impose martial law to regain control of the streets.

Seven hours had passed since Bourdeaux had called Palenski with the news that Marcos Dominguez had been assembling nuclear bombs in Louisiana. Three hours had passed since the Department of Energy had informed the Bureau that two satellites had detected an unusual amount of radioactive material just outside Baton Rouge, at the same plantation that the Mossad operative had identified. One hour had passed since DOE Secretary Patrick O'Keel had called Palenski to inform him that the most recent satellite pass over the area indicated that the level of radioactive material had substantially dropped. But some hardware still remained inside the large house. He had urged Palenski to be cautious.

The report in Palenski's hands outlined the current strike plan of the team deployed outside Baton Rouge to storm the plantation. Palenski didn't expect to find Marcos in the mansion. He didn't even expect to find a bomb, but just the leftover hardware—the radioactive material detected by the Lacrosse satellites. Seven hours was more than ample time for the legendary terrorist to vanish, but probably not long enough for Marcos to fully sanitize the place before leaving. Palenski hoped his team would find at least one clue to Marcos's or the bombs' whereabouts.

14

THE DREADED EVENT

When the Trumpet sounds a single blast; when earth with all its mountains is raised high and with one mighty crash is shattered into dust—on that day the Dreaded Event will come to pass.

—The Koran 69:15

OUTSIDE BATON ROUGE, LOUISIANA.

At the edge of the sugarcane plantation outside Baton Rouge, across from the Mississippi, the FBI special agent in charge did not like the way things were going this afternoon. After spending twenty years in the Miami resident agency before his current assignment to head the New Orleans Field Office, the veteran agent had gained a sixth sense for smelling trouble, and the odor emanating from the plantation made him nauseous. Although the order had come directly from Roman Palenski himself, the SAC still didn't feel comfortable with the situation developing in front of him. The word was out among the FBI ranks that as recently as seven hours ago, Marcos Eduardo Dominguez had been assembling three nuclear bombs on that plantation. That information alone had been reason enough to deploy all available agents from the Baton Rouge, Lafayette, Shreveport, and Alexandria resident agencies and from the New Orleans Field Office, which was over twenty times the size of the resident agencies.

In all, nearly one hundred agents had circled the plantation for the past two hours, along with dozens of deputies from the Louisiana State Police, who had informed the FBI of the helicopter accident and the recent shooting in the plantation, which, according to the Baton Rouge Police, had been blamed on an attempt to steal very expensive helicopters used for crop-dusting the sugarcane fields.

Without spending any time issuing warnings, two heavily armed FBI teams of twenty men each approached the mansion at the far end of the plantation, one from the east, the other from the north. Sharpshooters hid in the trees on the opposite bank of the Mississippi to cover the rear of the mansion. The SAC didn't feel like taking any chances. He would deal with this problem in the only way he knew how: with an overwhelming use of force. It wasn't going to be pretty, but it would get the job done.

A second set of teams followed the first as backup a hundred feet behind. In all, eighty armed agents, dressed in black uniforms with the letters FBI stenciled in white across their backs, closed in on a mansion that so far appeared to be abandoned—aside from the nuclear hardware detected by the most recent satellite pass. Three Nuclear Regulatory Commission vans packed with radiation-proof suits and Geiger counters stood fifty feet away from the SAC. The bulky suits would be distributed as soon as the plantation was secured. Right now only the team scheduled to break into the place wore skintight versions of the suit—courtesy of the Nuclear Regulatory Commission. The rest of the team was forbidden from entering the mansion until an NRC team on standby near the van could go inside the antebellum house and take actual measurements.

With his eyes focused on the seasoned teams and his ears listening to the conversation over the mission frequency, which linked all agents on the ground together, the SAC silently prayed nothing went wrong.

Inside the mansion, Amal Saffah prayed to Allah for the strength to pull the trigger. In front of him was an old, paperback copy of the Koran, which his brother Walid read out loud.

Three days ago, Amal and Walid had received a phone call from the Iraqi ambassador to the U.N., who had ordered them here from their dorm at Louisiana State University in Baton Rouge. Amal and Walid were both graduate students in physics at the university, and today they would prove themselves worthy of entering Allah's kingdom. The infidels would die today.

The brothers were ready. In fact, they had been ready for a very, very long time. Since their parents had perished at the hands of the Americans during the War of 1991, Amal and Walid had been ready to avenge their deaths.

Amal felt fortunate that he and his brother had been selected on this steamy Louisiana afternoon to be the instrument of justice of Saddam Hussein, a man who had confronted and defeated all the armies of the world, a man who stood as a living example of what a Muslim could achieve with enough determination and a little help from Allah.

Amal listened to the voice of his brother Walid as he read the Koran. Amal lost himself in the Word of Allah, as revealed to the Prophet Muhammed by Angel Gabriel fourteen hundred years ago.

In the middle of the second story loft, kneeling in front of the backpack, his right hand clutching the pistol attached to a stainless steel tube connected to the main bomb assembly, Amal raised his left hand to the Heaven his soul would soon reach, tears filling his eyes.

"None but the perverse turn away from the true faith," Walid read, tears rolling down the sides of his young face. He was only twenty years of age. Amal was twenty-one. "Perish the liars, who dwell in darkness and are heedless of the life to come!

" 'When will the Day of Judgment be?' they ask. On that day they shall be scourged in the fire, and a voice will say to them: 'Taste this, the punishment which you have thought to hasten! The righteous shall dwell amidst gardens and fountains, and shall receive what their Lord will give them.' "

Amal's index finger began to apply pressure on the trigger as his ears discerned noise outside. But he would not stand. They both had been instructed by Kemal Ramallah to remain low, out of sight from all windows, where they could fall victims to the bullets of a sniper before being able to carry out their holy mission.

Let them get near, Amal. Let infidels come and meet their destiny!

A noise downstairs. Broken glass, followed by footsteps on the oak floors.

Amal Saffah looked into the tanned face of his younger brother one final time before closing his eyes and pulling the trigger.

Perish the liars, who dwell in darkness and are heedless of the life to come!

The slug of enriched uranium struck the neutron initiator with a velocity of nearly one thousand feet per second. Made of beryllium and buried at the center of the sphere of uranium 235, the neutron initiator released a single neutron into the two-kilogram mass of radioactive material surrounding it. The neutron struck its first uranium atom with a force large enough to split it. The fission, or splitting of the uranium atom, caused the uranium atom to release two neutrons, as well as energy in the form of heat and light. The free neutrons struck two other uranium atoms, causing further fission, which resulted in the release of four neutrons, more light, and more heat. The chain reaction continued at lightning speed, striking neighboring atoms and releasing more and more light and heat. Some neutrons missed their uranium atom targets and attempted to escape the sphere, but were reflected by the enclosing shell of graphite and gold, which acted as a tamper device or nuclear reflector. The maverick neutrons bounced back into the uranium mass and finally found targets, maximizing the efficiency of the chain reaction, which took just under one-hundredth of a second to absorb the entire mass, releasing the equivalent heat and light of an explosion of forty thousand tons of TNT, twice the size of the one that leveled Hiroshima.

The blast vaporized all of the FBI agents and police officers in the area as the expanding fireball covered the entire plantation in the first two-tenths of a second. In another half a second, most of central and western Baton Rouge had been incinerated as temperatures across the capital of Louisiana rocketed past two thousand degrees Celsius. Birds ignited in midair, crackled, and vaporized. On the streets of Baton Rouge, pedestrians were burned to a cinder, the fireball flashing their photograph on the charred sidewalks. Automobiles turned into high-temperature ovens, carbonizing their passengers, all of whom shrank in size as their viscera boiled away in the intense thermal energy. Farther out, in the suburbs, the flash heated all exposed human flesh to just over 150 degrees Celsius for a fraction of a second, leaving its victims burned and severely blistered, but alive. By the time the initial flash ended after one second, there were no creatures or vegetation—on land or in water—alive within two miles of Ground Zero. Ships and barges cruising the boiling Mississippi or docked at nearby Port Allen were either on fire or sinking as their steel hulls turned liquid for a few seconds before solidifying again into a new shape. The shock wave that followed the initial explosion swept away from the hypocenter at over three miles per second for the first five hundred yards, leveling every single structure in its path, before slowing down to the speed of sound, destroying most houses and a large percentage of the buildings within a four-mile radius, and breaking the windows of houses as far as ten miles away. Small boats were lifted right off the water two miles away from Ground Zero and thrown onto land. The afternoon traffic on Interstate 10 simply ceased to exist a mile on either side of the blast. At two miles, charred vehicles held carbonized passengers. At three miles away, cars caught fire and were turned in every direction or flipped upside down, the wounded crawling out of their vehicles, some partially blinded from having looked directly at the flash, others on fire, and others simply in shock. Surviving motorists four miles away got to see the rising mushroom cloud with the shaft of debris and smoke hovering over where the city had been twenty seconds before, but most of them would die within the next twenty-four hours from their burns or from radiation sickness caused by the lethal gamma rays pounding their living tissue. At ten miles out motorists stopped their cars and got out to see the cloud, alive with streaks of yellow and red, reaching an altitude of almost six thousand feet, which, in the flatlands of southern Louisiana, would make it quite visible for many miles around.

In the parking lot of the Church of St. George in east Baton Rouge, a Catholic priest lay by a warm pool of bloody water and vomit. Dazed, hurt, confused, wondering how his surroundings had changed so abruptly in one instant, he turned to the sky and gazed at the crimson cloud menacing the demolished city. Billowing fires spewed orange-and-yellow flames near the interstate, a few blocks away. Vehicles burned on the crowded highway, on the mall's parking lot across the interstate, on the access roads. Buildings crumbled away, changing into avenues of rubble, of smoke, of debris.

He slowly sat up. The vision of burning vehicles on the interstate and the crumbling building on the other side of the wide highway added to his confusion. He had never been able to see the interstate from the church's parking lot. The trees had always blocked the view—*the trees!*

The narrow forest that separated the church's grounds from the highway had been leveled. Several pines had been uprooted and thrown over the traffic, fueling the inferno, creating whirling clouds of black smoke.

The priest felt the intense heat, wondered how he had survived this . . . this apocalyptic madness. Turning around he understood. He remembered now. The funeral. He had been giving a sermon by the memorial wall on the south side of the church. The granite wall. Fifteen feet tall. He had been right next to it while addressing his parishioners . . .

His glaring eyes studied the wall, still intact, unlike the leveled church, which had been turned into a mountain of glass, wood, concrete, and twisted steel beams. Only the large steel cross next to the building still stood, albeit leaning slightly in the direction of the shock wave that had destroyed this society.

Shirtless, and with his pants torn below the knees, the priest began to walk toward the interstate, but he tripped on something and fell headfirst into another puddle of reddish water. Turning around he discovered, to his horror, that he had tripped over a man's head, a parishioner, someone who had stood just ten feet from him a minute ago.

"I'm sorry . . ." he apologized to the dead man, whose dead, glassy eyes stared at the boiling clouds of dust. "Oh, God, I am so sorry. I am sorry."

The wind carried the cries of the wounded. The priest slowly became more and more aware of the new landscape. Much had changed, but he staggered up and began to look for survivors among the dozens of parishioners spread across the parking lot.

He found no one alive at the church. He could barely recognize fewer than half of them. Their swollen heads, their burned hair, their nakedness . . .

He heard an agonizing scream through the smoking rubble, beyond the fallen trees. Another scream pierced the afternoon in an earsplitting crescendo, then another, and another. They came from the interstate, from the access roads, from the smoldering men, women, and children moving away from their vehicles, some staggering, others crawling, all crying the cries of the dying, the screeching wail of the most inhumane of torments.

The priest's legs trembled. He felt weak, afraid, lacking the spirit of his profession. But the words from one of the psalms of David slowly came to him, filling not just his mind but also his very soul with the strength he would need to endure this nightmare.

The Lord is my Shepherd; I shall not want. Even though I walk in the dark valley I fear no evil; for you are at my side with your rod and your staff that give me courage.

The priest took a step toward the interstate, then another. He walked through the dark valley almost in a trance, nearly hypnotized by a sight that belonged in Dante's *Inferno.*

"The Lord is my Shepherd . . . I fear no Evil."

"The Lord is my Shepherd . . . I fear no Evil."

He repeated the words over and over, again and again. His lips never ceased to move, sometimes just whispering the words, other times almost screaming them out loud. But his legs did not stop moving, kept him walking in the direction of the macabre vision his eyes took in with the same intensity as he breathed in lungful after lungful of heated, dusty, dead air.

He reached the first victim, a woman crawling on her belly away from a burning van . . . or was it a man? He couldn't really tell until he turned the person over.

"Easy, my child," he said as a pair of webbed hands reached out for him. And it was at that moment that the priest saw that the woman—for it was a woman after all—had no face left, just two small orifices for a nose, a pair of bloated lips, and empty eye sockets. Charred flesh underneath loose skin covered the rest of her face and upper chest, the smell of burned hair reached his nostrils. He momentarily looked away in horror, toward the leaning steel cross next to his fallen church, visible through the smoke and the haze.

"Hurt . . . it hurts . . ." she said, trembling, shivering, dying.

The priest slowly made the sign of the cross and quickly began to perform the Anointing of the Sick, the sacrament given to someone who is dangerously ill due to sickness, injury, or old age. The priest lacked blessed oil for the anointment. Neither did he have a crucifix, two lit candles, and some holy water, but he knew it would not matter. The flames of the burning vehicles would be his candles. The leaning steel cross would be his crucifix. The blood and water dripping from his hands after he soaked them in the reddish puddle next to him would replace the blessed oil and holy water.

He rubbed a wet thumb across her forehead and said, "Through this holy anointing may the Lord in his mercy help you with the grace of the Holy Spirit."

Next, he smeared her hands and recited, "May the Lord who frees you from sin save you and raise you up."

The woman died a minute later. The priest, tears welling in his eyes, set her down on the asphalt and made the sign of the cross on her forehead before moving on to the closest victim, this time a young boy, probably not older than nine or ten, crying next to his scorched parents. He raised his little red arms to the priest. The blistered skin covering most of his body tore the priest's heart in two, but he could not show a single ounce of weakness now. Not while the grotesquely burned child, his brown eyes lifting up to meet his, wrenched out of his lungs a hellish howl unlike any tormented cry the priest had ever heard in his life. The priest needed savage self-control, and he found it in the same words that had gotten him this far.

"The Lord is my Shepherd . . . I fear no Evil."

"The Lord is my Shepherd . . . I fear no Evil."

In the swimming pool of an apartment complex outside Louisiana State University, around one and a half miles from Ground Zero, a woman struggled to swim to the edge of the pool, where she had dived as the weapon detonated across the river.

The few burns covering her legs—the only exposed surface of her body as the heat flash swept across the area—contrasted sharply with the half dozen bodies ablaze on the shimmering sundeck next to the pool.

She trembled at the sight. The crackling hair, the stench of scorched flesh, the charred, frozen figures sprawled on the decks, the rubble of the collapsed apartment complex—all under Hell's sanguine shadow, under a scorching Heaven.

Her scream filled the silence that had followed such instant destruction. Tongues of fire licked the reddish clouds as a nearby gas station exploded with the same intensity as those blazing bodies.

Everywhere she looked destruction reigned.

Everywhere.

And somehow she had been spared. Soaked blond hair stuck to her tanned, unscathed back, framed her triangular face, fell over her forehead as her blue eyes took in the destruction with terrifying awe.

What in the world happened? And how did I survive this?

And the answer quickly came to her: *I was underwater! The pool!*

The large mass of water had reached the temperature of a heated spa in less than one second as the firestorm swept across Baton Rouge, but it had ended a second later.

She reached the end of the pool and placed a hand on the edge but quickly jerked it back.

"Aghh!"

The pool deck was boiling hot! The world seemed on fire, except for her pool, her pocket of life in the middle of a field of death.

Considering herself lucky, she swam to the middle of the pool and decided to wait for the rescue crew to arrive. But what she did not know was that there would not be any rescue crews for many hours. And besides, she would not live past another thirty minutes. The same water that had saved her from the initial heat flash would now slowly kill her in a way far more inhumane than the heat flash that consumed the bodies blazing on the pool deck. Those were the lucky ones, the victims who had ceased to exist in the first second of the explosion, the ones who had been spared the horror of surviving—if only for a little while.

The woman immersed herself in the heated waters and forced her mind to relax. The water would keep her alive until the rescue crew arrived, she thought. But soon the cramps would come. Soon blood would reach her throat and she would convulse and vomit. She would then bleed from her nose, ears, vagina, and rectum, staining the pool with the same crimson hue of the cloud covering the city. She would bleed to death in minutes, until her lifeless, shriveled body floated still, inert in a pool of heavily radioactive water.

When the city worker climbed out of the manhole and up to the street, he found himself not in downtown Baton Rouge, but in the middle of Hell. Just ten minutes ago he had parked his truck next to this manhole, lifted the round metal cover, and gone down the built-in ladder to repair a faulty power distributor. Then the sky, as seen through the round hole fifteen feet above him, had turned red with flames and a violent shock wave followed, making him lose his footing on the metallic ladder. He had landed in two feet of sewage water as the infernal flash on the surface disappeared as fast as it had come.

Rubble, fire, black smoke. Destruction. Total destruction filled his eyes as he took a faltering step away from the hole that had spared him the fate of the dozens upon dozens of bodies alive with blue flames, their hair flaring, their skin peeling off like thin, burning paper, which the wind carried up to the dark sky. Many of the corpses still stood, like black statues frozen in time, their feet fused with the charred sidewalk, dark smoke whirling up to the colossal cloud hovering over Baton Rouge. City buses and cars burned everywhere, some overturned, others standing straight up. But all in flames. All of them.

A terrible feeling of loneliness overtook him. The entire world appeared to have died except for him. He could hear no screams, no agonizing shrieks, no sign of another human life, just burning corpses everywhere.

Feeling utterly alone, the nauseating stench of scorched flesh reaching deep inside him, the city worker dropped to his knees, praying the nightmare would soon end, praying for *anything* but being there at that moment—even if that meant praying for death itself.

But the city worker was already dead, only he did not know it. He had died not when the bomb exploded, but the moment he had left the protection of the underground sewer, where six feet of concrete had shielded him from the gamma rays now destroying his living cells at a staggering rate.

In another minute the abdominal pains would come, making him vomit blood, which would then flow freely from his nose and ears. His dying eyes gazed at the menacing mushroom cloud, fed by column upon column of billowing smoke from all the destruction surrounding him, from the blazing ruins of downtown buildings, from the crimson-and-orange flames stabbing the sky above the perishing city.

Outside Lafayette, Louisiana.

Kevin Dalton bolted out of bed when he heard an explosion in the distance. It sounded like nothing he had ever heard before. Khalela also woke up, her sleepy eyes on him.

"What is wrong, Kevin?"

"Just heard a weird blast outside."

"The termination team? Marcos?"

"No, nothing like that. It sounded distant. As if something big just went off several miles away . . ." Kevin suddenly brought both hands to his face. "It *couldn't* be!"

Getting up and dressing, the two of them went outside, where a commotion of truck drivers pointed at something in the distance. Kevin saw the unmistakable reason for the explosion that had awakened him a minute ago.

Jesus Christ!

"That's a nuke!" a man screamed.

"Looks like it's over Baton Rouge!" another shouted as a crowd gathered in the parking lot outside the diner.

A truck driver hauled a portable radio out of his truck, set it on the ground, and turned it on. He switched through all the Baton Rouge radio stations but only got static. As the truck driver tuned in a Lafayette station, Kevin heard the high-pitched tune of the Emergency Broadcasting Signal, followed by an announcer telling everyone to remain calm and stay clear of Interstate 10. The entire Lafayette area was safe, and there was no reason for alarm. Emergency teams were heading toward Baton Rouge from Lafayette and also from New Orleans. The state police were already putting up roadblocks fifteen miles in every direction from Baton Rouge to keep citizens out of the danger zone.

Kevin Dalton closed his eyes at the impossible sight in front of him. *It's happened! It's actually happened. Saddam Hussein has finally done it!*

A large cloud of smoke began to rise in the distance. Whatever had survived the explosion was now ablaze.

Khalela pulled Kevin away from the crowd, a pained expression on her face. "We must get away from here, Kevin," she said. "There are two more bombs headed north."

Shocked by what he had just seen, and also realizing that part of it was his fault for interfering with Khalela's work, Kevin Dalton brought a hand to his face, muttering through his clenched jaw, "It's all my *fucking* fault!"

"No! Do not even say this," she begged him, as her arms embraced him. "It is not so. Saddam and Marcos did this, not you. If it was not Baton Rouge, then it could have been any other city. There is nothing we can do here. The damage has already been done. But there is much we can do to prevent another disaster from happening."

Kevin raised his gaze and locked it with hers. Khalela was right. There was no sense in self-pity when two maniacs were hauling nuclear weapons.

First things first.

He turned around and headed back to his motel room. "Come," he said.

"Where are you going?"

"To call Bourdeaux and get the hell out of this place."

NEAR LAFAYETTE, LOUISIANA.

In a small airfield north of Lafayette, Kemal Ramallah landed the small crop duster helicopter he and Irina had used to get away from the plantation.

They saw and heard the explosion as Kemal made his approach to the airfield from the west. He had circled it a few times, looking for signs of trouble. With a warhead in his possession over twice as powerful as the one that had just leveled Baton Rouge, the former Iraqi pilot couldn't be too careful.

"That is Marcos's hangar. Yes?" Irina said, pointing to the blue hangar Marcos had told them would be located next to the field's main terminal building, a two-story, redbrick structure. In front of it was a concrete ramp with about two dozen small planes, mostly single-engine.

Using the Unicom frequency—the standard radio frequency of 121.0 MHz in use on all airfields in the United States that lacked a control tower—Kemal steered clear of the air traffic and put down the chopper in front and slightly to the right of the blue hangar.

Irina jumped out, hauling the backpack. Without securing the helicopter, Kemal also left the craft. The former KGB agent pulled out the key Marcos had given her and unlocked the hangar. Kemal helped her move the large sliding door aside.

Inside they found a twin-engine Cessna 421, a nine-seat light transport aircraft. Kemal walked around it, inspecting the plane while Irina pulled down the side door/ladder and hauled the backpack inside.

"Let's go," she told the Iraqi.

"I need to preflight it," Kemal responded.

"Why?" she said. "Marcos told us he always kept it fueled and ready."

"Go inside the plane and see if there are any navigation charts of the states between here and Virginia."

Exhaling heavily, Irina disappeared inside the plane, coming out a minute later holding a dozen folded charts. "I found these."

Kemal briefly inspected them. "These are no good to us unless you want to head for Mexico. Stay here. I will go inside the terminal. Keep your weapon ready, but out of sight."

Irina burned him with a stare of pure female contempt. "I *know* how to handle myself."

Kemal went inside the redbrick building. A snack bar was to his right, next to a counter sporting an advertisement for flying lessons. The clerk behind the counter, a blonde with large breasts who was chewing gum like a cow chewing its cud, regarded Kemal with an indifferent glance before turning her attention back to the small radio on the counter, where an announcer commented on the blast. To his left was another counter, behind which Kemal found what he was looking for. A number of shelves displaying flying gear, including flight computers, logbooks, headsets, and navigation charts.

He approached it. A young black man probably not a day older than twenty listened to his Walkman, his eyes wide in surprise. He removed the headphones at the sight of Kemal.

"May I help you?" he asked.

"Yes, please," Kemal responded in the strong British accent he had gotten from studying at Oxford.

A minute later Kemal returned to the plane. In his hands he held a dozen charts, which he would use to map his route across five states.

After handing the charts to Irina, Kemal spent the next fifteen minutes doing the walkaround, the external preflight of a plane he had never flown before. But just like the crop duster helicopter, he had flown something close enough to get airborne, get where he needed to get, and land. Checking ailerons, elevators, the rudder, both fuel tanks, the oil level in both engines, and removing the covers from the airspeed indicator probe and the stall probe, Kemal climbed inside and pulled up the ladder, which also acted as the door, and locked it in place.

Irina was already sitting in the copilot's seat.

"What took you so long?" she asked. "This entire state will be swarming with policemen looking for us."

Kemal looked at the pale Russian woman with faint distaste before he began to look for the preflight checklist, which he found stuffed in a pocket on the side of her seat. He handed it to her. "Here," Kemal said. "Read the items one by one, and do not skip any. I have never flown this kind of plane before."

Irina snapped the laminated sheet of paper from his hairy hands and, with a hitch of the shoulder and a twist of the lips, began to read.

"Master switch on."

Kemal looked for the switch that would bring battery power to the avionics. He found it and threw it. As expected, the electrical components came to life.

"Check," he said.

"Auxiliary fuel pumps on."

"Check."

"Navigation radios on."

"Check."

They continued until Irina read the last item on the list, at which time Kemal adjusted the fuel/air mixture and cranked the left engine. It started on the first try. Marcos indeed kept this airplane in top shape. The second engine also started without a hitch. The only problem Kemal did find was a slightly low reading on the oil pressure for both engines, but it was nothing that would prevent him from flying out of the state.

Using the rudder pedals and the throttle, the large Iraqi taxied the airplane out of the hangar and onto the ramp, which led to a long taxiway ending on the main runway. Again using the Unicom frequency, Kemal checked for traffic before getting on the runway and taking off.

He used the electrical trim as he cut back throttles and leveled off at seven thousand feet heading northeast, toward Mississippi, doing 275 knots, the normal cruising speed of the Cessna—according to the manufacturer's specs he had read on the reverse side of the laminated checklist.

Night began to fall. Far away, toward the southeast, Kemal could see the distant fires consuming what was left of Baton Rouge. The flames reminded him of the day his family perished at the hands of the Americans. He watched them in silence.

THE WHITE HOUSE. WASHINGTON, D.C.

Black rain clouds began to break up over the nation's capital, giving way to streaks of moonlight that cast a grayish glow on the south lawn of the White House. The stiff wind of just minutes ago had given way to a light breeze, gently swaying the drenched branches of nearby trees.

President Bill Clinton saw it all through the Armorlite windowpanes behind his desk in the Oval Office. The ultimate nightmare had unfolded itself in Louisiana, sending a clear message all the way to this office: the terror had begun. Four hours had passed since the explosion, and the situation worsened by the minute.

Riots broke out in New York, Miami, Los Angeles, and a dozen other cities protesting against the Clinton administration for failing to protect the citizens of this country. In Washington, police had a hard time dispersing large crowds gathering in front of the Capitol before protesters organized a large demonstration down Pennsylvania Avenue, toward the White House. In Houston, people overturned a dozen city buses and set them on fire. At the University of Miami, two Iranian students, armed with automatic weapons, fired into a crowd of students while screaming that the end of the Great Satan was nearing. In Detroit, a bomb exploded in a department store at noon, killing over forty people and wounding a hundred others, bringing back images from the Oklahoma City bombing. Similar bombings took place in Palm Springs, Portland, Nashville, Tampa, Boise, Denver, and even Anchorage. In Dallas, three Syrian students attending SMU medical school took control of a radio station at gunpoint and began broadcasting messages of Arab liberation and of the end of the evil American society. A group of Iranian-born oil workers in Alaska killed themselves while blowing up five hundred feet of Trans-Alaska pipeline, pouring tens of millions of barrels of crude into the hills that led to the Gulf of Valdez before emergency crews could stop the flow. The black liquid cascading into the gulf dwarfed the damage done by the Exxon tanker some years before.

And CNN was everywhere to capture every gruesome detail in living color, along with the ghastly images of Red Cross workers, the National Guard, and the U.S. Army as they rescued and treated tens of thousands of burned victims from the holocaust that was Baton Rouge. Louisiana not only didn't have a capital anymore, but the state also had no leadership. The governor, lieutenant governor, and hundreds of other high-ranking state officials had perished during the explosion.

Like a brushfire in the middle of a drought, nationwide violence spread from larger cities to the smaller ones, and local police simply could not cope with the surge in crime. Images on television showed a level of looting and vandalism that brought back memories of Los Angeles in the early nineties, after the trial of the police officers charged with the beating of Rodney King. Homeowners across the country, armed with handguns and rifles, shot looters and rioters as they tried to vandalize their neighborhoods. There were bodies sprawled on streets and sidewalks from Washington to San Francisco, and from Maine to Key West. Hospitals and the American Red Cross simply couldn't keep up with the wounded. The president had declared martial law two hours ago, and he had ordered the Army and the National Guard to gain control of the streets and restore the peace.

In Colombia and Bolivia, drug barons had taken advantage of the chaos in the United States to launch their own offensives against local government officials and to increase shipments into the U.S. and Europe. In the Philippines, the newly elected civilian president was assassinated and a military junta took control of the nation in the early hours of the morning. In Germany, an American Airlines DC-10 was hijacked by Lebanese terrorists and ordered to fly into Libya. But the Libyan government, afraid of a U.S. retaliation, had refused the DC-10 permission to land. The jetliner, out of fuel, failed to reach Rome, and was forced to make an emergency landing in southern Italy. The plane had broken apart during the landing and caught fire. There were no survivors. In Ireland, a surge of riots, beatings, and public killings had forced the government to declare a state of emergency, suspending all constitutional rights and imposing martial law.

Dear God, what a disaster.

Grimacing, President Bill Clinton turned away from the windows and sank into the leather chair behind his desk. He was alone now, his staff had left the office ten minutes ago carrying long lists of action items to implement to bring the domestic situation under control, particularly in southern Louisiana, where the seriously wounded now reached close to one hundred thousand. There was no possible way to provide so many people with proper medical attention so quickly. The system wasn't designed for disasters like this. Help continued to flow into the stricken area, but there just wasn't enough medicine or facilities to assist everyone, especially since there were so many other disasters.

The president rubbed a hand over his sternum. A burning pain was making it up his chest at the thought of such widespread world violence. But as Commander in Chief of the world's strongest superpower, the American president had to look beyond the current wave of violence and focus on the root of the problem: Saddam Hussein. He was at the heart of Clinton's problems. It was the Iraqi tyrant who had purchased the Russian hardware, got the bombs assembled, nuked his own people, and then went on to nuke Baton Rouge.

Clinton briefly glanced at a pair of satellite images, which the president had used during his twenty-minute address to the nation—ironically just an hour before the atomic explosion in Baton Rouge. At this point in time he couldn't care less if the world still thought he had nuked Iraq. He had his own disasters to deal with. But somewhere in the corner of his mind still lingered the statement made by Director of Central Intelligence Joseph Goldberg before he'd left this office accompanied by the Defense Secretary and FBI Director Roman Palenski. *Saddam still has enough hardware for many more bombs. We must take that capability away from him.*

The CIA had apparently identified the place where it all was happening. Bourdeaux had a man near the area in northern Iraq trying to get confirmation before he called in an air strike and eliminated Saddam's nukes.

But in Clinton's tired mind, he wanted to do much more than just take away Saddam's ability to assemble and deliver nuclear weapons. Clinton wanted to eliminate Saddam, erase anything and everything the Iraqi tyrant stood for. He wanted to do away with the entire fucking country by using a few twenty-megaton thermonuclear warheads, each as powerful as five hundred Baton Rouges. He wanted to push the button so badly he could taste it. Saddam deserved that and much more for what he had done. An hour ago CNN showed a day of celebration across the Middle East. In Baghdad, Teheran, Amman, Beirut, and Tripoli, crowds took to the streets in celebration of the nuclear blast in America. Clinton and his staff had watched the broadcast right after the images of hell from Baton Rouge and the rest of the nation filled every square inch of the color television screen inside the Oval Office.

Russia, China, England, and France had urged the United States to refrain from retaliating with nuclear weapons. The requests had come just over an hour ago, while Clinton and his staff were in the middle of a brainstorming marathon to formulate solutions to the long list of problems facing his country.

Clinton's response to the other members of the United Nations Security Council had been simple. With his staff in the Oval Office, he had informed the nation that as president, he felt compelled to retaliate in any way he felt was powerful enough to discourage further attack on American soil. The United States of America had not been in such turmoil since the days of the Civil War, and President Clinton had no choice but to use every power available to him to bring the situation under control and prevent a calamity of this magnitude from ever happening again.

BAGHDAD, IRAQ.

Sitting at the head of a long mahogany table in one of the Presidential Palace's conference rooms, Saddam Hussein smiled broadly while watching yet another CNN broadcast in the presence of an interpreter and of seven of his top military leaders, including General Sa'dun Mustafa, who sat at Saddam's right.

Although the destroyed city had not been New York or Washington, it was after all an American city, and he had eliminated over 250,000 Americans at the last estimate, with close to 100,000 wounded.

America was suffering. Clinton was suffering, and his suffering made Saddam Hussein's ego grow larger than life itself. He was in control. He was in command. Now was the time to invade Kuwait. The Americans would be too busy with their own internal problems to interfere. Clinton had his own domestic problems to worry about a deployment of 100,000 troops heading south to reclaim the tiny country, which in Saddam's mind had always belonged to Iraq.

He could only wish his most-trusted Jafar Dhia Jafar were here with him to celebrate this historical moment, but his subordinate had flown back to Tikrit to personally oversee the assembly of the next bombs, which Saddam planned to smuggle into every nation that had participated in the failed attempt to destroy Iraq in 1991.

Yes, Saddam thought. *Soon I shall send more messengers to other parts of the world, messengers of destruction.*

"My leader," said one of the junior generals sitting at the table.

"Yes? What is it?" responded Saddam without taking his eyes off the television screen.

"The American president, Great One. He claims that we detonated the weapon on our own troops in southern Iraq."

Saddam snapped his head at the nervous general, his soft brown eyes lowering when confronted with Saddam Hussein's armor-piercing stare. This general had lost a younger brother in the blast.

"A lie!" Saddam said, slapping the table with the palm of his right hand. "The evil Clinton does not speak the truth!"

The general nodded in agreement but made the fatal mistake of mumbling something.

"Speak up, General!" Saddam commanded. "If you have something to say, say it now!"

"No—nothing, Great One. Nothi—"

Saddam abruptly stood and reached for his Makarov. "Speak up now or I will put a bullet between your eyes this moment! There shall be no secrets among us!"

The general swallowed hard as he put his trembling hands in front of him, sweaty palms facing Saddam Hussein. "I . . . the helicopters, Great One. My brother was the pilot of one of the Hinds. He called me on the radio right before the explosion to tell me that—"

"You trust the word of the evil Clinton over my own! You dare disgrace me in front of all these men!"

"Oh, Great One. I shall never even think to—"

The sound of the gunshot reverberated inside the conference room, the round striking the general in the left eye, pushing him into the swivel chair, which rolled several feet back. His hands jerked for a few seconds before he went limp.

Six bodyguards burst into the room, their AK-47s searching for any general holding a weapon. One of the guards made the mistake of accidentally pointing his Kalashnikov at Saddam for a fraction of a second and was instantly shot by another guard. The unlucky bodyguard never knew what happened. His limp body crashed over the smooth mahogany surface with a loud thump, his dead eyes staring directly at Saddam.

"Clean up this mess!" Saddam commanded, as he holstered his weapon and walked out of the room.

After Saddam left, while the guards picked up the bodies and dragged them out of the room, General Sa'dun Mustafa leaned back on his chair and slowly shook his head. *Could it be true?* Did Saddam indeed order the deaths of his loyal troops?

Mustafa had never hesitated following Saddam's orders before, but this went beyond his limits. Killing forty thousand Iraqi soldiers with a nuclear device? And all for what? To satisfy a personal vendetta against the American president? Those had been real human beings who perished in the explosion. Mustafa had visited the army hospital in Basra where most of the survivors were being flown, and the macabre sight had turned his stomach inside out. Mustafa had seen more than his share of violent death in his days, but this went far beyond anything he had ever experienced. The apocalyptic vision had changed him, turned him into an opponent of the weapon, for he had seen firsthand what it could do. But he would never be so stupid as to confront Saddam with his suspicions. Not while he stood disarmed and Saddam kept that Makarov strapped to his belt.

Intending to get to the bottom of this and then to follow his heart if the claim turned out to be true, General Sa'dun Mustafa stood and also left the conference room, a hundred questions bombarding his mind. He was a powerful man with a big ego and a strong will, one which at times had come close to colliding with Saddam's. But a voice inside of him always pulled him back. This time, however, if it indeed turned out that Saddam had ordered the deaths of so many of Mustafa's people, including three of his brothers, Sa'dun Mustafa doubted his inner voice would be able to control his feelings.

NEAR JACKSON, MISSISSIPPI.

Inside a small hangar at a secluded airfield thirty miles north of Jackson, Mississippi, Kemal Ramallah cursed the evil Cessna plane. A sudden drop in oil pressure had forced him to land at this desolate field, and also to pay a small fortune to the mechanic working on the plane's right engine. Kemal could have easily forced the man to fix the plane while holding a gun to his head, but Irina had convinced the Iraqi that it was better this way. The last thing they needed at this moment was unwanted attention, particularly with the havoc going on across the country.

Keeping a low profile now was the general rule, one which Irina Bukovski played like an ace. As her Iraqi friend paced the concrete next to the tall rudder, Irina checked out the young mechanic wearing oil-stained blue jeans as he bent over to pick up a wrench before going back to work on the engine.

Irina approached him. "Is it going to take long?" she asked, her blue eyes studying the young, black-haired man with the neatly trimmed mustache, and muscular arms and chest under a thin white T-shirt with the sleeves cut off. He looked as if he had graduated from high school the day before. Irina decided the mechanic was harmless.

"It'll be several hours, ma'am. You got yourself a serious leak in here."

Nodding, Irina walked over to where Kemal still paced.

"Take it easy. Yes? You are making me nervous."

The large Iraqi stopped pacing. He looked disgustingly messy. His hair was uncombed, his eyes bloodshot, and his body odor! Irina could barely take it.

"You need to freshen up. Why don't you head over to the hangar and ask if there is a rest area and try to take a nap? We still have a long way to go, and I cannot help you flying this thing. Maybe you can even find a shower, or at least wash yourself in a sink." She crinkled her nose.

Putting his hands on his waist, Kemal slowly nodded. "I guess you are right."

"The mechanic said it will be several hours. I will use the phone in this hangar to call my people. Then I plan to remain with the plane and the cargo," she said.

Kemal nodded once more and walked away.

Irina made a long-distance phone call to Atlantic City and spoke with

Viktor Kozlov for less than a minute, ordering him to kidnap Kate Marston, use chemicals to extract anything of value from her head, and then kill her with an overdose.

Katrina, Katrina, thought Irina Bukovski. *You will pay dearly for what you have done to me.*

After hanging up, Irina eyed the mechanic one more time before going inside the plane.

AL JABER AIR BASE, KUWAIT.

Lieutenant Colonel Diane Towers sat alone in her tent. She had actually been alone for a very long time, ever since her father had died in Beirut. Like herself, her country also stood alone in this mess. As the huge armored units of the Republican Guard drove south with a clear objective, the petite but muscular female warrior contemplated the possibility that she might not survive the next twenty-four hours. The odds certainly were stacked against her, and from the looks of it, reinforcements wouldn't get here fast enough to change her destiny.

Getting up from the canvas cot, Diane stretched her arms and yawned. This was the best sleep she had gotten in the two days since she returned to the small air base after surviving the nuclear blast. The Marine surgeon who had examined her following her arrival had indicated that although the short-term effects of the radiation might be fairly negligible, the long-term consequences could be quite serious. Her risk of breast, ovarian, and uterine cancer had increased by an order of magnitude, basically canceling any plans she'd ever had of having a family. The Marine surgeon had brought in a local gynecologist, who explained to Diane that her ovaries could have been irreversibly damaged during her short exposure to the lethal gamma rays. There was also the risk of leukemia, salivary gland cancer, cataracts, and thyroid cancer.

"Ma'am?"

Diane's thoughts were interrupted by the voice of Major Blue Jeans Levi.

Levi and eight other Hornet pilots had been lucky enough to be out of the circle of death when the nuke went off. They actually saw it in the distance, as it lit up the night sky over southern Iraq. The ten surviving single-seat F/A-18Cs Hornets under her direct control represented most of the American land-based air power in the region. None of the Eagles at Salman Assad had survived the air strike. All of the A-10 Warthogs and most of the Kuwaiti Hornets had been destroyed by the nuclear blast. But help was on the way. Hundreds of fighters and bombers from all over the United States and Europe were heading to the Middle East to keep the new wave of Iraqis heading south from reaching Kuwait.

"Come in," she replied. "What's wrong?"

After saluting Diane, Levi ran a hand through his hair, which he always kept longer than regulation. His light brown, oval face was somber in the dim light. The black mustache covering his upper lip dropped at the ends as he grimaced. Outside, a soft breeze swept through the small air base, swaying the canvas walls of her tent. "Ah, nothin', ma'am. I reckon there ain't nothin' really wrong. Just wanted to stop in and see how you're gettin' by."

She turned her hazel eyes to a man who didn't resemble the stereotypical U.S. Marine but just the opposite. The laid-back Levi belonged on the catfish farm where he had been born and raised near Beaumont, Texas. Diane pulled in her mouth at the corners. "Well, there are one hundred thousand Iraqis heading our way, and aside from the *Kennedy,* we're it in terms of air support until reinforcements arrive. I say I'm feeling pretty fucking bad. What would you say?"

With color coming to his cheeks, Levi slowly shook his head. "Well, Miss Towers, all of the guys realize our situation, and we aim to do what we can to keep them Iraqis corralled north of the border. We were just wonderin' how you're feein' after . . . well, you know."

"It feels like crap to get nuked, if that's what you want to know. You lose your appetite and it's hard to keep anything down. But you can tell *the boys* that my command and flying abilities have not been impaired one bit, so relax and don't waste your energy worrying about me when we have plenty to worry about."

Diane actually felt bad for answering that way. In reality she liked the Texan Marine.

"Ma'am, me and the guys just wanted to let you know that we're behind—"

"Thank you, Blue Jeans. I think you better leave now. I'm getting tired and we have quite a bit of work ahead of us."

"Yes, ma'am."

Snapping to attention and saluting, Levi did an about-face and left the tent.

After zipping up the tent to get some privacy, Diane removed the white T-shirt she wore over a small white brassiere. She brushed her short hair back with a hand before leaning over the stainless steel bowl of white water on the table next to her foot locker. Cupping cool water with both hands, she closed her eyes and splashed her face a few times before also wetting her hair, neck, and underarms.

Reaching for a small blue towel next to the bowl, Diane toweled her head dry. As she was about to use the same towel to dry her underarms, she froze at the amount of short brown hair on the towel.

Dropping the towel and running both hands through her hair resulted in more hair falling out. The palms of her hands were covered with it, her naked shoulders were covered with it. Looking at herself in the small mirror hanging over her cot, Diane saw sections of scalp through her thinning hair.

Oh, damn!

Frowning and slowly shaking her head, the Marine aviator pushed out her bottom lip as she stared at the image of her face and upper chest. And it was at that moment that she also noticed a few spots of darker skin right above her breastline. Pressing them with a finger had no visible effect. The spots, a bit purplish in color, remained in place. The surgeon had warned her about the possibility of mild skin purpura, quite common among the survivors of Hiroshima and Nagasaki. Diane also ran a high risk of developing oropharyngitis, an inflammation of the mucous membrane of the mouth and a portion of the pharynx, near the soft palate. She could also get hematuria, which occured when blood was discharged into the urine.

Closing her eyes and swallowing hard at the cards life had dealt her, Diane forced back the tears. She could not afford to show any signs of weakness now. As much as she simply wanted to cry and have someone console her, Diane Towers knew she had no one. Only her father might have been of some help at a time like this, but he was gone. He had been gone for a very long time.

Brushing off her fallen hair and throwing it away, Diane buried her face in her hands and began to cry, wishing she were home, away from all this madness, back in her cabin outside San Diego, California. The one she had built with her own hands during the long, quiet years following the death of her father, when it seemed as if she had all the free time in the world. She had been young and proud back in those days. A Marine full of dreams and aspirations. A woman who loved the wilderness as much as she loved flying. Life had been easy in those days for Diane Towers, whose only worry during the second-to-last decade of the twentieth century had been her practice missions at Marine Corps Air Station El Toro, and the physically rewarding work at the cabin. Those long weekends clearing land, chopping wood, and building something with her hands had given her a sense of accomplishment she could never dream of getting out of flying. For once in her life she had actually built something, instead of simply pressing a button on some control stick and blowing it to hell.

But that didn't mean she thought any less of her flying. For Diane, flying was like a drug. She simply couldn't get enough of it. She had to fly faster and harder than before, had to push those metallic birds to the outer limits of the design envelope. As a pilot she truly believed that was her job. As a Marine, that was her duty. The world always changed for Diane the moment she got behind the control column, and she viewed everything through the information projected on the Heads-up Display. At that instant she wasn't Diane Towers any longer. The moment she felt the restraining harness wrapped around her, holding her back against the hard flight seat, the untamed pilot in Diane took charge. The noise of afterburning turbofans drowned her fear, quickly washing it away in the slipstream as her jet broke through the sound barrier and shot high above the clouds.

A part of Diane loved to fly, loved to feel the g's pounding on her as she pushed harder than ever before, forcing her plane to perform beyond its capabilities. The physical pain brought upon her by the ferocious g-forces were the dues she had to pay for belonging to a privileged class. Nothing came free. *Nothing.* Yet as with any drug, once the effects wore off, once her feet hit the tarmac at the end of a mission, she found herself alone, empty, with nothing to show for her efforts, without anyone to share her life. When she exited the euphoria of dashing above the grasslands at speeds that seemed faster than life itself, Diane found herself without a purpose, almost as if life rushed past her while she sat in the cockpit of countless craft over countless lands. It was at those moments that her maternal instincts overshadowed her love for flying, her love for the independent life she had chosen long ago. *But you simply can't have it all, Diane,* her father had once told her when Diane, merely twelve at the time, had shocked her parents by telling them that she wanted to become a Marine. *Life is full of compromises, and choosing a career with the Marines might compromise your private life. In fact, it might even compromise your entire life one day.*

His father had been correct. The military not only compromised her father's life in Beirut, but it was slowly compromising hers as the effects of the gamma rays ate her from the inside.

But it was all so downright unfair! her mind screamed. As a woman, she literally had to fight her way through a man's world. She had to endure countless jokes and put downs by one chauvinistic Marine officer after another. She had to take the mental punishment in a silent, resigned way. She was paving new ground for the female gender in this traditional field of macho men. But she'd hung tough, refused to surrender. She eventually overcame the jokes, the insults, the humiliations heaped upon her by men who felt threatened by her presence in the ranks. She had surpassed them all and proved herself worthy of not only belonging to the elite of the elite, but also of being able to lead them. Now, after all the hard work, after all the sacrifice, the sweat, the tears, and the agony, Diane Towers had to face a new kind of demon. An evil force buried deep inside her, quietly but steadily taking her apart. One hair here, one eyelash there, a purple spot above her right breast, a little blood in her urine, the radiation demon would tear her apart piece by piece.

Drying up her tears with the sleeve of her T-shirt, the Marine aviator tightened her fists and pounded them hard against her thighs. An inner voice began to come through, and Diane knew it was the voice of her father, the voice that always came at every crucial moment in her life. It was part of her inner fire, part of the Towers's legacy of Marines. Her grandfather had perished at Iwo Jima, her father in the rubble of Beirut.

Sooner or later her turn would come, but she would be damned if it would come because of a disease. If she was going to die, she would do so as a Marine, in the line of duty.

Diane swore to keep her worsening medical condition a secret. As long as she felt physically fit and capable of flying, she could not care less how many hairs she had on her head or how many purple dots appeared on her chest. She was a Marine, and she had a job to do.

BETHESDA, MARYLAND.

Kate Marston listened to Bourdeaux's voice on the answering machine and hammered her small fists on the kitchen counter. She was running out of time and could not wait much longer.

Reaching into her purse, she pulled out the audiotape she had recorded the other night and stared at it long and hard. In it was her ticket to a new life, but only if she could act fast enough. She could sense the *Komitat* closing in on her. At any moment the Ukrainian would return and demand information, presenting Kate with the same choice given to her before: information or violent rape.

She could chose to buy a gun and kill this man, but that would result in her execution. If the *Komitat* was indeed as powerful as Irina had led her to believe, they would catch up with her and execute her. But if she could tip the Americans and use them as a shield while she got away, then perhaps she could make it out of this mess alive.

But she had to act quickly. *Dammit, Robert! Where are you?*

15

THE EQUALIZER

When the first angel blew his trumpet, there came hail and then fire mixed with blood, which was hurled down to the earth. A third of the land was scorched, along with a third of the trees and every green plant.

— The Bible, Revelations 8:7

Near Lafayette, Louisiana.

Under a blanket of stars, Kevin Dalton walked in a nightmare that did not belong to this earth, a sight of Biblical horror. He walked in a sea of burned victims filling the parking lot of a truck stop outside Lafayette. The numbing pain that had crushed his heart when he first laid eyes on the victims arriving from Baton Rouge several hours ago was now a distant memory. His mind had to overcome such feelings in order to be of any use to the victims of a weapon whose ability to inflict misery and pain on an entire society he only now had fully begun to comprehend.

The people by his feet were Americans, some of them college students from LSU or Southern University. Others were businessmen, housewives, children, or senior citizens. But the people by Kevin Dalton's feet did not look like people. most of them did not have any hair because their hair had burned off. The faces of many were red and very swollen, with blistered lips and skin hanging off foreheads, cheeks, and chins. And those were the ones who still had a face.

Old and young, tall and short, rich and poor, they all lay side by side weeping, suffering, many unable to move, others not fully realizing what had happened to them. An entire society had been equalized as naked, burned human beings.

"Please . . . help me," came the faint cry of a girl to Kevin's right.

Kneeling, Kevin forced back his tears and put a hand behind the girl's swollen head. She was probably about ten, naked, with blistered burns covering most of her skinny body. The Red Cross medic, who had given Kevin a bottle of Percodan for those who could swallow, had told him that most of these victims would die by morning. If the burns didn't kill them, the radiation sickness would. They were essentially doomed and nothing anyone could do would save them. All Kevin could do was make their final hours as comfortable as possible.

But there are so many!

Kevin brought the canteen to the girl's blistered lips. Her eyes were closed. She managed to swallow a few sips, and Kevin put a pill in her mouth.

"For the pain," he said in a calm tone of voice. "Try to swallow it, honey."

After taking the painkiller, the girl put a small webbed hand over Kevin's. The fingers could not be told apart, and the skin of her thin arms hung loose. Like most victims, the thermal flash had blistered her skin, and the shock wave that followed had torn it loose.

"Thank you, mister," she whispered.

"You're welcome," he responded, taking her hand in between his and holding it for a few moments before getting up.

"My parents," the girl said. "Are they all right?"

With his voice about to break, Kevin swallowed hard and said, "Sure, angel. They're fine. They'll be with you shortly," before starting to walk away.

"That's good," she muttered. "That's good."

Kevin moved on, a tear rolling down the side of his face. A young National Guard reservist, his face frozen in horror, had told Kevin that the girl's parents were found charred standing frozen in running postures outside the girl's home, blue flames consuming their arms and heads, a brown liquid slowly flowing from their carbonized chests. They had looked like black statues, their feet fused with the charred ground. The girl had been inside and had been spared the initial flash, but she had fallen victim to the heat and shock waves that burned the house to the ground.

Kevin heard a suffering infant, in the hands of a naked woman with no hair, making a groaning noise. The child's balloonlike head jerked as the mother, crying and sobbing, tried to put a burned breast in the infant's mouth.

Kevin approached them and offered the woman some water. She put the canteen to her lips and took a swig, keeping the water in her mouth as she pressed her lips against those of the screaming child and forced some water inside his little mouth.

"The people were passing . . ." the bald woman suddenly said to Kevin after swallowing the water and wrestling with the infant, tears running freely out of her puffy eyes, which did not look directly at Kevin, but with a sideways glance. Like many victims who had looked directly at the initial explosion, the flash of light had gone through her pupils and left them with a blind spot exactly in the center of her visual field, forcing her to turn her head and use her peripheral vision to see straight ahead. "Their skin, their flesh," she continued, "it hung off like paper . . . just like paper . . . they didn't speak a word . . . they wouldn't help my baby . . ."

Kevin moved on from victim to victim as Red Cross workers came in hauling stretchers, taking away the ones with the best chances of survival. On the other side of the interstate, the Louisiana State Police had improvised a helipad to airlift victims to nearby Lafayette, where the hospitals were already jammed to maximum capacity and the victims were being flown to a number of high school gyms, movie theaters, stadiums, and any other place that was fit for use as a makeshift medical unit. New Orleans to the east, where a large portion of the victims were also being taken, was in similar shape, with too many wounded arriving in too short a time to assist them effectively.

A group of reservists from the National Guard, mostly young men in their early twenties, also walked around with stretchers. Their job was to take the dead behind the motel, where Kevin had seen a mountain of burned corpses already piled up next to the swamp that bordered the truck stop to the north, many of them already rotting in the hot and humid Louisiana weather. Kevin had seen officers from the Army Corps of Engineers calling for bulldozers and fuel to start mass cremations and prevent the spread of disease.

All the victims, stripped of their clothes and personal identification by the thermal wave, had basically lost their identities. Aside from the ones that had managed to identify themselves to the Red Cross workers airlifting them to New Orleans or Lafayette, the rest were just bodies, which upon dying made it to the official list of the dead kept by two Army officers. Kevin had taken a glance at the list, a handwritten scribble on a yellow notepad with columns for WOMAN, MAN, GIRL, BOY, INFANT, and SEX UNKNOWN.

Looking over his left shoulder, Kevin caught a victim, a young woman, getting up and beginning to stagger toward the helicopters across the interstate, peeled-off skin hanging in flaps from her back and hips. The woman held her arms in front of her naked chest, also as badly burned and discolored as the rest of her. Her hands pointed downward. She moved slowly toward the interstate, like a sleepwalker, keeping those arms in front.

Kevin reached her side and slowly guided her back to her spot on the parking lot.

"Please, kill me," the woman asked, her swollen lips distorting her voice. "I do not wish to live like this."

Kevin looked at her face, the left half grossly disfigured by the flash. Her left eye was missing, along with her left ear and the left side of her nose. The right side, however, had survived without a trace of injury. Kevin realized she had been a beautiful woman, fair in skin, high cheekbones, a somewhat pointy nose. Her undamaged right eye, hazel in color and slanted in shape, studied Kevin Dalton's unblemished face, and for a moment Kevin thought he had seen envy in her stare. A number of strands of blond hair still attached to the right side of her head.

"Now, now," Kevin said. "Why don't you sit back down. Would you like some water?"

The woman sat and took the canteen in her burned hands, but missed her mouth, the water dripping over her chest. Her left breast, purplish, shriveled and sagging, looked in sharp contrast to the creamy, uptilted right breast, a pinkish nipple pointing straight at Kevin, who helped guide the lip of the canteen to her quivering mouth, also putting two Percodans on her tongue.

"The pills will help alleviate the pain," he said, kneeling in front of her.

"The fire came," the woman said, swallowing the pills. "It darkened the sky almost as if someone had thrown a blanket over me . . . like a blanket of hot oil . . ." Tears welled in her right eye, her swollen lips trembling. Kevin put his arms around her, and the woman began to cry on his shoulder. "Everything just crumbled away . . . I opened my eyes and realized . . . and realized I could only see out of my right eye! Everyone around me was grossly burned . . . everyone. They all held their arms in front of them . . . walking . . . slowly. Wherever I walked I met these silent, naked people . . . slowly wandering around the rubble and the fires without purpose, without a voice. They walked slowly . . . very slowly . . . and I suddenly realized I was one of them! Oh, God! Please help me! Please! I don't wish to die! Please!"

Still holding her, and with his heart already ripped to shreds so small that Kevin wondered if he would ever be able to piece it back together again, the former naval officer waved at another volunteer to get a medic over to him. A minute later a Red Cross worker came and inspected the woman, and a minute later she was taken on a stretcher across the interstate. Her hazel eye never left Kevin's as she disappeared into a waiting helicopter.

Kevin Dalton walked to the truck stop diner, where Khalela and a few other women kept filling the canteens with water and handing them to a few dozen men consoling the wounded waiting to be airlifted, or waiting to die. A few medics went from burn case to burn case. Once in a while they would send for a stretcher and the lucky victim would be taken across the interstate.

Kevin wondered who the lucky ones were. The ones behind the motel, or the ones who would have to live with the horror of surviving their disfiguring wounds. He then realized that the truly lucky ones had been vaporized in the first fraction of a second following the blast.

Khalela and Kevin exchanged a brief, somewhat vacant glance before he went back to the parking lot and she to filling canteens.

The screaming mothers, who kept getting up to search for their little ones, were the hardest to convince to sit or lie down, sometimes requiring a medic and a tranquilizer shot in the arm before they would obey. Some could no longer bear the heat and would take Kevin's canteen and bathe themselves with it. Kevin would simply take the empty canteen back to the women by the diner and fill it up again.

At some point in time he had started to count victims in the parking lot, but gave up after the first hour. There were simply too many, and the number kept changing with so many of them dying and so many more arriving in Army trucks, their engine noise mixing with that of arriving and departing helicopters, landing lights and headlights crisscrossing in the night, fields of tall grass swirling to the rhythm of the hovering craft.

Once in a while his mind would acknowledge the wound in his leg, quite microscopic in comparison to the misery surrounding him. But he could not even think about resting. Dear God, how could he?

Several Catholic priests had arrived an hour earlier and were hearing confessions and administering last rites to the dying. The priests walked around blessing the dead, making the sign of the cross, carrying wooden crucifixes around their necks for the victims to hold and kiss as they wept and confessed their sins. One of the priests had been himself a survivor of the disaster. He had miraculously escaped with only minor burns. Kevin had helped the priest to a waiting helicopter, which took him to New Orleans a couple of hours ago. Even as the priest, already too weak to walk, was being carried out of the parking lot in a stretcher, he kept blessing the wounded as he passed them by.

The Lord is my Shepherd . . . I fear no Evil.

The Lord is my Shepherd . . . I fear no Evil.

Kevin remembered those words that holy man had spoken time after time, over and over, until the thundering helicopter had drowned them out. He vividly recalled how that priest, weakened by his injuries and radiation sickness, had blessed hundreds of victims before the other priests arrived and relieved him. Every time the priest had encountered a case far more shocking than the previous one, the same words would come to his lips.

The Lord is my Shepherd . . . I fear no Evil.

A large black man, the skin of his back and legs peeling like a potato skin, screamed for his wife and kids. He began to attack one of the reservists, but was instantly overcome by Kevin and two civilian volunteers. Between the three of them they carried the shouting man to the side. As burned and disfigured as he was, he exhibited remarkable physical strength, nearly escaping Kevin and the other two, both of whom were truck drivers with thick forearms and strong hands.

A Red Cross medic came running and plunged a hypodermic into the man's right arm. The effect was almost immediate. He relaxed, and the trio carried him back to the main waiting area.

Another victim, an old man, pressing both hands against a wound on his side, from which blood dripped, regarded Kevin in silence with a sideways glance, another victim who had stared at the flash. "The river . . . the bodies in the river . . ." the man said more to himself than to Kevin, who knelt in front of him and tried to bring some water to his swollen lips.

"No . . . no water," the old man said. "The water is full of them . . . full of them, don't you see?"

Regarding the disfigured stranger with puzzled eyes, Kevin remained still as the man talked about the rotting, bloated corpses of victims that had jumped into the Mississippi to escape the scorching heat, many of them lacking the strength to swim and drowning. There were thousands of them, the man told Kevin. All floating downstream, all dyeing the water red.

Kevin called for a medic, but the Red Cross worker dressed in stained white shorts and a white shirt simply shook his head. Kevin understood and was about to move on when a commotion broke out in the outer perimeter of the camp, near the edge of the swamp. Unlike the rest of the truck stop, that area was not well lit by the parking lot's mercury lights.

Several victims screamed while others staggered up and moved away from something. The beams from the flashlights of three volunteers pierced the night and converged on the reason for the panic.

Kevin saw three alligators moving on all fours toward the wounded, many of whom could not even see, much less get up and run away. This was the section that the Red Cross had selected for the worst victims, the ones that didn't have long to live. When they died, they could be carried away without having to pass through the middle of the main group.

Another group of alligators feasted on a victim, a woman they had managed to drag away to the edge of the clearing. One alligator grabbed an arm and went into a roll, tearing it off her body. The woman's loud scream ended as another alligator clamped its jaws over her head and dragged her below the surface of the swamp.

Kevin tried to scare away the three incoming alligators but failed. The reptiles had smelled blood and would not turn back.

"Get a gun over here!" screamed Kevin as one of the alligators snagged the leg of a badly burned boy, who apparently was too close to dying to know what was happening.

A shot echoed across the swamp, the round striking one of the two alligators in the head, which exploded in a small cloud of blood. Its companion, along with the rest of the reptiles, quickly vanished into the swamp.

After deciding to post an armed guard at this end of the group, Kevin, his hands trembling, picked up the canteen and the bottle of Percodan and headed back to the group.

A woman with a grossly swollen head, her jaw missing and her tongue just hanging out of her mouth, had gone into convulsions and was kicking a toddler in front of her. The toddler's father picked up a rock and bashed the woman's head before Kevin or any of the other volunteers could save her. As the woman's brains oozed out of her burst skull, the father went back to hug his boy, who Kevin saw had no face. The kid lacked eyes, ears, nose, and lips. He looked as if someone had literally erased his face and painted it purple. The father, with his flapping skin, no hair, and large purple blotches covering his back and neck, wasn't in much better shape either, but at least his face resembled that of a human.

Kevin stood in front of the man and was about to say something, but the ice-cold blue eyes that stared sideways at the former naval officer conveyed so much hatred and pain that Kevin turned and left them, just as two workers put the woman on a stretcher and took her behind the motel, where the funeral pyre grew even larger.

Bringing a hand to cover his nose and mouth as he walked back there, Kevin gasped at the size of the pile of bodies. Only two hours ago it had been half its size, now it rose fifteen feet high and extended for almost the entire two-hundred-foot length of the motel. Two armed reservists guarded this side to prevent alligators from claiming the dead.

The smell grew unbearable in the next hour, to the point that he felt like protesting to the Army officer in charge for taking too long to dispose of the bodies, but then realized that the only ones complaining about the stench were everyone but the victims.

Kevin felt ashamed of himself for being so selfish. He also felt guilty for not being one of the victims, for looking like he looked, for wearing clothes, however soiled and dirty, for having hair, for having a face that people could look at without feeling sick. A sudden sense of despair descended over him as the reality of what he was living through momentarily sank in, making him aware of the fact that he had fallen right into the middle of an apocalyptic, man-made hell. Many of the volunteers had already broken down and had been taken to Lafayette. They had been quickly replaced by Army and National Guard reservists, who kept taking turns walking among the victims, working the helipad section, or directing Army traffic.

But Kevin couldn't quit. Remaining with these burned figures bathed in yellowish light was the only thing he could do to alleviate the nightmare Kevin still felt he had a hand in creating. And there was no immediate place to go for Kevin, who several hours before had briefed a stunned Robert Bourdeaux by using an Army satellite radio after flashing his CIA credentials to the Army officers in charge. In five brief minutes he had summarized the situation. Bourdeaux had indicated that he would send for Kevin and Khalela in the next day or so. He had also told Kevin that the situation in the Middle East was worsening again. Saddam had rapidly deployed around one hundred thousand troops south, clearly with the intention of invading Kuwait while the United States was plagued with its own problems. In Kuwait, a massive exodus had begun, as Kuwaitis, their memories of August 1990 still alive in their minds, fled for Saudi Arabia.

President Clinton was in the process of formulating a response, which
Bourdeaux indicated could include the use of nuclear weapons.

Kevin thought about his conversation with the DDO while he began to
pray—something he had not done for many years. As the words from that
priest reverberated in his mind, Kevin prayed for the souls of the victims
vaporized in the first second of the blast, he prayed for the survivors, for
the men and women raising their arms to him, begging for water, weeping,
aching, their loose skin flapping in the soft, predawn breeze. He prayed for
the children, many of whom had lost their parents. Their faces were red
and swollen, their bald heads turned sideways to Kevin as he walked with
faltering steps, his knees beginning to buckle at the dreadful sight, his body
on the verge of collapsing from the frightful vision of burned, webbed
hands clasped and reaching up to the stars. Their imploring cries and
screams stripped him of his sanity just as the heat flash had stripped them
of their skin, layer by layer, deeper and deeper, burning their bodies to a
cinder, opening them inside out, robbing them of their dignity, their
self-respect, their pride.

Kevin saw it all, heard it all, smelled it all. The faces, the bodies, the
sideways glances, the frightfully injured forms crawling by his feet, the
bloated corpses piling up behind the motel, creating a mountain of human
flesh rising to the heavens.

The dark sky changed to a deep violet. Streaks of yellow and orange
brushed the indigo sky, shedding sunlight on the decimated crowd of the
dying, giving an eerie amber cast to the dead, to the heavy fog lifting off the
alligator-infested swamps, to the menacing vultures overhead. The Red
Cross medic had been right. Only a fraction of the victims had survived
the night. The rest had mercifully died or were receiving proper medical
care in Lafayette or New Orleans.

The carrion birds circled the camp on their massive six-foot wingspans,
waiting, floating, riding the thermals. Their descending spirals brought a
dozen of them atop the pile of corpses. Sinking their beaks into the pile,
losing themselves in a black whirling gyre, the scavengers began to feed.

Warning shots from a National Guard reservist did little to break up
the feeding frenzy. Another reservist took aim and fired repeatedly, but
not above the row of vultures. He had centered his sights on the birds
themselves. Almost in unison, terror possessing them by the sudden death
of some of their comrades, the dark flock took wing and flapped skyward
in a single, screech-filled moment.

Kevin breathed in the horror he had witnessed as Khalela walked by
his side, placing a hand on his shoulder, her face totally devoid of
expression. Her green eyes lacked emotion, stared vacantly at the survivors. Kevin realized at that moment that he wore a similar mask of gloom,
a reflection of his hollowed-out heart, squeezed clean of any emotion by
the reality of what they had witnessed.

The circling scavengers started another lazy descent. Three alligators testily left the safety of the swamp and began to crawl toward the dead. Reservists took aim and fired into the bloodthirsty creatures.

The Lord is my Shepherd . . . I fear no Evil.

The Lord is my Shepherd . . . I fear no Evil.

Kevin knew then he would take this memory to his grave.

SOUTHERN IRAQ.

On the other side of the world, another man walked through the same nightmare that Kevin Dalton was witnessing. General Sa'dun Mustafa had returned to Basra under the excuse of providing moral support to the three thousand survivors of an attack he feared had been ordered by Saddam Hussein. Most of the survivors had been taken to a huge warehouse usually used for storing rice, wheat, and other agricultural products harvested in the vegetation-rich lands surrounding the Euphrates.

Mustafa took in the smell of body odor mixed with that of burned flesh and mildewed sacks of grain.

Look at them, Allah! There are so many of them!

During his first trip here there had only been a few hundred survivors, and they all had been inside tanks at the periphery of the blast. Most of them were either partially blinded or losing their hair because of radiation sickness. There had been few burn victims. Now the warehouse was filled with them, their naked, burned bodies a living proof of the infernal heat flash that had stripped them not only of their uniforms, but also of their skin.

The deep sense of compassion he felt, however, did not show externally, as General Mustafa proudly walked up to one of the Red Cross workers, who pointed the general to the ground crew that supported the Hind-Ds that were providing air cover to the now-vaporized army.

Mustafa found two men, both wearing their uniforms while sitting up next to some sacks of grain stacked ten feet high. One of them recognized him as he approached them.

"General!" the soldier said, snapping to attention a fraction of a second before his companion, who also jumped to his feet.

"At ease, my brothers," Mustafa said while crossing huge arms in front of his body. "I have come here to find the truth about what happened out there."

The soldiers looked at one another. The one that had recognized Mustafa spoke. He was probably in his early thirties, with a dark mustache and long sideburns on his weathered face.

"What is it that you wish to know, General?"

"The helicopters," Mustafa said waving a hand in the air. "You were in charge of fueling them and arming them. Did you notice anything strange?

Any special cargo you were ordered to load onto them during the hours before the blast?"

The older soldier regarded Mustafa with questioning eyes, obviously not fully understanding where the tall, powerful general was leading.

"Describe to me the events that took place that afternoon and evening then," Mustafa said, when he realized the crewmen were confused.

The older soldier spoke for nearly thirty minutes, telling the general everything that went on with uncanny detail. At times he would glance over to his fellow soldier, who Mustafa learned was the older soldier's assistant for fueling and loading stores onto the Hind-D's underwing hard points.

"So," said Mustafa after the soldier finished. "Roughly one hour before the explosion two Hinds left fully fueled toward the front lines but without carrying any practice rounds or dummy bombs?"

"Yes, General."

Mustafa shook his head. "But that defeated the purpose of the war exercise, correct? The idea was to run the war game close to the Kuwaiti border to make them nervous."

"True, General. But in this case, the pilots told me they had been ordered to pick up a civilian and his cargo near the front lines and then hover over the middle of the advancing column until they needed to refuel."

"What kind of cargo was this civilian carrying?"

"We do not know, General. But one of the pilots told me it was very special, very expensive, and very secret."

"And what happened to the Hinds? Did they ever return from this mission?"

"No, sir."

Mustafa thanked the soldiers and walked away. He had obtained his proof. The civilian had to be one of Jafar's scientists, and the cargo the bomb that eliminated so many Iraqis.

Briefly closing his eyes in sheer disbelief at what his leader had done, the veteran officer left the warehouse and headed back to Baghdad. He had a new mission in life. His world had taken a sudden turn and he found himself incapable of going back to the way things were before the explosion. Saddam Hussein had crossed the line, and Mustafa could not join him on the other side.

THE WHITE HOUSE, WASHINGTON, D.C.

President Bill Clinton slowly shook his head. Saddam Hussein's troops were heading south at a staggering speed. The defense secretary had just spent the past hour with Joseph Goldberg and Robert Bourdeaux explaining the situation to the president, as if he didn't have enough fires on his desk to also have to deal with the recalcitrant dictator's troops one more time.

"The Republican Guard's front lines will reach the border with Kuwait in another twelve hours, Mr. President," said the defense secretary, his bloodshot stare landing on a president who had not slept a single hour in the past twenty-four—along with every member of his staff, foreign or domestic.

Getting up and walking around his desk, Bill Clinton, casually dressed in a pair of navy blue slacks and a white polo shirt, put a thumb against his chin, inquisitive eyes landing on the defense secretary. "Is the *Kennedy* ready to launch the first strike?"

"Yes, sir,"

"What's the situation of our troops in Kuwait?"

"They're ready for the worst, sir. Heavily outnumbered, but armed to the teeth with our latest weaponry."

"Will they hold the line?" asked Clinton.

"Long enough, sir."

Clinton nodded. His forces in Kuwait would not have to hold on for long. Clinton was about to deliver Saddam Hussein a message the Iraqi leader would not be likely to forget for the rest of his miserable existence.

"What's the situation on the domestic front?" Clinton asked.

The defense secretary stood up from the sofa. "Most Army and Marine divisions have been deployed across the country to keep the population under control. The initial reports show that some level of peace has already been restored in several major cities. The situation should improve vastly in the next twenty-four hours."

"The situation will improve," added Clinton, "assuming that there are no other nuclear detonations in this country."

The defense secretary silently agreed with his superior before sitting back down.

The president remained still. His country had been turned upside down through the actions of one man, and up to this point his administration had not done a single thing right to prevent the terrorists from striking another target.

With the eyes of his most trusted foreign policy advisers converging on him, the president of the United States closed his eyes, a single thought filling his mind.

God Almighty, please help us.

BAGHDAD, IRAQ.

Saddam Hussein reached for the phone to give the order to his troops stationed in the port of Umm Qasr, just thirty miles from the American fleet. As much as he hated the Jews, Saddam recognized the value of the

Israeli strategy of preemptive attacks on the enemy, a tactic that had saved the life of the Jewish nation time and again. Tonight, Saddam prepared himself to apply that same strategy against the Americans.

Another message was about to be delivered to President Bill Clinton.

UMM QASR, SOUTHERN IRAQ.

The young Iraqi captain in charge of the secret deployment of Exocet II missiles in Umm Qasr had received his confirmation orders from Saddam Hussein himself just thirty minutes ago. The Exocet II was a vast improvement over the original Exocet first introduced in the summer of 1977. Unlike its predecessor, the new Exocet could be launched from air, sea, or land. Today the missiles would be launched from the edge of a hill overlooking the Gulf.

As his subordinates wheeled the sixty twenty-foot-long missiles his government had kept totally secret since their delivery six months before, the captain felt the power of Allah surging within him. Somewhere out there was the American carrier fleet. He had seen the distant silhouettes of the ships by using a powerful telescope earlier that day, and he estimated the vessels to be no more than thirty miles from shore, well within the seventy-mile range of the French-made missile.

Flanked by the missile launchers painted in a desert camouflage pattern, the captain gave the order for the operator in the van next to him to activate the large radar dish above the vehicle. The Electronique Marcel Dassault Adac active-radar seeker began to saturate the air over the Persian Gulf with energy.

The captain walked into the rear of the van and nodded approvingly when the operator's large monitor came alive and began to display the search, acquisition, and tracking data from the radar returns of the large vessels. The advanced system could automatically acquire and track a maximum of twenty-five different targets and pass that information to the missiles stored in the multiple launchers.

The captain's ears rejoiced with the sound of the computer equipment automatically feeding acquisition and tracking telemetry data to the electronic brains of the missiles. He also realized that they were now in great danger because the Americans had no doubt detected his radar emissions. Fortunately, the French system had been designed to operate under this condition, and it completed the acquisition of the nine surface vessels in under thirty seconds. The automatic target partition software took the total number of missiles available, divided it by the number of targets, and then made adjustments according to the size of each target to determine how many missiles would be fired at each ship.

In seconds, the firing solution flashed across the screen and the operator turned around and gazed into his commanding officer's eyes. A single nod of the captain's head, and the operator typed in the launching code.

The ground began to rumble as Exocet IIs, each packing five hundred pounds of high explosives, broke through the plastic membranes sealing the launching tubes, shed their protective launching shrouds, and accelerated into the night.

From where he stood, the missile exhausts looked almost like tongues of fire streaking across the dark sky to destroy the Great Satan.

The Iraqi captain smiled broadly. Tonight Allah's will would be done. *"Allamdu li Allah!"*

"Mother of God!" screamed the radar officer on the bridge of the USS *Ticonderoga,* an Aegis missile cruiser escorting the *Kennedy.*

Captain John Peterson, who had just placed the ship on Condition I and ordered the crew to their battle stations the moment he received multiple warning messages from the crew of an E-2C Hawkeye-II and from his own radar officer, fast-walked to the radar officer's station.

As a commander aboard the USS *Stark,* when it got hit by an Exocet accidentally fired by an Iraqi MiG on May 17, 1987, Peterson was well aware of the damage missiles could do to a ship. He vividly remembered the sea-skimming missile hitting the *Stark* broadside, killing thirty-seven of his fellow sailors. But whoever it was that had the boldness to paint the carrier fleet with radar energy was about to become the victim of the ordnance of a pair of F-14 Tomcats flying Combat Air Patrol for the carrier fleet, which consisted of two destroyers, three missile cruisers, and three frigates shielding the *Kennedy.* The escorting vessels were positioned to provide the carrier with maximum protection from Iraq and Iran. Since the *Ticonderoga,* with its state-of-the-art Aegis Combat System, had the longest missile range of any other vessel in the *Kennedy* carrier battle group, it was positioned closest to the Iraqi shore. The other vessels followed in a conical pattern, with the *Kennedy* sailing farthest from the threat.

"What? What?" Peterson asked, reaching the radar station.

"Incoming missiles, sir! Close to sixty of them!"

Peterson momentarily froze. The carrier fleet had Tomcats ready to intercept incoming fighters, and the fleet's missile defense system could handle many incoming missiles in a single wave. *But sixty? Christ!*

The phase-array radar count came up at exactly sixty missiles less than thirty miles away and closing in at Mach 1.5. At that point the initial line of defense of the carrier fleet rested in the hands of the large computer-controlled multifunction phase-array radar and fire control systems of the Aegis air defense system.

The Aegis system produced and steered multiple beams for target search, detection, and tracking. After evaluating the incoming missiles and arranging them in priority, the Aegis system produced target designation data for the Raytheon target illumination radar.

Stored in vertical boxes with lids flush with the deck of the *Ticonderoga,* eighteen Standard SM-2 MR missiles were fired by tandem boost motors in rapid succession. The missiles tilted over and accelerated to Mach 2, skimming the water surface under the power of their solid propellant rockets. Their solid-state homing units remained slaved to the Raytheon target illumination radar.

Eighteen Standard missiles. Eleven hits. Of the other two cruisers, three frigates, and two destroyers escorting the carrier, nineteen more Standard missiles found their targets. Still, the battle group had thirty incoming missiles fifteen miles away.

Short-range Sparrows went next, nearly forty of them, simultaneously leaving the sizzling octal launcher boxes off the decks of destroyers, cruisers, and frigates. Their white-hot tails briefly disappeared in the night just before the entire horizon came alive with explosions. Many of them lit up the sky in pulsating shades of orange and red, like a stroboscopic sunrise.

With his eyes on the phase-array radar counter and on the radar itself, Peterson waited for the surviving missiles to enter the two-mile perimeter of the carrier group, the inner circle of the task force defense system. This was the killing zone of the Navy's gun systems.

More flashes in the distance foretold interceptions by the short-rangers. Peterson watched the counter drop to sixteen incoming missiles in six seconds.

The two starboard Phalanx 30mm Close-in Weapon Systems came alive with an ear-piercing noise. The self-contained installations unloaded heavy rounds at the rate of six thousand per minute. The projectiles left the six-barrel gun with an initial velocity of thirty-six hundred feet per second. Although it appeared that the Phalanxes fired at random, the gun system followed the commands of the Rapid Engagement search and track antennae on the radome above the gun emplacement.

The horrendous noise shook the entire cruiser as the weapons projected a wall of depleted uranium rounds in front of each incoming missile acquired by its sophisticated radar. Two sporadic flashes filled the night, both of them right above the waters as the sea-skimming missiles got dangerously close to the fleet.

With an elevation range of plus or minus eighty degrees and an incredibly fast transition speed of two hundred degrees per second, the gimbal-mounted muzzle became nearly invisible, changing targets in fractions of seconds. The system worked in a superfast morbid harmony of selecting, aiming, and firing, before the lightning cycle started over again.

With the missile exhausts visible in the dark skies, a half dozen seamen ran to the starboard side of the ship carrying Stinger shoulder-launched missiles, and quickly selected their targets and fired. The last-ditch group of interceptors left the launchers and streaked toward the incoming missiles while the Phalanx systems continued to pound away.

One more explosion in the distance. A missile plunged into the ocean as a Stinger exploded next to it a hundred yards from the ship's stern. The blow rocked the ship. Waves slapped the steel hull, creating a cloud of mist and foam. The Phalanxes fired their final rounds and went dry.

A second went by. Peterson closed his eyes and prayed, but the explosion came. One blast. He rolled on the floor as the ninety-six-hundred-ton cruiser rocked to a dangerous angle after absorbing one hit. Alarms blared as more explosions filled the air, but not from his ship. Other ships were taking the rest of the blows. Large fires started at the bow of the cruiser. Peterson could see a few vessels ablaze in the distance.

He reached for the radio. "Damage report! Now!"

"The missile struck our bow, right above the waterline, sir. Can't get a good view with the flames."

Peterson turned to his executive officer. "What's the word from the *Kennedy?*"

The XO slowly shook his head. "Two hits, sir. Several fully fueled jets blew up, setting her deck ablaze."

"Dammit! What about the others!"

"Sounds like two more ships ate some too, but it's hard to tell with all the noise, sir," said a radio operator sitting next to the radar officer.

A cloud of sparks and fire broke out of the radar station on the far left side of the bridge.

Peterson let out a short breath. "Get that fire under control!" He walked outside and watched the chaos of a direct hit on his vessel. *His vessel.* His responsibility. *Damn!*

He also heard the cries of men. Some ran to the bow, ablaze, as a dozen more raced after them with hoses and blankets.

Insanity. Madness!

The world burned around Captain John Peterson. It seemed to collapse around him as the crimson flames of defeat reached out into the night sky, like a powerful claw grabbing hold of his pride—the Navy's pride—before quietly pulling it below the calm, peaceful surface of the treacherous Persian Gulf.

As he stood on the bridge of his flaming vessel, Peterson pressed the rubber ends of his infrared field binoculars against his eyes. Ships burned in the distance. Navy ships. The carrier burned. One destroyer and another cruiser burned. Peterson felt the burning agony of war, tasted the bitter misery of defeat.

The White House.

President Bill Clinton had remained quiet and very pensive since his arrival at the Oval Office ten minutes before. No one had dared say a word until the president spoke. The defense secretary, Roman Palenski, Joseph Goldberg, and Robert Bourdeaux remained silently staring at the carpet. The secretary of state, who had just returned from his short-lived trip to New York City, also sat on one of the sofas.

The president, wearing a perfectly starched white shirt, dark blue slacks, and a blue-and-maroon tie, turned around and faced his nervous audience. "One carrier, one destroyer, two cruisers, and twenty-seven planes," Clinton said in a low, ice-cold voice. "That's not counting one hundred seventy-eight casualties and over five hundred wounded. Gentlemen, who wants to start?"

The defense secretary straightened up his posture and lifted his chin before addressing his Commander in Chief. "Plain and simple, Mr. President, Saddam Hussein set up a trap and we fell into it with both feet. We never thought they could get their hands on so many of those missiles. We received no warning from any of our intelligence agencies in regard to even the remote possibility of Saddam having access to them. We basically underestimated them. It was a terrible mistake."

The president turned around and faced the windows behind his desk. Large demonstrations both against nuclear weapons and against his administration had been gathering outside the gates for the past twelve hours, and this new disaster, once it reached the news, would cause another wave of upheaval. The political pressure from Congress and the private sector to cut American losses and leave the region would be immense. The United States had already suffered enough at the hands of Saddam Hussein. Let him have Kuwait. Get our boys home. Clinton did not have a force strong enough to face the incoming Iraqis, and America's available air power in the region had just been cut down several notches, leaving only a small group of Marine Corps Hornets in Kuwait to protect his troops until Clinton could get Air Force jets over there.

But pulling out now would mean letting Saddam have his way and take Kuwait, which would have devastating long-term consequences.

Once again, President Bill Clinton had reached a crossroads in his presidency. He had to hang tough. He had to do what was right, not what the political pressures of the moment wanted him to do.

"Gentlemen," Clinton said, "our involvement in this conflict will continue. It will continue in spite of expected congressional opposition. It must continue to prevent the loss of Kuwait and to send Saddam a strong message about our position in the region. Our plan to counter his attack and to retaliate for Baton Rouge remains as is."

Pausing for a second before focusing on his defense secretary, Clinton said, "How long before the Air Force jets reach the area?"

"Twelve more hours, sir. We have several groups of Eagles and Falcons heading there as we speak. I strongly feel those jets will keep the Iraqis at bay, and maybe even force them to turn back."

"But they need to get there first," Clinton said. "And in the meantime, General Grogan in Kuwait will have to do his best to contain one hundred thousand Iraqis."

Defense slowly nodded. "I'm afraid so, Mr. President. All he has for air support is a small group of Hornets, which are in the midst of launching a preemptive strike on Iraq's air force."

"What is the situation with the *Alaska?*" asked Clinton, referring to the Ohio-class nuclear-powered submarine cruising the Mediterranean.

"They're in position, Mr. President. Just waiting for the order to fire."

Clinton put an index finger against his chin while biting his lower lip. The crew of the *Alaska* had been on red alert for the past twenty-four hours. The president might loose a Trident missile on those Iraqi troops the moment it became evident that his conventional forces could not stop them. The missile's twenty-megaton thermonuclear warhead should definitely send Saddam the ultimate message, but Clinton didn't want to resort to that weapon just yet. He wanted to keep his options open. If he could contain the Iraqis with conventional weapons, that would give Clinton the flexibility to use a nuclear warhead on another sector of Iraq. The CIA claimed to have found the location where the bombs were being assembled. Officer Donald Bane was trying to confirm the claim. One possibility Clinton had already considered was to strike this safe house with a nuclear-tipped Tomahawk and make it look like Saddam's scientists had accidentally detonated a weapon while assembling it. Another possibility was to destroy the safe house with a conventional bombing run and use a nuke against Baghdad, or another major city in Iraq. However, doing so would carry terrible long-term consequences for the United States not just in the Middle East, but across the entire world. The American government still carried the scars of Hiroshima and Nagasaki. Openly attacking an Iraqi city with a nuclear warhead not only would reopen such wounds for many generations to come, but it could also escalate the nuclear proliferation business to an unprecedented scale, particularly after it became evident that the only way to protect yourself against a nuclear attack was to retaliate with a nuclear weapon of your own. In fighting fire with fire, President Bill Clinton would be setting the worst possible example for the entire world to follow.

I have to hold on, Clinton thought, fully aware that the use of a nuclear weapon had to be a last resort, but one he would not hesitate to use if he found himself out of choices.

Turning back toward the windows facing the White House lawn, President Clinton's heart went out to those brave soldiers in Kuwait who faced the strong possibility of being hopelessly overrun by the massive wave of Iraqi armor heading their way.

OUTSIDE TIKRIT, NORTH CENTRAL IRAQ.

Surrounded by four bodyguards, Jafar Dhia Jafar left the limousine that
had driven him from the small airfield outside Tikrit. He walked toward
the heavily secured entrance of the assembly building.

Iraq's top scientist was dressed impeccably, in a dark Armani suit, a
white shirt, and a narrow maroon tie. His Italian leather shoes quickly
became layered with the dust covering the clearing that separated him
from the safe house.

His strides long and confident, Jafar smiled. His efforts were finally
paying off. As he reached the entrance and was welcomed by the cool
temperatures inside the spacious room, he readied himself to assemble
more weapons of respect for his leader.

Up on the hill, Donald Bane rubbed his eyes in disbelief. He had done
it! He had verified the existence of the hardware. The face he had seen
departing the limousine belonged to none other than the famed Jafar Dhia
Jafar, Saddam's top nuclear scientist!

"Son of a bitch!" he whispered.

"Uh?" asked André Boyabat, half-asleep under the Rover. "What?"

"I just saw Jafar Dhia Jafar."

André quickly woke up, rolled away from the vehicle, and crawled by
Bane's side.

"Where?"

"He just went inside the building."

While André looked through the binoculars, Bane went back to the
truck, reached for his satellite communications gear, and called Langley.
He spoke with Robert Bourdeaux for five minutes and hung up, a frown
suddenly covering his face.

"What is wrong, my friend?" asked the Turk, before putting the
binoculars back to his eyes and surveying the valley.

"Bourdeaux wants us to stay put for another twenty-four hours. He's
gonna contact the armed forces and order an air raid on the place.
He wants us to verify the destruction of the house before leaving the
area."

The Turk, fully awake by now, put the binoculars down and sat by the
exasperated Donald Bane, who now had a ring of rash around his neck,
which he constantly scratched.

"You should get some sleep, my friend."

Bane sighed. "You try to sleep with your neck on fire. Fucking camel
hair!"

"I am sorry about the coat, but the border is no place to purchase
clothing."

"I just want to leave, André. We've accomplished our mission. Problem's the chief doesn't think so."

"It will be over soon," said the Turk, rubbing the sleep out of his eyes.

"Not soon enough," Bane said, as he turned around and faced the clearing once more. *Another twenty-four hours of this shit! Damn!*

CIA HEADQUARTERS. LANGLEY, VIRGINIA.

Robert Bourdeaux fast-walked toward Goldberg's office. The news could not have been better. Bane had found the place where Saddam was assembling the weapons. All they would have to do now was order an air strike and at least that part of the problem would be in the bag.

He reached the reception room and was surprised not to see Kate behind the desk. Instead, a blond secretary who usually worked in the Directory of Science and Technology sat in her place. Her blue eyes met with Bourdeaux's puzzled stare.

"Where is Miss Marston?"

"Just left sick, Mr. Bourdeaux," replied the blonde. "I'm filling in for her. I'll ring Mr. Goldberg now, sir."

Sick? Bourdeaux made a mental note to stop by her place later. He went inside the DCI's office.

While Bourdeaux related Bane's latest discovery to his superior, Kate Marston drove her Honda right up to Bourdeaux's car, which the DDO had parked in his assigned spot on the side of the old CIA building in Langley. She couldn't wait anymore to see him and give him the tape. It was just a matter of time before Viktor Kozlov returned and demanded more information. The sooner she could confess everything to Bourdeaux and get away from this place, the less the risk of getting cornered by the *Komitat.*

Pulling out the extra key to his Ford Bourdeaux had given her, Kate Marston stepped out of her car, walked to Bourdeaux's sedan, unlocked and opened the driver's door, and set the tape and a small note on the seat.

Good-bye, Robert.

Kate Marston got back into her Honda and drove around downtown Washington for an hour, until she felt certain no one was following her. Then she drove to the nearest grocery store and parked her car in front. Pulling out an ATM card, she went inside, walked up to an automatic teller, and withdrew three hundred dollars, the maximum amount she could take out from the machine in one twenty-four-hour period.

Before leaving, she paid cash for a pair of scissors, a bottle of hair coloring, shampoo, a hairbrush, styling gel, and some makeup. She needed a change in looks but didn't want to return to her town house, where the *Komitat* could be waiting for her. A hotel would have to do.

She went back into her Honda and drove to a nearby Holiday Inn, where she paid in cash for a single room. An hour later, Kate left the elevators and walked across the carpeted lobby of the hotel. Her short, wet hair, which she had toweled furiously after taking a hot shower, was blond, courtesy of the bottle of hair coloring she had stuffed down a large garbage bin outside her room, along with the scissors and seven inches of cinnamon hair. Kate's lips and eye shadow were as dark as her punkish-style hair was bleached blond, giving her a younger, mischievous look.

First she had to reach her bank, close the account, and take a taxi to the airport, where she would buy a ticket on the next plane leaving for California.

Sunlight shafted through the windows facing the parking lot. Dropping her room key at the front desk, Kate pushed one of the glass doors leading to the parking lot and began to walk in the direction of her car.

White, puffy clouds dotted a blue sky this cool, breezy morning. Feeling naked as the wind caressed her exposed ears and neck, which hadn't seen daylight for many years, Kate ruffled her hair with a hand to dry it in the wind.

She heard a noise behind her and began to turn around when an arm grabbed her across the neck from behind and lifted her off the asphalt. The pressure against her throat choked her. Before she got a chance to react, to scream, to do anything, a second arm came into her field of view, a handkerchief grasped by a large, hairy hand. It was the hand of Viktor Kozlov.

The skies, the clouds, the scattered cars on the parking lot vanished as the white cloth swallowed her face.

Chloroform!

Holding her breath, Kate Marston began to kick wildly, her mind flashing to the chloroform-soaked cotton balls she had dropped inside a jar holding a small frog, as part of a school project in Moscow decades ago.

She inhaled once, instantly regretting it. Her throat and lungs felt on fire. Kate lifted her hands and grabbed the arm locked around her neck, long, red fingernails digging into the Ukrainian's flesh.

"Astarozhna!"

The pressure around her neck intensified, her larynx about to give. She began to feel weak, light-headed, the Russian word shouted by Viktor told her how foolish she had been for thinking she could escape the powerful grip of the *Komitat Gosudarstvennoi Bezopasnosti.*

You can never leave the Komitat, *Katrina Markarova. Never.*

The shouts and curses from the Ukrainian behind her slowly faded away. Her hands began to tremble. Her legs tingled. Another deep breath, and Kate stopped kicking, her body quickly going limp, but not her mind. It struggled for a few more seconds, fighting to remain focused, thinking of a way out, dreading the pain in her future. Visions of the frog in that glass jar came back. The amphibian fell to its side after a few minutes of breathing the chemical. Katrina Aleksandra Markarova had dissected it.

NORTH OF WINCHESTER, VIRGINIA.

The bedroom's curtains were drawn over a pair of large windows facing the woods south of the safe house Viktor Kozlov had chosen to use for this interrogation session. Katrina's semiconscious body lay on a tan leather recliner chair next to a stand, where two intravenous containers hung, one filled with sodium pentothal, a strong barbiturate, and the other with Dexedrine, an amphetamine. The containers connected to a clear tube through a valve that controlled the flow from each. The thin tube ended in a needle inserted into Katrina's femoral artery.

Viktor stood in the space between the recliner and a queen-size bed, the floral pattern of the comforter matching that of the curtains. A large Oriental rug covered much of the recently finished hardwood floors, giving the room a warm, cozy feeling. A large oil of a landscape hung over the stone fireplace on the wall opposite the bed. A good fire now burned, casting dancing hues of orange and yellow throughout the room.

Irina Bukovski had had this cottage built as her personal retreat, away from everyone, including her own network. Few people knew of its existence. Today the three-bedroom safe house served a different purpose. Irina believed that Katrina was the main reason the CIA had shown up at Marcos's plantation. Her superior needed answers, and quickly. Irina suspected the CIA had to be on the move to put an end to Saddam's plans in the United States and in Europe, and Irina believed some of the answers were locked inside Katrina's head.

"Is she ready?" Viktor asked.

"Yes, sir," responded the keeper of the safe house, a short, bald, Russian man. Once an average doctor in Moscow during the mid-eighties, the Russian had made an allegiance of convenience with the KGB to improve his standard of living. The KGB used his medical services to interrogate the enemies of the Communist Party. After the fall of communism, he became an outcast and was forced to leave Russia or risk imprisonment. He joined Irina Bukovski shortly afterward and came to America to become her secret physician. "She should remain in a fairly responsive state for about thirty minutes."

"Thank you."

Viktor waited until the doctor left the room before approaching Katrina, slouched on the sofa, eyes closed, breathing steadily. Her blue jeans lay folded on the floor next to the recliner. Bronze, shapely legs were sprawled open to allow for the IV needle and plastic tubing connected to the inner side of her left thigh, her cotton shirt just barely covering a triangle of curly hair. A number of bruises on her upper thighs marked the spots where Viktor had grabbed her while he'd forced himself inside her an hour ago.

"Can you hear me, Kate?"

No response.

Viktor got closer.

"Hello, Kate, I'm a friend. I would like to know if you can hear me."

Her voice was weak. "Friend . . ."

"Yes, friend. I am here to help you. Do you understand that?"

"Yes . . . help . . ."

"Correct. Now tell me your full name."

"Kate Marston."

"And how old are you, Kate?"

"Forty-five."

"You are very pretty, Kate. Has anyone told you that before?"

"Yes."

"Who? Robert Bourdeaux?"

"Robert . . ."

"Is that your boyfriend's name?"

"Robert . . ."

"Where is he now?"

Katrina didn't respond.

Viktor frowned. There was a good chance she actually didn't know where Bourdeaux was. He decided to take a different tack and probe for information that might be beneficial to Saddam's network in Europe and the Middle East.

"Do you know CIA Officer Donald Bane, Kate?" Viktor asked. The Soltnevo Group had informed Irina's network that Bane had survived the frozen woods outside of Serpuchov, and there was a possibility he might be closing in on the latest shipment of nuclear hardware into Iraq.

"Bane . . . yes."

"Where is Bane now?"

No response. Her eyes opened halfway and closed again. Viktor realized he had asked a question that required a complicated answer. During this type of interrogation it was best to stick to questions that could be answered with a simple yes or no.

"Donald Bane was tracking a shipment of nuclear hardware out of Russia. Yes?"

"Yes."

"Did he leave Russia?"

"Yes."

"Where did he go after Russia."

Katrina squirmed on the recliner, a hand running over her upper thigh. Her subconscious realized she was naked from the waist down and the hand pulled down the shirt to cover herself. But a second later she let go and ran the same hand over her abdomen, pulling the shirt back up. A light moan escaped her lips and she opened her eyes again. She was beginning to come around.

It was crucial that her subconscious did not realize who was interrogating her. Viktor Kozlov adjusted the valve to give her another dose of sodium pentothal. The effect was almost immediate. Katrina breathed deeply and settled down.

"Where did Donald Bane go after leaving Moscow, Kate?" Viktor repeated.

"Tur . . . Turrkeey," she responded while moving her head from side to side. Viktor Kozlov cursed silently. Bane was really tracking the hardware.

"Where is Bane now?"

No response.

He was losing her. The barbiturate dose had been a bit stronger than necessary, and she was falling into a deep sleep. Viktor readjusted the control valve and gave her .5cc of Dexedrine. The amphetamine took several seconds to revive her, and she began to move a bit on the recliner.

"Can you hear me, Kate?"

"Kate . . . yes."

He smiled. "Is Donald Bane in Iraq?"

"Yes."

"Where in Iraq, Kate?"

"Irraaaqq . . ."

Her speech began to slur, a sign of the excess sodium pentothal in her system, which also explained the twitching in her cheeks. He had to hurry. "Yes, Iraq. Where is Donald Bane inside Iraq?"

It took Viktor just five additional minutes to pinpoint the location, along with another dose of sodium pentothal, before he removed the IV from her leg. Drenched in sweat and convulsing, Kate Marston turned sideways, braced herself, and brought her legs up to her chest.

"Cold . . . cold . . ." she said, shivering in a fetal position.

Viktor stuck his head outside the room.

"I will be making some phone calls, and then I will start a second interrogation session."

The doctor slowly shook his head. "A second session might kill her."

"That is of no importance. I will interrogate her as many times and as necessary to get my answers. This woman is nothing but a cheap whore for the CIA and the FBI. Irina believes she almost ruined our plans. She is a traitor and will be shown no mercy. Come in here in thirty minutes to reconnect the IV. Until then, I do not wish to be disturbed," he told the Russian doctor standing outside the door, before closing it and walking to the telephone on the desk next to the bed. He had to reach Baghdad immediately. The safe house outside Tikrit had been compromised.

But Viktor couldn't just pick up the phone and call Saddam Hussein, or anyone else in Iraq for that matter. The National Security Agency would nail him within hours.

Viktor would have to use a method devised by the *Mukhabarat* in order to send messages out of America that could not wait for the encoded ads in *The New York Times*.

The Ukrainian wrote his message on a sheet of paper, using as few words as possible. After two revisions he had the message down to just twelve words. He then used the encoder given to Irina Bukovski by Marcos Dominguez six months ago. It allowed Viktor to scramble the message in such a way that it would not make any sense to anyone but the intended receiver.

Such a strange phone call placed overseas might arouse suspicion if the call were actually monitored by the NSA, but it would meaningless, just random English words.

Viktor picked up the phone and called a number in Washington, D.C.

The phone rang three times, and a receptionist came on the line. "Black Youth of America. How may I help you?" she asked.

"Extension four four four, please."

Three more rings, and a man with an Egyptian accent said, "Your password?"

"Rodina."

"Your message?"

"Feast in fall gathered to wealth along the tracks of the night."

"Repeat for accuracy."

Viktor repeated the encoded message.

"Understood," was the Egyptian's reply.

Viktor hung up the phone and ran a hand through his hair. In twenty minutes a New Islamist International soldier would reach an apartment in the outskirts of the city, where he would place a long distance call to Lisbon, Portugal. The apartment, which was being leased on a monthly basis under a fake name, would never again be used by the NII. In Lisbon, the same tactic would be used. The Lisbon telephone number would never again be used by the NII. At least a dozen numbers existed for this type of emergency communication.

From Lisbon, the message would be conveyed to Athens. From Athens to Damascus, and from Damascus to Baghdad. Exactly two hours after Viktor Kozlov placed his original call, a phone rang at Saddam's Presidential Palace. The message had reached its destination.

An hour later Kate Marston became aware of her surroundings. The strong mixture of sodium pentothal and Dexedrine that had kept her in a state of semiconsciousness during the interrogation now began to wear off at a rate faster than Viktor had anticipated.

Slowly, Kate began to realize that she was in a strange room, and that she was not alone, a cloudy vision of someone sitting by a desk across the room talking on the phone kept her from moving a finger. The longer they thought she was out, the longer it would be before they stuck that IV in her again.

She felt awful. Her head throbbed, her eyes burned, her tongue was numb, and her limbs felt quite sore.

How long have I been out? Kate didn't remember much after a short man wearing a lab coat had injected her with a clear liquid, and that had been in another room, a basement or cellar of some sort. Not this warm, cozy room.

At the time, Viktor Kozlov had ordered her to disclose everything she knew about a CIA plan to intercept the nuclear hardware leaving Russia. At her continued refusal he had raped her twice in thirty minutes. When it became clear that Kate would not yield in spite of the sexual abuse, Viktor had called the little bald doctor, who had appeared in the cell holding a syringe already filled with the clear liquid that had knocked her out until now.

Her ears suddenly tuned to the voice of Viktor Kozlov across the room. His back was to Kate. For a moment the thought of getting up slowly, dashing across the room, and hitting the rapist on the head with something crossed her mind. But she quickly discarded it when she realized that she had probably been out for some time and her limbs were not likely to respond on demand yet.

She began to feel light-headed again, and even though she had her eyes closed, she felt everything spinning around her. She fought it, but her mind grew blurrier, confused, tired. The chemicals in her system drew her back down to a level of subconsciousness she did not want to reach again.

Exactly what information did she release to them during the chemical interrogation? The man in the lab coat had smiled before plunging the syringe into her, his words, calm and reassuring, still echoed somewhere inside her dizzy mind. *You mustn't worry, Katrina Aleksandra. Now you will speak the truth. Now you will speak the truth.*

Her body was unresponsive, and she could no longer hear a word spoken inside the room. But she did feel someone next to her now. Kate couldn't see the face but recognized the white lab coat. It was the Russian doctor, and he plunged an IV into her thigh again. A burning sensation smothered her leg, slowly at first, and then with growing speed, absorbing her waist, abdomen, and lower chest like a cloud of fire.

Almost instantly, the spinning in her head grew, pushing all the visions to the periphery of her mind, leaving her core empty, dark, alone. Kate Marston felt herself surrounded by a sea of darkness before everything faded away.

A few hours later, Viktor Kozlov, driving a Federal Express truck, pulled up in front of Robert Bourdeaux's home, located in the middle of a tree-lined street in Bethesda, Maryland, exactly where Katrina Markarova had told him it would be. This had been part of the little information the former KGB operative had revealed over the course of the short-lived second chemical interrogation session. Katrina had died from a drug overdose just five minutes into the session. Although Viktor never did learn the extent of the information Katrina had divulged to Robert Bourdeaux, the DDO was the next logical link in the liability chain.

The vast number of magnolias, cypress, and oaks shielding the house from the street made Viktor feel comfortable. Trees gave him a place to hide as he approached his target. The plantation-style home had four fluted columns across the front, each towering from the floor to the roof of the two-story structure. Long windows, flanked with dark shutters, ran the entire front of the house on both floors. A narrow cobblestone walkway connected the street with the front entrance hidden behind the trees.

Dressed in a freshly starched uniform, Viktor took a small bag from the rear of the truck and walked toward the house. Although Katrina had mentioned the absence of guard dogs, the Ukrainian moved cautiously, his right hand clutching a spray can of Mace, his ears listening for the sounds of a running canine. Security agencies had been known to surgically remove the vocal cords of guard dogs, increasing their chances of surprising a thief.

He approached a window near the back of the house and checked along the edges until he found what he was looking for: the window switch of a built-in alarm system. Placing a small suction cup on one of the eight-by-ten glass panels closest to the window's edge, Viktor took out a professional diamond-tipped glass cutter from the bag and made a small circular cut around the cup. After softly tapping the edges of the cut with the glass cutter's handle, he gently pulled back the suction cup and, with a barely audible sound, the circular section of glass snapped off the glass panel. He paused momentarily but, as he had expected, there were no vibration sensors on the glass.

Viktor Kozlov put the cup on the ground, removed a small magnet attached to an adjustable Velcro band, and inserted it through the circular opening. The alarm system's window switch had two components. One was stationary and fixed to the windowsill. It housed a contact switch, which had a pair of spring-loaded contacts. The second one, attached to the window, was a magnet located within a half inch of the contact switch when the window was closed. The magnet kept the contacts from closing, but the moment the window opened, the magnet would move away and the spring-loaded contacts would close, triggering the alarm.

He secured his magnet to the contact switch, using the Velcro strap. He then unlocked the window and slowly raised it. No alarm.

Slowly, he checked the carpet directly under the window for pressure sensors but found none. He stepped in and scanned the spacious living room: a couple of black leather couches over an Oriental rug facing a large fireplace. He examined the walls, looking for infrared sensors or motion detectors. He found none.

Viktor slowly moved through the living room, the kitchen, and into the dark foyer, where thick curtains covered large windows facing the columns in front. Three track lights on the left side of the ceiling faced the entrance. He decided that Bourdeaux would definitely have to turn on the track lights first to avoid tripping on something when entering the house.

Viktor reached into his bag, removed three light bulbs, and carefully inspected the highly flammable substance inside of each, making sure that at least part of the napalm was in contact with the light bulb's filament. The few ounces of napalm in each bulb, when ignited by the red-hot filaments, would result in a deadly bath of fire for anyone standing in that foyer.

Satisfied, he placed them on the foyer's floor, walked to the dining room, brought a chair over, and placed it exactly under the track lights.

Slowly, he unscrewed all three bulbs and replaced them with his own. He put the other light bulbs in his bag, put the chair back, and headed for the living room window.

He scanned the room once again. Pleased with his work, he crawled back outside, closed and locked the window, and removed his magnet. Finally, he reached down for the suction cup and pulled out of his left pocket a tube of clear cement.

After carefully applying the cement to the edges of the glass, Viktor inserted the circular piece back in place and removed the suction cup. The instant cement bonded the circular piece to the glass panel in seconds. He tapped on the glass and nodded approvingly.

A minute later, he returned to the truck, got in, and dialed an unlisted number in Maryland.

"The electric repair has been completed. I'm waiting to see if the customer is satisfied."

"Good. Report back when it's over."

Viktor hung up the phone and checked his watch.

16

THE STAND

Laws are silent in time of war.
　　　　　　　　—Cicero

SOUTHERN IRAQ.

The Teledyne Ryan BQM-145A Unmanned Aerial Vehicle separated from the solid rocket booster assembly after reaching the apex of its parabolic flight. The single static-thrust turbofan jet engine kicked into life, providing 970 pounds of thrust, and propelling the composite-skin craft to five hundred knots. The UAV's twelve-foot-span wings tilted to the right as the American-made craft turned to a northerly heading in response to its inertial navigational system's receiving constant updates from the Global Positioning System stored in the probe's center fuselage.

Twenty miles to the south, outside Kuwait City, Lieutenant Colonel Diane Towers sat inside a large rectangular tent with the ten surviving pilots of her flight group. Tired but otherwise in good enough health to continue flight operations, Diane readied herself to strike back with decisive force on this cool and windy night. Her mission was to take out a large Iraqi air base, which military intelligence believed would support the initial strike against General Oliver Grogan's 52nd Tank Regiment just south of the border with Kuwait.

Diane's mission was particularly critical because General Grogan's forces were vastly outnumbered and reinforcements would not arrive in time before the Iraqis struck. According to her recent radio conversation with the sixty-year-old general, the battalion of tanks would have a chance of containing the initial wave only if the United States had air superiority over the battlefield.

As Diane's eyes drifted to her new wingman, Major "Blue Jeans" Levi, the seasoned lieutenant colonel decided that this time things would go differently.

Although temperatures had already dropped well into the fifties, the cool, refreshing weather had no apparent effect on Diane, whose penetrating eyes remained glued to the large color projection screen, which, divided into four windows, displayed in real time the data collected by the UAV's sensors. The upper left window showed the probe's position in relation to a built-in color map of northern Kuwait and southern Iraq. Next to it Diane saw a real-time image from the probe's image-intensifier visual camera. Below that window, she saw the equivalent infrared image of the surveyed area. The lower leftmost screen displayed telemetry data, consisting of altitude, speed, fuel, and a number of other operating parameters. Both visual and infrared data were stored on tape for later analysis.

Diane looked at the position marked on the map on the screen, the place which a KH-12 satellite had identified as the location of the air base. Under different circumstances, the satellite data would have been sufficient for Diane and her team to commence the air strike, but not on this cool night. Not after hearing the news that the *Kennedy* would not be able to launch any planes, its crew still battling the damage sustained twelve hours ago. Diane needed to confirm the satellite data because she knew she would only have one shot at striking the Iraqis. Once her squadron became airborne, she would have to reach and destroy the Iraqi air base immediately, before the Arabs detected them and got their MiGs airborne. According to the CIA and the satellite data, the base had over seventy-five MiG-23s and many more MiG-21s being fueled and armed to provide air cover for Republican Guard divisions poised to strike General Grogan's forces in Kuwait. The general would be facing a formidable invading force as it was, even without the support of the MiGs. And reinforcements seemed unlikely to arrive for the next several hours. C-5 Galaxy transports were due to arrive in Kuwait hauling another twenty thousand troops by noon, but they wouldn't do General Grogan any good during the morning battle.

If those MiGs got airborne before Diane could destroy them, the Marine Corps lieutenant colonel and her team would be hopelessly outnumbered in aerial combat. But stealthiness was her team's credo. Striking at night in their Hornets was what this group of leathernecks did best, and tonight, Diane would put all the hours of practice and hard work to the ultimate test.

"How long before the probe reaches the target, Blue Jeans?"

"Just a couple more minutes, ma'am," responded Major Levi, without taking his light brown eyes off the screen.

Diane nodded while focusing on the upper right window. The image, thanks to the half-moon and the advanced optics of the sensing lens, which amplified the available light to enhance the viewing resolution, gave an amazingly clear picture of the terrain. She briefly eyed the infrared underneath.

"What's the optical resolution of this thing?"

"If anyone's smokin' inside a hangar on that base, I reckon we oughta be able to see him from the IR signature," Levi said, pointing to a satellite photo next to the screen.

Diane took in a deep breath of cool air. It was already one o'clock in the morning, and it was going to be a long night. She tilted her head and glanced at Levi. "How hard is it for the Iraqis to detect the probe?"

"Hard's catchin' a runnin' chicken, ma'am. The UAV's too small, and it's coated with the latest radar-absorbent stuff. That, plus the fact that it's black, and it has a high-bypass turbofan, sure in hell makes it damn near invisible at night."

"Let's hope so," Diane said. "The last thing we need is for those Iraqis to figure out our plan and launch an early attack on Grogan."

Diane Towers crossed her thin but firm arms and briefly closed her eyes. She felt weary and nauseated from lack of sleep and also from the residual effects of the radiation dose she had endured. She now wore a Marines baseball cap to hide her thinning hair, and her flight suit was zipped all the way up to her neck. She didn't want anyone to see the purple blotches that had taken over most of her upper chest. The tissue in her gums had also begun to decay, resulting in very painful toothbrushing sessions and a lot of blood, which she also found in her urine. She had come close to informing the squadron flight surgeon but decided against it. The surgeon might ground her at a time when her country needed her most. She would deal with the effects of the radiation later. Right now she had a mission to fly.

For the past thirty minutes the group had listened to Major Levi's detailed briefing on the SAM installations surrounding the Iraqi air base, and of the forces on the base itself. Now the probe was finally about to reach the target and hopefully confirm their satellite data.

"We're there," Levi said. Diane opened her eyes and studied the rapidly changing image on the screen.

The UAV's sharp nose bit into the air at four hundred knots while maintaining a shallow left turn. With the quiet turbofan now on idle, the eighteen-foot-long, honeycomb-structured plane slowly descended from five thousand feet while its Advanced Tactical Airborne Reconnaissance System's electro-optical and infrared sensors scanned the valley underneath. As the craft's passive wings—a design derived from NASA's supercritical wing design for better range and fuel economy—maintained a steady fifteen-degree angle of bank, the sensors went to work, providing real-time images of the terrain below. The instant the UAV reached an altitude of one thousand feet, the constant-motion elevons, located outboard of the two vertical fins, became flush with the streamlined design, leveling out the probe. The single rudder, located on the left fin, stopped the shallow turn and pointed the nose to a westerly heading. The turbofan didn't kick in right away. The craft glided for another minute at the rate of thirty feet forward for every foot of altitude—another advantage of the NASA wing design. The moment the Global Positioning System told the inertial navigation system that the craft had reached the three-mile mark from the target zone, the turbofan accelerated, but not to full throttle, just enough to maintain a two-hundred-knot escape velocity without losing any more altitude. At the ten-mile mark, the single engine's low hum increased to a mild whine as airspeed jumped to five hundred knots and the remote probe headed home.

"That was fast," said Diane.

"Yep, but sure was long enough," Major Levi responded as he approached the small portable control console built into a metallic briefcase, and replayed the fifteen seconds of low altitude surveillance in slow motion. The visual and infrared images confirmed the KH-12 data. Warm turbofans told them the planes had been flown recently, most likely in war exercises. In addition, the short aerial pass also revealed four underground fuel storage tanks, from which a number of hoses currently serviced dozens of fighters. Thermal images of about a hundred men moving around the parked fighters further confirmed the satellite data. The base was indeed getting ready for a morning assault.

"All right, Blue Jeans. Looks like the satellite data was accurate."

Levi ran a hand through his close-cropped brown hair and continued, covering in fine detail the numerous SAM batteries surrounding the base, as well as additional detail on the air base itself.

"Thanks," Diane said, checking her watch before getting up and scanning the group, mostly young pilots, but their age was not to be confused with the training and combat time they had under their belts.

"All right, gentlemen. We'll be flying top cover for General Grogan's 52nd Tank Regiment. Although we'll be carrying a full load of ammo for the cannons and a couple of air-to-airs, most of the load we'll be hauling are air-to-muds. Make no mistake, SAM facilities and the air base are where your ordnance goes. You must unload all of the bombs on the targets before engaging Iraqi MiGs, which I know will be a headache if they get airborne before we get there, although I'm sure the Iraqis will have some jets already on patrol. The timing here's critical. Our intelligence believes the Iraqis will attack the 52nd at dawn and aren't expecting an American strike tonight. Those MiGs on the ground are loaded with fuel and ammo for the morning. This is our best chance, so hit hard and decisively. Just as during our practice runs, we'll work in five sections of two. Blue Jeans, you'll be my wing. The rest split as we discussed before." Diane checked her watch once again. "If you have to go and relieve yourselves, do it now. Let's move out."

The pilots, already wearing their G suits and life vests, and carrying their helmets and oxygen masks, got up and headed outside. A few stopped by trees at the edge of the clearing to urinate, well aware that few things in this world were as uncomfortable as a full bladder in high-g situations.

Diane slowly walked to her single-seat version of the Hornet, the F/A-18C. Her ground crew finished up last-minute details to get the thirty-three-thousand-pound fighter-bomber ready for action, a task that involved filling up empty fuel tanks, replenishing the single 20mm cannon's magazine, securing missiles and bombs onto stores hard points under the short wings, and doing a number of "tweaks" to the avionics. The ground crew resembled a well-orchestrated play, with each of the five members performing his duty with grace and a high degree of effectiveness. There could be no mistakes here. No missiles left unsecured. No jammed cannons. No malfunctioning avionics. The Hornets had to be perfect for battle. Perfect to fight an enemy armed with the latest Russian technology.

The ground crew chief approached Diane. "Your plane is ready, Colonel."

The crew chief handed Diane the acceptance form and a pen. The lieutenant colonel grabbed them and began her walkaround, carefully examining all control surfaces, weapons, and panels. Satisfied, Diane signed the form and passed it back to her subordinate before climbing up the special ladder rolled up to the F/A-18C.

Diane strapped herself into her seat, plugged the combination oxygen-intercom lead, which fed her mask communications system, into the connecting block on the left side of the seat, and threw the jet fuel starter switch. At once, the auxiliary power unit housed in between the pair of turbofans came to life, bringing the generators on line to provide enough electrical power to allow Diane use of the intercom and cockpit instrument displays.

Instantly feeling at home, Diane went down the pretaxi checklist, verifying functionality of the central CRT, the radar, and the color map. She threw the Heads-up Display switch and confirmed that the projected telemetry and symbology data on the canopy matched that of the CRT. After adjusting the brightness of the HUD, Diane used the auxiliary power unit to engage the starboard turbofan while her eyes scanned the engine-related data shown on the upper right corner of the CRT. The low whine grew into a steady whirl. Diane kept the throttle on idle and started the port turbofan. She shut down the auxiliary power unit and turned her attention to the control surfaces' checks. Outside, her ground crew moved in harmony once more, visually checking the response of the ailerons, elevators, rudder, and flaps, reporting the results to Diane through the intercom system.

Diane enabled the Built-In Test Equipment, a program in which the onboard computers automatically examined all avionics and weapon systems. BITE came back green, and Diane dialed in the mission's Identification Friendly or Foe code into the transponder, permitting the other Hornets to "interrogate" her Hornet and verify it as a "friendly."

Diane placed both hands against the canopy so that they could be clearly seen by the ground crew as they removed the safing devices inhibiting accidental missile or cannon firing. The moment the crew backed away from the F/A-18C, she activated the radio and spoke into the small microphone built into her oxygen mask. "Strike Leader. Radio check."

"Five . . . two . . . four . . . three," came the response from the other teams.

The ground crew chief walked in front of the Hornet, snapped to attention, and saluted Diane. The Marine Corps lieutenant colonel saluted back.

With the brakes released and a gentle push of the side-by-side throttles to her left, Diane taxied her jet clear of the trees and toward the short runway. Levi followed her. Together they made the first "section" of their flight group.

Diane let her wingman catch up, and the pair rolled onto the runway. After a power check and a quick exchange of hand signals to indicate that all was well, both Hornets hurtled forward under the power of their turbofans. Diane slowly advanced the throttles to build up forward airspeed without much concern about the rapidly approaching sand dunes at the other end of the four-thousand-foot-long runway.

She broke ground as her airspeed continued to increase.

One hundred twenty knots . . . 170 . . . 210 . . .

Diane leveled off at two thousand feet holding 320 knots and put on her night goggles, instantly turning the world around her a palette of greens.

"This is Strike Leader. Stay close. Stay low," Diane said as she inched the centerstick forward, dropping down to two hundred feet, hugging the desert floor. Levi's Hornet flew slightly behind her and to her right. The color map told Diane the exact range to the Iraqi air base.

"Roger," she heard Levi respond.

Diane checked her mission timer clock. *Right on time.*

Speed 320 knots. Perfect. Everything seemed perfect. The jet was a work of art, the product of two decades of American engineering targeted at creating the ultimate advanced tactical fighter. In it, Diane knew she was nearly untouchable and almost invisible, especially if she maintained this altitude.

As an ocean of green-stained sand rushed under her, Lieutenant Colonel Diane Towers allowed herself the simple pleasure of briefly gazing at the crystalline sky, the adrenaline boost from the mission forcing her mind away from her decaying medical condition.

"Pickin' up some fast movers, Lead," reported Levi from Strike One

One Seven. *"Three MiGs at your two movin' in a parallel course in the opposite direction at fifty thousand. I reckon they can't see us while we're so close to the ground."*

Diane quickly checked the optical radar to the right multifunction display, confirming Levi's finding. The MiG trio flew too high for their lookdown radars to pick out their Hornets from the ground clutter. Although the MiGs were pounding the region with E-band radar energy, their searching beams were way too wide to pinpoint Diane's squadron. They were simply doing a large-area sweep. "Confirmed, One Seven. This is Strike Leader. Be aware of three MiGs thirty miles east of the target. Ignore unless they narrow their beams. Your ordnance's spoken for."

Diane heard confirmation from the other four elements of her group while keeping an eye on the optical radar for any sign of disturbance from the enemy fighters. She could hear their radars making a sweep every thirty seconds.

Beep . . . beep.

The MiGs continued their flight until disappearing from the screen a minute later.

Just as suddenly, Diane's radar warning receiver told her she was being "painted" on E-band by another radar. The narrow beams indicated that in spite of the Hornet's low altitude and speed, somehow the Iraqis had detected her, were currently tracking her, and had probably passed the information on to the nearest SAM systems and the air base.

"Hot damn!" Levi said over the radio. *"Bastards found us, and right over the sand!"*

Diane nodded. "This is Strike Lead. All elements to Mach one point five. The mission is a go. Lock in your targets and unload your stores before the Iraqis get here. Repeat, lock in your targets."

"Roger," came the unanimous response from the other elements, which Diane had spaced by twenty miles to maximize the chance of the elements reaching the target. Her plan would have to change now. She had to drop her load to give the Hornet the maneuverability necessary to engage with the fast and highly maneuverable MiGs adequately.

"Incoming missiles! Two, no . . . three!" reported Levi as Diane pushed full throttle and climbed to three thousand feet while tracking the incoming SAMs on the optical radar, which showed the tracking vectors of the Iraqi missiles.

"Got them. Follow my lead, One Seven. Countermeasures!"

"Confirmed, Lead."

As the pair of Hornets got within fifty miles of the base, Diane activated the electronic countermeasures and chaff dispenser system. The missiles, less than five miles away, approached them head-on. On the night vision goggles, the SAMs looked like shooting stars in the distant sky, almost blending themselves with the real ones.

The internal countermeasures system released two dozen five-foot-long Mylar strips coated with a microfilm of aluminum oxide. At the same time, the powerful ALE-905 system began to electronically pound the homing brains of the Iraqi missiles to provide them with a hundred virtual targets.

"Chaff released. Break!"

As the cloud of chaff washed away in the slipstream, Diane pulled the stick to the left while pushing full power. The g's tore at her as the jet cut left at great speed. Her G suit inflated to prevent her legs from becoming pools of blood, but even that didn't keep her upper extremities from tingling because of lack of circulation as her vision narrowed. The ensuing shock wave from the combined explosion of three warheads inside the cloud of chaff pushed her jet even harder to the right.

"One Seven, Leader. Damage report?"

"None, Lead!"

Diane cut back throttles and leveled the wings. She briefly checked her radar as it began to make wide sweeps searching, acquiring, and tracking ground targets, which were then passed on to the fire control computer. In an instant, over a dozen targets, labeled according to a priority system based on the highest probability of kill, peppered the Heads-up Display.

"One Seven, Strike Lead. Drop them as you see them."

"Targets acquired. Going shoppin'."

As Levi broke right, heading for the targets within his area of responsibility, Diane pulled the centerstick back and the Hornet went vertical to five thousand feet. The g's remained with her as she flung the stick forward, and the negative g's took over, pushing her upward against her restraining harness. Blood rushed to her head, making her eyeballs feel ready to explode. With the world turning shades of red, Diane forced her disciplined mind to ignore the g's and scan the information painted on the HUD. Throttles at half settings—540 knots—altitude 5,200 feet.

Pushing the nose over to a forty-five-degree angle, Diane heard her two tail sensors going crazy. Someone had sneaked up behind her and was trying to get a lock. *Too bad.* She pushed full throttles and the earth filled her windscreen.

A single depression of a red button on the sidestick, and one HARM antiradar missile left in a blaze before she began pulling on the stick. The g's hammered her as she kept up the rearward pressure. The Hornet jerked back up into the murky sky. A fiery ball of flames behind her told Diane the HARM had reached the SAM system.

The tail warning momentarily stopped. The goggles gave her superior vision for a night air-to-air engagement. Perhaps the MiG hadn't been able to pull up as hard and had lost her in the darkness. It didn't matter. She climbed up to three thousand feet and followed a new vector to the next SAM emplacement, which she locked in moments later. Once more she dropped on it like a hawk, releasing her second HARM from the rightmost underwing pylon, and a few seconds later she verified the secondary explosion.

Once more the tail sensor went crazy. Its high pitch told her the pursuer was close. Real close. Diane still couldn't engage in a dogfight, not with ten thousand pounds of explosives under the wings. She noticed the increased aerial activity near the air base twenty miles away. Blips began to appear on the radar.

"This is Strike Lead, sky's getting dirty. Drop your loads before the MiGs get airborne."

"Roger."

Ten miles. Diane pressed full power and the Hornet rushed past Mach 1.5. Nine miles. Eight . . . seven . . . six . . . five.

With the threat temporarily lost in her supersonic wake, Diane eased back throttles as the base loomed in plain view thanks to the goggles, which also told her of the half dozen MiGs that had just gotten airborne, and the many more taxiing into position on the crowded air base.

Diane dropped to five hundred feet while decelerating to six hundred knots. She armed the dozen Snakeye smart bombs on the multiple ejector racks under both wings as the fire control computer calculated her firing solution.

Antiaircraft fire broke out from several places at once, resembling streaks of lightning to the NVGs, filling the sky with light beams reaching out for her. Feeling the slight vibration on the stick from the explosions of near-misses, Diane popped up to seven hundred feet and gave the system a few more seconds to achieve total lock. The symbology projected on the HUD told her that twelve ground targets had been identified, and in the following second, she pressed the release button on the centerstick, and pulled up as she flew right above the base.

The g's pounded her. With her vision narrowing, Diane saw thin streams of vapor pouring off the wing roots as the pressure blasted against the composite surface of the Hornet.

The Snakeyes continued their ballistic trajectory. Multiple explosions turned the night into day as fighters went up in flames, creating instant havoc.

Her Identification Friendly or Foe system detected Levi's Hornet as it made its pass over the blazing airfield. Antiaircraft fire had decreased significantly, and that suited her just fine, Diane decided, as she rolled her craft to get a better view of Levi's run.

Unlike Diane, Levi flew in at treetop level—a necessary approach owing to the nature of his stores. Levi carried one large cluster of cratering munitions, which contained a shaped charge designed to drill through the runway to allow a second charge to detonate below the surface. The resulting craters made airfield repair specialists truly earn their pay. In addition, her subordinate carried two Rockeye II cluster bomb dispensers, designed to go off fifty feet above the airfield. The resulting shrapnel could damage an area the size of a football field.

Levi maintained his low approach at high speed until reaching the edge of the airfield, where he popped up to three hundred feet and released his load. Inflatable "ballute" tails stuck out the back of the bombs to increase drag and give Levi a chance to get away from the ensuing inferno.

As the runway, surrounding planes, and ground crew disappeared behind a sheet of fire, Diane saw two fighters closing in on Levi's tail. MiG-23s.

"Leader to One Seven. Got two MiGs on your . . . one of them just fired, Blue Jeans! Two, three missiles. Get the hell out of there!"

Diane hadn't finished speaking when Levi's Hornet went vertical a fraction of a second after releasing a cloud of chaff. Two missiles went under, the third remained locked on her subordinate's tail.

Diane pushed full throttle and went after the two MiGs following Levi, who rolled his craft and executed an inverted loop after popping more chaff and a cluster of infrared flares. That did it. The last missile went astray, but the MiGs stayed with him.

"Can't shake them bastards!"

"Hang in there, Blue Jeans. I got them."

Diane followed the inverted caravan down to five hundred feet, where her subordinate leveled off and pulled the tightest loop Diane'd ever seen. Both pursuing MiGs overshot the loop, losing the Hornet in the dark. Diane smiled as the Iraqi pilots obviously realized they had been outperformed.

The MiG-23s simultaneously executed a vertical corkscrew to five thousand feet, and Diane took pursuit with Levi now glued to her starboard wing.

"Bastards sure are fast," she heard Levi say as the MiGs split in a Y at the apex of their ascent. Both Hornets remained with the left MiG as it tried to go supersonic, but to do so, the Iraqi first had to push full afterburner to achieve the required supersonic transitional speed, and when it did, Diane locked a Sidewinder heat-seeking missile on its white-hot nozzle.

She fired and followed the river of smoke as it sprinted across the sky.

A cloud of infrared flares left an underside pod of the MiG-23, but it was too late. Although the Iraqi fighter hurtled downward to attempt fooling the missile into the floating countermeasures, the missile's infrared homing unit had too good a lock on the afterburning tail. Diane saw the missile detonate alongside the starboard aft fuselage section. The blast effect peeled the vertical fin, along with the starboard elevator, causing an immediate loss of control. The MiG-23 rolled and pitched nose-downward as an explosion in the aft fuselage caused fragments of the warhead to penetrate into the fuselage, impacting the turbine blades with disastrous results. The thrown blades, still rotating at thousands of revolutions per minute, shredded nearby fuel lines. The engulfing fire that followed quickly spread to the wings as the burning fuel moved toward the main tanks. The MiG broke apart in midair just seconds before striking the ground.

Diane saw no ejection.

"Strike Three to Lead. MiGs, MiGs. Three at my six o'clock! Bastards are right on my tail! My wingman just disengaged with a downed turbofan!" Diane heard the lead pilot of the group's third section shout over the radio.

"Confirmed, Strike Three. Coming back around. Got an approach vector. Be there in twenty seconds," Diane responded as she turned into the vector and pushed Mach 2, with Levi glued to her side.

"I don't know if I can hold them, Lead. The bastards . . . oh, shit. Missiles! Two closing at Mach four!"

"Get out of there!"

"Chaff's out!"

Diane saw the air show in the distance. The two missiles followed the Hornet as it tried to lose itself in the ground clutter. It worked. The missiles went astray in a cloud of chaff, but the pursuing MiGs kept the pace. Diane played the throttles and centerstick to close the gap. One of the Iraqis broke left.

"Stay with the two on Strike Three's tail, One Seven!"

"Lead, Lead, the third's loopin' around," said Levi. *"He's gonna try to—"*

"I know, One Seven. I know. Just stay with the two MiGs. Strike Three, Lead, over."

"Lead, can't get them off my tail!"

"Relax," responded Diane as she unsuccessfully tried to saddle in for a missile shot. "I'll clear them for you. Too close for missiles. Switching to guns!"

Strike Three executed a vertical corkscrew and the two MiGs followed. Diane pulled on the stick and added throttle to go vertical and float her fighter right up to the left MiG-23, before lining up the craft on the HUD's crosshairs and pressing the trigger to the first detent.

The 20mm cannon kicked into life, firing rhythmic bursts of ten rounds each every two seconds. The NVGs allowed her to see the bursts as strings of light projecting toward the MiG. Diane used the luminous beams to adjust her fire, and watched in satisfaction when the MiG's turbofan began to smoke as the caravan reached forty-five hundred feet.

Diane's tail sensor went red again as the third MiG completed the loop and tried to get a lock on her Hornet.

"Gotta move, Lead. The bastard's going to get an angle on my ass," Levi said.

"Break hard left, Strike Three," Diane told the pilot of the lead Hornet. "Get him when he overshoots. I have to take care of a MiG on my tail."

"Confirmed, Lead," responded Strike Three's pilot.

"Okay, One Seven. Stay with me. Let's see what this guy can do."

The pair of Hornets left the tail of the MiG following Strike Three by executing an inverted dive. Suddenly, instead of following Strike Three, the second MiG joined the one following Levi and her.

"Lead, now we got both of 'em bastards on our butts!"

"We have to separate, One Seven. Break left on count!"

"Roger, Lead."

Diane pulled out of the inverted dive and broke hard right while applying full throttle. Eight g's blasted on the composite skin of the F/A-18 as Diane forced the Tactical Fighter to the outer envelope of the design. The trick worked again. The Iraqi overshot the turn and came out of it five hundred feet ahead of Diane, who managed to fight the high-g–induced tunnel vision enough to lock him in the crosshairs and fire, but the MiG-23's pilot anticipated Diane's attack and broke left just in time. The Iraqi then inverted and shot straight down. Diane followed and switched to missiles. In order to pull out of the dive and maintain that forward airspeed, the MiG would have to use afterburner. Diane smiled when the MiG-23 rolled out and started a tight right turn and climb in full afterburner.

Diane heard the loud buzz of the heat-seeking head of her second missile, and fired. The Sidewinder left in a blaze and closed in at Mach 3, got momentarily lost in a cloud of infrared flares left behind by the departing MiG, but quickly reacquired and closed in for the kill. This time, the missile disappeared into the MiG-23's exhaust, and a second later the entire sky in front of Diane became a ball of bright NVG green light as the Iraqi fighter blew from its core out.

After making a sharp right turn to avoid the burning debris, she scanned the radar for signs of Levi, who had already taken care of his MiG and was returning to her side.

"Good shooting, One Seven."

"Ditto, Lead."

Diane verified that the remaining craft in the area were friendlies. "Leader to Strike group, Leader to Strike group. Confirm touchstone on red, over."

"Three . . . Four . . . Five . . . Two."

All SAM systems had been destroyed. The base was in flames. All enemy fighters that had managed to get airborne had been downed. General Grogan would have air superiority during the initial Iraqi attack in the morning.

The trip back took only ten minutes as the Hornets cruised in a straight line at Mach 1.3, depleting nearly ninety percent of their fuel by the time their landing gear struck the runway.

Under the dim lights of the base, Diane taxied her Hornet back to the shelter, where the ground crew chief already waited with his team and the rest of the pilots. Diane performed a tight 180 turn using the rudder pedals, leaving her jet on the clearing with the tail facing the desert. A diesel tower with a nosewheel adapter came around and pushed the craft into the temporary shelter, which had a roof made of heavy camouflage mesh over a waterproof canvas.

As the ground crew chief pulled the ladder out from the left side of the fuselage, Diane powered down, lifted the canopy, and unstrapped herself. On the ground, Levi ran to join the other pilots, who cheered their victory.

Diane removed her helmet and quickly put on a green cap to hide her thinning hair before climbing down the ladder. The small crowd surrounded her.

"Yes, Colonel, we really did it to them this time, didn't we?" one pilot said.

Diane, helmet in hand, rubbed her eyes and said, "It's too early to call it a victory, isn't it? Particularly with the Republican Guard heading this way."

Smiles vanished in a flash as most of the pilots lowered their gaze. Levi glanced at Diane, who simply raised a fine eyebrow while tilting her head.

"Gentlemen, no one celebrates in this place until that maniac is back in his little shithole in Baghdad. No one. Today we just scratched the surface. It's going to take a lot more flawless, top-notch flying to keep those Iraqis at bay, and I can tell you it's not going be easy. Today we lucked out. The timing was just right. Another ten minutes and we would have found ourselves fighting dozens of Iraqi MiGs instead of the few that managed to get airborne before we got there. Tomorrow this place is going to be swarming with Air Force planes on their way from the States. But before that, we have another sortie coming up to support General Grogan. I suggest you get something to eat and grab some sleep before reporting to the briefing tent. Dismissed!"

The pilots looked at one another, half in disbelief, half in bitter understanding of their commander's words, before slowly walking away from the makeshift shelter.

Diane remained behind, standing next to the F/A-18C as the ground crew began to haul carts loaded with 20mm ammunition and missiles. As she watched it in silence, Diane's prayers went to General Oliver Grogan, who somehow had to hold back the Iraqis until reinforcements came. Defeat meant the imminent loss of Kuwait, and the beginning of another long and arduous campaign to eject the Iraqis from a country that never belonged to them in the first place.

17

THE LINE IN THE SAND

Oh war, thou son of hell!
—Shakespeare

KUWAIT-IRAQ BORDER.

On the battlefield, there are two areas of particular concern to the brigade commander or battalion commander: the "Area of Influence" and the "Area of Interest." Area of Influence is defined as the operational area assigned to a commander in which he is capable of fighting the enemy using manpower and equipment assigned to his command. The Area of Interest extends beyond the Area of Influence to comprehend any enemy forces capable of directly or indirectly affecting the commander's current operations within the Area of Influence. Areas of Influence and Interest vary in size from brigade to brigade, and within a brigade, from battalion to battalion. Typically, a twenty-four-hour Area of Influence and a seventy-two-hour Area of Interest allow the commander to concentrate his forces effectively, fighting the enemy that can be acquired in the next twenty-four hours while keeping an eye on the enemy within seventy-two hours' reach.

The 52nd U.S. Army Division's current position in the field was ten miles south of the forward elements of the Iraqi offensive echelon. Division Commander General Oliver "Buck" Grogan's mission this overcast morning was to defend his line in the sand and push back the Iraqis from a sector of desert north of the Kuwaiti border. His twenty thousand men, their fighting and transportation vehicles, and four hundred Advanced Multiple Rocket Launchers faced a formidable adversary made up of more than forty thousand Iraqis and their fighting hardware, just the first wave of an ocean of Iraqi forces Grogan hoped would not reach him before reinforcements arrived. Although his task had been made easier by the U.S. Marines' successful elimination of the Iraqi division's air support, the threat from the Iraqi army up ahead was significant nonetheless.

Standing next to his Chrysler M1D Abrahms tank positioned on a small hill overlooking his wedge-shaped defensive force, the seasoned general, a tall, elegant man with a full head of sandy hair, thick mustache, and a booming voice that went well with his ice-cold blue eyes, counted on Lieutenant Colonel Towers's F/A-18C squadron to maintain close air support over the combat zone and delay enemy land forces within the Area of Interest and Influence, to allow the 52nd enough time to complete its initial defensive maneuvers until squadrons of F-15s and F-16s from the States reached the area at midday.

Divide and conquer. That was the way Grogan preferred to fight battles, particularly when outnumbered by the enemy. The forward echelon elements consisted of just under forty thousand Iraqi army regulars. Information extracted from satellite photographs before the gray clouds had descended over the valley enabled him to make a preliminary determination of his Area of Interest and Influence. Once that determination was made, he ordered the deployment of five Remotely Piloted Vehicles from their launchers five miles behind his front line.

A couple of minutes later, the Kevlar-armored, angular-shaped craft darted across the sky at two hundred feet, closely following the contours of the terrain below. Single pusher propellers thrust them forward, in spite of heavy crosswinds swirling down the hills to the northwest. The craft, flying 120 knots, climbed to 850 feet as they approached the far section of the division's current Area of Interest.

Unlike the older, operator-driven versions of the RPVs, the fully autonomous observation vehicles provided Grogan with a panoramic view of the valley without having to commit any of his men to battle.

He kept his eyes on the portable nineteen-inch monitor system in front of him as the planes reached the other side of the valley, where onboard cameras scanned the area below, generating real-time images of the enemy's defensive front, and provided valuable target acquisition information, through microwave downlinks, to the 52nd's rocket artillery.

Grogan stepped away from the radio and waited for the AMRLs to open fire, with coordinates devised to cut the Iraqi offensive's primary echelon in order to isolate their front from the rest of the column.

Behind him the AMRLs started their hellish sounds as hundreds of self-propelled rounds zoomed overhead, partially blocking the sky. The heavy shells pounded the far eastern section of the valley in a perpendicular line between two low hills, creating a wall of fire and debris right in the middle of the Iraqi first echelon. Through the RPV cameras, Grogan saw the massive destruction from the mixed array of warheads fired from most of the AMRLs in unison.

The data acquired by the RPVs provided initial acquisition and tracking for the wave-active radar-guided submunitions housed inside the multiple rockets flying overhead. The moment the rockets reached the target area, a time fuse released the weapons, which immediately began to glide while allowing their radars a few seconds to acquire their individual targets—the Russian-made T-72 Iraqi tanks. On acquisition, the submunitions initiated their terminal top-attack dive on the targets, detonating their shaped-charge warheads on contact with Iraqi armor.

In the first thirty seconds, over one hundred tanks caught fire while many more blew up when they ran over an array of mines and minelets deployed by other self-propelled rounds.

Although that initial strike took care of a significant percentage of enemy tanks, the AMRLs alone couldn't stop the advancing Iraqi column. A second wave of tanks slowly made its way past the burning wrecks of the frontal line. Another thirty seconds, and the Iraqi tanks broke the nine-mile mark from the 52nd's own front line.

Grogan turned to a young captain sitting behind a portable radio console and nodded. The captain activated the UHF radio designed to trigger the U.S. Army's newest and most accurate and lethal unmanned battlefield weapon to date: the Sensor Fuzed Weapon.

In an instant, hundreds of submunitions hurtled upward over the battlefield under the power of their own solid rocket motors. The SFWs, set in place on the low hills along both sides of the valley during the past twelve hours by U.S. Army scouts, reached an altitude of 450 feet directly in front of the advancing Iraqi tanks and slowly descended by parachute. Ten feet above ground the SFWs jettisoned the chute, and, as they reached ground, the smart weapons righted themselves with spring-loaded feet. Using both acoustic and seismic sensors to detect the approaching Iraqi tanks, the SFWs fired secondary rocket motors to propel a cloud of submunitions above the incoming enemy. Each submunition released four skeets with infrared sensors, which, upon detecting a target directly below them, fired an explosive that collapsed the copper in front of it into a projectile. A rain of copper slugs, traveling at over five thousand feet per second, penetrated the armor of dozens of tanks in the first few seconds of engagement. Explosively formed penetrator warheads sliced through the thick armor of tanks along the entire width of the Iraqi divisions to create a sheet of fire and debris that rose up to the sky.

"Dear God," murmured the young captain while Grogan stared at the screen in sheer disbelief. The manufacturer of the SFW had provided the U.S. Army with specifications on the capabilities of their product, but it wasn't until today that more than a just a few of the very expensive weapons were tried at once.

"They're still coming, sir," reported the captain. Grogan brushed his mustache with an index finger as the real-time image from the still-circling RPVs revealed yet another wave of Iraqi tanks crashing through the inferno fueled by their own hardware.

"Enable the WAMs," Grogan commanded a major who was operating out of the back of a truck.

Another secured UHF code came to life, enabling another wonder weapon, the Wide Area Mine, which was not a mine in the formal sense of the word since the WAM did not operate from below ground.

Using Texas Instruments C30 computer chips, the WAMs—spread in a gridlike pattern across the eight miles now separating the two armies—began their digital processing to detect incoming heavy vehicle targets. The moment an Iraqi tank came within range of a WAM, the fully automated unit rotated its single skeet into the best firing position. A second later, an explosive charge propelled the skeet upward over the tank. Using a two-color, lead-based infrared sensor with multiple detectors, the spinning skeet searched in a conical pattern for the tank before firing its deadly heavy metal tantalum projectile.

In the next few minutes over two hundred tanks succumbed to the WAMs.

Then Grogan saw a missile hit one of his own tanks. Then another missile struck another tank, which went up in flames, quickly followed by three others.

Colonel Muhammed Hassani, along with his wingman and four other MiGs from his base outside Baghdad, had joined forces with sixteen MiG-23s from a base in Northern Iraq to provide air cover to Republican Guard elements after the devastating attack on the regional air base the previous night. They flew in at treetop level, softly grazing the valley's contour until a minute ago, when his radar detected the multiple incoming self-propelled rounds from the American defenses. He had then pulled up to ten thousand feet, disappearing in the thick clouds before firing radar-guided missiles on the American tanks.

"Come, my brothers," Hassani said on the radio. "Come and let us carry out our holy orders! The wrath of Allah shall descend over the satanic Americans today, just as it descended on their blasphemous base at Salman Assad! Let us avenge the deaths of our beloved comrades, who perished during the American's cowardly attack! Let us destroy them just as we destroyed their fighters at Salman Assad!"

"*Inshallah!*" came the response from the other MiGs.

"Remain by my side," he ordered his wingman. "The blasphemous Americans shall not prevail today! The spirit of Islam is with us!"

"*Yes, sir!*"

Hassani circled the American front lines before dropping on them with his guns alive with fire, his narrowed eyes absorbing the information painted on his Heads-up Display, his mind replaying the agonizing images of his Samia, of his Khalil. His heart burned with an insatiable desire to achieve retribution against a country that had taken so much from him. As the rest of his flight group provided cover against enemy fighters, Hassani and his wingman engaged the Americans. The Iraqi colonel silently thanked Allah every time an enemy tank fell victim to his rockets and to the explosive rounds of his 23mm cannon.

"Dammit, get those planes over here this minute! I thought we had air superiority in the region!" Grogan thundered into the radio as another five of his tanks disappeared behind a column of fire. He had just received confirmation of Iraqi fighters flying overhead, and Grogan was all too aware of the devastating damage those MiGs could inflict on his army.

Over on the hill opposite his, across the valley, the silhouettes of Iraqi Hind-D gunships flew downhill, grazing the sand dunes. As soon as they reached the valley, they increased the distance between them and turned west toward the front line, also using their missiles and cannons to blast his tanks.

"Shit!"

He raced to the radio to alert Stinger teams. He knew he couldn't touch the MiG-23s overhead—as a matter of fact, he could barely see them because of the cloud cover—but he could do something against the Iraqi heavy assault helicopters.

Out of the corner of his eye, he saw one of the Iraqi gunships blow up in midair. "What the hell?"

He strained to see what had attacked the gunship. The other two had turned around and were flying uphill, away from his troops, but didn't make it far before also exploding in midair.

Suddenly he heard a light zoom. It quickly became louder, sounding like jet engines, but much quieter.

"Oh, shit!" he screamed as he dropped to the ground. He noticed all his staff on the hill doing likewise.

An F/A-18C flew up the side of the hill at fifteen feet above them while topping six hundred knots. Grogan watched, in total awe, as the streamlined shape of a Hornet darted through the sky right over them, disappearing as abruptly as it came. *Dear Lord!* he thought. *I'm glad they're on my side.*

"Redeye, Redeye, this is Strike Leader, and we have you covered," Lieutenant Colonel Diane Towers said over the radio as she set her F/A-18C vertical in full afterburners while her fire control computer got a lock on the MiGs circling overhead. She noticed in satisfaction as Major Levi did likewise, gluing himself to his superior's right wingtip.

"Strike Leader, Redeye," came the voice of General Grogan through Diane's headset. *"They're all over the place. My tanks are blowing left and right!"*

"We have you covered, Redeye. We have you covered. You just hold your ground and don't stop shelling those Iraqis on the ground. We'll handle their MiGs."

Diamonds flashed on Diane's Heads-up Display, showing her the closest targets, which the Identification Friendly or Foe system had already detected as unfriendlies.

"Got them, One Seven?" Diane asked Major John Levi, still fixed to her right side.

"Affirmative, Lead. Got a lock on two MiGs. Five miles dead ahead. Them bastards haven't even attempted to evade!"

"Too bad." Diane advanced the throttles and the Hornet bit into the wind and hurtled past Mach 1. The HUD symbology projected small blinking squares surrounding the diamonds. She had a lock on both—

"MiGs, MiGs! Three at our seven!" screamed Levi as Diane's aft sensors went crazy.

"Where'd they come from?"

"Hell, I ain't got a clue!"

Diane checked her range to the two MiGs straight ahead. Three miles. She also noticed three blips following her two miles behind, and she pushed full throttle, grazing Mach 2.

Hassani's early warning buzzer ran inside the cockpit. He quickly shut it off. The American fighters were going to spoil his ground attack with their inopportune timing. In the single minute since his engagement with the enemy's front line, his fighters had managed to destroy a mere seventeen of the hundreds of tanks preventing the advance of the Iraqi offensive echelon. He decided to risk it, and remained engaged for a few more seconds.

The steady beeping in her helmet told Diane she had a solid lock on both Iraqi jets circling dead ahead. She cut back throttles and her airspeed plummeted to six hundred knots. "Got a lock . . . fire!"

She saw the contrails of the missile propagating toward the left MiG of the two-plane formation. Levi fired on the right one.

"Pull away! Pull away!" Colonel Muhammed Hassani screamed to his wingman while applying rearward pressure to the sidestick controller without adding throttle. The MiG-23 went vertical without the use of afterburner after releasing dozens of infrared flares. In ten seconds he broke through the clouds and sunlight filled his cockpit.

"Those cursed American fighters!" he heard his subordinate complain as both missiles went astray.

"Concentrate on your flying!"

"Yes, sir!"

"Stay with me!" Hassani commanded, as the American pursuers broke through the clouds and closed in at great speed.

Diane cursed out loud when she saw her missile going for the stream of flares. Not only did she have to catch up with the two climbing MiGs, but she also had to contend with the three locked on her tail—the three Iraqi jets that had just broken through the clouds and continued dashing upward after her and Levi.

Suddenly, the two leading MiG-23s split.

"Stay on the left one, One Seven!"

"Roger," Levi responded as both F/A-18Cs cut into a left turn to catch the MiG-23 broadside, but instead of completing the turn, the Iraqi pilot, seemingly anticipating that move, abruptly pulled a hard right turn while going for a steep dive.

Checking the airspeed readout, Hassani noticed both F/A-18Cs staying with him after he broke away from his wingman's jet. He headed directly toward the thick layer of cumulus two thousand feet below.

Diane shoved the centerstick forward and to the right. In an instant, the Marine Corps pilot felt her hastily eaten breakfast rising up to her throat the moment two negative g's pushed her upward. The restraining harness held her firmly in place and allowed her to continue the tight right turn and dive.

"Stay with me, One Seven!" she shouted, as the clouds quickly accelerated toward her. She saw the MiG-23 go in, and soon the clouds engulfed her as well. Thermal imaging took over, and she saw the MiG-23 pulling out of the dive while inverting and doing a 180 turn, defiantly approaching Diane head-on.

"That Arab has balls!" Diane said as she switched to guns and lined up the incoming MiG on the crosshairs. "Fox three!"

She had not even pressed the trigger when the MiG-23 broke left. Diane followed, feeling the g's as she pushed the Hornet into a tighter turning circle than the departing MiG.

Missile warnings filled her cockpit. "Shit, One Seven. Three missiles! I have three missiles locked on me!" She added throttle while pumping out chaff and flares as the ECM tried to jam the missiles' computer brains electronically.

"Break left, One Seven. Get the hell out of here!"

"No way, Lead! I'm stayin'!"

Diane checked her radar. Although she had already pushed through Mach 1.5, the missiles continued to close in. "Dammit, Blue Jeans! I just gave you a direct order. Break left and come back around. Try to get some of those Iraqis off my tail. Now move it!"

As Levi's Hornet went subsonic and executed a left turn, Diane noticed in satisfaction two of the missiles going for the chaff. The third temporarily lost lock, but then reacquired. Ten seconds to impact. She waited while her finger softly rubbed the chaff button on the sidestick. *Get closer, you bastard. Yes, a little more . . . now!*

In the same swift motion, Diane released another cloud of chaff, cut back throttles, and shoved the stick left and forward, and a few negative g's pounded on her, flooding her head with blood. Straining against the spectacular pressure, Diane scanned the sky behind her for the missile, and exhaled in relief when she caught it going for the chaff and exploding in a small orange ball of flames. She also noticed that only two MiG-23s remained with her. In addition, the HUD no longer showed her a diamond for the MiG-23 she had been pursuing.

"I'm comin' back around, Lead," Diane heard Levi say while she devoted precious seconds to consider her options.

"Get the hell out of there, Blue Jeans. Don't get behind them!"

"But, Lead, the—"

"Dammit! Get the fuck away from their tails!"

As Levi's Hornet banked right of the three-craft caravan, Diane leveled off at three thousand feet and cut back throttles to let her pursuers get closer. The tactic worked. Both MiGs closed in within a thousand feet of her. Abruptly, she jammed the throttles forward and broke hard left. Blood rushed to the right side of her body from another nine-g turn. One of the MiG-23s overshot, rushing past her on a wider circle. The second managed to hit the speed brakes in time and remained behind her.

Ignoring her pursuer, Diane switched to guns as she pulled directly behind the runaway MiG, which suddenly executed a vertical corkscrew. Hitting the throttle and jerking the centerstick back, Diane rushed after it. Because of the superior thrust-to-weight ratio, the Hornet quickly gained ground on the rocketing Iraqi as both jets zoomed through the layer of clouds and reached ten thousand feet.

With the MiG-23's tail filling her field of view, Diane managed to get an angle for the cannon, which she took full advantage of by pressing the trigger to the second detent, unleashing twenty 20mm rounds each second.

As the tracers reached the trailing edge of the MiG's port wing, Diane saw a river of holes lacerating the white-painted surface, peeling off bits of material, some of which struck Diane's armored canopy before washing away in the slipstream.

Smoke. Diane saw dark smoke coming out of the turbofan, quickly followed by flames as the canopy blew open and the pilot ejected. The burning plane arced down back toward the clouds below. A bright red parachute deployed at the apex of the Iraqi pilot's short parabolic flight.

While continuing to hurtle upward, she saw the trailing MiG-23 running out of steam and heading back down. She smiled as she cut back throttles with the Hornet still pointing straight up. The American fighter remained suspended in midair for a second, before Diane banged the stick forward and to the right, inverting the F/A-18C and dropping like a bird of prey over its victim.

Under her oxygen mask, a smile flickered across Diane's face the moment she saw the Iraqi pilot making the cardinal dogfight mistake. In trying to go supersonic, the MiG first had to go into full afterburner. The mistake the Iraqi pilot made was that instead of trying to outmaneuver

Diane with aerobatics, he too quickly reached for the throttle handles to use speed as a means to shake off the Hornet—a fine tactic as long as the enemy wasn't too close.

In Diane's case, the moment the MiG-23 attempted to go supersonic, she locked a Sidewinder on its sizzling-hot afterburning exhaust and fired from a mere seven hundred feet away. From such a short distance all of the infrared flares in the world couldn't disguise the MiG's scorching tailpipe, which disappeared from Diane's sight the moment the proximity fuse of the seventy-pound warhead exploded just aft of the engine, blasting melted metal into the turbine at lightning speed. Bursts of orange flames pulsated off the wounded engine for a few seconds as the fighter trembled before it came apart. The resulting cloud of fire and debris would have engulfed Diane, had it not been for a last-minute inverted turn.

Laboring against the massive g-forces squashing her deep into her seat, Diane focused on the symbology projected on the HUD. The IFF system told her of six other MiGs in the region. She quickly turned the Hornet's nose toward a MiG-23 in pursuit of Strike Three Two Eight, piloted by the youngest member of the Strike Team, First Lieutenant David Katz.

His finger on the control stick trigger, Colonel Muhammed Hassani maneuvered himself right up to the tail of the American fighter, which abruptly cut hard right. Reducing throttles to avoid overshooting, Hassani could not prevent the American from increasing the gap during the hard turn, which the Hornet followed with a vertical climb.

Slamming the throttle forward, he shot upward after it, cutting the distance back to three hundred feet, when his aft sensor began to beep and the information projected on the Heads-up Display told him a Hornet had sneaked up behind him and was trying to get a lock.

"Two Eight, this is Strike Leader. Roll out and break left!" Diane shouted, as she unsuccessfully tried to get a blinking square over the rapidly moving diamond on the HUD.

"Can't shake him, Lead. He's gonna fire! He's gonna fire!"

"Break left, dammit! Trust me!"

Katz inverted and pulled the Hornet's nose down and to the left in full afterburner.

"No, no! Don't use the burners!"

Hassani smiled at the Hornet's white-hot tail, which screamed for an infrared missile. A green diamond projected on his HUD turned blinking red. Thanking Allah for this gift, Hassani pressed a button on the control stick between his legs.

Diane saw the river of white propagating directly toward Katz's Hornet. A cloud of flares and a tight left turn didn't work. Lieutenant David Katz had also made that fateful combat mistake. The ensuing explosion streaking across the twin outwardly canted vertical fins threw the jet into an unrecoverable flat spin just seconds before the F/A-18C disappeared in a ball of flames.

Diane watched first in relief, then in horror as the burning ejection seat shot away from the midair inferno and into a parabolic flight that did not end with a deployed parachute, but grew into a flaming comet streaking downward and ultimately disappearing in the cumulus below.

With tears of rage rolling down the sides of her oxygen mask, Diane sought the assassin MiG, but it had already joined the fight below. As her Hornet cut hard right to avoid the scorching wreckage plummeting down to Earth, Diane decided that it didn't matter if she didn't know which of the MiGs had been the one. In her mind they were all responsible. Every single one of those Iraqi fighters had pulled the trigger.

Without another thought, she pushed the stick forward and nose-dived over the combat zone, hunting for prey.

Major John Levi pulled back throttles to idle to prevent his jet from overshooting his prey's tight left turn. Levi kept his eyes on the sneaky Iraqi fighter as it briefly leveled off before banking hard right. He shoved the stick to the right and cut in full military power before switching to guns. The Iraqi was too close for him to use a missile.

The crosshairs popped onto the HUD, and Levi maneuvered himself into a shot, but the catlike moves of the MiG-23 pilot kept ruining his angle. A left turn, followed by a short dive and a half-inverted loop, and both jets flew right under the clouds.

"Steady, you Arab bastard," he urged, while following the inverted jet. His finger pressed the trigger, but with just a few tracers reaching the MiG's tail, the jet pulled out of the roll and shot up into the clouds.

Alarms blared inside his cockpit. *Missile lock.*

Cursing his bad luck, Levi shot up, careful not to use afterburners to give the Iraqi an even better lock on him. The clouds came and went, and as he topped seven thousand feet, he inverted and cut left, but the MiG stayed with him, obviously waiting to get the best angle.

Levi let his airspeed rebuild to 430 knots before rolling the plane on its back and pointing the nose toward the earth. The MiG followed and loosed a missile on Levi's jet.

Alarms filling his cockpit, Levi pressed a button on the centerstick and released a trail of infrared flares, rolled out of the vertical dive, and held the jet inverted to keep his exhausts from facing the missile.

The maneuver worked, and the missile went under. Levi breathed easier, but not for long. The MiG-23 closed in once more, this time using guns. The left pressure he applied to the stick while pushing full right rudder forced the fighter into a horizontal corkscrew, which quickly became vertical as Levi added rear pressure to get out of the line of fire.

Levi leveled off at five thousand feet and noticed the MiG doing likewise. "Well, ain't you the persistent little dirty bastard?" he murmured without altering his flight, letting the MiG close the gap to under a thousand feet.

Just a few more seconds . . . reverse now!

With the MiG-23's thundering cannons ringing in his ears, Levi idled the jet, dropped the landing gear, and engaged the speed brakes.

His body shoved forward from the monstrous deceleration, Levi watched in satisfaction as the MiG-23 surged past him at great speed. Its pilot's head snapped back in sheer disbelief.

Without a second thought, Levi pushed full throttle, raised gear, released the speed brakes, and bolted after the Iraqi, the target designation diamond projected on the HUD soon superimposed upon by a red blinking square. A steady beep sounded inside his helmet and he released a Sidewinder, which hurtled across the sky at Mach 4, ignoring the Iraqi's countermeasures, and blasting through the MiG's fuselage before the pilot had a chance to eject.

The fighter broke apart and turned into flaming debris at the blink of an eye, forcing Levi to cut hard left into another high-g–pulling turn.

Levi saw two traces on the radar screen and his warning lights told him of the nearing threat. Two MiGs closing in. One MiG he felt certain he could handle, but two? He spoke into his microphone.

"This is One Seven. Got me some real problems!"

"Blue Jeans, this is Strike Leader. What's your situation, over?"

"Got two of them MiGs on my butt, Lead . . . shit! They just fired! Three incomin' missiles!"

"Hit the ground! Fast as you can!"

Releasing a chaff stream out of the Hornet's integrated ECM dispenser, Levi yanked the stick forward, pushed full power, and felt the crushing negative g's tear at him, making his head feel like a balloon ready to burst. His vision reddened to the point that he could barely see the information on the HUD, which told him he had just pulled two and a half negative g's.

Diane saw the small flashes followed by the bright contrails of the Iraqi missiles propagating toward the F/A-18C, which released a cloud of chaff and went vertical.

Diane managed to sneak behind the Iraqis, which quickly did a Y and broke away. She stayed with the one that followed Levi's Hornet. Levi inverted and dived. The MiG did the same, and Diane went after them. The three-plane caravan dropped to one thousand feet before Levi pulled out of the dive and leveled off, momentarily giving the MiG a great shot, but Diane had long since gotten the desired angle on the Iraqi fighter, and she pressed the control stick trigger to the second detent.

Smoke quickly belched from the single turbofan, along with debris from the MiG-23's tail falling away. With images of Katz's Hornet bursting in midair in her head, Diane refused to let up, pumping nearly one hundred rounds into the light composite fuselage until it came apart in a blast. She easily avoided the flaming debris with a tight right turn, positioning herself in front and to the left of her wingman.

A brief check of her radar told her all she cared to see. "This is Strike Leader. Four remaining MiGs are pulling out. Situation report, One Seven?"

"Thirteen enemy fighters destroyed, and two downed Hornets, Lead," Diane heard Levi's voice crackling through her headset. *"Fuel situation turnin' nasty."*

Diane nodded. Although they had gotten to the area less than fifteen minutes ago, the dogfighting had taken its toll on the group's fuel tanks. She spoke again. "Strike Leader to 52nd, over."

"Go ahead, Strike Leader."

"Surviving MiGs have pulled out. Running on vapor."

"No problem, Strike Leader. Situation on the ground is stable for now. Broken initial Iraqi offense. Currently shelling the second echelon. I've just been informed that the first squadron of F-15s will be here within the hour. Thanks for your help."

"Anytime, 52nd. Out."

With that, Diane Towers and her flight squadron turned back to their base.

Colonel Hassani, his wingman, and two other MiGs headed back north to refuel and rearm. The Americans had won the initial battle, but in Hassani's mind that was only one of many that would be fought before the Americans were ultimately defeated and Iraqis marched triumphantly into Kuwait. *Soon. Very soon.*

Outside Tikrit, North Central Iraq.

Donald Bane simply couldn't stand waiting any longer. He hadn't heard from Bourdeaux in hours, and he hadn't seen a single plane anywhere in the area.

Frustrated and quite hungry, Bane had forgotten how much he hated this aspect of fieldwork. André Boyabat, who was peacefully snoring away, had endured the trip far better than the tired and hungry CIA officer, who for the last two hours had stood behind a line of tall bushes observing the safe house. Jafar Dhia Jafar was still inside.

Taking in a full breath of cool and dry desert air, Bane was about to bring the binoculars back up to his face, when he felt a muzzle jammed against his back.

"Shit!" he said, dropping the binoculars and turning around, only to be welcomed by the wooden butt of a rifle.

His knees gave and he fell to the ground, where a black leather boot swung in the direction of his stomach.

"Aghh!" The expulsion of air was mixed with the cries from André, as Bane, stunned and light-headed, gazed around the moonlit clearing and saw at least a dozen armed men dressed in khaki uniforms and black berets. Some were kicking André in the face and sides while others pointed their rifles at them.

"Stop," Bane said. "We surrender!"

Another boot struck him in the abdomen just as another wooden butt crashed against his left eye. Bane braced himself as he felt the pain from a blow to his testicles streak up his body.

"Aghh, shit! Stop!" he screamed, but the blows kept coming from the side, from above, from behind, making him roll over the dusty clearing. The sky and the shadowy shapes of his attackers mixed with the cloud of dust lifting around himself. Another blow to his head followed a boot kicking in his rib cage, making him vomit blood. Then the kicking stopped and the Arabs tied their hands behind their backs and dragged them down to the valley.

His face already badly swollen from the repeated blows he had endured thirty minutes earlier, Donald Bane was forced to his knees as he watched a shirtless Jafar Dhia Jafar walking outside. The CIA officer was in bad shape and he knew he faced an even worse future. André Boyabat hadn't even made it this far. During the kicking drill on the mountainside, one of the Iraqis had broken the Turk's neck. Two guards had already thrown him in the Tigris and let him float downstream.

You're fucked, Don, he thought, as Jafar stepped in front of him while two of his guns threw the eavesdropping gear and the portable satellite communications equipment on the ground next to him.

"What is your name?" asked Jafar.

Bane, who could only keep one eye half-open—the other had already swollen shut—glanced up at the Iraqi scientist.

"I asked you your name!" Jafar snapped.

"Go to hell," Bane said.

"Tell me your name, or by Allah I will have these men beat it out of you!"

"Mickey Mouse, asshole," Bane responded.

Jafar's jaw tightened as he slapped Bane hard with a backhand.

Bane licked the blood dripping from his lips and said, "Fuck you, raghead. Fuck you and your whole fucking country."

Another slap, and Bane gave Jafar another defiant stare.

"When did you contact your people last?" Jafar asked.

Bane remained silent.

"Tell me and I promise I will kill you quickly. Resist and I will kill you so slowly you will wish you were never born!"

"All right," Bane said, his face suddenly becoming serious. "I will tell you."

Jafar put a knee to the ground, and Bane took the opportunity to spit on his face. "Go to fucking hell, asshole!"

Slowly getting up as one guard kicked Bane in the ribs, Jafar said, "Stop! Bring him inside. I will work on him."

Dazed from this last blow, Donald Bane felt a pair of arms lifting his heavy frame off the dusty clearing and hauling him inside the safe house.

BAGHDAD, IRAQ.

Gazing at the night sky over Baghdad, Saddam Hussein listened to the voice of Jafar over the speakerphone on his desk. The information he had received from America via Lisbon, Athens, and Damascus was true. Apparently the Americans had located the safe house outside Tikrit, but the captured infidel refused to talk.

"Do not kill him," Saddam said over the phone. "Bring him to me."

"Yes, Great One," responded Jafar.

"He will talk," the Iraqi tyrant added. "Colonel Karrubi will make him talk."

"I shall put him on a plane as soon as one is available. What about this safe house?"

"That place is compromised," said Saddam. "You must move to a new location immediately."

"My men are in the process of transferring the hardware to the transport plane. The infidels will not get a chance to rob us of our weapons of respect. I have assembled three more warheads. These new ones have timers incorporated into the trigger mechanism. They will give our men time to escape the blast."

"Well done, Jafar. Bring the bombs and the infidel to Baghdad."

"Yes, Great One."

Saddam hung up and stared at the stars.

NORTH OF JACKSON, MISSISSIPPI.

Irina Bukovski was furious. It had taken the useless mechanic over twelve hours to fix the oil leak, time she had spent mostly protecting their precious cargo while Kemal slept in the small terminal building. At one point in time the mechanic had decided to take a little break and had gone inside the plane and attempted to make a sexual pass at Irina. The former KGB operative had pointed him back toward the broken engine, but not before he got a chance to see the contents of the red backpack Irina had been inspecting at the time.

Now, with sunlight shafting through the open hangar door and Kemal counting up the money to pay off the mechanic, Irina wondered if indeed this was the best way to handle this man, who had seen their faces, their plane, and had taken a glimpse at their cargo.

"Wait, Kemal," she said.

The large Arab, his eyes clear after sleeping steadily for almost twelve hours, gave her a curious look.

The field was still empty at this early hour of the morning, and aside from the night clerk at the terminal, she hadn't seen another soul in the area.

"I don't think we can afford to leave a trail," she said, suddenly reaching down for the stiletto strapped to her calf under the blue jeans.

The mechanic, eyes and mouth wide open, tried to run away but the huge hands of Kemal Ramallah held him in place.

"Wrong place at the wrong time," Irina said, as she approached the American kid and slit his throat.

Kemal let him fall on the oil-stained concrete floor as he made groaning noises for several seconds, his hands on his own bleeding neck, before going limp.

"I will be right back," Kemal said, cocking his pistol and heading for the terminal.

Irina went inside the plane and waited for the gunshot, but it never came. Instead, she watched Kemal race back to the plane, close and lock the door, and get in the pilot's seat.

"Hurry," he said as Irina, already strapped in the copilot's seat, put a hand up in the air, palm up.

"What happened?"

As he went down the preflight checklist himself, the *Mukhbarat* colonel said, "Americans, about a dozen of them in the terminal building!"

Kemal threw the master switch on and the avionics came to life. He flipped on the navigation and communications radio and adjusted the fuel-to-air mixture.

"Let me drag the mechanic in here to cover our trail."

"No time! Besides, there is too much blood. The police will know either way. We need to get out of here!"

"Let's go then!"

Kemal started the starboard engine. The oil pressure quickly reached the normal level. He did the same to the port engine before looking at Irina.

Five minutes later they were airborne, heading northwest. After trimming the plane to maintain his altitude and heading, Kemal pulled out the navigation charts and plotted them a course toward Birmingham, Alabama, where they would have to stop and refuel before continuing through South Carolina and into North Carolina. Victor Kozlov would be waiting for them at a small airfield outside of Raleigh.

18

ENCOUNTERS

Sitting in the rear seat of an Army Jeep, Kevin Dalton held Khalela's hand as they left the nightmare of the truck stop and headed for a small airfield north of Lafayette, where a chartered propeller plane waited to take them to Virginia.

Thoroughly drained, both physically and emotionally, Kevin stared blankly at the swamps and fields of sugarcane zooming by, the wind swirling Khalela's hair as she rested her head on his shoulder. In the back of his mind Kevin prayed that he'd never have to see this state again.

A large billboard from the Louisiana Tourist Bureau on this side of the interstate showed a fisherman cruising through a swamp. Kevin shook his head at the sign above the boat. *Come to Louisiana, the Sportsman's Paradise.* Then he noticed the picture of a couple of alligators at the bottom of the sign, swimming in the boat's wake. They were smiling.

Kevin Dalton's eyes filled.

Twenty minutes later they reached the airfield, a single runway with several hangars on both sides of the paved landing strip. The chartered plane, a white-and-blue twin-engine Piper Navajo, stood in front of the two-story, redbrick building that served as a terminal.

The Jeep came to a stop next to the plane. The pilot already had the engines running.

Holding hands, and with no personal luggage, Kevin and Khalela got off the Jeep and began to walk toward the plane. At that moment, Kevin caught something in the corner of his eye that looked oddly familiar.

"What is it, Kevin?" Khalela asked.

But Kevin Dalton had already let go of her hand and was running toward the small helicopter standing in front of a blue hangar next to the terminal building. He reached it thirty seconds later. His instincts had been correct. The two rows of stainless steel tubes with spray nozzles under the chopper's fuselage confirmed his suspicions.

Khalela reached his side and immediately went on to inspect the machine under the curious eye of the Navajo's pilot, who had already walked out of the plane and was approaching them.

"Something wrong, sir?" asked the pilot, a tall man with bushy sandy hair, a heavily pockmarked face, and a long jaw. He regarded Kevin from behind a pair of Ray-Bans.

"You from around here?" asked Kevin, as Khalela kept looking around the helicopter.

"Yep," responded the pilot. "Lived here since '77, when I retired from the Navy. I teach flying lessons over there." The pilot pointed to a brown hangar across the narrow runway. Kevin spotted a couple of small Cessna trainers.

"Used to fly for the Navy myself," Kevin said while shifting his gaze back to Khalela, who was looking at him from under her thick brows while nodding and pointing to a few buckshot cracks on the large Plexiglas bubble of the helicopter.

The Navajo pilot smiled. "Small world! Didn't know I was gonna be carrying a fellow aviator. What'd you fly, buddy?"

"Ahh . . . Tomcats from the *Ranger.*" Kevin felt his heartbeat going back up again. This was one of Marcos's helicopters. *Shit!*

"Flew Intruders in 'Nam. Name's Jake Sasso." The pilot extended his hand.

"Nice to meet you. I'm Kevin Dalton," he responded while pumping the man's hand.

Sasso suddenly let go of Kevin's hand and took a step back. "You shitting me? You the fellow that flew that F-14 into Iraq last year and blew up . . . what'n the heck was the name of that place?"

Kevin smiled. "Allahbad?"

"Yeah, that. Them raghead names all sound alike. So you're the guy?"

"Afraid so. Fucked up my back big-time though."

"Yeah, I read about it in the papers. Tough break, pal."

Kevin raised an eyebrow and sighed, his eyes shifting back to the helicopter.

"What's with the chopper?" asked Sasso.

"Know the owner?"

"Nope, but I do know the fellow who owns the hangar. He rents it out by the month. Why you ask?"

Kevin Dalton looked at Khalela and then back at Sasso before giving the former Intruder pilot a smile.

* * *

Thirty minutes later, after having a conversation with a black guy behind the counter while Sasso contacted the hangar's owner and got all the information on the current tenant, Kevin called Bourdeaux. It took him ten minutes to bring his superior up-to-date.

"Are you serious?" asked Bourdeaux.

"Damned serious, Bob. I want those bastards."

"Easy now, Kevin."

"Fuck easy, Bob. You weren't here last night. I saw what those motherfuckers did. I'm telling you, seeing this shit changes you."

"All right, all right. I'm with you."

"They're headed north, Bob. They're gonna go for New York and Washington, and if they get their way, they're gonna nuke them."

"Give me that plane number again."

"November One Seven Five Yankee Sierra."

"Got it. I'll call the FBI and we'll put every man we've got available calling all the damned airfields between here and Louisiana."

"You do that, Bob. The plane you chartered for us has got a phone. I'll call you after we're airborne. Maybe we can catch these assholes after all."

After hanging up, Kevin looked at Sasso, whose long face regarded Kevin with a curious look. "Now, you mind telling me what that was all about?"

"You want to help us catch the assholes who nuked Baton Rouge?"

Removing his sunglasses, Sasso cocked his head at Kevin, wrinkled eyes glinting with sudden anger. "You bet your ass I do."

CIA HEADQUARTERS. LANGLEY, VIRGINIA.

Robert Bourdeaux couldn't take it anymore. He needed to sleep, if only for a few hours. The stress of not closing his eyes in almost forty-eight hours was slowly driving him to the edge.

After hanging up with Kevin, he had spent the next fifteen minutes on the phone with Palenski to bring the FBI director up to speed.

Bourdeaux was very exhausted, and he also felt quite guilty for ignoring Kate during the past two days. But the situation was quickly getting out of control, basically absorbing him.

Only then did he remember that Kate was supposed to have been sick.

Damn, Bob! You idiot! You could have at least sent her flowers and a card!

Cursing himself for forgetting about the conversation he'd had with the blond receptionist, Bourdeaux unlocked his car and stared at the audio-tape and the yellow note attached to it.

His first reaction was to call security. Someone had been inside his car. But then he read the note:

To my dear Bob,
I will always love you.
Your Kate

Remembering that Kate kept a set of his keys, Bourdeaux's surprise was quickly replaced with curiosity. What was Kate up to?

He got in and cranked the engine. He slipped the tape into his car's stereo and adjusted the volume as her voice came clear through the speakers.

"My dear Robert," the tape began. "This is the most difficult thing I have ever done in my life, but I am left without choices and must tell you the truth about me. I was born in Moscow under the name Katrina Aleksandra Markarova. At the age of eleven, I was taken away from my parents and sent to a special school owned by the KGB . . ."

By the time Bourdeaux left Langley, his trembling hands were already reaching for the bottle of Motrin. His eyes began to tear as he got on the Georgetown Pikeway, the aberration of the words spoken by Kate Marston in a Slavic accent was like a cold chisel against his heart. Each word shaved off a layer of his sanity as a nightmarish scenario unfolded in front of him. *Kate a Russian spy? Dear God, what have I done? What kind of secrets did she pass to the other side? And who is the other side?*

Bourdeaux continued to listen as he cruised through the light morning traffic. The trained professional quickly pushed his emotions aside and concentrated on the information being revealed to him. The Russian Mafia in America was at the heart of this. He heard about a club in Atlantic City, about another former KGB agent by the name of Irina Bukovski, about a relationship with the Arab community in America, with the Soltnevo Group in Moscow, and with Marcos Eduardo Dominguez.

Dear God!

The deputy director finished listening to the confession as he turned down his street, deciding that a hot shower and a nap would have to wait until he got a chance to call the FBI.

Leaving the tape in the car's stereo, Bourdeaux pulled up his driveway and got out, deeply breathing the morning's cool air. His mind was in turmoil, his heart was broken. He felt stunned, dizzy, almost as if someone had just hit him across the face with a baseball bat.

He searched for the key and inserted it into the high-security lock of the heavy wooden door. Stepping inside, he reached for the nine-digit keyboard on the wall behind the door and punched in the alarm-deactivating code before putting a finger on the light switch and flipping it on.

A deafening blast preceded a shower of ignited napalm, turning Robert Bourdeaux into a ball of fire as a blanket of flames descended over him.

In a desperate attempt to remain in control in spite of the agonizing pain, Robert Bourdeaux ran outside, threw himself on the recently watered lawn, and rolled on it to no avail. The napalm continued to burn his flesh at an overwhelming rate. Colors wildly exploded in his mind as the searing pain intensified before everything turned black.

BAGHDAD, IRAQ.

General Mustafa knew he would die today. From the moment he had become a general in the Republican Guard he knew his fate was sealed. It didn't matter how well Mustafa had performed his assigned duties. That was not how Saddam measured the worthiness of a subordinate. The first item on Saddam's list when judging his generals was the threat they presented to him. The more the troops liked a particular general because of his leadership abilities, battles won, or fairness, the warier Saddam would become of that general. At some point in time, as that general grew in popularity, Saddam would either throw a false charge of treason at him and execute him on the spot, or arrange his death in a staged accident. Either way, the life expectancy of popular generals was quite short in Iraq.

On the other side of the spectrum were officers who performed poorly. Those Saddam wasted no time eliminating because they tended to slow down the Iraqi war machine, like the dozens of colonels and generals Saddam had executed one by one a year ago for failing to protect Allahbad. That left those generals who played the middle of the road, not excelling, but not failing. Those who kept the machine moving without becoming an immediate threat to Saddam.

Sa'dun Mustafa had forced himself to become one such general for many years, until word of his good judgment in the battlefield and his fairness to the troops eventually brought him the popularity he had desperately tried to avoid.

Mustafa did not doubt that he would die one day, but he had decided to make that day today. If he had to die, he would do so on his own terms. Mustafa planned to assassinate Saddam Hussein today. Whether he succeeded or failed did not matter as far as his life was concerned. Mustafa would die either way. If not from a bullet from Saddam's Russian-made automatic, then from the hollow-point rounds of his guards' AK-47s.

But if given a choice, Mustafa would prefer to kill before being killed. But to do so he had to be careful, he had to use his wits, his experience, his instinct. Mustafa had to tap into the small safe in his basement office in the Presidential Palace and pull out a very special weapon, one that Abu Ibrahim, the legendary Iraqi terrorist himself, had designed and built. It was a weapon made to fool the metal detectors at international airports—the same metal detectors used by Saddam's bodyguards to prevent any man meeting with the Iraqi leader from smuggling in a weapon.

The small pistol was actually quite primitive in operation. Made of fiberglass and capable of firing two .45-caliber hollow-point rounds, it was slim enough and small enough to be carried in one of the coat pockets of his military uniform. But Mustafa would take better precautions in case a suspicious guard decided to frisk him in addition to using the metal detector on him.

Along with designing the weapon, Abu Ibrahim had also built a special forearm holster, which secured the tiny gun to a person's forearm and could be covered with a long-sleeved shirt. A simple flexing of the forearm in a specific way would cause the holster to release the weapon, which would then slide down the inside of the shirtsleeve and right into the assassin's waiting hand.

After checking the firing mechanism and loading two rounds, Mustafa checked the holster's release mechanism a dozen times, until he felt comfortable with it. Then, after a short prayer to Allah for the strength to carry out and succeed in the most important mission of his life, Mustafa left the room and headed for Saddam's office.

CENTRAL IRAQ.

Colonel Muhammed Hassani raced toward the bunker protecting his MiG-23. He had just received the most important phone call of his life. Saddam Hussein had personally ordered Hassani to protect a highly secret warehouse right outside Tikrit. The eminent Jafar Dhia Jafar himself was in the process of moving nuclear hardware from the safe house to a cargo plane at a nearby airfield. Two Americans spies had been captured while stalking the building. The operation had been compromised and had to be moved elsewhere immediately. Hassani's mission was to keep the area clear of enemy aircraft until the cargo plane took off. Saddam had then ordered the Iraqi colonel to escort the plane until it safely arrived at a new safe house outside of Baghdad.

The future of our country depends on you. Those had been Saddam's words, and Hassani understood their hidden meaning only too well. Succeed and you shall be promoted to general and be rewarded with privileges known only to those belonging to Saddam's inner circle. Fail and you and your family will be shot. There was no middle ground, no compromise. Such was the luck of those officers who came under the spotlight for excelling in previous missions. In Hassani's case, the destruction of Salman Assad had brought that unwanted attention to him. Other officers would have been flattered and rejoicing at the chance to move up the ranks in such cutthroat environment as the Iraqi military service, but Hassani knew better. He had seen too many of his superior officers go this same route only to end up at the receiving end of Saddam Hussein's Russian pistol.

Draining his thoughts of all emotion, the Iraqi colonel reached his MiG and began barking orders to his flight crew, who jumped to their feet and began readying the jet for the new mission.

AL JABER AIR BASE. KUWAIT.

Sitting behind a small wooden table in the middle of a tent at the far south side of the Marine airfield outside Kuwait City, Diane Towers's mood slowly turned gloomier. U.S. forces were barely containing the large wave of Iraqis heading south. Even with Air Force fighters and bombers dropping load after load of ordnance on Republican Guard armored divisions, there were just too many tanks, personnel carriers, and soldiers heading south to handle in too little time. It had taken the well-orchestrated effort of the huge coalition forces many weeks of pounding the Republican Guard during the air war portion of Desert Storm to bring it to its knees. The United States and its recently arrived groups of aircraft had only a small chance of success.

And to top it all off, she had received an order to send one of her Hornets on a bombing mission in northern Iraq.

Northern Iraq! Far away from where the real action was, far away from where she needed to be.

Dammit, why? she wondered, as a middle-aged man in civilian clothes walked inside the tent carrying a map, which he set on the small table in the center of the tent, underneath the yellowish glow of a single light bulb hanging at the edge of a coiled black cord. His square face was pitted, as though from a bad case of acne in his youth. His eyes, narrowed and brown, gave Diane Towers a brief glance before he sat down.

"Hello, Colonel," Squareface said, without introducing himself, which told Diane almost immediately she was dealing with a CIA spook. "I have been asked by your superiors to brief you on what will be one of the most important sorties of your military career."

Diane leaned back on her chair and pushed out her lower lip at the comment, fine brows rising to the middle of her forehead. This looked bad. Real bad, but she also knew she had been handpicked because she was one of the best pilots the Marines had to offer.

"What's my target?" she asked as Squareface regarded her with suspicious eyes. Diane felt she was being sized up by this stranger.

"Saddam's latest location for assembling nukes."

The spook had Diane's undivided attention from that point on.

Thirty minutes later Diane walked outside and went directly to the adjacent tent, where she donned her G suit, collected her helmet and sidearm, and tested her oxygen mask equipment. After that, she headed for the camouflage shelter of her fighter.

Diane found Major John Levi inside the cockpit of her Hornet.

"Something wrong, Blue Jeans?" Diane asked.

"No, ma'am. Just personally triple-checkin' things. The ground crew chief wasn't feelin' good, so I told him to go take a break." The Texan got up and walked down the side ladder before pointing to the underwing stores.

"You got yourself a heavy load here. Two Paveway IIs, two drop tanks, two Sidewinders, and a full load of ammo. You better use the burners durin' takeoff, just in case."

"I'll try to remember that," she replied with a smile, as Levi shoved both hands into the side pockets of his flight suit and kicked the front wheel of the Hornet.

"I can tell something is bothering you, Blue Jeans."

Shrugging, Levi said, "Well, ma'am. I know it ain't my place here to speak my mind, but I still think this deal of you goin' alone is for the birds. You sure I can't go along to watch your back?"

Diane put a hand on Levi's right shoulder. "Thanks, but my orders are pretty clear. I have to fly alone to keep the element of surprise."

"What if them Iraqis surprise you instead? What then? You ain't got but a couple of heaters and the cannon to cover ya."

Diane nodded. "That's a risk I'm just going to have to live with, Blue Jeans."

With a heavy sigh, Levi handed Diane the fighter acceptance form and a pen. Diane took them and did a thorough check of all control surfaces, underwing stores, and general aircraft integrity. The large Paveways were attached to the outer underwing pylons. The drop tanks, each holding 292 gallons of JP4 fuel, were attached to the inner pylons. The Sidewinders were loaded on the wingtips.

Diane signed the form and handed it back to Levi.

"Ma'am?"

Diane was about to reach for the ladder of the F/A-18C. She turned to her subordinate. "Yes? What is it?"

"Good luck."

Diane smiled, went up the ladder, and strapped herself in her seat. Quickly going down the checklist, Diane engaged the turbofans, verified the functionality of the three multifunction displays, and enabled the Built-In Test Equipment. BITE came back clean, and after dialing the night's Identification Friendly or Foe code into the transponder, Diane placed both hands against the clear canopy while Levi removed the safing devices from the ordnance and the 20mm cannon.

Finally, Levi walked in front of the Hornet, snapped to attention, and saluted Diane. The Marine Corps lieutenant colonel saluted him back. She was combat ready.

Thirty minutes later, Diane flew a terrain-hugging approach to Tikrit at a mere four hundred knots to avoid detection by the Iraqis. She had kept her radar off and had maintained radio silence since leaving Kuwait.

So far her flight had been uneventful. The desert sand, painted in shades of green by her night goggles, extended as far as she could see, until slowly melting away with the mountains of western Iraq, by the border with Iran. Cruising this low and this close to the mountain range significantly reduced the chances of someone spotting her.

This was actually a mission that screamed for an F-117 stealth fighter, but the black jets, as they were usually called by the pilots who flew them, had not yet arrived from Nellis Air Force Base in Nevada, making Diane and her Hornet the next best choice for the job.

As she reached the fifty-mile mark from her target, Diane turned west, toward Tikrit. She suddenly heard the slow sweeping beep of an Iraqi E-band search radar increase in frequency. In another thirty seconds the radar beeps grew louder and louder, until the lieutenant colonel decided she had been found. She cursed into her oxygen mask, suddenly wishing that she had taken Levi's offer.

Switching on her own radar, an action that gave away her position, although it really didn't matter anymore, Diane gave the green tracks on the color radar a quick scan. Four Iraqi MiGs, which had been flying over the region at forty-five thousand feet, were not turning in her direction.

Diane dropped her tanks and pushed full throttles. The Hornet accelerated to Mach 1.1, about the top of the speed envelope while hauling the huge Paveway laser-guided bombs. This meant she didn't have much time. The MiGs, which trailed her by forty miles and were closing, would catch up with her jet in less than a minute.

Colonel Muhammed Hassani felt the powerful boost of the engine rocketing him to Mach 2.2, and with such tremendous speed came a pink glow on all leading surfaces, particularly the jet's nose. Bordering on the maximum-rated speed for the MiG-23, Hassani felt a slight vibration on the stick created by a microscopic oscillation of the wings that the engineers at Mikoyan-Gurevich could never iron out of the naturally unstable wing surface, but one that provided the MiG-23 with superb maneuverability for a fighter of its class.

Hassani's Heads-up Display projected the blue diamond corresponding to a single American fighter. The diamond began to blink as he closed the gap to fifteen miles. The enemy fighter remained on course, vectoring directly for Tikrit.

I have found him.

After ordering his squadron to intercept, Hassani thanked Allah. This mission was of the utmost importance.

I'm being tracked, thought Diane, as she reached the twenty-mile mark and broke left. Forcing her disciplined mind to ignore the incoming Iraqi MiGs, Diane focused her attention on the fire control computer as her target loomed in the distance.

Alarms suddenly filled her cockpit. One of the pursuing MiGs had fired two missiles at her. Diane scanned the night sky for the incoming contrails as she released dozens of aluminum oxide-coated strips of Mylar while shoving the stick left.

Nine g's drilled her with monstrous force, squashing her into her seat as her vision became a foggy tunnel. The G suit inflated and the maximum-g alarm went off inside the cockpit, telling a fainting Diane that she had pushed the jet beyond the design envelope.

As the Hornet vibrated from the fierce explosion of both missiles flying into the cloud of chaff three hundred yards away, Diane breathed deeply and leveled off just as the thundering cannons of the MiG rang in her ears.

Instinctively pulling up and shoving full power, Diane went vertical. As both planes broke through six thousand feet, Diane continued full thrusters until she outran the MiG, which had a lower thrust-to-weight ratio. A few more seconds and she cut back the throttles at nine thousand feet, pushed the centerstick forward and to the left, but instead of going after the falling MiG, she pointed the nose toward her target.

In full power, Diane lowered the nose and reached Mach 1.4. The trembling stick told her she had exceeded the maximum speed of the Hornet while hauling underwing stores, but Diane had no choice. She had to make up the lost time, and so she chose to lower the nose ten more degrees, adding another 240 knots to her forward airspeed. With the stick's vibrations increasing, Diane saw the nose and leading surfaces turning soft pink.

Grazing Mach 1.7, she reached her target in thirty seconds and eased back throttles as she closed the gap to three miles, popped up to two thousand feet and enabled the laser designator. The crosshairs came alive on the HUD, and she centered them on the nearing target.

Her tail sensor warning her that the MiG had closed on her again, Diane dropped the Hornet's nose over her target while cutting back throttles to keep from going supersonic.

A cannon thundered, and Diane watched in surprise as a river of bullets ripped across her port wing. *Shit!*

Shoving full throttle, she pulled out of her bomb run. The MiG stayed with her, obviously trying to regain the angle for the guns.

Diane turned back toward the target. She could wait no longer and, applying full throttle, she sprinted after it. Twenty seconds later, she had the target in sight once more—but again, the MiG opened fire.

His tracers streaking toward the American fighter, Colonel Hassani saw the pilot constantly adjusting his altitude in an obvious effort to evade him.

Roads and houses dashed fifty feet below him as the pair of fighters approached within twenty miles of Tikrit.

Hassani frowned as the thought of failure entered his mind. The grave consequences chilled him. *I must stop him!*

Some of the rounds managed to pierce the skin of the agile American fighter, exploding in tiny bursts of dark gray composite material. *Blow, infidel! Blow!*

Telemetry data popped on the HUD, telling Diane of the destruction of the bomb-release mechanism on the starboard wing. Forcing her mind to remain focused on the target dead ahead, Diane played the stick and throttles to maneuver her Hornet into a shot without immediate regard to the pursuing MiG, which had slowed down the firing to controlled bursts to avoid running out of ammunition.

Staying on target, Diane dropped over it like a hawk, maintaining the laser spot on the building and releasing her only functional Paveway. But she didn't pull up. She stayed with the falling bomb all the way to four hundred feet. She had to make sure it reached its target. She had to make sure the facility didn't produce another nuclear bomb. She briefly closed her eyes as the Paveway malfunctioned and detonated prematurely, roughly a hundred feet off the target.

Damn!

Donald Bane had been beaten so badly that he barely saw the Jeeps parked thirty feet away, under the lights of the stars. But he could still walk, and he could still hear the Iraqis. They were angry at his stubbornness, meaning that in the espionage game he was still winning, he had not yet been broken. But that could soon change. According to Jafar, Bane would be taken to a location near Baghdad, where he would be tortured by the *Mukhabarat.* For the past hour, the soldiers had been loading the hardware and assembly equipment inside the safe house onto trucks, which hauled it to the waiting transport plane parked at the same airfield to which Bane was headed. In fact, the CIA officer suspected he would fly out in the same plane carrying the three warheads Jafar Dhia Jafar had so proudly shown Bane a half hour ago. *Look, infidel! The people of Allah have the means to fight back against your evil nation!* Jafar had said to him during the interrogation.

The two soldiers that followed him, muzzles pressed against his back as he walked with his hands on his head, screamed and spit at him. Twice already they had tripped him from behind. The skinned knees and elbows didn't bother him as much as his throbbing face. But he would not talk. He would tell these idiots nothing, regardless of the pain.

Just as they reached the Jeeps, he heard jet engine noises nearing. A moment later a loud explosion ripped the night in half, the shock wave sending Bane and the two Iraqis rolling over the sand.

Survival instincts surfaced through the bruised skin of Donald Bane. The two guards, distracted by what they had just seen, momentarily forgot about their prisoner. And that was all the time Bane needed to kick one in the groin and the other behind the right ear. As both guards rolled on the sand, one unconscious and the other screaming with both hands on his testicles, Bane grabbed one of the AK-rifles and fired repeatedly at them.

Bastards!

As the Paveway detonated in wild yellow-and-orange flames, Diane pulled back the stick and pushed the throttle to the top as another river of bullets cut across the starboard wing. She had failed to destroy the target and now the MiG closed in for the kill as her Hornet flew through a cloud of flaming debris that rose up to the sky.

Diane was thrown against the restraining harness as the debris from the explosion broke off the Hornet's starboard wing. The night engulfed her as the goggles ceased to operate, and she pulled on the ejection handles.

The jet, the sky, the desert below, everything around her went up in flames as the ejection seat shot her up at great speed. The immediate windblast caught underneath the NVGs, forcefully ripping it and the attached helmet from her head.

Emerging from the cloud of fire that suddenly turned into a brilliant explosion that shoved her even higher, Diane struggled to remain conscious. The shock wave pushed her up, and to the side, and turned her upside down several times. Her watering eyes captured images of the clouds in between flashes of fire as she shot upward in a parabolic flight to nearly one thousand feet. Bolts of pain rushed through her body, and the smell of burned flesh made her realize that she'd been hit by some of the debris and that her flight suit had briefly caught fire before the solid rocket booster got her out of that inferno below.

As she reached the apex, the flightseat automatically disengaged and a hard tug told her of the parachute safely deploying. The pressure gave way to a cool breeze that seemed to caress away some of the burning pain coming from her smoking chest and legs. Too tired and dizzy to check out her wounds, Diane simply let the wind carry her. She reached the ground; a pounding headache drilled her into near-madness as she felt the tug of the nylon strings of the still-inflated canopy.

Feeling dizzy and nauseous, Diane managed to free herself from the harness and staggered to her feet, letting the wind carry the canopy into a nearby tree.

Pulling out the Model 39 from a Velcro-secured pocket on the side of her flight suit, she disabled the automatic beacon and silently began to scan her surroundings.

Muhammed Hassani watched the American eject. He ordered his flight squadron to circle the area at twenty thousand feet while he headed for the small airfield. The Iraqi colonel planned to fly over the field, determine if the runway was long enough to land his MiG, and then proceed with a

short field landing. That cargo plane would leave for Baghdad as scheduled, even if it meant Hassani had to personally protect the loading
operation. Nothing could go wrong. Nothing. The lives of his Samia,
Khalil, and Jazmine depended on how he handled this situation.

His body aching but his mind thrilled at the prospect of living a long and
prosperous life, Donald Bane turned to the sky and silently thanked the
American pilots who had just saved his butt.

With one Kalashnikov strapped across his back and the other clutched
in his hands, the CIA operative dropped to a crouch and silently moved
over the sand, crossing the clearing in under a minute, just as a half dozen
Iraqi soldiers ventured outside the compound.

Bane was ready, unloading the contents of one AK-47 at waist level.
Four men went down in the first five seconds. The other two tried to turn in
Bane's direction, but their chests exploded in a cloud of blood before they
could line up their own Kalashnikovs.

Quickly dropping the first AK-47 and bringing the second one around,
Bane fired directly into the face of another guard, who had just come out
the door. The guard's head jerked back and struck the wooden door before
cracking open and spraying Bane with a red mist.

Donald Bane was now operating entirely on instinct. Over two decades
of experience in the espionage world guided him as he jumped over the
collapsing guard and landed on his side by the entrance, the stinging pain
from his bruised ribs drowned out by the adrenaline boost.

Two pilots came into plain view. Bane recognized them as the ones who
had arrived two hours ago and had participated in the evacuation effort to
move the hardware to the transport. Both of them reached for their
sidearms.

Bane didn't want to shoot. He needed a pilot to fly him and the
hardware out of Iraq. But the pair in front of him didn't give him a choice.
He fired a half dozen rounds into their chests.

Slowly getting up, Bane kept the AK-47 trained on the last figure inside
the safe house: Jafar Dhia Jafar. Bane scanned the murky room where he
had spent the past few hours getting the hell beat out of him by the dead
guards. A quick count of the dead told him he had taken care of all of
them. Just Jafar Dhia Jafar remained, and whatever many soldiers were
protecting the transport plane. The Iraqi scientist stood on the side of the
room with a hand on the receiver unit of a portable radio.

Bane pointed the Kalashnikov at the radio and blasted a few rounds.
The Iraqi scientist jumped back, his stare burning Donald Bane.

"You better leave while you can, infidel," Jafar said, while slowly
moving toward Bane. "A detachment of troops is on the way from Tikrit."

Bane didn't flinch at the comment made by the shirtless man who had
punched him in the face so many times in the past few hours. As tired and
hurting as he was, Donald Bane simply didn't feel like putting up with the

cocky Arab, who had already caused so much destruction in the world. He knew he couldn't let him go alive. Without Jafar's intellect, Saddam would have a hell of a time assembling more nuclear weapons. On the other hand, Jafar would make an excellent hostage, particularly if a detachment of soldiers was indeed on the way from Tikrit.

"You know, asshole," Bane said, while training the Kalashnikov back on Jafar, "I say it's about time you meet Allah."

Jafar froze and gave Bane a suspicious look. Bane fired once, striking the wood plank by Jafar's left foot. The Iraqi jumped up and Bane fired again, by Jafar's right foot. This time Jafar tripped over one of the dead pilots and landed on his back. Bane approached him and struck him in the back of the head with the Kalashnikov, not very hard, just enough to knock him out for a little while.

Bane glanced at the empty tables, and he realized what he had to do. He had to haul Jafar to a Jeep and drive them to the airfield, where, somehow, he would have to figure a way to get inside that transport plane and fly out of there. *But how, Don? You shot the fucking pilots!*

In a way that gave Bane some relief, because it meant that the plane wasn't going anywhere. On the other hand, the lack of a pilot presented him with serious difficulties. *One thing at a time, Don! First get to the hardware!*

Just then, he heard a noise outside.

Dropping to a deep crouch while pivoting on his left leg, Bane brought the weapon around, training it on the doorway, which he reached a moment later. He pressed his back against the side while peeking over his left shoulder. There was someone outside, a small figure approaching the house from the right.

Who could it be? Not the Iraqi guards. Bane knew he had finished them off. Certainly not the troops that Jafar had warned him about. Bane expected a detachment of soldiers arriving in Jeeps and trucks, with plenty of noise to warn him. *Who then?*

He was about to fire but didn't. Something didn't feel right. The same instincts that had made him mow down the Iraqis without warning now held him back from firing on the figure just over fifty feet away, carefully moving across the clearing while inspecting the dead Iraqis sprawled in front of the house.

Bane decided to wait it out, letting the figure get closer while he hid on the other side of the doorway. A minute went by. The figure approached the entrance. Bane held his breath as the shadow peeked through the entryway.

Reaching for the figure with his left hand, Bane grabbed an arm and pulled hard, lifting the stalker off the ground and throwing him across the floor. The sidearm fell from the figure's hand and landed by Bane's feet. He left it there and watched the stalker crash against a table a few feet away from the unconscious Jafar.

"Aghh . . . shit!" the figure said in a feminine voice as she reached for her head and rubbed.

Bane dropped an eyebrow at the petite woman in a flight suit staring back at Bane with a mix of surprise and contempt.

"Who are *you?*" Bane said, his half-shut eye suspiciously inspecting his prisoner.

Sitting up, the woman briefly glanced around the room, finally landing her gaze on Bane and his AK-47.

"Who are *you?*" she asked.

"Sorry, lady. Doesn't work that way," replied the CIA officer. "I got the gun. Now, would you please answer the question?"

Still rubbing her head, the woman curved her lips into a frown before saying, "Lieutenant Colonel Diane Towers. U.S. Marine Corps aviator. And you will have to kill me before I tell you anything else."

Bane smiled at the small woman with the pale face and strangely thinning brown hair. She was attractive all right. Her hazel eyes under fine brows defiantly glared at Donald Bane. "Easy, Colonel. We're on the same side. I'm Donald Bane, CIA."

Her stare softened as she said, "The way you look, I'm not sure if I want to be on your side," before slowly getting up.

"You all right?" Bane asked, moving toward Jafar, an escape plan quickly taking shape in his mind.

"Been better," she replied. "May I have my weapon back, please?"

Bane nodded and pointed at the door. As she walked over to get it, Bane grabbed some wire from a nearby table and bound the wrists of Jafar Dhia Jafar behind his back.

"This place is empty. I thought these people were assembling nukes in here," said Diane, pointing at the empty tables while Bane went outside and dragged in the dead bodies of two guards. One was as big as he was. The second was short and thin.

"They were," Bane replied, as he undressed the guards. "There was enough stuff here to nuke quite a few cities. Here put this on, and hurry. We don't have much time." Bane handed Diane a bloodstained Iraqi uniform.

She crinkled her nose while inspecting it. "Time? Time for what? And where is the hardware now?"

"Inside a transport plane at an airfield less than a mile from here. Now, please. No time to argue. Put this on," said Bane as he turned around, removed his pants and shirt, and donned another bloody uniform in less than thirty seconds.

"Meet me outside when you're finished," he said, without looking back.

"I'm done," Diane replied.

Bane turned around and saw she had put the uniform on right over her flight suit. Slinging the Kalashnikov across his back, Bane lifted the limp body of Jafar and threw him over his left shoulder, wincing in pain as his body reminded Bane of his wounds.

"For being so short, he sure weighs plenty. Follow me," he finally said, shivering the pain away.

"Where are we going?"

"To the airfield. I didn't bust my butt across Russia and Europe to let that shipment get away from me."

Diane shook her head at this man. "What happened to your face?"

"Long story. Let's just say you got here barely in time to keep these ragheads from hauling me off to Baghdad for some serious torturing."

"Glad to be of help, Mr. Bane."

As she said this, Bane heard the sounds of trucks in the distance. He closed and locked the door as soon as they left the safe house. With some luck, the locked door should distract the soldiers long enough for Diane and Bane to reach the airfield. "Name's Don," he said with a frown. "And I hope you don't mind me calling you Diane. We're stuck in the same boat and there's a storm heading our way. First names always work better in these situations."

"Soldiers?"

Bane nodded as he jumped over three dead guards and began to walk quickly toward the Jeep. "A bunch of them. This guy here called them right after you dropped your bomb."

"You killed all these people?"

Shrugging, Bane reached the Jeep and grunted in relief as he dropped Jafar in the rear seat. He got in the front seat, cranked the engine, put it in gear, and waited until Diane climbed in next to him before taking off toward the airfield, the rear tires kicking up a cloud of dirt and gravel behind the departing vehicle.

"Here!" he shouted over the noise of the engine and the wind, handing Diane the AK-47. "It's got a half magazine left. Hopefully you won't have to use it."

The Marine took the weapon in her hands, removed the magazine, inspected it, and snapped it back in place. "How many do you expect to be guarding the transport?" she shouted as Bane steered the Jeep down the dusty road, which veered around the side of the hill behind the safe house.

"Not that many," he responded. The cool wind felt great on his bruised face. "I think Jafar kept the number of soldiers to a minimum to maintain the secrecy of the place. In fact, I doubt if any of the soldiers coming from Tikrit know what they're protecting."

"Who's Jafar?"

Bane extended the thumb of his right hand and pointed behind him. "That guy back there. He's Iraq's top nuclear scientist, and close friend of Saddam Hussein. He'll make a great hostage . . . we're there."

With his one good eye, Bane carefully studied the small field. There was a good chance that the incoming troops had warned the two soldiers standing guard by the side entrance of the transport, which Bane now recognized as an American-made C-130 Hercules, a leftover from the billions of dollars in military aid the United States had given Saddam during the Iran-Iraq war of the eighties.

Bane decided not to stop the Jeep. Instead, he accelerated toward the plane, flashing the high beams while keeping his left hand pressed against the horn. Both guards turned to them.

"What are you doing?" Diane screamed, her hands clutching the Kalashnikov, her thin hair swirling in the wind, her lips drying and her heart pounding at the incoming threat.

"Trust me! We're dressed like Iraqis and driving an Iraqi Jeep. We're supposed to be hurt, remember? Just act the role and blast them as soon as they're in range!"

Leaning forward to pretend to be injured, Diane slowly took a deep breath and noticed that the guards, although looking straight at them, kept their weapons pointed at the ground. The moment the Jeep got within twenty feet of the Iraqi pair, Diane decided not to risk it and fired four short bursts at chest level. The vibration of the Kalashnikov in her hands brought back memories of her early days in the Marines, before she joined the ranks of the aviators. It had been that long since she had fired an automatic weapon like this.

Bullets bursting their chests open, both guards fell back, crashed against the fuselage, and rolled on the dust by the landing gear.

"Good shooting," commented Bane, as he stopped the vehicle next to the side door by the rear of the plane. "You go first. Go in there and get this thing ready to fly."

Diane stopped. "You want me to fly *this?*"

As Bane reached for the limp Jafar and slung him over his left shoulder, he gave her a suspicious look. "Aren't you a pilot?"

"Well, yes, but—"

"Then get in there and get this thing rolling. We don't have much time! And keep that weapon ready. There might be guards hiding inside."

Diane went up the steps and disappeared inside the Hercules.

His shoulders and his ribs burning, Donald Bane staggered to the Hercules as shouts and gunfire in the distance told him that the soldiers had reached the safe house.

Throwing Jafar inside the plane, Bane walked under the fuselage, removed the wood blocks in front of the landing gear, and climbed inside, closing and locking the door from the inside.

The cargo section of the plane consisted of an aluminum-floored room with bare walls of green-painted metal. Cables and hydraulic lines ran exposed across the walls and ceiling. Dim yellow lights, spaced every couple of feet, ran the entire length of the cargo section along both walls. There were no lights on the ceiling, just an assortment of pipes.

Close to the door that led to the cabin compartment, Bane saw a half dozen seats bolted to the floor. In three of the seats Bane found the canvas backpacks he had seen Jafar working on right after he was dragged inside the safe house. The bags were strapped to the seats with regular safety belts. Behind the seats, the Iraqis had stacked a half dozen boxes, probably filled with the balance of the hardware that had filled the tables of the safe house.

He patted one of the canvas bags as he opened the door that led to the cabin section. The C-130 cabin was divided into two sections. The rear section contained two bunks, a small closet, and a galley. The forward section was the flight deck, with seats for the pilot, copilot, and navigator.

Bane entered through the rear section, which faced a set of access steps leading up the flight deck. To his immediate left, directly across from the steps, was the crew entry door, which was locked from the inside.

Bane went up the access steps, past an oval connecting hatch, and up to the flight deck. Diane Towers was already sitting in the pilot's seat going through the checklist.

"Better hurry," Bane said. "Just crank up the engines and get us out of here."

Diane turned her head and burned Bane with a stern glare of narrowed hazel eyes. "You want to do the flying, mister?"

Bane grinned and raised both hands. "Sorry."

Diane exhaled heavily as her hands went back to turning knobs and flipping switches, motions which did not accomplish what Bane desperately wanted them do to: start the fucking engines!

Patience, Don. Patience. She's a professional. She knows what she's doin—

He heard shouting outside, and, peeking over the side windowpane of the Hercules's cabin, the CIA officer saw to his dismay a dozen trucks and Jeeps driving up to the plane. Thirty seconds later over two dozen armed soldiers surrounded the transport. Bane then heard nearing jet engine noises.

Bane tugged on Diane's shirt. "We're not going anywhere. Come on, let's get out of sniper range."

The Marine pilot nodded and followed Bane out of the exposed flight deck, down the access steps, and into the cargo area.

Her inquisitive eyes, displaying a hint of fear absent until now, turned to Donald Bane.

"Sounds like we're trapped in here," Diane said.

"Yep. Us two, the towelhead, and three assembled nuclear warheads in the middle of Iraq. Not a pretty picture. That doesn't even take into consideration the hardware inside the boxes, probably enough to make ten more bombs."

"What do we do now?" she asked.

"One thing we're not going to do is let them have this stuff."

Diane nodded. "I second that. I got a chance to see the effects of a nuke firsthand."

Bane looked up in surprise. "You did?"

"I guess I won't be needing this uniform anymore," she said as she removed the shirt and the pants, and unzipped a few inches of her flight suit, showing Bane a few purple blotches. "I was near the blast in southern Iraq a few days back."

"Jesus. I'm really sorry," he said, also understanding the reason for her thin hair.

"I'm actually quite pissed, and I'll be damned if those bastards outside are going to get their hands on these weapons. I'd rather blow it all up before letting them have them," she said, one hand holding the Kalashnikov, the other in front of her, an index finger cocked at Bane.

Bane stared at her long and hard. This woman had guts. "And that's exactly what we might have to do," Bane added, as a hard knock on the rear entry door made him snap his head in that direction. A booming voice speaking Arabic crackled through the door.

"They want us to open the door and surrender," Diane said to Bane.

"You speak the language?"

She nodded.

As shouts and warnings from the soldiers outside echoed inside the cargo area, Bane picked up Jafar Dhia Jafar and slapped him across the face several times. The scientist began to come around.

"Diane, tell them that we've got the eminent Jafar Dhia Jafar with us, and that I will kill him if they attempt to attack this plane."

As Diane blasted away in Arabic, Donald Bane dragged Jafar to the cabin section. "Let's go, asshole. It's showtime for you! Diane, tell them to look at the cabin. I will show them Jafar!"

More Arabic flowed back and forth as Bane forced Jafar up the steps. "Here, asshole. Look pretty for your people." Bane shoved him against a side windowpane as a group of soldiers gathered on this side of the plane. Bane had Diane's cocked sidearm pressed against the side of Jafar's head. At that moment a dozen Iraqis swung their weapons in Bane's direction.

"No one fires!" shouted Colonel Muhammed Hassani as he walked away from his MiG and took command of the deployment of troops that had surrounded the Hercules. "You!" he screamed at a young lieutenant, who wore a mask of surprise on his boyish face. "Who's in charge of this operation?"

"I . . . I am, sir," responded the lieutenant.

"Not anymore, Lieutenant. I am Colonel Muhammed Hassani! How many men do you have here?"

"I'm not sure, sir. We just got a call from our captain to come and protect Jafar Dhia Jafar from the infidels."

Hassani listened to the words being shouted from inside the plane. The voice belonged to a woman speaking broken Arabic with a heavy American accent. The Iraqi colonel glanced at the scientist and the American by the windowpanes, before turning his attention back to the lieutenant. "There are at least two infidels with Jafar. The man by the windows and the woman shouting instructions. I want a report on our situation immediately, Lieutenant! I want to know how many men you have here, what kind of weapons they have, and what kind of training they have with those weapons. I don't want to have a bunch of inexperienced soldiers guarding one of our country's most coveted possessions. I also need a field telephone. I must reach Baghdad immediately!"

The lieutenant snapped to attention, saluted Hassani, did an about-face, and began to walk away. After five or six steps, he turned around. "Colonel, sir?"

"Yes, what is it?" Hassani asked as he scanned the area, his trained military mind already deciding on the best locations to place machine guns to protect the plane from further attacks.

"Exactly what are we protecting, sir?"

Hassani shook his head. His government never ceased to amaze him. The very troops that were not only guarding the life of Iraq's most prominent scientist, but also his precious cargo, did not have a clue what they were protecting. *In the name of Allah!*

But at least he was here now. He knew what was at stake, and only he would decide on the best use of his limited resources until he could get word to Baghdad and request further instructions and reinforcements.

"That is not of your concern, Lieutenant!" shouted Hassani. "Do as you've been told!"

The lieutenant ran away and began to gather the information Hassani had requested. Less than a minute later, Hassani was on the phone to Baghdad. It took him just another minute to explain the situation to one of Saddam's top generals, who put him on hold. A few minutes later the same general was back. He conveyed Saddam Hussein's message to Hassani. The Iraqi leader felt the Americans were bluffing.

Bane pulled Jafar back. "All right, asshole. They've seen your pretty face. Now, let's head back to the cargo area."

Diane met him halfway up the access steps.

"They're not buying it," she said. "They'll storm the place in one minute unless we open the door."

Bane frowned. He needed more ammunition to keep those guards from attacking the plane until he could figure a way out of here with the hardware, or a way to detonate it and blow it all to hell, including Diane and himself. Bane could not let them take possession of the weapons.

Think, Don. Think!

Suddenly, André's words came back to him. Bane and Diane were right outside Tikrit, just over a mile from the place, definitely well within the radius of death of one of these bombs. And Saddam considered the place holy, sacred. It was the place from where he got his most trusted advisers.

In the twilight of the access steps, with Jafar's dazed face inches from his and Diane only two steps below, Donald Bane smiled.

"What's so funny?" she asked, placing fine hands on her small waist.

"Tell them there is a nuclear bomb fully assembled in here, and that I know how to set it off. Tell them that if they storm this place, we'll nuke Tikrit. Tell them Saddam won't be pleased at all."

Diane nodded and headed back down the steps and into the cargo area, where Bane joined her a few seconds later, with Jafar in tow.

She screamed in Arabic for a minute. Her words were met with silence. Bane looked at his watch and waited one full minute, but nothing happened. The deadline came and went. Bane relaxed and sat Jafar in one of the empty seats. The Arab's hands were still tied behind his back. Bane secured a safety belt over his lap.

"They . . . Saddam will kill you for this . . . infidel," Jafar muttered as he slowly came around, the dark eyes glowing with hatred, the carefully clipped mustache moving over his upper lip as he spoke.

"I piss on you and your Saddam Hussein, asshole," Bane said. "The way I see it, I've got all the cards. I got the bombs and Saddam's top scientist, and I got me a plane."

"They will . . . they will never let you leave alive. You are doomed."

Bane ignored the Iraqi and turned to the Marine officer.

"They're probably calling Baghdad now," he said as he stood next to Diane. "That reminds me," he said to the startled Diane. "You've got a call to make. Why don't you try to use the plane's radio and see who you can reach, and hurry. Those troops out there might try to shoot off the antennas."

Diane Towers nodded and headed back up to the front while Bane walked up to one of the canvas bags and opened it.

"All right, asshole. How does it work?"

Jafar gave Bane a smirk of a smile. "Do you really think I will tell you, infidel? I will take that secret with me to the grave."

Bane shrugged. "And that might be sooner than you think."

The CIA officer carefully lowered the canvas cover, exposing an odd-looking apparatus: a metallic sphere roughly the size of a soccer ball with a metallic cylinder attached to one end. Connected to the cylinder was a small digital timer welded to what appeared to be the muzzle of a revolver. A closer inspection confirmed his initial observation. It was the muzzle of a gun. The handle and the hammer were missing, but the barrel was still attached. His years with the CIA plus his work with Krasilov gave Donald Bane the knowledge to recognize this as an implosion-type bomb. The twisted pair coming out of the side of the timer connected to a tiny triggering device, which would fire the revolver, shooting an enriched uranium slug against the neutron initiator in the core of the bomb, thus starting the chain reaction.

"Pretty smooth, asshole," Bane commented, disconnecting the twisted pair from the timer and the triggering device. He then flipped on the timer and played with the controls until he figured out that the timer worked much in the same manner as a regular digital alarm clock. He even set it once for fifteen seconds and watched the timer count down until the display flashed 00:00.

"Boom," he said to Jafar. *"Adiós muchachos.* Good-bye Tikrit."

The Iraqi scientist frowned in anger and turned his head away from Bane, who switched off the timer, reconnected the twisted pair, and unstrapped the safety belts of all three weapons just as Diane came back down from the cabin.

"Well?" he said, shouldering one of the bags and feeling the weight. "Reach anyone?"

"One of our AWACS. I passed our coordinates and our situation to the crew. They're currently relaying the information to our guys by the border. They told me to call back in twenty minutes. If communications broke down, they told me to check the Guard frequency on my portable radio every ten minutes for news on a rescue attempt. I told them we didn't have much time. What are you doing?"

"See that?" Bane said, pointing to the cabin. "I read somewhere that the entire cabin area is bulletproof in the Hercules, but not the cargo area. That cabin could very well turn out to be our last line of defense if the Arabs actually find the balls to storm the place, and I'll be damned if I'm gonna run in there without these."

They spent the next five minutes hauling not only the three assembled nukes inside the cabin, but also Jafar, whom Bane tied facedown on one of the bunk beds in the lower cabin section. Then Bane and Diane spent an additional five minutes rummaging through the half dozen boxes behind the seats in the cargo area. Bane picked out the uranium spheres, already enclosed in their protective nuclear reflectors. He counted seven of them.

"Let's just take the spheres," he said. "Without them, the rest of the hardware is useless."

After securing the hardware in the rear of the deck, Bane sat on the flight deck, his back against the center panel in between the pilot and copilot's seat, well below the line of fire of the Iraqis outside. Diane sat next to him.

Running her hands through her thinning hair, an action that resulted in a few dozen brown hairs sticking to her palms, the Marine aviator loudly let go a breath of air. "That damned nuke," she muttered between her teeth. "I'm losing all my hair."

"Well," Bane said, briefly getting up, grabbing a white sheet from the upper bunk bed, and sitting back down next to her. He pressed a section of the clean sheet against his face and grimaced at the bloody imprint of his facial features. "I wish I could tell you that you might live long enough to see it all grow back again, but our situation looks pretty grim."

She nodded. "You know, I usually despise your kind."

While lightly pressing a clean spot of the sheet against his face, Bane turned his half-shut eye to her. "Excuse me?"

"You know, you spooks. I usually hate your kind."

"Oh, yeah? Why's that?"

"Because more than once I've seen good soldiers die from poor intelligence gathering before a mission. Take the blast in southern Iraq, for example. Why weren't we informed of the possibility that the Iraqis had a nuke with them? We would have opted for carpet bombing the bastards with B-52s from forty thousand feet."

"Intelligence gathering and interpretation is not an exact science, lady," Bane said. "Just like it's not a sure thing that your bombing runs will hit the mark."

Diane's thin lips curved up a notch. "You have a point," she responded, before standing up in front of him, releasing the small pouch strapped to the back of her flight suit, and kneeling in front of Bane.

"First aid kit," she said in response to Bane's puzzled stare.

Ripping open a small pack of peroxide-soaked paper towels, Diane put a hand on his right shoulder. "Close your eye and don't move. This might sting a bit." It took her just over a minute to disinfect his face. Bane didn't even flinch, remaining perfectly still even though a couple of times she touched a seriously tender spot on his left cheek.

"Not bad for a spook," she finally said, sitting back down. "You take the pain well."

Bane opened his one good eye and shrugged. "You get used to it after a while."

"What's your guess on what's gonna happen to us?"

Cautiously feeling his facial bruises with an index and a middle finger, Bane said, "They'll probably come back and give us the false option that if we surrender, they'll let us walk. However, that's not a real choice because we've seen this arsenal. Saddam would never let us live. If we give up, we'll wind up in some torture chamber in Baghdad. Like I said before, not a pretty picture."

Seeing the sudden flash of fear on her hazel eyes, Donald Bane reached for her and put a hand on her shoulder, giving it a soft squeeze. "What I'm trying to say is that we don't have a choice. They can't take us alive and they can't have the hardware."

Diane nodded. "That narrows it to one option, doesn't it?"

"Afraid so," he said, looking over to the Arab. "It's just a matter of time now. Let's just hope that our guys at the border can send help our way pronto."

Diane checked her watch, rose to a deep crouch next to Bane, and reached for the radio. She turned it on, frowned, and glanced back at Bane while slowly shaking her head. "They cut us off."

"Shit," Bane said as Diane sat back down next to him. "Guess we're banking everything on that little radio of yours."

Diane Towers took the PRC-112 in her hands, flipped it on and turned it to Talk—two-way communications—but was unable to reach anyone. A minute later she switched it off.

"Doesn't look good," she commented. "Just promise me they won't capture us alive."

"If it comes to that, I promise you I'll do us both, and also take all of those bastards out there with us."

BAGHDAD, IRAQ.

Saddam Hussein quietly listened to the voice of Colonel Muhammed Hassani. This time around the Iraqi leader had come to the phone. He had to handle this matter personally.

Saddam doubted that the infidels could actually detonate a bomb. The cautious Jafar would have been smarter than to let an easily triggered nuke just sit on some table waiting for someone to come and push a button.

No, Saddam reflected. *The Americans are bluffing again, perhaps trying to buy themselves some time. That is all.*

It came down to a matter of priorities. His first impulse was to negotiate for Jafar's release, but what about the bombs? Could someone else, like one of Jafar's hundreds of students, be capable of completing the assembly? Jafar was indeed a valuable asset for Saddam Hussein. The scientist not only knew how to assemble bombs small enough to make them portable, but he also had the wits to orchestrate the purchase and delivery of the hardware into Iraq. Saddam needed Jafar as much as he needed to hang on to his arsenal.

Saddam, his decision made, said, "Storm the plane. Try to capture the Americans alive and also save Jafar, but that is a second priority to regaining control of the hardware."

AL JABER AIR BASE. KUWAIT.

The lulling sound of the AC window unit inside the communications tent was really making Major John "Blue Jeans" Levi sleepy. The Marine major had been depressed since his commanding officer had disappeared from the AWACS's radar just over an hour ago. But as it turned out, the same AWACS had picked up a transmission from Diane five minutes ago. After listening to the AWACS crew relate her bizarre situation over the radio, Levi had wasted no time in coming up with an ingenious rescue plan.

Around the small table were four of his men, also Hornet pilots. Next to them were the pilots of a pair of Hercules transports, which had been used for the past few days to haul troops back and forth from bases in Europe. Tonight they would serve a different purpose.

The native from Texas stood at the head of the rectangular table inspecting a large map of Iraq. A single pair of fluorescents hung a few feet over the wooden table.

"That's the place?" asked one of the C-130 pilots, a major, while leaning over the table.

"Yep. Small base. Secluded, poorly defended, and poorly lit at night."

"Guess that works in our favor," responded the major.

"Uh-huh." Levi checked his watch.

The game plan, as Levi had just explained it to his men, seemed a bit crazy when he first conceived it, but the more he thought about it, the more it made sense. Diane Towers and the CIA officer were out of time. The U.S. military did not have days to plan a better, more-comprehensive rescue operation. The U.S. had just a few hours, if not less, to get the mission going or risk losing the opportunity to rid Saddam Hussein of his nuclear arsenal.

NEAR TIKRIT. NORTH CENTRAL IRAQ.

His face and ribs on fire, Donald Bane sat next to Lieutenant Colonel Diane Towers in one of the seats in the main cargo area, by the door leading to the access steps of the forward cabin. The seats were far more comfortable than the floor by the flight deck.

He briefly closed his one good eye while leaning his head against the seat. The news Diane had picked up on the Guard frequency had been encouraging. There was a rescue attempt on the way, and with some luck Bane and Diane could be out of this predicament in another hour. All they had to do was hold off any attacks for that long.

But Bane didn't think they would last another thirty minutes. The level of activity around the plane was increasing. From metallic banging under the fuselage to men shouting and running about, Bane suspected that a raid was in the making. He wondered how the Iraqis would storm the place. Would they come from the rear or the front? Would they blast a tear gas canister through a windowpane in the cabin or would they blow a hole in the underfuselage and storm the cargo area from underneath? The banging could have been associated with the placement of shaped charges at strategic spots on the underfuselage to blow an entryway for the raid team.

Bane checked the ammunition clip of Diane's Model 39 and frowned. They had little ammo left. Bane had eight rounds in the automatic, and Diane had fewer than twenty in the AK's magazine. The contents of the canvas bag in between his legs would be the final line of defense against the Iraqis.

"You look like you've been around the block," Diane said, her hazel eyes on Donald Bane. "What's your story?"

Bane tried to smile but it hurt too much. He settled for a slight grunt before saying, "You don't really want to know that. Pretty boring."

"Try me," she said. "Besides, there's nothing better to do before those men out there storm the place."

Bane gave her comment a painful smile while slightly shaking his head from side to side. This woman never ceased to amaze him. "In short, I joined the FBI when I was nineteen, left the Bureau for the CIA in 1988, and have been a 'spook,' as you called me earlier, since."

"Any family? Wife? Kids?"

"Used to be married. No kids. Got divorced six years ago."

"I'm sorry to hear that."

"It was bound to happen," he said. "I spent too much time on the job and not enough with her. She got fed up and left. Worst mistake I've ever made."

Her hazel eyes glinted with warmth as she put a hand on his right shoulder. "You loved her?"

He nodded. "Didn't show it, though. That's what counts. And that's enough about me. Your turn."

Diane put both hands behind her head while leaning back against the seat. "For me it's been just the Marines. My dad and my grandfather were also Marines. Dad died in Beirut, Grandpa in the Pacific. I guess it's in the blood. No personal life, though. Never seem to have enough time or stay in one place long enough to get anything going. Besides, as a woman, I'm always too paranoid of getting involved with another officer just to have him make fun of me if we ever broke up. Too risky. Can't have it both ways."

"Well, Diane," Bane said, "if we ever get out of this one alive I'll be more than happy to take you out to dinner. You seem nice enough."

The Marine officer turned her head toward the nearly disfigured Donald Bane, her mirror-brilliant eyes glistening in the wan reddish light of the Hercules emergency-lighting system. "Are you asking me on a date, Donald?" Her lips slowly twisted into a smile.

Bane shook his head, feeling too old to date. He did manage another smile of swollen lips—at the price of yet another jolt of pain on both cheeks. His half-lidded eye inspected her naturally beautiful face. Her thinning hair was a mess, but when combined with the way her soiled uniform followed the smooth contour of her slim body, and the way those fine brows adorned the inquisitive grin on her dirty face . . .

"Yes, Diane. I guess I'm asking you on a date. I just hope that we live long enough to—"

The shouting started outside.

Diane cocked her head toward the rear door and listened for a half minute before turning to Bane. "They've called Baghdad and they still want us to surrender, or they'll storm the plane."

Bane's right hand automatically tightened its grip on the pistol while his left reached for the timer on the canvas bag. He turned it on and set it to go off instantly at the push of a red button on the side. "Looks like we lose. No one's coming to our rescue soon enough," he said, lowering the bag on the seat next to him and putting a hand on her shoulder. "And that's just too bad."

She put a hand over his. "Doesn't seem fair, does it?"

He slowly shook his head. It sure didn't feel fair to Donald Bane for everything to end this way, but even the seasoned dinosaur in him couldn't see a way out of this alive. "This is a pretty unfair game, Diane."

Diane slowly nodded, the Kalashnikov firmly held in front of her, an index finger fixed on the trigger.

"One thing I can promise you, though," Bane added. "It's not going to hurt. It will last less than a sec—"

Gunfire suddenly exploded outside, pounding against the thick rear door. A loud explosion underneath the Hercules shook the entire plane.

Another explosion threw them to the side of the craft, and they skittered across the floor, bouncing against the opened boxes of stolen Russian hardware as the rear door blew open and the compartment began to fill with thick smoke.

"Shit! Cover your mouth and nose. The bastards are gassing—"

Before he got a chance to say another word, a figure appeared through the rear door.

Bane swung the Model 39 toward the back and fired once, twice. The report echoed loudly inside the plane. The figure arched back.

Another figure replaced the first. Bane fired twice more and the man dropped. The sounds of Bane's gunshots hammered his eardrums.

"Run to the front, Diane! Hurry!" he screamed over the noise and the gunfire that now burst through the side windowpanes, showering Bane with broken glass.

With Diane racing to the front, Bane leaned down and, with his right hand, grabbed the canvas bag, keeping the weapon in his left hand trained on the door.

His ears rang from the gunshots. The smell of gunpowder, burned plastic, and smoke filled his lungs. Bane moved back as fast as he could, kicking his legs over the metallic floor.

Another explosion, this one blowing a huge hole in the side of the craft, just a few feet from the door that led to the cabin. Three figures jumped in, but they were pushed back by the bullets from Diane's Kalashnikov.

"Donald! Get in here!"

Momentarily confused by the smoke and the noise, Bane turned around. Three men crawled up through the large oval hole on the floor behind the two rows of seats. Bane moved his weapon in their direction and fired twice before a piercing pain on his shoulder made him drop the weapon.

"Donald!" Diane screamed as she turned her AK-47 on the surviving figure and fired twice into his chest.

Feeling light-headed, Bane threw the canvas bag to Diane, who pulled it up the access steps. Bane felt his legs about to give. He was just a few feet away from the door leading to the access steps. In one motion, he jumped sideways, landing on his side next to the door and crawling inside.

Diane pulled him by the lapels with one hand while firing the Kalashnikov with the other. The moment Bane's legs were out of the way, the Marine officer shut the heavy cabin door and locked it in place. The door was made of reinforced steel and was bulletproof. He heard the heavy banging on the other side a few seconds later, but it was of no consequence. The cabin section was lined with sheets of Kevlar and steel. They were temporarily safe as long as they remained in the rear section of the cockpit, away from the windowpanes in front, which were also bulletproof.

"You've been hit!" Diane said as fire subsided and she helped Bane up the access steps and into the flight deck, where he sat down on the armored floor with his back against the center console.

"No shit," responded Bane as the pain streaking up and down his shoulder pushed him near the brink.

Breathing deeply as he felt Diane tearing open his shirt with her Gerber knife, the CIA officer couldn't believe he was still alive.

"The Iraqis," he mumbled, as his good eye slowly closed and darkness engulfed him.

"We're safe," she replied.

Diane inspected the wound and noticed that the bullet had only grazed the shoulder. Blood, however, poured freely out of the half-inch-deep track the bullet had carved on Bane's flesh. Diane made long strips of cloth from the shirt and shoved them inside the bullet hole. She wasn't that concerned about disinfecting the wound as she was about stopping the bleeding.

The stream quickly decreased to a trickle of blood as she applied pressure with both hands against the cloth. She temporarily secured the cloth with a strip of medical tape from her first aid kit.

"I'm cold," Bane mumbled. "So . . . cold."

Diane stood and walked to the rear section of the cabin, where she stripped one of the bunk beds of its linen and used it to cover Donald Bane. She also cut a piece large enough to wrap tightly around the wound to minimize the blood loss.

That finished, Diane Towers checked on Jafar before taking a seat next to Bane. Putting an arm around him, she let him rest his head against her shoulder.

"Quite . . . the nurse," he mumbled.

"What did you say?" Diane asked.

"You're quite . . . the little nurse . . . aren't you?"

"Shut up and go to sleep," she responded.

"Yes . . . ma'am."

Diane listened to the Iraqis outside, but the soldiers had apparently quieted down. They were probably calling Baghdad for further instructions. If there was one thing she had learned during her years in the region, it was that no Iraqi officer in the field ever did anything without first checking with Baghdad.

Bane's breathing grew steadier. The physical abuse had finally caught up with the CIA officer. Diane laid him on his side. After checking the magazine of her AK-47, she reached for the canvas bag by her feet and inspected the red button on the side of the timer. If the Iraqis attacked again, she would be forced to press it. The half dozen 7.62mm rounds left in the magazine would do little to fend off another wave of soldiers.

She closed her eyes and prayed for the rescue team. They were running out of time.

Colonel Muhammed Hassani watched the dead soldiers being carried away from the plane. He was furious at the poor performance of his soldiers. His plan had failed miserably and in the process he had lost nearly a third of the men on the base.

"Dammit, Lieutenant! I thought you said these men were properly trained!"

"Sir . . . I—"

"Silence! I need silence to think this through!"

"Yes, sir." The lieutenant snapped to attention and remained next to Hassani as the colonel stood roughly fifty feet in front of the Hercules staring at the cockpit's windowpanes and the small entrance below and to the right of the last bulletproof pane.

"How thick is that door?" Hassani asked out loud, even though he was asking himself the question.

"Sir?"

Hassani gave the young lieutenant a sideways glance. "I thought I told you I needed silence! What are you still doing here?"

"Sir . . . I—"

"Get back to your men, get the dead and wounded out of the way, and get ready for a second strike!"

"A second strike, sir?"

"Are you deaf, Lieutenant?"

"No, sir. I just—"

"Go! Now!"

The lieutenant ran back toward the plane and began barking orders to his men while Hassani crossed his arms and kept on staring at the plane and talking to himself. He had to find a way out of this predicament. He had to get inside that plane and recover those nukes—or die trying. Hassani figured that if he died while trying to recover the nukes, Saddam Hussein might spare his family.

At that moment, Hassani got the answer he was looking for. In the end the outcome of this mission could be one of two. Either recover the nuclear hardware, regardless of what happened to Jafar, or fail but perish in the process. He could not fail and survive. Failure and survival would mean not only his death, but also the death of his family.

"Lieutenant!" Hassani shouted. "Get back over here!"

WASHINGTON, D.C.

Working under Roman Palenski's strictest orders, the female technician from the Microscopic Analysis Unit of the FBI carefully inspected the front seat of Bourdeaux's Ford with a magnifying glass for a second straight hour, looking for hairs and cloth fibers that might give the Bureau a lead in the investigation of the violent assassination of the CIA deputy director for operations. Another team of six technicians was combing the house and the front lawn.

Aside from a small love note addressed to Bourdeaux from someone named Kate, so far her search had been in vain. The slippery leather seats weren't very good for the accumulation of fibers. She would have preferred an upholstery cover, which would have provided a harsh surface for hairs and fabrics to attach themselves to.

She frowned. In addition to a poor working surface, the local police had failed to contact her unit immediately. By the time her team arrived at the scene, several police officers had been inside the automobile and the house looking for clues that are never obvious to the naked eye. Now she had the additional job of collecting hair and cloth fiber samples from every officer that had been inside the Ford to sort out the real evidence from the rest.

That is, if I ever get to find anything on these seats, she noted, completing her third sweep of both front bucket seats and sitting back against the passenger seat. The police report hadn't indicated anything of importance found inside the car. The focus of their report had concentrated on the assassination method: napalm-filled light bulbs. Simple but deadly. Once the jellied substance ignited, it was very hard to extinguish until it burned itself out. In this case it nearly consumed Robert Bourdeaux, whose mortal remains were also under analysis at the forensics lab.

The technician leaned down to start scanning the carpet when her head accidentally hit several buttons on Bourdeaux's stereo. Instinctively, she dropped the magnifying glass, brought both hands to her head, and softly massaged her bruised skull as she glanced at the fancy stereo system.

For a second, no more, she thought her eyes were playing tricks on her as she stared at the cassette that had just ejected from the stereo system. The word ROBERT was written across the front. For the past few hours the car had been scrutinized by police detectives, and she was utterly amazed that everyone had missed something so obvious.

Without a second thought, and wearing skintight plastic gloves, the technician softly grabbed a corner of the cassette with her index finger and thumb, carefully placing it inside a small plastic bag. She then walked back to her automobile and dialed the number Palenski had given her.

FBI HEADQUARTERS. WASHINGTON, D.C.

Roman Palenski sat behind his desk and hit the stop button on the portable tape player in front of him. He had already listened to the confession of Katrina Aleksandra Markarova three times. This, however, was Director of Central Intelligence Joseph Goldberg's first time.

The DCI remained silent, his legs crossed as the fingers of his right hand fiddled with a burgundy Mont Blanc pen. Slowly shaking his head while staring out the windows behind Palenski, Goldberg's pale skin grew redder.

"I was pretty damned angry myself, Joe," Palenski said. "But I figure we could put this information to good use."

"He was a good man," Goldberg mumbled in between clenched teeth. "A *damned* good man. And Kate! Christ Almighty! She had a security clearance high enough to guard the president himself!"

Palenski placed both hands on his desk and interlocked his fingers. "These things are always difficult to swallow. But we have to take this situation and make it work for us, otherwise Bourdeaux's death would have been in vain."

Goldberg tapped his right temple with the ink pen, regarding the director of the FBI with a curious glance. "What do you have in mind?"

"Remember what Bourdeaux told us right before he died? Kevin Dalton was after the terrorists."

"Right," Goldberg said. "And you've alerted every agent in the area to look for the missing twin-engine plane."

"That's right," responded Palenski. "Now, Bourdeaux also indicated that there were three bombs. One is gone, leaving us with the question: where are the other two going?"

"Well, New York and Washington, of course. Bourdeaux also told us this. What's your point, Roman?" asked Goldberg with a wave of the hand, an edge beginning to creep into his speech.

Palenski opened a green folder and pointed to a computer printout. "I got my men to run a full check on this club in Atlanta, and it turns out to be owned by Irina Bukovski. So that all matched. Next, I had them run a financial check on this woman, and she owns quite a bit of real estate in

New England, which includes over fifty condos and office suites in New York City alone. She owns an apartment complex in the Washington area, along with a few small office buildings and a dozen condos. She even owned the fucking mosque that just got blown up. Do you get my point now, Joe?"

Goldberg smiled "Perfectly."

19

FINAL FLIGHT

SUMMERVILLE REGIONAL AIRPORT, SOUTH CAROLINA.

Kevin Dalton hadn't been behind the controls of an airplane in nearly a year, and even though he wasn't piloting the plane but merely sitting in the copilot's seat, his mind couldn't help but focus on the smooth and experienced Jake Sasso as he lined up the plane with the runway's center line and lowered the flaps.

In the six hours since leaving the airfield north of Lafayette, Kevin had become quite familiar with the controls of the Piper, to the point that he had even flown the plane for about an hour while the former Intruder pilot took a nap in the rear.

The feeling had awakened the flying demons in Kevin's mind, and the thought of commercial aviation didn't seem all that farfetched.

Sasso made a perfect approach, sweeping right over the runway just as if he were trying to grab a carrier's arresting wire, except for the controlled crash. Sasso didn't slam down the plane and push full throttle as he would have in a carrier landing. The Vietnam vet softly floated the twin-engine over the runway and let it drop nicely and quite smoothly over the tarmac. The main gears hit first with a minor shake of the airframe. Then Sasso let the nose drop by itself as airspeed dropped below fifty knots.

"Here we are," Sasso said. "I hope your people are right about this place."

Kevin nodded. Three hours ago, as they flew over northern Mississippi, Kevin had received a report from Jackson about a twin-engine Cessna spotted on a field north of Jackson. One death was reported. Then another report from the Birmingham FBI Field Office indicated that the Cessna had stopped for fuel and left on a northeasterly heading, probably toward South Carolina.

The FBI and the armed forces had then swung into full action, with jets and helicopters converging from Air Force bases in South Carolina, Florida, Alabama, and Georgia. Every available agent in the southern states had started a massive "plane hunt" in the Carolinas, but so far the twin-engine Cessna hadn't been spotted.

But all that had changed thirty minutes ago, when Kevin Dalton picked up a radio transmission on the Unicom frequency. It was November One Seven Five Yankee Sierra, and it was about to land in a small field south of Summerville, a small city twenty miles northwest of Charleston, South Carolina.

Kevin had immediately phoned Langley, but had been unable to reach Bourdeaux. The DDO had been murdered. It took almost a full minute for Kevin to recover from that piece of news. Kevin got transferred to Goldberg who, after giving Kevin few details about the murder, promised to get the FBI and the Air Force to the airfield immediately. That had been five minutes ago.

With Baton Rouge still alive in his mind, Kevin had warned Goldberg against storming the place, an action that might result in another nuclear detonation.

Now they were taxiing toward the small terminal building, Kevin searching for any twin-engine planes in the area.

The Summerville Regional Airport was roughly about twice the size of the one near Lafayette, with a few hangars scattered on both sides of the runway and a main terminal building near the middle of the single landing strip.

"See anything?" Kevin asked over his left shoulder at Khalela, who sat in the middle row of the Navajo.

"Nothing yet," she replied, her green eyes also searching for the plane.

"It has to be here," Kevin said while narrowing his eyes and scrutinizing every airplane parked on the tarmac in front of the gray stucco terminal building. He knew it had to be here. Kevin had paid close attention to the Unicom frequency since listening to a man with a British accent call out the plane's number while approaching the field from the west. The plane landed and Kevin never heard him call out again before takeoff. *It's got to be here.*

"Over there!" Khalela shouted. "Kevin, I see it. It is over there!"

Kevin unstrapped himself and turned around. "Show me. Where?"

Khalela pointed at a twin-engine Cessna parked in front of a small hangar across the runway from the terminal building. A pair of single-engine trainers stood next to the larger Cessna, currently refueling from a blue pump station on the side of the metallic gray hangar. A black hose ran from the front of the pump to the left wing.

"They're taking some fuel. Looks like we're in luck," commented Jake Sasso as he turned the airplane around and headed for the hangar.

Luck? It was at that moment that Kevin Dalton realized he was within three hundred feet of at least one fully assembled nuclear warhead in the hands of terrorists.

"How are you going to play this out?" asked Sasso, shooting Kevin an inquisitive look.

Kevin Dalton reached behind his back and pulled out a Beretta. Khalela did the same.

"Oh, shit," said Sasso, as Kevin checked the ammunition clip.

"You don't have to stick around," Kevin said. "You might get shot at."

Sasso smiled. "Like I never got shot at while flying in 'Nam."

"All right, then," Kevin said. "This is what we should do."

Irina Bukovski stood right next to the Cessna while Kemal Ramallah chatted with the mechanic operating the pump. Something made her look toward the taxiway that connected this small patch of concrete with the runway. Maybe it was because she grew bored or even quite exasperated. Perhaps because she was tired of looking at the Arab's face and wished to get this business over with so that she could get back to her operation in Atlantic City. In any case, she had turned her attention away from Kemal and the mechanic, and toward the white-and-blue twin-engine plane heading their way.

She had noticed the conservative speed at which Kemal had taxied the airplane following their landing twenty minutes ago, and she didn't like the speed of the incoming plane, whose nose gear seemed about to jump off the tarmac.

Why is it going so fast?

Then she saw the airplane's side door swinging open as the plane reached the small ramp and cruised by them. Irina watched the American Kevin Dalton jump off the wing and land on the tarmac in a roll, followed by a woman with long black hair. Both held handguns.

"Kemal!"

By that time Kemal had already spotted them and, pulling out his own weapon, fired once into the mechanic's chest. The *Mukhabarat* colonel then raced toward the side of the Cessna as the second plane came to a full stop on the other side of the fuel pump.

Irina knew quite clearly what she must do to ensure their survival and accomplishment of their mission. She jumped out of the plane just as Kemal disconnected the fuel hose from the wing.

"Get inside and start the engines!" she commanded as she grabbed the hose from him. "I'll keep them away!"

Without a word, Kemal raced inside. While using the gas pumps for cover, Irina, fuel hose in one hand and a Colt .45 in the other, saw the two figures hiding behind the plane. She pointed the hose at them and released the valve.

The fuel poured over the concrete just as the Cessna's engines cranked into life. A highly flammable puddle quickly separated her from the enemy plane, whose pilot understood her tactic and began to rev the engines to get out of the way.

"Freeze!" screamed Kevin Dalton.

Irina smiled inwardly at the foolish American as she leveled the Colt at the plane's pilot and fired twice. The small cloud of blood behind the shattered Plexiglas told her she had reached her target. Slowly, the plane began to move forward, the pilot obviously no longer controlling it.

Kevin took cover the moment gunfire started. Concerned about shooting the gas pump, he didn't return the fire and chose to hide behind the rear landing gear of their Piper Navajo. Khalela knelt by his side, but then the plane began to move, leaving them exposed to the woman behind the pumps.

"Shit!" Kevin screamed, as two rounds struck the tarmac by his feet. "Move!"

Both of them ran alongside the Piper just as the puddle of gas turned into an inferno, its flames swallowing the area where they had been just a few seconds ago. The fire, however, provided them with temporary cover while Kevin jumped back inside the moving airplane.

"I'm going in!" Kevin screamed. "Cover us!"

Nodding, Khalela left the side of the plane and ran in a crouch parallel to the flames and the screen of black smoke curling up to the sky.

Breathing heavily and with beads of perspiration rolling down the sides of his face, Kevin scrambled to the front, where Jake Sasso, the back of his head blown open and scattered on the headrest, sat in his seat, his arms hanging off his sides like broken limbs.

Damn.

Kevin sat in the copilot's seat, placed his left hand on the dual throttle controls and his feet against the rudder pedals, which he used to steer the plane away from the flames.

Just then, the sound of revving engines made him turn his attention back to the other plane, which had already taxied halfway back toward the runway.

"You idiot! Wait for me!" screamed Irina Bukovski as Kemal left her behind. Her legs burning from the strain, her lungs taking in large gulps of air, the former KGB operative focused her attention on the still-open door on the side of the plane, now just twenty feet away from her.

As Kemal darted past another hangar, Irina watched the ground to her left explode a fraction of a second after her ears heard a gunshot.

Glancing over her left shoulder, she saw the long-haired woman thirty feet behind. Cursing the Arab, Irina cut left, toward the sheet metal protection of the hangar wall, which she reached in seconds, turned around, dropped to a crouch, and aimed her Colt at the incoming woman, but the woman was no longer in sight.

Where is she?

Quietly and swiftly Khalela Yishaid moved along the outside of the hangar, on the other side from which she had seen the small woman disappear. Anticipating the enemy's strategy was a law the Mossad engraved in each of its operatives, and in this case it had saved her life. But her training also taught her that the enemy would realize her tactic and counterattack. She had to remain alert, anticipating, planning contingencies. Her suspicious, green eyes scanned this side of the hangar, where one single-engine plane stood fifty feet away under the ardent sun. The ropes that tied its wings and tail to the ramp looked like flying snakes in the heat wave lifting off the blistering tarmac. A field of tall grass extended behind the hangar.

Wiping the film of sweat from her forehead with the sleeve of her T-shirt, Khalela reached the end of the wall. Pressing her back against the tin, she began to peek around the corner over her left shoulder, keeping the Beretta clutched with both hands over her right shoulder.

As her eyes gravitated from the grassy field to the rear of the hangar, an elbow struck the base of her nose, instantly bringing an ocean of tears to her eyes. At the same time, a sharp object struck her wrist, making her drop the Beretta, which skittered away over the concrete.

The Mossad operative knew she was in trouble. Blinking to clear her cloudy vision would take the precious seconds her attacker needed to terminate her. Instead, she reacted almost instantly, turning sideways to the blurry shape in front of her while coiling her left leg. With her face feeling on fire and blood dripping from her nose, she extended the leg out in a quick, single motion, toes pointed down, driving the heel into her opponent's abdomen.

The rapid expulsion of air detected by her ears told Khalela she had now bought the few seconds she needed to clear her vision and truly launch a counterattack. But the flow of tears would not stop. The blow had been more severe than she had originally thought, preventing her from fully engaging her opponent.

With the translucent figure bending over in pain, Khalela blindly pivoted on her left foot, bringing the right one up and around, striking the woman across the face with the edge of her sneaker, sending her rolling over the concrete. The strike, however, made Khalela lose her balance, and she too fell.

The boiling surface baking her right shoulder instantly placed the blow to her nose in second place. The tears dried and she staggered back up, blinking rapidly and readjusting her vision. The small frame of a pale woman with short, deep auburn hair came into focus. She had one knee on the concrete and was rubbing the left side of her face.

Weapons!

Khalela searched for hers and found it several feet to her left. The woman's pistol, which had apparently fallen from her hand somewhere during the short fight, was to Khalela's right, roughly at the same distance.

Their eyes locked. The pale woman slowly got to her feet and glanced at her weapon and back at Khalela, who kept her gaze on the ice-cold, blue eyes now darting back and forth between the weapon and the Mossad operative. But instead of going for the gun, the pale woman smiled as she pulled out a small dagger from under her red T-shirt.

A stiletto.

Still considering the possibility of going for her gun, Khalela watched the pale woman take a step toward her, then another, the stiletto's blade protruding from her fist like a deformed claw. Khalela spread her legs shoulder width apart and bent her knees slightly as she lifted her heels a bit off the ground and began to walk a circle around her.

The woman slashed with the stiletto once, but it was too far away from Khalela, who didn't flinch as her eyes concentrated not on her enemy's blue eyes or on the dagger itself, but on the woman's torso, keeping the actual position of the stiletto at the end of the right arm within her peripheral vision. The pale woman might be able to control the expression in her eyes before an attack. In fact, Khalela herself had learned to master such eye-deception techniques. But the torso didn't lie.

The Mossad operative, both hands bent at the elbow and slightly in front of her body, stayed focused on the curved lines between the pale woman's shoulders and her small waist. They would tell Khalela exactly what to expect next.

With her heartbeat drowning the sounds of gunned engines accelerating, Khalela bit softly into her lower lip as the circle closed.

The woman's upper body moved a dash to the right before swinging fully to the left and forward as the hand holding the stiletto stabbed the air where Khalela's neck had been a fraction of a second before. Khalela had already fully turned sideways to the incoming blade, striking the wrist with the palm of her left hand, which she then used to grab the wrist and twist it counterclockwise until the shiny blade pointed at the sky. In the same movement, Khalela's palm struck the elbow. The sound of snapping bones and ripping cartilage told the Mossad operative she had won this battle.

"Aghh!"

The stiletto fell on the concrete. Without letting go of the arm, now broken at a repulsive angle, Khalela turned her rear to the woman's side, recoiled her left leg, and side-kicked the right knee, its cracking sound similar to that of the elbow. A final palm strike to the area just below and behind the right ear, and Khalela let go of the wrist. The pale woman collapsed on the concrete without another sound.

Quickly racing for the weapons, Khalela shoved the Colt in the small of her back and pointed the Beretta at the still figure sprawled on the ground, the broken arm twisted behind her back.

Taking a deep breath of relief while also leaning down to grab the stiletto, Khalela turned to the ramp, where the flames were now dying out as the sound of sirens blared in the distance. *But where is Kevin? Where are the planes?*

Turning toward the runway, she saw the Piper Navajo taking off. The twin-engine Cessna was already airborne and turning northeast. At that moment she also saw three unmarked sedans coming to a stop next to the main terminal building. Six men in suits jumped out, all holding hand-guns, which were pointed at the Mossad operative.

"FBI! Freeze!" screamed one of them.

Khalela didn't move, letting the armed federal agents come closer as she gave the departing planes another glance.

Kevin Dalton pulled up the flaps, the landing gear, and turned the wheel to the right while applying right rudder, turning the Piper's nose toward the departing Cessna twin-engine, roughly a mile ahead of him.

He glanced at the gauges. Nine hundred feet at just over 145 knots. This thing was definitely no Tomcat, and at that moment he wondered what in the hell he was going to do. He certainly couldn't shoot the Cessna down. All Kevin could do was track and perhaps call in some interceptors to shoot it down.

He got on the radio but found to his surprise that it didn't work. The same gunfire that had killed Sasso must have damaged the communications gear.

Rats!

Pushing full throttle, Kevin leveled off at one thousand feet, roughly two thousand feet below the runaway Cessna. He let his airspeed build up to 295 knots before pulling on the wheel. A mild two g's descended on him as the plane gained altitude through the blue skies. He had to be careful not to exceed the 3.8-g limit of this plane or the wings would rip off. The light aluminum frame of this bird didn't come anywhere close to withstanding the ten-g rating of an F-14A Tomcat.

Airspeed quickly bled off as he came up to within three hundred feet behind and roughly two hundred feet below the runaway Cessna's tail section. Kevin adjusted the throttle and trim to close the gap slowly. He flew in the Cessna's blind spot. Unless its pilot inverted or took an abrupt turn, Kevin would remain invisible, the noise of Cessna's engines drowning his own.

One hundred feet.

Keeping his left hand on the dual throttle controls and his right on the wheel, Kevin Dalton floated his plane right up to the Cessna. Altitude:

thirty-five hundred feet. Speed: 275 knots. With the tall pines of Francis Marion National Forest slowly moving below him, Kevin struggled to bring the port engine right up to the Cessna's empennage. The maneuver reminded him of an air-to-air refueling session from his Navy days, where he had to line up his Tomcat refueling probe with the moving boom at the end of a hose trailing a flying tanker. Now it was the moving tail section of the Cessna that changed in altitude by as much as five to ten feet, forcing Kevin to adjust his altitude as well. This time, however, the target was much larger than the small refueling boom, and the clear disk made by the propeller gave him more play than the small refueling probe. He didn't have to be as accurate.

The shiny white tail moved down just as Kevin's port engine came up, its propeller grazing the bottom of the tail. The instant vibration of his plane mixed with the cloud of white debris and sparks generated from the one-second contact before the planes separated.

Kemal Ramallah cut left the moment he felt the noise behind him. Adding throttle as he turned a full circle, he caught a glimpse of the plane glued to his tail, also turning with him. The infidel was trying to collide with him!

As his MiG-29 training quickly resurfaced, Kemal pushed the wheel forward, pointing his nose toward the forest below. Airspeed quickly shot past three hundred knots. The vibrations inside the cockpit reminded the former Iraqi pilot that he had exceeded the maximum speed of the twin-engine. Cutting back throttles, he reduced speed as the plane dropped below three hundred feet over the tall pines carpeting the hills northwest of Charleston.

Leveling off, Kemal hugged the rugged terrain as he kept the nose pointed toward the city slowly looming in the distance. Glimpsing back, he looked for his pursuer but did not see him.

Kevin Dalton decided to change tactics in response to the Cessna's treetop flying. He kept his plane slightly above and behind it, his airspeed varying to remain with the Cessna. Slowly, he descended over the plane, but the pilot suddenly gained some altitude, the top of its cockpit slamming against Kevin's underside with a loud noise.

Pulling back on the wheel and breaking left, Kevin watched the top of the Cessna's fuselage and saw the scratched and indented surface reflecting the sun's light.

Kevin went after it again, playing the throttles and the elevators to force it down, but the Cessna cut left, ruining Kevin's approach.

Kemal smiled. He had seen the Piper trying to drive him into the forest and had reacted just in time, sending the pilot a message.

Now he pushed full throttles again, feeling the engines revving as the

RPM indicator shot past four thousand revolutions per minute, slowly creeping into the red. But the *Mukhabarat* colonel did not care. He had to gain speed, increase the gap between himself and his pursuer. If fate prevented him from destroying New York City, then he would use the weapon safely strapped to a rear seat to level another large American city.

The infidels will remember this day.

Back at Summerville Regional Airport, the FBI special agent in charge learned from Khalela Yishaid what had taken place. A brief call to Roman Palenski confirmed the woman's claim. He now got on the radio and dialed a prearranged frequency. He spoke for only thirty seconds, giving out the exact location of the last sighting. Four Apache helicopters from a nearby Army base responded and turned to intercept. In his rush to convey the information, however, the FBI agent failed to mention that only one of the twin-engines was to be shot down. The second was piloted by a CIA agent in pursuit.

The agent thought about switching to Unicom and warning Kevin Dalton to get out of the way, but in doing so the agent might also warn the terrorist, who could also be listening. With the knowledge that the terrorist could have at least one warhead in that plane, the FBI agent chose to take zero chances of that terrorist panicking and detonating the weapon before one of the Apaches could destroy him with a missile.

Kevin Dalton began to tire of the chasing game. He also pushed full throttle and went after the Cessna, which closely followed the contours of the hills with a skill that even Kevin found difficult to mimic. Barely grazing the treetops, the Cessna moved with the terrain, smoothly climbing and descending, at times disappearing from Kevin's field of view as it dropped behind a hill Kevin had not yet reached.

He had to change tactics to catch up. Pulling on the wheel and climbing to two hundred feet, Kevin positioned his Navajo twin-engine almost over the Cessna. Adding forward pressure on the wheel, the former Navy pilot descended in a straight line toward the Cessna, which continued to follow the terrain below. Airspeed climbed to 325 knots, but Kevin did not cut back throttles. He had to get rid of the Cessna this time around. Charleston was too close.

Kevin dived, accelerating past the maximum rated speed of the Navajo, his heart hammering his chest with the same intensity as the propellers of the redlined engines bit into the air. The vibrations on the wheel and rudder pedals intensified, the airframe trembled, but Kevin didn't care, couldn't care. The horror facing the population of this city had to be eliminated, and the horror was inside that Cessna.

Angered brown eyes focused like a laser beam on the empennage section, the most vulnerable spot in the entire plane, the place that governed heading and altitude, the area Kevin had to destroy to prevent that plane from reaching its destination.

The Cessna grew in size, it filled his windscreen. With the vision of victims sobbing and moaning in pain, Kevin turned the Navajo at the last possible moment, letting the port engine smash into the tail section of the Cessna, his propeller digging deep into the aluminum frame.

A cloud of sparks and debris crashed against the Plexiglas windshield, cracking it in several places before washing away in the slipstream. The same turn that had forced his plane into the Cessna now pulled him away from it.

Momentarily disoriented, Kevin simply pulled back on the wheel. He needed to climb. He needed altitude to keep from crashing against the sea of tall pines below. A quick glance to port showed him a disabled engine in the middle of his wing, the three-spoke propeller grossly bent back. But he still had control of the Navajo. The Cessna, however, had lost the entire rudder and one elevon.

Kemal pulled back on the wheel, but the plane did not respond. The nose was dropping, and he no longer could control his heading. The rudder pedals failed him as he tried to keep the plane flying toward the American city now just under five miles away.

Allah, I am so close!

With his plane just over twenty feet above the forest and dropping fast, he did not have time to reach for the backpack, load a uranium round and pull the trigger.

The nose dropped even more, pointing him directly toward the pine trees now grazing the underfuselage. In another second the turquoise sky disappeared as the evergreens swallowed him. A branch pierced the starboard wing, cutting right through the recently fueled tank.

Kevin Dalton managed to climb to seven hundred feet as a sheet of orange flames rose up to the sky from the fallen Cessna.

Got you, he thought as the forested hills gave way to the grass plains leading to Charleston.

Adding left rudder to compensate for the loss of his port engine, Kevin concentrated on finding a place to land his crippled bird. Although the plane was flyable with one engine, the stress induced on the wing, while the propeller chopped away the tail section of the Piper, could have created fractures in the honeycomb structure underneath the aluminum skin, meaning that the wing could just fall off without warning.

Cutting back throttle as he spotted a clearing a couple of miles away, Kevin also lowered the landing gear and went through the emergency landing checklist, which unfortunately did not include a fuel dump as it did on the Tomcat.

With the clearing now just over a mile away, and with his altitude back down to four hundred feet, Kevin saw the bulky shapes of four helicopters in the distance, coming toward him from Charleston.

Without warning, one of them fired a missile at him. Kevin estimated the helicopters to be a couple of miles away.

Trained instincts took over the second his eyes saw the wispy contrail leaving the helicopter, which he now recognized as an Apache.

Without flares and chaff to fool the incoming demon, Kevin inverted the Piper Navajo while redlining his starboard engine, squeezing every single ounce of power. The sky and the grasslands swapped places as he pulled the wheel toward him, forcing the craft into an outside loop, which dropped him to fifty feet in the time it took the missile to get dangerously close to him.

Subsonic. The missile had to be subsonic. Had it been a Sidewinder, his butt would have been roasted a few seconds before, but the subsonic missile had given Kevin the six or seven seconds that allowed him to drop so close to the ground that the missile passed him up a hundred feet above, going off in the forest behind him.

As he leveled off, the helicopters closed in for the kill. Out of options and without a radio to tell them he was the good guy, Kevin reached for the landing light switch, connected to the three halogen lights attached to the landing gear.

Kevin quickly switched them off and on. Three times fast and three times slow. Repeating the sequence over and over, he desperately hoped the choppers would recognize his Morse code S.O.S. and not fire again.

They did not, but they did circle Kevin, two of them keeping their guns and missiles pointed straight at him as they forced him to land on the field Kevin had originally spotted for this emergency landing.

Now came the hard part. It was one thing to take off and fly a plane. It was an entirely different story to land one, particularly one he had never flown before, and while flying single-engine. But at least the grassy field wasn't moving up and down like the heaving deck of an aircraft carrier.

Adding fifteen degrees of flaps while cutting back throttles to drop his airspeed below eighty knots, Kevin slowly brought the Piper down, keeping an eye on the altimeter and the airspeed indicator to avoid going into a stall.

The ground came up to meet him just as he idled the engine and softly pulled back on the wheel, bringing the nose up a second before the rear wheels touched the ground. The Piper started to vibrate as it cruised over the uneven terrain. Kevin kept the rear pressure on the wheel and let the nose fall by itself as airspeed bled off. The plane came to a full stop twenty seconds later.

The Apaches landed on the field in tight formation, their rotors' downwash creating a cloud of swirling debris. Kevin shut off the engine and glanced at the dead Jake Sasso, still strapped to his seat, before heading for the rear of the plane, unlocking and opening the side door, and walking down to the field of grass.

The cloud of dust rose up to the bright blue skies outside Charleston, a city that Kevin hoped would live to see many such beautiful days. Pulling out his CIA credentials, the former naval aviator walked toward the helicopters.

20

DESTINY

Dulce et decorum est pro patria mori.
It is a sweet and seemly thing to die for one's country.
—Horace

CENTRAL IRAQ.

Major Blue Jeans Levi piloted one of five F/A-18C Hornets escorting two HC-130N Hercules flying treetop over central Iraq. The Hornets were split into three sections. One section of two at the front of the convoy and another one five hundred feet to the left. Levi covered the rear.

The Marine pilot eased back throttles as the Hercules transports reduced their speed to 180 knots.

"Here we go again, folks," he said over the squadron frequency.

"Hate slow flights," commented one pilot.

"Especially in this wind," said another.

The high winds coming down from the Zagros Mountains to the east made the Hornet difficult to control at slow speeds. The F/A-18C was inherently unstable, particularly below two hundred knots.

Levi found himself fighting the controls. He hated it with a passion, and the thirty-knot crosswind didn't make it any easier either. The stall buzzer went off. Levi quickly lowered the nose and added power, recovering. He eased back throttles and tried to achieve the slow flight once more, but went into another stall.

"Hot damn!"

Again, he added throttle to prevent going into a spin. He could hear moans and complaints from the other Hornet pilots over the squadron frequency.

"Hercules Lead, Stingray Lead," Levi said into the voice-activated mike.

"Stingray, go ahead."

"Can't hold the slow speed on this bird tonight. Let's crank it up to four hundred knots." Levi knew that the higher speed meant a greater chance of being heard by the troops on that airfield much sooner than with the engines at half throttle. But he couldn't risk a Hornet losing control this close to the ground.

"Four hundred. Roger."

Levi smiled as he added throttle and the Hornet instantly became an entirely different beast, smoothly sailing through the night sky—at the price of doubling the amount of noise generated by the engines. A check on his radar, and he verified that the airfield was only fifteen minutes away.

Sitting on the aluminum floor of the C-130's cockpit with his back against the copilot's seat, Donald Bane could barely move. After a week of little sleep and hardly any food, plus a severe beating and, finally, a gunshot wound, he was ready to call it quits. The eyelid of his good eye grew heavy and he wasn't sure how much longer he could stay awake. The short nap he had taken right after getting shot had come to an abrupt end when Diane Towers informed him that the rescue team would be here in less than fifteen minutes.

"We have to get ready," he said, slowly getting up and testily moving his arm around.

"You shouldn't do that," she said, also getting to her feet and reaching for the portable radio, which she brought to her lips.

"Hercules One here, over."

"Hercules One. Strike Lead. Cargo ready?"

"Will be in a minute. What's your situation?"

"Cleanup pass in ten. Extraction pass in twelve."

"We'll be ready."

Bane grabbed the canvas bag and set the timer to go off in exactly twenty minutes. With the extraction in twelve minutes, that would give them eight minutes to get out of the range of the nuclear detonation. He closed the canvas bag and placed it under the control panel next to the navigator's seat, well hidden from view. Now all they had to do was wait for the rescue team to—

His thoughts were cut short by the noise of shattering glass behind him, immediately followed by a loud blast coming from the lower section of the cabin.

Hassani knew something was wrong when he heard the faint noise of jet engines in the distance. It was not his squadron. Hassani's MiGs had been forced back south to refuel fifteen minutes ago. *Are the infidels sending another strike so soon?*

Immediately he had contacted an Iraqi base fifty miles to the north, and he had been told that there were no other MiGs in the region. At his request, the base commander agreed to send a dozen MiGs to cover the airstrip immediately.

But that had not been enough for Hassani. He heard Allah's words echoing inside his head, and they told him to act quickly, to move in and recover the coveted weapons before it was too late. Allah told him those distant jet noises were the enemy coming to take his country's weapon of respect away from him, and that was something the large Arab would die to prevent. He could not fail Saddam Hussein.

And so he gave the premature order to storm the cockpit before he received confirmation from Baghdad. But the weapons would not be taken away by the Great Satan. No, the Americans would not touch the weapons or his country's top scientist.

As the loud report from a dozen Kalashnikovs cracked through the night like a whip and the shaped charge applied to the thick cockpit access door detonated with a bright flash, Colonel Hassani swore on his soul that the weapons would not leave Iraqi soil, and that Jafar would not go through the shame of being captured alive.

The earsplitting detonation still ringing in his ears, Donald Bane instinctively threw himself over Diane and rolled with her to the safety of the rear cockpit, crashing his back against the aluminum frame of the lower bunker.

"Damn!"

At that moment, an explosion coming from the lower section of the cabin rocked the transport.

"Donald!" Diane screamed as she jumped to her feet, the nearly depleted AK-47 clutched in her hands.

Stunned by the blow to his back and loss of blood, Bane did not react as quickly as Diane. By the time he staggered to his feet, Diane Towers had already reached the access hatch leading to the steps connecting the flight deck to the lower cabin section.

"They blew a hole in the bottom!" she screamed. "They're coming up!"

"Lock the access hatch!"

Diane, one hand firing down the steps, reached for the heavy D-shaped door. A few seconds later, Bane's hands joined hers and together they pulled the door down and over the incoming Iraqis, three of whom fell back, victims to Diane Towers's final rounds before her AK-47 went dry.

Just as the door was about to be slammed shut, a single bullet, fired almost by accident by one of the mortally wounded Iraqis rolling down the access steps, bounced off the edge of the closing door and ricocheted right into the middle of Diane's chest, shattering her sternum, the explosive round detonating inside her rib cage. The shot lifted her off her feet and threw her against the navigator's station, where she bounced off the seat and landed on the floor faceup.

"DIANE! NO!"

With the door locked and the Iraqi threat temporarily locked out of their Kevlar and steel sanctuary, Donald Bane knelt by her side on the aluminum floor. Blood gushed out of her chest, jetting against his shirt every time she coughed.

"It . . . hurts . . . hurts . . . Donald . . ." came the voice, a mere whisper in the stillness of the flight deck, a murmur that pierced Donald Bane's ears with an intensity a thousand times more powerful than the shouts coming from the other side of the locked hatch.

With tears filling his eyes, Donald Bane carefully zipped her flight suit down to her waist, exposing a chest covered with purple blotches and blood.

"The pain . . . Donald . . . Oh, God . . . the pain."

"I know, Diane. I know." Bane tried using the same white cloth with which he had wiped off the blood on his face to slow the blood flow. But the moment he even brushed the cotton cloth over her wound, Diane Towers arched her hips to the sky in one bloodcurdling shriek, tight fists pounding the floor.

Donald Bane felt an uncontrollable burst of anger swelling inside him. The Iraqis had taken her away from him! He felt life slowly escaping his soul with every drop of precious blood flowing out of her, out of the courageous Marine pilot who had saved his life and was now dying in his arms.

"Cold . . . I'm . . ."

Donald Bane lifted her slim frame off the floor and brought her close to him, very close. He could feel her breath on his neck, the shivering hands finding refuge on his wide chest. His shoulder wound no longer hurt, every single ounce of flesh on his body went numb at the thought of losing her, drop after drop, breath after breath, second after second.

Their eyes met. Diane tried to talk. Bane put an ear to her lips and felt them move, but not a word was uttered out of them. Not one more word ever came out of those fine lips.

Standing in the middle of the flight deck clutching this brave woman, Donald Bane began to cry. He cried the tears that only those who had lived and survived this uncertain world for decades knew how to cry. He felt her trembling, felt her shivering, closed his eyes at the irregular breathing that suddenly stopped, at the heartbeat that ceased to pound his own chest, at the hands that slowly fell to her sides.

Dear God, no! This cannot be happening!

But the sad reality of the moment stung him with the power of a hundred thorns, chilled him with the thunder of a thousand frozen rivers running through the middle of his shrinking heart, of his frantic mind, of his mournful soul.

Donald Bane took a deep breath, stared at those hazel eyes, her dilating pupils fixed on a spot on the cabin's ceiling, a trickle of blood running out of the corner of her mouth.

Good-bye, Diane Towers.

The sound of jet engines increased. The professional in Donald Bane slowly began to sweep aside the feelings he knew would interfere with his mission, with the reason Harvey Lee, André Boyabat, *and* Diane Towers had died.

Lifting his gaze to the broken windowpanes, he noticed a dark cylinder flying through one of the openings, landing between the pilot's and the navigator's seats.

Grenade?

With his mind working on automatic, Bane got up, painfully held Diane close to him, and jumped behind the navigator's station, struggling to get away from the range of the shrapnel, the pain shooting down his wounded shoulder crippling him. But he would not let go of her, would not let the Iraqis maim her further.

The grenade went off, and he braced himself, protecting Diane's body with his own, but the impact never came. Instead, smoke began to fill the cabin.

Gas!

His eyes began to burn.

It's fucking tear gas!

He set her limp body down, reached for the gas canister, and flung it out through a broken windowpane.

"Hercules One, come in, over."

The radio. Bane knew he had to reach the portable radio Diane had left between the front seats and tell them to hurry. A part of him actually didn't care anymore. He just wanted to detonate the weapon and vaporize himself in the process. But the operative in him could not allow this, and not just because of his own survival instincts. By prematurely detonating the weapon he would be killing the very same people who were risking their lives to rescue him. He had to follow through with his plan, had to reach that radio. But which way was the front? The cabin was filled with gas and he could not open his good eye. His shoulder burned and the warm liquid on his chest and back told him he had just reopened his wound.

"Hercules One, come in, over . . . Hercules One?"

Leaving Diane in the rear section of the cabin, Bane crawled across the metal floor until he hit something . . . a seat. He felt his way to the right and reached the center console. He grabbed the radio and brought it to his lips.

"Stingray Lead . . . hurry . . . tear gas . . . the gas . . . hurry."

Major John Levi heard just about all he cared to hear. "Breakin' formation and makin' a cleanup pass," he said over the squadron frequency. "Rest of you stay with the transports."

Without waiting to hear an acknowledgment, Levi lowered the nose while pushing full power, cruising up to Mach 1 while sprinting from under the caravan and toward the base, which the night goggles helped him find in seconds. In an instant, Levi could clearly see the base, the parked C-130, and a number of people surrounding the plane.

He enabled the 20mm cannon and the pipper came up on the Heads-up Display.

Cutting back throttles until his indicator read 450 knots, Levi flew right above the sand, the gunsight centered on the figures surrounding the transport plane.

Colonel Hassani heard the increased jet engine noise, but he had been unable to spot any planes in the dark sky. He had been disappointed in his men's inability to gain control of the Hercules.

The sound of jets went up several decibels, and Hassani still could not see the fighter in the dark sky.

He must be very—

A 20mm round scored a direct hit on the colonel's abdomen, cutting him in half. With a crippling, burning pain coming from his stomach, Hassani noticed that his legs no longer supported his upper body as he landed sideways in a pool of his own blood and viscera. Everything went dark for the large Iraqi, but not before he saw several of his own men being mowed down by the guns of the Great Satan. He had failed, but he was going to die in the process.

His last thought before dying was of his Samia, his Khalil, and his Jazmine. His death while fighting against the Americans would buy them their lives.

"Two minutes, Hercules One. Get ready to eject! Repeat, get ready to eject."

"Roger," responded Bane, before hurrying to the rear of the cabin. Donald Bane would not leave this woman behind. There was only one thing he could do for her: take her home and give her a proper military funeral. She was an American hero and deserved to be treated as such.

"Let's do it!" he screamed over the noise of the gunfire and the jet engines outside, his burning eye a mere slit covered with tears.

Holding her in his arms, Bane staggered to the front, sat her in the copilot seat, and secured her safety harness. Bane raced back to the navigator's station and took one last glance at the digital display in the canvas bag. Eight minutes. In eight minutes there would be a cloud of vapor the size of a thousand football fields.

He raced back to the front, got into the pilot's seat, and secured his safety harness. Through his tears, he spotted the ejection handles on the side of the seat. The moment he pulled on them, both Diane and he would eject. He could hear the commotion outside.

"On my mark, Hercules One," crackled the voice from the rescue party

through the radio speaker. *"Ten . . . seven . . . five . . . three . . . one . . .
now!"*

Bane pulled on the handles. A translucent vision of fire loomed
through the hazy room as the five-foot-square hatches above the pilot's
and navigator's seats were blown upward by dozens of explosive bolts a
second before the Martin-Baker GRU-7A ejection seats' solid-propellant
rockets kicked into life and shot them upward at great speed.

It was over before Bane's mind had a chance to register it. As he
overcame the initial g-force from the ejection rocket, Bane grew disoriented while spinning freely through the night air. Everything became
fuzzy, cloudy. His face and shoulders burned, his body demanded rest, his
mind screamed for peace. A hard tug told him the parachute had deployed.
It was his last visual input before he passed out.

At an altitude of seven hundred feet Levi saw the explosion above the
cabin and now watched the ejection seats—two of them—reaching the
apex of their parabolic shots, which left them at almost his same altitude.
The small chutes popped off the back of the chairs and dragged the main
canopies behind them. The moment they deployed, the heavy seats
automatically fell away, leaving both parachutes slowly gliding back to
earth.

But they'll never reach the ground again, reflected Levi as he watched
the first HC-130N Hercules—a version used for midair recovery of small
space capsules containing satellite data—lower the two large hooks used
to snag on to parachutes. Hercules Two dropped its nose before heading
directly toward the nearest parachute.

Making a steep right turn, Levi held his breath as the Hercules
approached the parachute and . . . hooked it in spite of the heavy
crosswind!

Incredible!

Craft and dragging parachute disappeared in the night sky as the
second HC-130N—Hercules Three—came into view, heading directly for
the next parachute, but the hooks missed the target by a few feet.

Hot damn! Levi thought. *It missed . . . and the parachute's only four
hundred feet from the ground!*

"Hercules Three, Stingray Lead. Missed it. Repeat. Missed the target."

*"Crosswind's too strong, Lead. Hercules Three going around for a
second pass."*

"Better make it a tight one-eighty, Hercules Three, or that guy's gonna
be on the ground by the time you come back."

"Roger."

The Hercules completed the one-eighty, came back around, and
dropped to 150 feet. Again Levi watched in silence as the gigantic craft
approached the fragile parachute and its cargo almost as if it wanted to

crash right through it, but the extra twenty feet of altitude kept the hooks aligned with the silk, which came in contact with the left hook, but not for long enough to snag it. Instead, the hook pulled on the parachute for ten feet before a small section of the canopy ripped free.

Levi cursed out loud as he watched a number of men emerge from somewhere and run toward the parachute, which landed on a patch of grass just left of the runway. He simply couldn't believe it.

The downed parachuter rolled on the grass as the canopy, still inflated from the strong winds, dragged the poor bastard over the runway.

"Hercules Three, Lead. Go one more time! Make a one-eighty and another pass. This one at ground level!"

"But the Iraqis . . ."

"I'll handle them! You just make sure to hook him up for good this time around!"

"Roger."

Donald Bane hit the ground hard. The painful jolt brought him back to consciousness, but when he opened his good eye all he could see was tarmac and swirling white silk as he felt dragged across the runway by the inflated canopy.

On his back, glaring at the cosmos, the CIA officer felt the flesh-tearing grinding of tarmac against the skin of his wounded shoulder and back.

God it hurts! his mind screamed.

The white sheet Diane had used to wrap the wound was now scraps of cloth around his arms and chest. But through the pain, Bane saw something else: figures running toward him. The silhouettes of men carrying automatic weapons aimed in his direction.

The first shot ricocheted off the tarmac to his left. A miss. Then more shots rang in his ears, but his mind was too cloudy now, the pain too intense. He prayed to lose consciousness, prayed to escape the numbing pain of burning flesh and bones ground against the tarmac where the Iraqi rounds exploded . . . the crippling pain nearly threw him over the edge. A round had grazed his right thigh. Bane could feel it, his fingers clumsily groped over the torn cloth and felt the same warm blood that continued to flow freely from his reopened shoulder wound.

The figures loomed closer, the firing intensified, the pain grew unbearable.

Soon, his mind said. *Soon there will be peace.*

Blue Jeans Levi swung the control stick to the right and rolled the craft on its side while adding throttle and dropping the nose. Airspeed increased to 450 knots . . . 480 knots. Levi watched the altimeter's needle zoom below three hundred feet . . . two hundred. He leveled the wings, pulled down the nose a bit more, and pushed full throttle. As the afterburner slammed him in the back, Levi watched the Hornet's airspeed climb to 640 knots.

He pointed the F/A-18C's nose at the dozen men rushing toward the parachute. He could see their muzzle flashes, but not toward him. The bastards had opened fire on the parachute!

Bastards!

With his anger spiraling, Levi fixed his index finger above the trigger casing on the stick, and he pressed it to the second detent.

The multibarrel 20mm gun came to life, vomiting rounds at the rate of three thousand per minute, but having a maximum load of 675 rounds, Levi limited himself to short controlled bursts. Six men dropped immediately. The rest began running the other way.

"Hercules Three, Lead. Coast is clear. Make your pass."

"Roger."

Levi made a tight 180 turn and the g's squashed his shoulders, but he maintained the rear pressure on the stick to keep the nose from dropping —something that at his treetop altitude would result in his immediate destruction. He pulled out of the turn and came back around. This time, however, he didn't use the guns. He didn't have to. The Iraqis were out of sight as the Hercules lined up the hooks with the overblown silk canopy.

Levi watched a cloud of sparks explode the moment the steel hooks crashed over the runway seconds before the Hercules approached the white parachute . . . and snatched it!

The Hercules's nose hoisted above the horizon, dragging the parachute and its wearer.

"Good fishin', Hercules Three! Damn good fishin'!"

"Thank you, Lead."

The caravan headed back to Kuwait.

Donald Bane floated in the dark. The strong but cool wind soothed his burning back. The sound of engine noises hammered against his eardrums, the throbbing from his thigh and shoulder numbed him. His rib cage felt on fire, and so did his face, but his mind was too tired to care, his body too drained to withstand the strain any longer.

But he refused to jump into the abyss of his unconsciousness. He could not do it until he heard the blast that would come soon, the sound that would make all the suffering worthwhile, except for her death. Nothing Bane could imagine would have justified Diane Towers's sudden death. *Nothing.*

The blinding flash in the distance brought a sarcastic smile to his lips, along with a jolt of pain. It was over. The thundering sound echoing across northern Mesopotamia with the force of a million sandstorms told Donald Bane that Saddam's weapons of mass destruction no longer existed.

The night surrounded Donald Bane. He saw Diane's hazel eyes

twinkling in the stars above. It was so peaceful, so perfect, so different from the nightmare that had been his life for the past days. Slowly, oh so very slowly, Donald Bane let the night air caress away the pain as his vision and his mind grew cloudier, before everything faded away.

BAGHDAD, IRAQ.

Saddam Hussein was shaking. He had not displayed such foolish behavior in front of anyone for a very, very long time, much less his immediate staff. But the news . . . *Why, Allah? Why must you punish me this way?*

The loss of Tikrit was total. His hometown, his roots, had been vaporized by his own weapons of mass destruction. It might as well have been him pulling the trigger. It was his money that had purchased the weapons. It was his mind that had conceived the plan to achieve revenge against Bill Clinton. And now it was his own fault that everyone he had ever held dear had been obliterated in the cloud of vapor that hung over his beloved birthplace.

As he sank into his swivel chair behind his desk, both hands on his face, Saddam Hussein's mind filled with visions of his past, of his childhood days, of his friends, family, of his uncle. Some memories were good, some bad, but they were all his. They all had shaped him into the powerful leader he was this day. Saddam remembered every street in Tikrit, every tree, every stone house, every face. He remembered the home where he grew up and the waterhole fed by the waters of the Tigris, where he and his friends swam and bathed. He remembered his school, his teachers, his beloved uncle. Now all of that was gone, and he could blame no one but himself!

"Great One," said General Sa'dun Mustafa from across his desk. The large general was flanked by two junior generals. "We are not making headway at the border. The American planes are keeping our front lines from advancing farther south."

Saddam Hussein barely heard him, his mind momentarily confused, his feelings temporarily turned upside down by a reality he refused to accept, by a change of fate he found too difficult to swallow. Then his ears heard another noise: the mechanical sound of the firing mechanism of a pistol as it was cocked. He had heard that sound many times before putting a bullet into an insubordinate's head.

Saddam put both hands over his lap and raised his gaze. General Mustafa held a small, yellow gun in his right hand and had it leveled at the Iraqi leader.

"We cannot go on like this," Mustafa said. "You are ruining our country."

Saddam's narrowed stare burned Mustafa, who took a step back as the other two moved to the sides, their black leather holsters empty, as they should be. Momentarily puzzled at how Mustafa had managed to sneak the small pistol through the security checkpoint, he finally said, "You dare point a weapon at me, *Kurf?*"

The general didn't utter a sound, simply keeping the weapon pointed at Saddam's face.

"I will not only tear you apart, piece by piece," Saddam said, "but I will also pull your roots. I will have every member of your family executed."

Mustafa remained frozen. His two companions did likewise, except for their eyes. They kept shifting back and forth between Saddam and the general's gun.

Saddam stood, a defiant grin flashing across his face as he reached for his own Makarov, freeing it from the holster and bringing it up.

A shot went off, the report blasting in Saddam's ears before he himself got a chance to pull the trigger. The impact pushed him back against the leather chair, forcing him to sit. The round had struck right below the chin. Warm blood gushed down his chest as he stared at his right hand, still clutching the Makarov he never got a chance to fire.

His gaze clouding, Saddam saw the general walking right up to the desk, the small gun still pointed at the Iraqi leader, thin smoke coiling upward from the muzzle. The general pressed the trigger again, but Saddam only heard the snapping sound of the firing mechanism. The small gun had malfunctioned.

The other two generals quickly distanced themselves from the assassin just as a dozen guards stormed the office, their weapons pointed at the generals.

"The infidel Mustafa has shot our leader! Kill him! Kill him, you fools!" one of the generals screamed.

Two guards instantly pointed their Kalashnikovs at Mustafa, still clutching the small weapon. Gunfire erupted, ripping open Mustafa's chest, and sending him flying to the other side of the office. The other two generals watched in silence.

The Iraqi leader couldn't mutter a single word. Although somehow he could still breathe, his body would not respond to his commands. The bullet had broken his neck, paralyzing him. Only his eyes moved, and they traveled from the shocked guards to the generals.

Imbeciles! Kill them too! They are his accomplices! Can you see this for what it is? And where are the medics, the doctors? I am dying!

But his thoughts remained unheeded as life quickly flowed out of his neck, down his chest and arms, and over the Makarov his stubborn right hand refused to release.

To his appalling shock, Saddam watched the guards lowering their weapons. One of them even kicked the dead general repeatedly while the others crowded around the dying tyrant.

"Do not leave us, Great One," one guard said as he dropped to his knees and began to weep. "We do not know the way to defeat the Great Satan!"

Idiots! I'm surrounded by idiots! Get me help, you imbeciles! Get me a doctor! Stop the blood loss! Kill the infidel generals! Kill their families!

Another minute went by before his personal surgeon showed up, screaming and shouting to get the guards out of the way.

"Air!" he screamed. "This man needs air! Move!"

The guards stepped aside and joined the two generals on the other side of the desk as the surgeon knelt by his side and quickly applied pressure to the neck.

Saddam Hussein found it difficult to breathe and suddenly felt cold, very cold. His eyes began to roll to the back of his head, and he fought it for another minute, his clouding gaze landing one final time on the two generals. Right before everything turned dark, Saddam watched the flicker of a smile flashing on one of them. Then all thought vanished and he ceased to breathe.

WASHINGTON, D.C.

Viktor Kozlov reached the twenty-ninth floor condominium in downtown Washington. The three-bedroom apartment with an excellent view of the Capitol had been leased to Irina Bukovski six months before. In his hands he carried a canvas bag housing enough firepower to demolish every structure in a two-mile radius and every living creature within four miles.

He walked out of the elevator and down the carpeted corridor, right hand holding the bag, his left inside his trench coat, the fingers holding on to the handle of a Browning automatic. His eyes scanned not just the long hallway but also the gold numbers on the white doors on either side of him. He stopped halfway down the corridor and knocked once on the door for apartment 2931.

"May I help you?" came the male voice from inside the unit.

Viktor expected the Persian-accented English, and he released the grip on the Browning. The Ukrainian man had been wary of this operation ever since Irina failed to show at the appointed rendezvous in North Carolina.

Viktor had waited for hours in a small field outside of Raleigh, but there had been no Irina. When he returned to the club in Atlantic City, the Ukrainian found a message from Marcos. The Chilean wanted to meet him at a secluded spot on the Jersey shore. The meeting took place as planned. Marcos did not know what had happened to the Russian woman after leaving the sugarcane plantation. The atomic bomb changed hands and then Marcos had disappeared.

And now here he was, ready to hand over the weapon to an Arab terrorist who would apparently sacrifice himself in order to fulfill Saddam Hussein's plans.

The door opened, and Viktor walked in slowly, taking in the short and bearded Arab with a curious glance. The Ukrainian had never before met someone destined to die by his own hand in order to accomplish a mission. Even in the KGB an operative would at the very least plan for a way out if a mission didn't go as planned. But this new wave of terrorists from the Middle East removed the factor of hope from a mission's equation and replaced it with the knowledge that they would have to perish in order to succeed.

Viktor shook his head at the thought and handed the bag to the Arab, who took almost a full minute to remove the bomb from the bag and inspect the firing mechanism.

"The uranium bullet?" asked the Arab, when he found the empty revolver chamber.

Viktor dug in his pocket and handed it to him.

The Arab brought the shiny round to his eyes and dropped his bushy brows while inspecting it. He then loaded it in the chamber and stared at Viktor. "How long do you need?"

Viktor reached for the door. "I will be out of range in fifteen minutes."

The Arab nodded. "Fifteen minutes."

Viktor raced out of the apartment and headed for the elevators. A minute later he reached his car. His driver had kept it double-parked in front of the apartment building for the past five minutes.

Inside the apartment, the Arab man removed the round from the revolver and handed it to one of several figures emerging from the bedrooms.

The figure, wearing a dark overcoat over an iron gray suit, inspected the round that would have triggered the devastating chain reaction.

"Amazing, isn't it, Joe?" the man in the overcoat asked another man standing next to him. "Just a few grams of this stuff fired at a specific velocity into the uranium mass and we won't even have time to bend over and kiss our sorry asses good-bye."

Joseph Goldberg took the round from Roman Palenski's hand and fiddled with it for a few moments. "We and the entire population of Washington, D.C." the director of Central Intelligence added in his rheumy voice, his sunken eyes glaring at the bullet. "What about the courier?"

Palenski shrugged. "His name is Viktor Kozlov, a Ukrainian immigrant and former member of the KGB. We have people following him as well as a hundred other selected immigrants from the former Soviet republics and close to five hundred men and women from the Middle East currently living in this country. Kozlov will be arrested within the hour. We'll move on the others within a week or so."

The DCI handed the round to one of the technicians from the Nuclear Regulatory Commission. The bomb was fully deactivated after the first thirty seconds, when one of the technicians removed the neutron initiator from the core, thus eliminating the possibility of accidentally triggering a chain reaction. It took a special team from the NRC just over five minutes to disassemble the basic components of the weapon, store them in carefully labeled radiation-proof containers, and haul them out of the apartment.

Palenski and Goldberg left the building last. Before they parted, a smile reached Palenski's face. Goldberg cocked his head at him.

"I don't think I've seen you smile in all the years I've known you, Roman."

The director of the Federal Bureau of Investigation raised an eyebrow. "I was simply wondering what is going through Viktor Kozlov's mind at this moment."

Goldberg checked his watch and realized it had been exactly fifteen minutes since the Ukrainian had left the building in a hurry.

They both glanced at the clear skies over downtown Washington.

EPILOGUE

CIA HEADQUARTERS. LANGLEY, VIRGINIA.
Six Weeks Later.

The gray-and-white marble floors of the lobby of the CIA headquarters sparkled as President Bill Clinton solemnly stood with Hillary by his side. Joseph Goldberg and Donald Bane flanked the First Couple. Outside, the rains had subsided and given way to beautiful skies and the cold breeze that swirled Bane's thin brown hair the moment two other men entered the building accompanied by their bodyguards. They were the secretaries of defense and state. Roman Palenski stood in the back, also paying his respects to a true American patriot. The same group plus a lot of high brass had attended a memorial service in Arlington for Diane Towers. Donald Bane had not been there. He had been in a coma for an entire week following the rescue mission. The extreme blood loss had nearly killed him. This was actually the first week he had been out of the hospital, his body healing at a rate much faster than his mind, which was still quite torn at losing her.

During the past weeks, Donald Bane had seen Diane Towers in his dreams almost every night. She had stood there, in the twilight of the flight deck, one hand holding the Kalashnikov and the other reaching for the steel door. Her hazel eyes, alive with a mix of fear and determination, locked with Bane's for a brief second, before the bullet came.

Bane briefly closed his eyes and said a little prayer not only for the most courageous woman he would ever know, but also for the soul of Robert Bourdeaux, one of the best officers the CIA ever had. As he listened to the short eulogy of the Episcopalian minister President Bill Clinton had asked to attend this ceremony, the newly appointed deputy director for operations finally understood the true meaning of his profession. It wasn't about spies, or surveillance, or intelligence reports. It wasn't about the killings, the counterintelligence games, or the President's Daily Briefs. His profession was all about human sacrifice for the benefit of others. Diane Towers had certainly lived by this belief, and so did the Turk André and the rookie Harvey Lee. They all had died because of that belief. With time Bane knew the sting of their deaths would pass, at least that of André Boyabat and Harvey Lee. He was not so sure about Diane Towers's. The handful of hours they had spent together, the final seconds of her life as he held her in his arms, had already become an inseparable part of him.

The eulogy ended and Bane watched Goldberg step forward and remove the red veil covering the CIA Memorial, exposing a shiny new gold star.

In between the American flag and the CIA flag, Donald Bane watched in silence the stars of fallen heroes, some of whom he didn't even know. Others, like Harvey Lee and Robert Bourdeaux, and the ones who would not even make it to this memorial, like André Boyabat and Diane Towers, would remain alive in Bane's memory for as long as he breathed. All of them had given their lives for the benefit of their nation. It was indeed too bad that no one would ever know about the great sacrifice Bourdeaux, André, Harvey Lee, Diane and so many others before had to endure to keep America free. Sometimes he wondered about the unfairness of his profession, questioning if he indeed belonged to this world of deception and death.

This round had been a close one for the American intelligence community. Terrorists had actually succeeded in detonating a warhead inside America, but fortunately, the other two bombs had been intercepted in time to prevent another disaster.

Disasters.

Bane slowly closed his eyes in respect for the people he had killed in Tikrit. Many innocent women and children had perished because of his act, but many more would have died if he had not detonated that weapon. As it turned out, Donald Bane indirectly stopped the bloodshed at the border with Kuwait. Just an hour after the destruction of Tikrit, an Iraqi military junta held a press conference at the Presidential Palace in Baghdad. Saddam Hussein had been assassinated by one of his generals. The reign of terror had ended for the Iraqi people, and the generals promised to restore the peace with their neighbors and put to a halt the pursuit of nuclear weapons.

As the ceremony ended and the president and his staff left, Donald Bane and Joseph Goldberg looked at one another.

"We supposedly won, sir," commented Bane, while shifting his gaze back toward Bourdeaux's gold star. "But the problem is that this whole thing just doesn't feel like a victory."

"There are no winners in a nuclear war, Don," said Goldberg in his rheumy voice.

Bane inspected his aged superior with a melancholic stare.

"President Kennedy once said this in no uncertain terms," continued the old director of Central Intelligence. "He said that in a nuclear war even the fruits of victory would be ashes in our mouth. He couldn't have been closer to the truth."

Bane watched the old man walk away toward the elevators across the lobby. He thought about following him but decided against it. The DCI needed time alone.

With one final glance at the memorial, Donald Bane walked outside the building. The air was cold and dry. He breathed it deeply as he slipped on a pair of Ray-Bans and stared at a line of visitors, mostly kids from a local elementary school on a field trip.

"Look, Tommy, there goes a spy!" one of the kids shouted to a friend, while pointing at the seasoned officer.

"Do you carry a gun, mister? Do you? Do you?" shouted a girl, before their teacher told them to be quiet and stay in line.

Smiling, Donald Bane pulled back his coat's jacket and let them have a glance at his chest-holstered Colt. The expression flashing across the kids' eyes was all the gratitude Donald Bane needed to keep plodding ahead. That alone made up for all the sacrifice, the pain, the suffering, the tears. This is what Lee, Bourdeaux, André, Diane and so many others had died for.

With a final wave at the kids, Donald Bane walked toward his car, truly realizing that his profession was indeed the best profession of all.

NORTHERN VIRGINIA.

Kevin Dalton never saw Khalela Yishaid after the near-disaster in South Carolina. By the time the CIA officer managed to get a ride to the small airfield, the FBI had already taken the Mossad operative back to Washington, where she was put on the next plane to Europe. This time, however, two federal agents escorted her all the way to Germany.

Kevin resented the Feds for doing this, and he had let his opinion be known to Goldberg and Palenski, both of whom tried to explain to the young CIA officer that it had been out of their hands. The prime minister himself had called President Bill Clinton and requested the safe and immediate return of his operative.

Kevin Dalton had taken a one-month leave of absence and headed for Louisiana as a Red Cross volunteer worker. It was the least he could do for the survivors. At the end of the month he had returned home and began working under Donald Bane.

Briefly glancing at the slow-flowing waters of the Shenandoah beyond the forest surrounding his house, Kevin stretched his back and grabbed a red brick from the stack to his left. He set it over the thin layer of mortar he had just deposited on the broken section of the wall of his house.

Wearing a pair of jeans, a white sweatshirt, and sneakers, Kevin decided to get this job over with before January came. It was late December and the Virginia countryside had been blessed with a warm front unusual for this time of the year. Temperatures were in the mid-fifties and that suited the CIA officer just fine. He hoped they would hold for another two days, which was how long he estimated it would take him to repair the fifteen-by-seven gap the old oak had created almost two months ago.

He actually welcomed the work. It kept his mind from drifting back to Khalela Yishaid. Glancing toward the forest as he reached for the bucket of mortar, Kevin Dalton saw a figure emerging from the tree line.

He momentarily froze. The thought of racing inside his house and grabbing his Beretta jumped into his mind, but it quickly washed away as the vision of her filled him.

Impossible!

Kevin Dalton slowly took a step in her direction, then another, then broke into a run as Khalela also ran toward him, arms stretched out, a radiant smile flashing across her face.

The embrace came, and Kevin closed his eyes as her body pressed hard against his. Her touch, her smell, her hair caressing his face. Kevin let it all go as her body drowned him with his one true reason for living, for breathing.

Slowly pulling away, she regarded him with a slanted stare before saying, "I missed you, Kevin Dalton."

Kevin cupped her face, keeping it just inches away from his. "Are you here to stay?"

Khalela slowly shook her head. "No, Kevin. *I* am not here to stay. *We* are here to stay," she said, taking one of his hands and lowering it to her stomach.

He hugged her again as a tear escaped the corner of his eye. The sun, the clouds, the soft aroma of her hair. Kevin Dalton filled his lungs with the promise of a new beginning.

FIC   Pineiro, R. J.   23 95
Pineiro
             Retribution.

DATE			